A DEADLY DISCOVERY . . .

Emma looped the end of Oliver's lead around the gatepost. Then she took a deep breath and put her hand on the gate. "Wish me luck, Oliver. Here I go."

But right then, a breeze whirled around them and Oliver's nose shot up. "Something's wrong."

"What is it, Oliver?"

"Wrong, wrong! Bad!" Oliver charged, right under the gate. The loose knot on the lead came undone immediately, and he bolted for the cottage door, barking at the top of his lungs.

"Oliver!" Emma struggled one-handed with the gate latch, praying that she didn't drop the scones, and also praying that Victoria Roberts was hard of hearing. "Quiet, Oliver!"

"I can't! I can't! Something's wrong!" Oliver scrabbled at the doorjamb.

Emma hurried up the garden path. This was not like Oliver. Something really might be wrong.

"Okay, okay, easy, Oliver. Calm down."

"I can't! I can't! Something's wrong! It's wrong!" He kept barking, but he did back away, giving Emma room to get to the door.

The old cottage didn't have a bell that Emma could see, so she knocked. "Ms. Roberts?" There was no answer. She knocked harder. "Ms. Roberts?" she called again. She also rattled the knob. Much to her shock, it turned in her hand.

The cottage door creaked as it opened. Oliver was inside before Emma's eyes could adjust to the dim interior.

The cottage was the sort with a long central hall between the sitting room and the stairs. At the far end, watery daylight filtered through the neatly curtained window above the sink.

There was a clock ticking, and Oliver barking, but no other sound.

A chill ran down Emma's spine.

To Fetch a Felon

JENNIFER HAWKINS

BERKLEY PRIME CRIME
New York

BERKLEY PRIME CRIME
Published by Berkley
An imprint of Penguin Random House LLC
penguinrandomhouse.com

Copyright © 2020 by Penguin Random House LLC
Penguin Random House supports copyright. Copyright fuels creativity, encourages
diverse voices, promotes free speech, and creates a vibrant culture. Thank you for buying
an authorized edition of this book and for complying with copyright laws by not
reproducing, scanning, or distributing any part of it in any form without permission.
You are supporting writers and allowing Penguin Random House to continue to
publish books for every reader.

BERKLEY and the BERKLEY & B colophon are registered trademarks and
BERKLEY PRIME CRIME is a trademark of Penguin Random House LLC.

ISBN: 9780593197080

First Edition: December 2020

Printed in the United States of America
1 3 5 7 9 10 8 6 4 2

Cover art by Daniel Liévano
Cover design by Judith Lagerman
Book design by George Towne

1

"YOU, THERE!" THE SHOUT EXPLODED IN EMMA'S EAR.

"Gah!" Emma jumped half out of her skin. Beside her, Oliver barked and jumped as high as his stubby legs allowed.

A woman popped up from behind the ancient garden wall along the side of the old high street and pointed her muddy trowel directly under Emma's nose.

"That dog must be on a lead!"

Oliver, the dog in question—specifically the brown and white Pembroke Welsh Corgi in question—barked again.

"I told you, Emma!" he said. "I said somebody was there!"

He also wagged his curling tail and opened his mouth in the way that made corgis appear to be laughing and always charmed the onlooker.

Well, usually charmed the onlooker. As it was, the gardening woman glowered at Oliver like he'd just dragged something unmentionable across her carpets. She had a round face, a stout build, and a mop of gray curls held back in a blue bandana. She wore a faded blue blouse with the sleeves rolled up and a flowered apron. Taken all together, she looked like someone who should be baking ginger biscuits for her beloved grandchildren.

At least, she would have, if she didn't also look like she'd be willing to lace those biscuits with a dose of arsenic.

"You need to be careful with this one," Oliver went on. "She's not happy. And she's rude."

Fortunately, the only person who understood Oliver when he spoke was Emma herself. This woman, whoever she was, would probably not appreciate his current line of commentary.

"Ah, um, hello!" Emma plastered a polite-apology smile on her face. She also reached down and patted Oliver's head. "Not now, please," she whispered.

Now was not a good time for a person who might become a neighbor to start noticing Emma was . . . quirky. That being the polite term for a person who heard her dog—not to put too fine a point on it—talk.

"I'm so sorry, I didn't see you there," Emma added to the gardener. "You startled us a little."

The gardener sniffed. It was a sharp, eloquent sound, and it probably had the capacity to wilt the resolve of grown men. After twenty-five years in London's financial sector, however, Emma was not intimidated. At least, not very.

Oliver growled uneasily. "We shouldn't stay here."

"Quiet, Oliver." Emma gave his head a final rub. "Good boy," she added for affect.

"And you're right, of course," Emma said to the gardener, a little more loudly than she needed to. "He should be on his lead, and I do have it here—" She pulled the bright red lead from her overstuffed handbag.

"But you just thought you'd let him race about and get into people's gardens to destroy years of hard work!"

Emma took a deep breath and concentrated on keeping her tone level. "I understand your concern, but he's really extremely well-behaved . . ."

"He's a public menace! And plainly takes after his owner," sneered the woman. "Like every other day-tripper who comes traipsing through here!" She waved her trowel up the curving high street toward the village center, scattering clods of soil in all directions.

"Oh, I'm not a day-tripper, I'm moving to Trevena." Emma bit her tongue, because she had the sudden feeling now was not the best time for this woman to find that out either. "I'm opening a tea shop," she added.

From the woman's look of terror, Emma might have just as well have added, "And I plan to make meat pies of the neighbors."

"A tea shop!" she cried. "Well, we'll see about *that*." She leaned forward over the wall. "You're one of Maggie Trenwith's Londoners, aren't you?"

Emma felt her spine stiffen. As a matter of fact, Maggie Trenwith was the estate agent she'd been working with, but what did that have to do with anything? Who, exactly, did this woman think she was? Emma had dreamed of owning her own tea shop for years. Trevena, the site of her summer holidays as a child, had seemed the perfect choice to make that dream come true.

She hadn't entirely reckoned on the idyllic Cornish village having its own local busybody.

Emma opened her mouth, but the woman made a slashing gesture with her trowel. "Don't bother. I can spot one of you a mile way. Maggie Trenwith will rent to anybody. Probably didn't even get proper references. But you'll see I'm not so easily fooled." She brandished the trowel again. "I've got my eye on you now, and that dog. You make sure he stays off my property, or I'll call the constable on you both!"

Of course, that was the moment Oliver decided to charge the garden wall.

2

HUMANS, AT TIMES, COULD BE QUITE BEWILDERING.

Take this strange lady human who smelled of earth and roses, fertilizer and all sorts of plants Oliver couldn't name. What in the world was she so angry about? They were in the middle of an excellent place. If she and Emma had been sensible creatures, they would have been playing together by now. But all she did was shout and wave her arms and that digging thing.

Humans wasted so much *time*. The air was full of green, growing and salty smells—even more smells than Hyde Park on a Sunday—and they weren't paying attention to any of them. There were dog smells as well, lots and lots of friendly dog smells, new and old, all up and down this wall. Every part of him wanted to follow the trail and investigate all its layers.

Of course, being a corgi, Oliver was a dog of noble warrior heritage. His foredogs had sailed with the Vikings, and his royal brothers guarded the Queen's Majesty every day, just like he guarded his best human, Emma.

So, obviously, Oliver was not about to leave Emma's side at this crucial moment. In fact, his first instinct was to make it clear to the angry digging lady that it was not acceptable to shout at Emma.

But noble warrior corgis absolutely never barked or growled or bared their teeth when their special human needed them to keep quiet. They certainly did not run under closed gates, even if they *could*. Noble corgis stayed at their posts, no matter what, and . . .

What's that? A new smell on the breeze, a wild, bitter, copper-tinged smell, a . . .

"Better watch your step there, mate."

A fox.

Oliver dropped his muzzle and pricked up his ears. There was a hole in the stone wall, low down near the walk. The fox crouched on the other side, grinning.

Fox! Instinct shouted. Duty pressed it back down. *Stay!*

"This one, she really don't like your sort," said the fox.

A noble warrior corgi stays at his post. A corgi is strong and disciplined. A corgi is . . .

"Fox!"

Oliver charged, barking. Shouty Lady screeched, but that wasn't important. Now Emma was the one shouting. Oliver still couldn't stop. His paws were moving faster than his brain.

Fox!

He dove through the hole—at least, he tried. His nose made it, and the hole smelled of lots and lots of fox, and if he could just dig a little more room, he'd be on the other side and then and then . . .

"Oliver! No!"

But just a little farther . . .

"You get that dog out of here!" screamed the shouty lady. Emma grabbed his scruff and dragged him backward as he paddled the air frantically.

"But I can get him! I can!" Oliver barked. "Fox! Fox!"

"Oliver!" shouted Emma. "Sit! Bad dog!"

"But there's a fox!"

Emma put her hand on his back and pushed, and Oliver knew she meant it. Worse, she was right.

"But . . . I mean . . . Oh, crumbs." He slumped down onto his belly. "Sorry, Emma." He put both paws over his nose.

"I'm calling the police!" shrieked the woman. "I'll have him put down!"

Emma was busy untangling the Lead. A small whine escaped Oliver, which was not noble either, but he couldn't help it.

"I'm so sorry," Emma gasped as she clamped the Lead onto his collar. "Really. He must have caught a scent . . . maybe a fox . . . ?"

"Out!" screamed the bad lady, waving her digging thing. "Out!"

"Of course. Come on, Oliver." Emma tugged on the Lead. She smelled worried. He jumped to his feet. "Again, I'm so—"

"Out!"

Emma hurried down the street and Oliver trotted to keep up, watching her anxiously. Emma shouldn't be worried. He'd keep her safe from the shouty woman.

And the fox. That fox was still out there. Next time, he would not get away.

3

EMMA REED HAD NOT ALWAYS BEEN ABLE TO TALK TO THE animals. Well, she didn't actually *talk* to the animals. She spoke with her corgi, which was different, although the results did not change. To her, Oliver—an otherwise perfectly normal corgi dog—spoke perfectly comprehensible English.

As a puppy, he had only said a word here or there, and the incidents were scattered enough that Emma had been able to tell herself it was her imagination. But as Oliver got older, he started speaking in—or at least, she started hearing him in—complete sentences, spoken with an ever-so-slight hint of a Welsh accent.

Still, she actively avoided explaining that to people, because it never failed to sound just a teensy bit mad.

She had tried to bring the subject up with her brother, Henry. Sort of. Over the phone.

"So, Henry, do, um, you know if we'd ever, I mean, maybe Mum and Da, um, were there ever any relations we might have who were a little . . . different?" Henry was seven years older than Emma, and he knew more of the family myths and legends than she did.

"Different how?" She could hear him frowning through the phone.

"Oh, you know, just . . . eccentric?"

Henry had laughed. Emma's brother was unimaginative and utterly dependable—the epitome of the old-school stiff-upper-lip sort. When their father had retired, Henry had taken over the family accounting firm like he'd never thought of doing anything else, which he probably hadn't. He even went around the house in a cardigan and slippers. A generation back, he probably would have smoked a pipe, but his wife, Vivian, would have none of it.

"Come on, Em. You know none of our lot was ever rich enough to be eccentric. Now, mind you, Mum did say her aunt Margery was a little strange. Did you ever meet Margery? I think I remember she died when you were pretty young. Anyway. Mum never said she was dangerous or anything. Just, well, quirky."

"Quirky how?"

"Firmly believed she could hold actual conversations with her Jack Russell terrier. Harmless enough, I suppose, but Mum did say it could get a little awkward at Sunday lunch."

Emma thanked him and immediately asked about Vivian and the kids and the junior football league Henry coached on Saturdays, then made sure to hang up before he could remember to ask why she'd wanted to know about quirky Great-Aunt Margery.

The conversation with Henry didn't actually change anything. It had been five years since Emma and Oliver found each other, and she still heard him talk. She also loved her feisty, gossipy, zoomy corgi and wasn't going to give him up for anything. So, in the end, she decided she was simply going to have to learn to live with it.

And truth be told, it was nice to have someone to talk to on Sunday walks who didn't want a choc ice every five minutes, like her nieces, or wasn't trying to hide their disappointment with the fact that she wasn't slimmer, younger, and/or richer, like some of the men she (very occasionally) tried dating.

"Where are we going now, Emma?" Oliver trotted happily beside her. His pointed ears barely reached her knees, and his legs were so short he couldn't get up on the sofa without help, but that never stopped him trying. "That garden was infested with dangerous and shockingly rude vermin, and what I mean to say is, there was a fox. Did I tell you there was a fox? I could have got him. I did try, but I was interrupted," he added pointedly.

"I know, I know." Emma sighed. "But we couldn't . . ."

But Oliver had already started pulling hard on the lead.

"Ooo . . . that's a good smell! That's fish! Fish! *And* a fish lady!"

Trevena village was old Cornwall with all the trimmings. The village meandered along the rugged coastline. The ancient cottages nearest the cliffs put their backs to lanes of clapboard, brick and whitewashed stone buildings that dominated the high street. From here, Emma could even make out the battlements of the truly ludicrous building that had been the pet project of a long-dead sweets manufacturer who had wanted to re-create "King Arthur's Castle."

Hedge-lined fields spread out over the hills like massive coattails. Farther up in the hills, tracts of semidetached houses clustered in places where they could have a view to go with all their modern conveniences. A local boom sometime in the nineteenth century had given birth to a few grand stone houses that still stood between the modern estates.

When Emma was little, her family had holidayed here every year. Emma had spent summers playing in the ruins of the medieval fortress on the spit of land that stuck out into the sea. She had devoured *Rebecca* and *Jamaica Inn* at what was probably an inappropriately young age and would hang about the docks for hours, trying to spy on the locals to see if any of them were still smugglers or, better, wreckers. She begged to be allowed to explore Merlin's Cave just once. That was strictly forbidden, so she'd spent her time diving into every nook and cranny of the landscape she could get to on her own, giving her parents and her staid older brother fits when she vanished for hours at a time. She always cried when it was time to go home.

When she finally decided it was time to get out of London and finance, Trevena was the first place she thought of.

Emma and Oliver had reached the point where the winding country road turned into cobbled high street. A woman stood in the doorway of the chip shop that occupied the corner of a row of low, whitewashed buildings. The hanging shingle above the door read THE TOWNE FRYER. The scent of hot oil, battered fish and potatoes, which Oliver had detected several meters back, reminded Emma how hungry she was.

"Welcome to Trevena village!" the woman said. "Every new arrival comes with a free scolding by Victoria Roberts."

Emma froze in her tracks. "I'm sorry. Did you say that woman was Victoria Roberts?"

"I did. Something wrong?"

Emma felt the blood drain out of her cheeks. "I . . . oh, heck. Yes. There is, rather."

"Emma?" Oliver bumped his nose against her shin. "Emma? What's the matter?"

"Here, you look like you've just seen a ghost. Come on in out of the sun." The woman gestured for Emma to come into the chip shop.

"No, I'm fine, thank you, erm . . ."

"Genevieve Knowels." The woman introduced herself and held out her hand. "Everybody calls me Genny."

"Emma Reed." They shook hands. Genny was middle-aged and a little taller than Emma. She had dark blond hair pulled back under a white cap, a healthy tan, broad hands and a sparkle in her blue eyes that managed to be cheerful and slightly ironic at the same time.

Emma referred to herself as a "faded ginger." Her red hair, which she wore long, was now flecked with gray, and her angled face showed evidence of a lifetime of both laughter and a few sleepless nights. Her skin was the kind of pale that burned bright red in summer. She had long ago come to terms with the fact that she was forever zaftig, and she tended to dress as comfortably as appropriate for the circumstances.

"Nice to meet you, Emma. And really, you shouldn't let the Roberts bother you." Genny waved over Emma's shoulder. Emma glanced back up the sloping street to see Victoria standing at her garden wall, openly glaring at them. When Victoria saw them looking back, she lifted her nose in the air and ducked down beneath her wall. "It's a good bet that whatever set her off probably wasn't your fault, or your dog's." She bent down and ruffled Oliver's ears. "Who's this lovely little fellow, then?"

Oliver plopped his hindquarters down on the cobbles. "Emma, I do believe it would be acceptable to form an acquaintance here."

Emma smiled. "This is Oliver. And it's not that she"— she gestured down the street—"bothered me. It's . . ." Emma took a deep breath. "I'm moving to Trevena and I have plans to open a tea shop . . ."

"That's wonderful! There hasn't been a place in town to get a decent Chelsea bun since Penhallow's closed . . ." Genny's sentence trailed off. "Oh. Were you hoping to re-open Penhallow's?"

Emma grimaced. "Well, I'd been thinking about it. It's a prime location." In fact, she could see the shop, right up where the high street took a tight bend. The faded sign with what had once been a jaunty teapot painted on it swung back and forth in the fresh breeze.

"And, of course, Victoria owns the building," Genny sighed.

"I guess she has a lot of property around here." As it happened, Maggie Trenwith had been grumbling about it.

"Only about half the village." Genny made a face. "And she's always looking to buy the other half."

"Emma?" Oliver bumped his nose against her shin again. "Emma? Perhaps we should get some fish, Emma. It has been a long time since breakfast, don't you think?"

Oliver was not wrong, and Emma had more questions for Genny, who seemed ready and willing to join in a good bit of gossip.

"Are you open?" Emma asked her. "We've been sightseeing all morning." If tossing the ball for Oliver on the beach and then finding the most wonderful little twisty footpath up the cliff could be considered "sightseeing." "We didn't get lunch, and I'm supposed to be looking at a cottage to let in—" She glanced at her watch. "Oh, lord. Less than an hour. I totally lost track of time."

"No worries," Genny told her. "We are definitely open, and I've just put a fresh basket in the fryer." She beckoned Emma to follow her inside. "I hope you like haddock?"

"Love it."

Emma paused to loop Oliver's lead around the bike rack next to the café tables set up on the cobblestones. "Stay here, that's a good boy." She gave his head a firm scratch.

"Emma, you *know* I'm always on the alert," he said loftily. "Ooo . . . that's nice, right there . . ."

Emma grinned and followed Genny into her shop.

4

......

THE TOWNE FRYER WAS A CLASSIC SMALL CHIPPERY—LITTLE more than a service counter, a set of fryers and a second counter by the window where three, maybe four customers could stand and eat, if they were very good friends.

Genny worked the fry baskets and loaded a paper-lined basket with golden chunks of fish and fried potato. She sprinkled a healthy dash of salt over everything. But she just shook her head when Emma held out her credit card. "Can't let Victoria Roberts be your only welcome to Trevena."

"Oh, no. I couldn't. . . ."

"Of course you could." Genny set the basket on the counter. "Besides, you'd be doing me a favor. This is a new curry batter I'm working on, and I need a test subject."

"Well, in that case . . ." Emma bit into the crisp, delicate fish and immediately sucked in a breath to cool her mouth. "Delicious!" she exclaimed, or tried to, around the mouthful. "Just spicy enough."

"Marvelous. For that, you can stay." Genny waved to one of the outdoor tables. Emma went back out into the glorious, and highly unusual, Cornish sunshine. Genny followed behind, with two mugs of tea.

As soon as Emma unclipped his lead, Oliver plopped himself down beside the table.

"That fish smells truly exceptional. Is it?" He wagged his entire bottom. "Because it does smell that way, and perhaps I should just check for you. You know, Emma, you do sometimes have difficulty detecting when the fish is less than fresh. It's not your fault, it's just that human nose of yours . . ." He wagged harder.

Emma handed him a bit of fish, which he wolfed down straight off her fingers. She put down a couple of chips as well. Their London vet—who regularly lectured her on the importance of a carefully balanced canine diet—would be appalled.

"I promise, I've tried to teach him not to beg at the table," she said to Genny.

"It's hard, isn't it?" Genny smiled sympathetically. "I've got an Irish setter, and I swear he's spoiled worse than my kids." She took a swallow of tea.

"You know, Emma, it's been a very long day," whined Oliver at her feet. "And that fox might be back any moment, and I should keep my strength up, don't you think?"

"You want more fish?" Emma asked.

"I want more fish," agreed Oliver.

Emma rolled her eyes, but she broke off another bit of fish and set it on the pavement.

"So what made you choose our fair village?" Genny asked. If Emma noted a slight hint of suspicion in Genny's question, she could excuse it. Probably she was not the first Londoner to watch one too many episodes of *Escape to the Country* and decide it sounded like a good idea.

"My family used to holiday in Trevena every year, and I always loved it." Emma helped herself to a perfectly crisp, gloriously salty chip. "And, to be honest, I'm forty-five years old, and I've spent twenty-five of those years in the financial sector. And the past ten of those years have been spent training boys who all just *somehow* got promoted over me, and then all just *somehow* came back to beg me to take care of the problems they caused because they wouldn't listen . . ." *Or didn't want to hear.* "It was just time to go."

There was no need to go into the details of the last fight with her boss, or the anguished, weepy nights on the sofa with her best friend, Rose, not to mention the angry phone call from Henry demanding to know what on *earth* had possessed her. To be fair to Henry, once she explained what was actually going on with her former employer, he quickly issued multiple apologies and an assurance that there'd always be a place for her in "the old family firm."

"So you've decided on a second act?" Genny raised her mug to Emma in salute. "Good for you."

"Ta." Emma raised her own mug in answer. "I mean, I know it sounds silly, a grown woman chucking a perfectly good career to go muck about with cakes"—which had been Henry's reaction when she told him what she was planning—"but it's what I've really wanted to do since I was a girl, and now I'm taking my chance."

"It doesn't sound silly at all," said Genny, firmly. "It sounds like you're ready to open yourself to some new chances and some old dreams."

Which was exactly right, but it was a relief to hear somebody say it out loud. Emma gave Genny a grateful smile and received a friendly grin in return. While they each helped themselves (and Oliver) to more chips, a cherry-red two-seater sports car came into view up the narrow, crooked high street.

To Emma's surprise, the car pulled up outside of Victoria Roberts's cottage and parked.

"Well, well, this could be interesting," murmured Genny.

The car's passenger-side door opened, and a thin older woman whose curls had been dyed solid black got out. The driver emerged next—a stout, pink-faced young man with butter-yellow hair. As they approached the gate, Victoria Roberts popped up from behind her wall like a foul-tempered jack-in-the-box.

Victoria said something to the pair of visitors and then turned on her heel and marched into the house.

The younger man wrestled with the gate latch for a minute before hurrying up the path to follow Victoria inside. The black-haired woman trailed behind. Even from this distance, Emma could tell she would have really rather been someplace else.

Oliver's head and ears strained forward. Emma could tell he felt as curious as she did.

"That's Jimmy Lambert, Victoria's nephew," said Genny, with the air of someone announcing the players as they ran onto the pitch. "He had been working in the States. Some big video game company out in San Francisco. But he's staying with her now that he's back home."

"And who's the woman?"

"Louise Craddock," Genny said. "She's Victoria's best friend—her only friend, really, except maybe for Ruth Penhallow."

"Ruth Penhallow? As in Penhallow's tea shop?"

Genny nodded. At that same moment, the cottage door slammed loud enough that they could hear it from where they sat. Startled, Oliver jumped to his feet.

"Bad!" he barked. Oliver's "words" could fail him if he got agitated. "Wrong! Bad!"

"Easy, Oliver. It's okay." Emma patted his back until he settled down. She also gave him another bit of fish. "So, why'd you think that might get interesting?" *Not that I'm the overly curious type, you understand.*

Fortunately, Emma had been right about Genny. She was in fact perfectly ready to engage in a spot of local gossip. "Well, I can't say for certain, but there've been a few arguments between the three of them now. Poor Louise has always been a nervous soul, but at the Tesco the other day, I bumped her shopping trolley on accident, and the poor thing about jumped out of her skin! And nobody's had a pleasant word out of Jimmy since he got back, and that's almost been a year now."

"I wonder what . . ." Emma shook her head. "Sorry. None of my business at all." But Genny just laughed.

"It's a *village*," she said. "Everything is everybody's

business. But, I'd better warn you, apart from the Victoria Roberts show, I'm afraid you're going to find Trevena pretty dull after London. We're very much geared toward the tourist trade and the farms here, with not much else on the go."

"Believe me, after twenty-some-odd years in London finance, 'pretty dull' sounds perfect. I'm just sorry I've gotten off on the wrong foot with Victoria." She nodded toward the cottage. "I don't suppose there's anything I could do to make it up to her?"

Genny looked into the bottom of her tea mug, considering the problem. "Hard to say. The truth is, I really don't know what goes on in Victoria's head. She's always had a short fuse, but I swear it's been getting worse. On the other hand, she's a sharp businesswoman. She bought the Penhallow's building before she'd even finished at uni. I think it might even have been the start of her little local real estate empire."

"So why's it been empty for so long? Maggie, my estate agent, says she's let it sit empty for over a year now?"

"Nobody seems to know. Unless . . ." But Genny stopped and shook her head.

"I'm sorry—unless . . . ?" prompted Emma.

"Nothing. Old news. If I had to guess, I'd say Victoria hoped Ruth would come back," she said, but Emma was left with the feeling that it wasn't what she'd planned on saying at first. "Victoria hates change. But really, the whole town was devastated when Ruth closed up shop and moved down to Torquay. But she'd broken her hip, poor thing, and just couldn't keep up anymore."

"But why didn't she just hand the business over to someone?" Genny's little "unless" had sparked Emma's curiosity. So did the little furrow in Genny's brow as she looked up the street toward the shop.

"Well, Ruth's rather elderly now, and what family she has is mostly in Devon and Torquay. I'm sure she assumed Victoria would find a new tenant pretty quickly. And maybe . . ." There it was again, that little hesitation, like she was stopping herself from saying something. Emma's curiosity sat up, as attentive as Oliver at the sight of a fresh sausage.

But Genny just shook herself and checked her watch. "Gosh, look at the time." Genny drained her tea mug. "I'm afraid I've got some work to get in before the teatime rush. Martin, my husband, he's out picking up a delivery, and our assistant, Becca, is out on an interview, so I'm on my own today. It's been lovely meeting you, Emma, and I wish you the best of luck wherever you land. You too, Oliver." Genny rubbed the corgi's head.

"Oh, yes, we will come back soon, won't we, Emma?" Oliver laughed and rolled over, exposing his belly to the sun. "She smells good! Fish and vinegar and warm feelings! Ahem." He righted himself again. "Yes. Excellent."

Emma laughed. "Oliver says thank you."

"He's a darling."

"Yes, he is." She rubbed Oliver's head.

Oliver put his nose in the air. "*He* is a noble corgi, the original warrior dog, and . . ." His head whipped around. "Oooo . . . something smells good . . . !"

"He says thank you again." Emma popped the last chip in her mouth and got to her feet. "Come on, Oliver."

Emma slung her handbag back over her shoulder and paused to make sure Oliver's lead was firmly clipped to his collar. As she did, movement caught her eye.

Up the road, the cottage door burst open. Louise Craddock raced down the garden path, quite literally wringing her hands.

And who wouldn't, with Victoria Roberts right on her heels?

". . . after everything I've done! All these years!" Victoria roared. "You have the nerve to try to defend him now!"

"Aunt Victoria, please . . . !" Jimmy stumbled out of Victoria's cottage behind her.

But Victoria wasn't listening. "How much did he pay you?" she shouted as Louise scrambled to get into the car. "How much did it take for you to sell us all out?"

Louise slammed the car door.

"Please, Aunt Victoria!" cried Jimmy. "Whatever happened, it wasn't—"

"Why should I trust anything you say?!" Victoria rounded on her nephew and shook her finger right under his nose. "I never thought I'd see the day when you would be so *ungrateful!*"

"That is not a nice woman," muttered Oliver.

"Yes, Oliver," breathed Emma. "I do believe you're right."

5

· · · · · · · · ·

"I LOVE IT!"

Emma turned around in the cottage's front room, trying to take in everything at once.

The estate agent smiled. "I thought you might. Some people are just meant to be in old houses. It's as if they understand each other. Which is probably just me being overly sentimental." She shrugged. "But what's the harm?"

Maggie was a thin woman, about Emma's age, with dyed blond hair and a sharp chin. She dressed in brightly colored trouser suits and cultivated an estate agent's professional friendliness, mixed with a touch of flattery for the clientele. Emma had actually first contacted her a couple of months ago. She'd come to Trevena over a bank holiday, just to clear her head a bit. Instead of her head clearing, however, her imagination woke up, and she started making notes and lists of what it would take to actually make the move to a new life, one where she was finally able to explore her passion for sweets and baking.

Step one had been putting together a plan, and a budget. Step two had been contacting an estate agent to find a house and a shop space to lease.

"Nancarrow's a beautiful house," Maggie went on. "And

I've always felt it deserved better than to be just another holiday cottage. It should be a proper home. And I think your dog approves." She nodded toward Oliver, who was darting back and forth and every which way, shoving his nose into all the nooks and crannies, wagging enthusiastically the whole time.

"Yes, yes, excellent," he huffed. "Very good—ooo . . . what's that?"

Emma laughed. "I think I can say with great confidence that he absolutely loves it."

Nancarrow cottage was a traditional stone cottage, halfway up the long hill that rose from the village center. Probably it had once been home to generations of shepherds or cattle farmers. Most of the land around it had been sold off long since, and now it just perched alone on a weedy half acre at the end of a rutted drive.

But for Emma, the isolation was part of the charm, and the cottage had charm to spare. Despite changes in styles and building codes, the owners had kept the diamond-paned windows. Most of the downstairs was taken up by a front/living room with flagstone floors. The walls had been freshly painted white and the door was a cheery royal blue. The exposed oak roof beams and window frames had been blackened by centuries of smoke from a stone fireplace big enough for Emma to stand up in. At some point, someone had rigged a wood-burning stove in the middle of it, probably in a bid to increase heating efficiency and keep down the threat of fire.

Despite her declaration that it was perfect, Nancarrow did have some flaws. The cottage's furnishings were—not to put too fine a point on it—dreadful. It was all cheap stuff meant to be used hard by a parade of holidaymakers and their families and replaced frequently. Emma added the option to refurnish to her mental list of requests for her new landlords.

Then there was the kitchen, which waited directly on the other side of the chimney from the front room. It had its own lovely hearth, but the cabinets and counters had obviously last been updated in the midseventies, and that included the cooker.

Emma decided she could live with them for now. The avocado green might even grow on her in time.

Well, maybe we don't have to go that far. We'll have to talk upgrades as well as furnishings.

And then there was the garden. Or, rather, the complete lack thereof. What waited outside the kitchen door was a sad rectangle of weedy grass bordered by a badly maintained stone wall. A trio of yew bushes clustered at the far end like they were huddling together for warmth.

Right now, though, Emma was determined to ignore the depths and concentrate on the heights—like the open staircase leading to the upstairs, with its low-ceilinged bedrooms and the slope-roofed bathroom. The ancient claw-foot bathtub in there had no doubt been an expensive luxury to the cottage's original owners, and now it just looked perfect for a long soak after a hard day.

Emma had been in Trevena the better part of a week now, and Maggie had shown her half a dozen houses and flats. Despite its shortcomings, this was the first one she could really see as the foundation of her brand-new village life.

Oliver, of course, had his own opinions.

"I'm sure the garden needs a thorough investigation before we make any final decisions." The corgi trotted over to the kitchen door and wagged.

"Yes, okay, Oliver." Emma opened the door so Oliver could head outside. The stone wall was a little saggy, but it looked solid enough to keep one overly curious corgi from wandering off onto the open heath.

While Oliver began his detailed investigations of wall and grass, Emma stood in the doorway to take in what really set the cottage apart from anyplace she'd ever lived—the view.

From here, Emma could see down the whole sweep of the hillside, all the way to Trevena and the sea beyond. She could even make out the ragged black line of the rift with its rapid freshwater stream. The distant clusters of the housing estates felt like an afterthought, dropped in among the ancient walls and hedgerows. The hills rose up over all of them, dark and solid and, to Emma, reassuring in their permanence, just like the sea below.

Emma felt a wave of contentment wash over her. The view above Trevena's rooftops gave her the sensation of being in a secret tree house. She could already picture herself sitting beside the hearth stove with a cup of fresh tea and leafing through Mary Berry's latest cookbook while Oliver stood at the garden door and let the local crows know exactly what he thought of them.

Emma turned to face Maggie. "It's exactly what I was hoping for."

"Excellent." Maggie took a seat at the battered, and incongruously modern, kitchen table with its cracked blue-checked oilcloth. Emma sat across from her.

"You said the owners would be willing to do a longer-term lease?"

"Oh, yes. They believe, and rightly so, that a stable tenant will be a better value in the end."

Meaning less trouble, and cheaper, Emma thought to herself.

"Plus, of course, having someone living in the property full-time is simply better for the house itself." Maggie pulled a pair of black cat eye glasses from her blazer pocket and shoved them onto her narrow nose. "Now, I'm obliged to tell you Nancarrow cottage is a little short on the modern conveniences. The water heater's new from last year, but the last time the roof was redone, Churchill was still in office. You can read the details here." She passed Emma a stack of papers.

"And the furnishings?"

Maggie glanced across to the particularly hideous flowered sofa and matching armchairs. "Yes, I did mention to them that any long-term tenant would probably want to bring in their own things. They're willing to work with you on that."

Emma pictured long, lovely afternoons browsing an-

tique shops and jumble sales for the perfect pieces. Maybe
Rose would come down from London and help. Rose was
currently subletting Emma's London flat. So Emma bringing down her own sparse Swedish-modern furniture wasn't
an option. Besides, none of it would fit in with Nancarrow's
character. Fortunately, she'd budgeted for the possibility of
having to fix up her new place when she'd started making
her plans to move.

"And the kitchen?" Emma asked. "That very much needs
an update as well." It had only been a few days, but Emma
was already missing having a kitchen of her own. Baking
was so much a part of her life that even a week's hiatus left
her feeling restless.

Rose said Emma had a butter-dependency problem.
Rose was not entirely wrong.

"Kitchen, right." Maggie made a note. "I'm sure we can
come to an agreement. Perhaps a cost-share, if you want
new appliances." She scribbled down a few more words.

"Perfect." Emma paused and took a deep breath.

Maggie raised her eyebrows. "I hear a 'but' coming."

"Oh, no. Well. Yes. But it's not about the house. I wanted
to talk about finding a space for the tea shop. You know I
said I wanted to look into the Penhallow's building?"

"And I think I told you there might be problems with it."

"Yes, well, I met one of those problems, and I, erm,
think I made things worse."

"Ah." Maggie nodded. "You mean you had a run-in with
Victoria Roberts."

"Oliver tried to get into her garden."

"Well, that explains it." Maggie pulled off her glasses
and tucked them away in her pocket. "The old dear"—she
dropped the last word like a curse—"rang me while I was
on my way here and gave me a proper earful about my ir-
responsibility, and how I was driving Trevena into the dirt
by working with any unsavory character who might wander
by with a checkbook." With each word, Maggie's voice
grew harder and more bitter, until her voice, and her eyes,

filled with real anger. "That garden is sacred ground for Victoria. Her roses have won the local fete for ten years running. Frankly, I think it's because the judges are scared of what she'll do if they award the prize to anyone else." Maggie glowered down at her notes, and Emma could feel the frustration radiating out of her.

"There are a lot of vacant buildings in Trevena right now," Maggie said, almost to herself. "But I just hate the idea of you not having the best possible place for your shop because Victoria Roberts . . . because she's decided she needs a fresh grudge to hang on to." She lifted her gaze. "I understand you want to get things moving right away, but can you give me a couple of days? I may be able to work out a deal for you."

"Well . . ." Emma hesitated. "I really can't afford too much of a delay on the shop."

"Just a week, at most," said Maggie. "And I'll draw you up a list of alternatives that you can go over while you're getting settled here, just in case."

Emma sensed there was a great deal Maggie wasn't saying. Had she stepped into a rivalry between the two women? It seemed very likely.

If that was true, the smart thing to do was back out. Getting in the middle of other people's grudges was never a good idea.

Except she did want Penhallow's. She remembered having tea there as a girl, and how Ruth Penhallow never minded if she lingered at the table over a slice of cake bought with her own money. She could spend hours on a rainy afternoon just watching people and cars going past the windows and writing (truly fantastic) notes about what she saw, or thought she saw.

At the same time, Emma remembered Genny's hesitation and evasion when she talked about the shop, and Ruth Penhallow and Victoria.

"Do you know, I met Genny Knowles a little earlier today. She seemed to think there was something wrong with the property? I mean more than structurally." Which might be a lot to hang on one hesitant "Unless . . ." But Emma wanted to see what Maggie had to say.

"Well, if there is, I don't know about it," Maggie told her firmly. *A little too firmly?*

When Emma didn't say anything immediately, Maggie leaned forward. "Listen, Emma, I'm going to be completely honest with you. Village life isn't nearly as simple as it looks on the surface. It can be a real minefield if you're not used to it. And, well, to put it bluntly, Victoria Roberts is a truly unpleasant old baggage, and everybody knows it, but she also wields a lot of clout locally. Half the council is terrified of her. But I'm not, and I see no reason she should always have everything her own way. Let me try to see if I can get you Penhallows. Just one week. If I can't work something out by then, we'll move on to other prospects. I promise."

Emma hesitated again. She'd be making waves before she'd even unpacked. Potentially serious ones. Would it be worth it?

But she also pictured Penhallows as she'd known it, with the sun flowing through the windows and the cozy little tables and the air full of the smell of warm sugar, chocolate and tea.

"Yes, all right," she said. "Please try."

"Excellent!" Maggie slapped both palms on the table. "You are the sort of person we need around here. Not dragged down by tradition or cringing in front of the local ogress. Now." She looked at her phone. "Good lord! How long have we been at this?" The room had faded to twilight without either of them noticing. "I should get going. I've got a late client meeting . . ." She began hastily gathering up her papers and folders. "You're staying at the King's Rest, right? Can I drop you?"

"No, thanks all the same. I'll walk." Emma paused. "Would it be all right if I stayed behind, just for a few minutes?"

Maggie hesitated. "Well, I really shouldn't, but it's not as if there's any silver to steal, even if I thought you were so inclined . . ." Maggie laid the key on the table. "Just be sure you lock up and drop the key in the lockbox on the door handle. I'll give you a call tomorrow about the lease on the cottage after I've had a chance to talk to the owners, all right? I'm sure they'll be delighted to have you as a tenant."

"Perfect."

They said goodbye. As soon as she closed the cottage door behind Maggie, Emma went straight into the garden. The village spread below her, a scene out of an old novel set against a backdrop of molten silver. It was almost too lovely to be real.

Then Emma noticed Oliver was nowhere in sight.

"Oliver!" she called. "Oliver! Here, boy!"

The yew bushes rattled and Oliver emerged, shook himself, scratched, sneezed and trotted to her side.

"An excellent place," Oliver whuffed and sneezed. "Are we staying? I believe we should stay. Will we stay?"

Emma breathed in the scents of salt and green and damp earth that were so very different from London's summer pong. She also shivered from the brisk breeze that wafted straight up off the sea. How wonderful it would be when this place was all hers. She could light a fire in the hearth stove, wrap herself up in an old quilt and sit with her books and her tea. There'd be no spreadsheets. No Kenneth calling every five minutes to demand to know where his new report was or reminding her the partners' meeting was happening in less than twelve hours. Nothing to keep her up late nights except testing new cake and bun recipes.

"Yes, we're staying," Emma said firmly. "We're home, Oliver."

6

FROM THE MOMENT EMMA OPENED THE BACK DOOR FOR him, Oliver was surrounded by a whole new landscape of scents—warm, living smells; cold, stony smells; rich, earthy smells. After just one deep sniff, he knew he'd have a great deal to tell Emma when he returned to the house.

Except he might just possibly not tell her quite everything.

Of course, Emma was his special human, and of course, it was his duty to tell her about whatever he discovered. But if Emma had one tiny fault in her otherwise excellent character, it was that sometimes she left him behind in the house or garden when anyone ought to be able to see that it would be far better for her to take him along. How could he properly guard and advise her if she wouldn't let him go places with her?

These were the times when it was a corgi's duty to look out for their human in spite of themselves. In a new place, with so much still unknown about it, this might just possibly involve having a secret way out of the garden. Just in case of emergencies.

So Emma did not really need to know about the hole in the garden wall. At least, not immediately.

Oliver had found the hole during his second circuit of the garden. He'd already begun the important work of dealing with the spiders and field mice that had been allowed the run of the place for too long. Then there was the matter of the Bit of Rubbish by the (unfortunately firmly closed and well-maintained) gate that had to be thoroughly investigated. All the while the wind coming up the slope kept bringing the most fascinating sorts of smells—humans, dogs, sheep, and far more wild growing things than Oliver had names for.

There were so many smells that it had taken Oliver a little while to realize some of them weren't coming from over the wall, but under it.

The yew bushes' bitter, piney odor masked the direction of the telltale scent cloud for a while, but corgis do not give up. It is not in their nature. Eventually, Oliver had to go down on his belly and creep beneath the prickly branches. This was uncomfortable, and an affront to his dignity, and the branches scraped at his sensitive ears, but it was worth it. Once he got under the bushes, he saw that three or four of the wall's stones had gone missing, creating a hole where the breeze blew through cleanly.

This hole, of course, could not be left to itself. Oliver needed to investigate its dimensions. If it was big enough, the fox might get in, or some strange dog or even a badger. Anything, really.

Oliver pressed himself as flat as he could against the damp ground and pushed and scrabbled forward. His nose made it fine. His ears brushed against cool stone. His shoulders were a squeeze, but once those were through, the rest of him followed quickly. A little too quickly, to tell the truth. Fortunately, there was no one around to see him tumble down into the little hollow on the other side and roll over, sit up, shake and sneeze.

Which was when he noticed his belly fur was now caked in mud.

Well, Emma would understand. It was all for her sake. Really. Because now he knew without question he'd have to watch this hole. If he could fit through, that fox definitely could. Or a badger. And there were badgers. He knew that smell. Oliver lifted his nose to the fresh breeze. And hedgehogs too, fairly close. He should find them. In fact, he should investigate this entire hillside so he could tell Emma about it later. Not, of course, mentioning how he came to be out here, but . . .

"You're new!" A dog's bark, and a dog's sharp scent, tumbled down the wind. "You're new!"

The interloper raced up the slope. He was a little brown and black Yorkshire terrier, smelling of lots of outdoors and mud and enthusiasm. With a terrier's typical lack of dignity, the little dog proceeded to run in circles around Oliver.

"You're new! You're new! Are we friends?" The terrier sniffed closely. "Let's be friends!"

Oliver saw no point in being standoffish and returned the little fellow's friendly sniffings. The terrier had clearly been on a long walk this morning, over quite a bit of the countryside, and . . .

"Percy! Percy, heel!"

The man came trudging up the hill, puffing hard. He was pale and smelled of closed rooms and hand sanitizer. And beer. Rather a lot of beer.

"Oh, heck." The terrier's ears drooped. "Thought I lost him."

"You *tried* to lose your human?" Oliver was aghast.

By then the man had reached them. "Making friends, are we?" The man laughed and scooped the terrier, Percy, up under one arm. "And who's the good boy, then?"

He also reached out his hand, fingers curled for Oliver to inspect. Oliver smelled gasoline and a whole set of heavy green flower smells that were familiar to him from gardens and parks. It would take time to sort them all out. There was rose and mint and lavender and . . . and . . . that was new. He didn't know that one . . .

"Yes, a very good boy." The man scratched Oliver's head, even managing to get the spot just behind his right ear.

Good human. Oliver leaned into the scratch and the man laughed again.

"All right, all right. Come on, Percy." He shook Percy. Percy kicked at the air and whined. "Back to the salt mines for us. See you later, little fellow." He moved one of Percy's paws up and down, making a human waving gesture. Percy growled impatiently.

The man carried Percy quickly away down the hill. In fact, he was jogging, even though he was still breathless, and Oliver could smell him starting to sweat.

Without thinking about it, Oliver started down the slope after the man, but at the last minute, he pulled up short. He'd been on this side of the wall a long time. If he stayed here, Emma might get worried and come looking for him. She might be angry that he'd got out. No. She'd definitely be angry. Emma was the best possible human, but she was still a human, and that meant sometimes she could be *most* unreasonable.

Quickly, Oliver wriggled and shoved himself back through the hole. He yawned and settled himself by the hole to deter the man, or the fox, from coming through.

An excellent afternoon's work. Oliver rested his muzzle on his paws and felt his ears and eyelids start to droop. But how much should he tell Emma?

Pondering this most important question, Oliver fell asleep.

7

THE ENGLISH LOVE THEIR DOGS, SO IT HADN'T BEEN TOO hard to find a bed and breakfast in Trevena with a pet-friendly policy.

The King's Rest Bed and Breakfast was a former public house on the far side of Trevena from Nancarrow cottage. A long two-story white-washed building, it nestled between the cliffs on the inland side of the motorway. A zebra crossing and a set of broad stone stairs led down to the pebble-covered beach. According to the framed magazine articles in the public rooms, that beach had been a favorite stopping point for smugglers, and pirates. Generations of tavern owners had helped them hide their goods, if not in the inn's cellars then in the seaside cavern known as Merlin's Cave.

These days, the public room held cloth-covered tables and comfortable chairs. The long stretch of polished oak that had once been the bar now held a bountiful breakfast buffet, as well as the urns and other appurtenances for coffee and tea service. Brochures for local attractions and services filled racks beside the doors and were scattered across the tables. There were several for Maggie Trenwith's firm.

One set of French doors opened onto the front of the building. A broad deck provided a space where guests could sit and have a view of the sea, interrupted only by the occasional lorry or motorist. If one preferred a view of the dramatic Cornish hills, a matching set of doors opened onto the back garden with its flagstone terrace and abundant shrubs and flower beds.

In this latest incarnation, the King's Rest was run by Angelique Delgado with help from her daughter, Pearl. Angelique was a tall, curvy, outgoing woman whose family had emigrated to England from Jamaica when she was four years old. Her husband ran a fishing and sightseeing boat, taking punters out for daylong trips around the bay or overnight stays on the nearby islands.

The Delgados had four children. Their three sons were all away from home. In positively vintage fashion, one had gone to university, one to the army, and one to seminary. Pearl was home for the summer holidays from the technical college in Edinburgh where she was finishing her degree in hotel and restaurant management. In fact, when she heard about Emma's background in finance, Pearl had asked if she could see a copy of the business plan for the tea shop.

It had taken exactly one and a half pots of tea after Tuesday breakfast to find all this out. Angelique loved a good natter as much as Emma did.

Last night, after returning from her appointment with Maggie, Emma had holed up in her room with Oliver for some quality cuddle time (not to mention a good going-over with brush, comb and towel). She watched old episodes of *The Great British Bake Off* on her laptop and happily daydreamed about the time when her scones would earn her the famous handshake from Paul Hollywood.

Of course, she'd also called Rose and filled her in on everything that had happened so far, including how Genny had gone all vague about the Penhallow building.

"Oh my lord, Emma!" Rose said, laughing. "Leave it to you to find a village mystery and set up shop in the middle of it!"

"Then you don't think I'm just imagining things?" Emma asked.

"Definitely not!" Rose told her. "Clearly there's something going on she didn't want to talk about there."

"The dark and suspicious demise of the previous owner?" Emma suggested.

"The vicar caught in a sordid tryst with a married woman?" countered Rose.

"A mysterious stranger making a payoff to the local council?"

"A ghost!" cried Rose triumphantly. "Penhallow's is haunted by the restless spirit of a sailor murdered by a smuggling ring because he was going to betray them to the revenuers!"

They'd shared a good laugh over that.

"But seriously, Em," said Rose when they'd calmed down. "You've spent your professional life dealing with shifty characters—"

"You mean rich punters and flash boys."

"I stand by my original phrasing. If you think there's something off, I'd bet money there is something. The question is, do you want to steer clear of it, or dive in? I mean really. You can always tell this Maggie Trenwith to back off. Just because she wants to score one against the local bully, it's no reason for you to get involved."

Rose's words stayed with Emma through the rest of the evening. They ran through her mind now as she lingered in the public room over a stack of notebooks and three-ring binders, as well as house-made toast and marmalade and a second pot of Darjeeling tea.

Oliver lay under the table munching biscuits, with the occasional bit of toast.

"Oliver, we keep eating like this, and we're both going to need a lot more walks," Emma murmured.

"Walks are an excellent idea," Oliver mumbled around his mouthful. "I'm always trying to tell you so. You should listen to me. We could go on a walk right now."

Emma looked out the French doors at the leaden sky. This morning, Cornwall had reverted to type. The sunrise shot red beams across the ocean, supposedly a sign of bad weather to come. That prediction seemed to be holding, because the view out the windows now featured a sky filled with ominous-looking clouds. The walking tourists and kayakers scattered around the breakfast room hunched over their phones, checking the weather and wondering to each other about changing their plans.

"Um, no," said Emma. "It's about to rain."

"I don't mind."

"I mind."

"You have a mac, and an umbrella."

She broke off another piece of toast and gave it to him. Oliver grumbled, but he munched, and then started nosing about the carpet for crumbs.

Slowly, the other guests started to clear out of the dining room. Emma, though, stayed where she was. Outside, the rain began a steady drumming against the windows. In answer, Emma tapped her pencil against the table and glowered at her books. She'd a good bit laid by from her years in the financial trenches, plus what Rose was paying to sublet her London flat, but she still obsessed over her budgets. Now that she knew she was renting Nancarrow, she wanted to go over the figures again, just to make extra sure everything was still in order, in case getting the shop set up took a little longer than she'd originally projected.

Which brought her back to thoughts of Penhallow's, and Victoria Roberts and Rose's question.

Do you want to steer clear of it, or dive in?

Obviously, steering clear was the smart thing to do. She should call Maggie and get that list of alternatives today. She had enough on her plate without poking the dragon that was Victoria Roberts.

But the idea that Penhallows might have a secret past was so . . . delicious. Emma sighed. Memory washed over her—of being a little girl crouched behind a pile of crates on the pier, her notebook stuffed in a book bag and her spyglass clutched in her hand. Every now and again, she'd peek out over the crates, looking for signs of "nefarious" activity on the part of the local sailors.

At least, until Henry caught her and dragged her back to the holiday flat where their parents were waiting.

The snitch. Emma shook her head.

Yes, she had to admit it, a mystery attached to a property was a selling point as far as she was concerned. It might not be rational, but there it was.

But that left a whole world of questions, starting with one in particular.

"What, exactly, can be done about Victoria Roberts?"

"You're not the first person to ask that."

Emma started and blinked. Oliver poked his head out from under the table.

Angelique was clearing off the buffet. Emma had been so lost in her own thoughts, she hadn't even noticed the B&B owner come in.

"Sorry." Emma felt herself blush. "Just talking to myself."

Angelique waved this away. "I did exactly the same thing when I was working out how to start this place. Even had my own pile of binders." She smiled. "And me daughter's following right along in the family tradition, I'm pleased to say. Oh, and thank you for letting her have that copy of your business plan. She's thinking there are opportunities to expand us, you see, and is looking for more examples of how to write her own prospectus."

Oliver trotted out from under the table to sniff around her ankles. Angelique chuckled. "No, I have not dropped anything for you, you greedy thing."

"Just checking," Oliver murmured, continuing his investigation. "One never knows, does one?"

"Did you have any run-ins with Victoria Roberts when you started up?" Emma asked curiously.

"Not directly." Angelique turned down the flame under the chafing dish for the sausages. "Fortunately, this was one of the few bits of property she didn't own in the village. So she complained, but there was very little she could actually do. Poor thing." The humor in Angelique's brown eyes faded.

"Poor thing?" said Emma, a little startled. "Why poor thing?"

"The only reason someone walks around carrying that much bitterness is because something bad happened to them." Angelique smiled ruefully. "At least, that's what I tell myself when I'm feeling charitable. Other times, I just suppose some people are natural-born sourpusses and there's nothing the rest of us can do but get on with things."

"Maybe she's just lonely," said Emma hopefully. "Some people get angry to cover how sad and frustrated they are."

"No. It's not that. It's . . . it's something more. Getting on her bad side can be dangerous."

"Dangerous?" Emma repeated, remembering Victoria's threat to have Oliver put down.

Angelique was silent for a minute, concentrating on stacking the empty chafing dishes, one into the other. Then she said. "There was an . . . incident, not too many years ago. The local supermarket manager wanted to expand the car park, but to do that, he would need some land Victoria owned. He made a big speech about it at the village council meeting, accusing her of standing in the way of progress and Trevena's welfare, all that. The next day, Victoria caught up with him in the middle of the store and said right out loud, 'If I were keeping two sets of books, I'd be a lot more careful about raising a fuss in council meetings, even if I were paying off half the members.'"

Emma felt her eyes go wide. Angelique just nodded.

When Emma regained her voice, she asked, "Was it true?"

"Turns out that it was." Angelique gave her a small, wry smile. "Including the fact that some of the council members had been getting their groceries for free. He served three years for fraud and moved to Canada directly afterward." She shrugged with one shoulder while she stacked the used serving spoons into the chafing dishes. "But that's why I say she's dangerous. She collects people's secrets with her parcels of land, that one. Then she uses them just as soon as she's ready."

Emma twirled her pencil nervously. After hearing that, a sensible person would just find a different spot for their tea shop.

But I'm starting a whole new life. I don't want to give up at the first sign of difficulty.

Oh, come on, Emma, she scolded herself. *There's character and curiosity, and then there's pure pigheadedness.*

She looked down at her notes again. "There must be some way to make a connection with her. If I could draw Victoria out of her shell, prove I'm not just some Londoner out to stomp all over village tradition . . ." Emma tapped her pencil again. "There must be some way to make a connection. Does she have a pet? A hobby?" The idea hit. The pencil stilled. Oliver pricked up his ears.

"Does she like cake?"

Angelique pulled her chin back. "Cake? I could not say . . . I do think I remember Ruth once saying how much Victoria loved her scones and jam, but . . ."

"That's it!" Emma jumped to her feet. "That's how I make friends with Victoria Roberts. Food. Food . . . and flowers!"

Angelique narrowed her eyes. "All right, Emma. You've lost me."

"Victoria loves her roses. They're prizewinners for her."

"This is true," agreed Angelique.

"Nancarrow's garden is . . . it's not even a disaster. It's nonexistent. I'm negotiating with the owners about letting me make some improvements to the cottage. I'll take her a plate of scones as an apology for yesterday and ask her for her advice on what to plant and where and how . . . Connection!" Emma pressed her palms together. "Angelique, I have a favor to ask."

Angelique drew back in a show of consternation. "What is it?"

"It's a dreadful imposition, and a little bit mad, I know, but . . . could I use your kitchen?"

8

EMMA HAD LEARNED TO BAKE FROM HER GRANDMOTHER
Phyllis. Among her friends, Phyllis Reed's scones were legendary.

Phyllis did not hold with putting "all them fancy sorts of
things" like lemon or crystallized ginger in scones. Phyllis
never understood why people insisted on mucking about
with what was perfectly simple, and perfectly good.

Emma might have disagreed with Nana Phyllis about
banishing red currants and lemon peel, but she had to admit
there was something wonderful about a simple scone. It took
just five ingredients for a good batch—flour, baking powder,
cream, butter and a dash of salt. Plus, Emma found the physical
work—crumbling in the butter, stirring in the cream,
pressing out the dough, and seeing it all come together under
her hands—uniquely satisfying. Emma planned on making
her scones the centerpiece on her tea shop menu. Right now,
however, they would be the opening salvo in her charm offensive
against Victoria Roberts.

Once she explained her plan to Angelique, Angelique
opened the kitchen for her, then stayed to help her find the
ingredients she needed, and the necessary pans, and show
her how to work the cooker.

Baking scones in a virtual stranger's kitchen to try to woo a prickly old woman was, of course, ridiculous. As a matter of business, it was unnecessary and contained a high risk of backfiring, especially with Maggie Trenwith out there trying her own methods.

Emma was doing it anyway.

Emma's life up to this point had been about making sure other people—her brother and his family, her parents, all the little overprivileged boys at work—had what they needed. She'd helped take care of her nieces when they were young, then cared for her parents while they aged. Even her choice of a career in finance had been a compromise. It was a way to follow in the family footsteps while still asserting some independence. It had also, incidentally, allowed her to gather a nest egg big enough that she had been able to help the family during the last financial crash.

But now her parents were gone, her nieces were on the brink of leaving for uni, and Henry was talking about taking on a new partner at the accounting firm. Emma wanted to build something new, something that was fully hers, and she would not waste any opportunity to get what she wanted.

When the scones finally came out of the oven, they were fragrant and warm and lightly browned. Emma broke one open to release the steam and check the bake. She handed half to Angelique.

Angelique blew on the hot scone and took a bite. "That's fantastic!" she exclaimed around the mouthful, and if there was a touch of surprise in her voice, Emma readily forgave her.

"It seems a shame to waste those on Victoria Roberts," Angelique went on as Emma continued her really unconscionable mooching and borrowed a tea towel to wrap the scones in.

"If you like, I'll make another batch when I get back."

"That'd be wonderful. Mmm." Angelique popped the last of her scone in her mouth. "If this is a sample of what you'll have at the new shop, I'll be first in line. Probably every day."

"Well, first I have to convince Victoria Roberts to let me have my space. Then, I promise, it's Nana Phyllis's scones all round!"

Angelique waved her hand. "If you can soften the Old Vic, you will be doing the whole village a favor. I wish you the best of luck."

CORNISH WEATHER WAS FAMOUSLY CONTRARY. BY THE TIME Emma had taken all her binders and notebooks upstairs and grabbed her umbrella, mackintosh and Oliver's lead from her room, the rain had let up. The clouds, however, kept a low, tight lid over the village. Emma tucked her umbrella under one arm, just in case. Oliver trotted obediently at her side, on his lead.

She'd really meant to leave him back at the B&B. He'd whined and begged so hard, though, that she gave in. Besides, after this morning, she really couldn't cadge yet another favor from Angelique by asking her to keep an eye on him.

"Oliver, you have to promise me you'll behave," she said as they walked briskly up the street. She'd bundled the scones up into one of her spare carrier bags for easier transport and also to protect them from the rain that would surely start up again any second. "You'll wait by the garden wall, and you won't even *try* to get into the garden."

"You have my solemn word. But if that fox—"

"No. No fox hunting for you. Anyone would think you were a beagle."

"Emma! How could you!"

Emma crouched down and rubbed his ears. "Please, Oliver? I need your help, okay? This is really important to me."

Oliver immediately put his paws on her knee and licked her cheeks. "I promise, Emma. Corgi's honor!"

"I can always count on you." Emma kissed his forehead, then rubbed his ears again for good measure.

They reached Victoria's gate. Her cottage was a stucco-sided house with low eaves and a mossy roof. The famous roses drooped heavily over the wall, filling the rain-washed air with perfume.

Emma had decided on a gradual approach. Today, she would hand over her apology scones. If there was a chance, she'd remark on the roses and mention the sorry state of Nancarrow's garden. If she played it right, she might just get Victoria to agree to talk with her again. Not today though. If invited in, she'd refuse, citing Oliver, which would demonstrate she respected Victoria's preferences and help show that she really could be trusted. She'd make plans to come back later, when she didn't have her dog.

Reviewing the plan now, Emma felt confident. When she saw the light shining through Victoria's front window, her optimism kicked up another notch.

"Great. She's home." Emma couldn't imagine Victoria as being the kind who would leave a light on when she wasn't there.

Emma looped the end of Oliver's lead around the gatepost. Then she took a deep breath and put her hand on the gate. "Wish me luck, Oliver. Here I go."

But right then, a breeze whirled around them and Oliver's nose shot up. "Something's wrong."

"What is it, Oliver?"

"Wrong, wrong! Bad!" Oliver charged, right under the gate. The loose knot on the lead came undone immediately, and he bolted for the cottage door, barking at the top of his lungs.

"Oliver!" Emma struggled one-handed with the gate latch, praying that she didn't drop the scones, and also praying that Victoria Roberts was hard of hearing. "Quiet, Oliver!"

"I can't! I can't! Something's wrong!" Oliver scrabbled at the doorjamb.

Emma hurried up the garden path. This was not like Oliver. Something really might be wrong.

"Okay, okay, easy, Oliver. Calm down."

"I can't! I can't! Something's wrong! It's wrong!" He kept barking, but he did back away, giving Emma room to get to the door.

The old cottage didn't have a bell that Emma could see, so she knocked. "Ms. Roberts?" There was no answer. She knocked harder. "Ms. Roberts?" she called again. She also rattled the knob. Much to her shock, it turned in her hand.

The cottage door creaked as it opened. Oliver was inside before Emma's eyes could adjust to the dim interior.

The cottage was the sort with a long central hall between the sitting room and the stairs. At the far end, watery daylight filtered through the neatly curtained window above the sink.

There was a clock ticking, and Oliver barking, but no other sound.

A chill ran down Emma's spine.

"Ms. Roberts?" She forced her reluctant feet to move forward, to carry her down the cool passageway and into the kitchen. "Victoria?"

Emma had the impression of broken crockery and glass. A flowered tablecloth lay crumpled on the floor, like it had been pulled off and dropped. A teapot lay on its side next to a broken cup. Brown liquid puddled on the linoleum.

In the middle of it all lay Victoria Roberts, facedown in the spilled tea.

Emma gasped.

"Victoria!" She charged forward, dropping scones and umbrella, and fell to her knees.

"Victoria?"

As carefully as she could, Emma turned the woman over. She saw her open eyes and slack, reddened mouth.

She didn't remember much after that.

9

"EMMA? EMMA?"

Something wet was patting at her face, accompanied by warm breath that smelled distinctly . . . *doggish.*

"Emma? It's all right, Emma!"

Then she wondered, *Why are my eyes closed?*

Emma opened her eyes. She was staring straight at a rosebush. She also seemed to be sitting down, in the mud.

"Emma? Wake up, you can do it." Oliver pawed at her shoulder. "Come on, time to wake up."

"I'm awake, I'm awake." Not only was she awake, but the details of what had just happened were flooding back. She remembered seeing Victoria stretched out across her kitchen floor, the broken teacup, the spilled teapot. Emma remembered running to Victoria's side and turning her over, and seeing her eyes opened and her mouth red and swollen . . . and . . .

And now she was sitting in the dirt beside the cottage door, probably crushing the herbaceous border. She didn't have her scones, or her umbrella, because she'd dropped them in the kitchen.

I must have run out here and . . . fainted. Good lord.

Emma gathered Oliver into her lap and buried her face

in the corgi's fur. She held him tight, absorbing his living warmth and steady affection.

"It's okay." Oliver prodded her cheek with his hard little nose. "It's okay, Emma. I'm here."

"Hello?"

Emma's head shot up.

A man with a round, flushed face stood on the other side of the garden wall. His dark hair was both retreating and going gray. He wore a green T-shirt and a brown bomber jacket. He also carried a wriggling Yorkie terrier under one arm.

"Is everything all right?" the man asked.

"Erm." Emma gently shooed Oliver off her lap and struggled to her feet. She swayed briefly, but was relieved to find her knees quickly steadied. "No. I . . ."

She pulled out her phone, trying to see if she'd managed to call 999 before she'd decided to imitate a heroine in a particularly bad Gothic novel and faint in the garden.

"Here, now." The man pushed the gate open and came up the garden path. He set the Yorkie down. The little brown and black dog immediately started nosing around Oliver, who returned the favor. "Has something happened?"

"Yes, it has. It . . . that is, I . . ." Emma took a deep breath. "I need to call the police." She punched the first two nines into the phone.

"The police?" the man exclaimed. "Is someone hurt? Can I help?" He started for the open cottage door.

"No. I . . . don't go in there!" Emma shouted. "She's dead."

The man jumped back a step. The Yorkie, as if sensing a chance for mischief, charged toward the cottage door, barking. Oliver darted into his path head down, herding him away.

"No, no, this way." Oliver nipped and nosed at the smaller dog. "You can't go in there. Emma says no!"

The Yorkie did not like this and responded with a sharp bark.

"Behave, Percy!" The man snatched him up. The Yorkie's little legs paddled at the air, but the man held him, gently but firmly.

Emma held up her phone again, but before she could touch the next digit, she heard Genny Knowles shout.

"Emma?"

Genny was hurrying down the street from the chip shop, holding on to her white service cap with one hand.

"What's going on? Is everything okay? Where's Victoria?" Genny saw the man standing with Emma and evidently didn't recognize him. "Um. Hello?"

"Ah. Hello. I . . ." The man held out his hand. "Parker Taite. I was just passing by, walking my dog." He patted the Yorkie. "Well, he's not really my dog. I'm watching him for my brother. I'm staying at the King's Rest and . . ."

"You are?" said Emma, startled. "I haven't seen you at breakfast."

The man shrugged. "Yes, well, I'm a writer. We're not usually morning people . . . Didn't you say you needed to call the police?"

"Oh! Gosh, yes. Sorry." Emma hit the final 9 and held the phone to her ear.

"Police!" cried Genny. "Emma, what's happened?"

"Nine-nine-nine emergency." The operator spoke with preternatural calm. "What is your emergency?"

"It's Victoria Roberts," said Emma to Genny. "She's dead."

Genny pressed her hand over her mouth.

"You need to report a death?" said the operator. "Are you currently in a safe location?"

"I'm really sorry," the man, Parker Taite, said to Genny. "Did you know her well?"

"Are you still on the line?" said the operator. "Have you taken steps to ascertain whether the person was still breathing? Was CPR administered?"

"Yes, I'm here," said Emma. "And yes, she's dead, and no, at least, I don't think so. I . . . it's all a little blurry."

"Everybody knew her." Genny frowned at the doorway. "None of us . . . Oh, God, this is so horrible."

"Do you require an ambulance?" asked the operator.

"Here, here, you better sit down." There was a bucket beside the door. Parker upended it to make a stool. "Or you'll faint, like your friend."

"It's okay, it's okay." Genny turned to Emma. "You fainted?"

"I fainted," Emma admitted.

"Do you need an ambulance?" inquired the operator again.

"I . . . no, sorry, that wasn't for you," said Emma into the phone. "I'm so sorry. I need the police. I think. I'm sorry. I . . . I don't know what to do."

Which sounded pathetic and ridiculous. She ought to know what to do. She wasn't sure why, exactly, but it felt like the kind of thing a person was supposed to know.

"Are you in a safe location?" asked the operator.

"Yes, yes, I'm safe."

"Of course you're safe," said Oliver stoutly. "I'm right here, aren't I?"

The operator ran down some other questions, like had Emma been hurt? (No.) Was there any possibility of an attacker on the premises? (No, at least, I don't think so . . .) Finally, Emma was instructed to remain at the scene and told the police would be there shortly, and asked again if she was sure she was safe.

Emma looked out at the lovely garden with its rainbow array of summer roses, the weathered gate, and the peaceful village road beyond. "Yes. Yes, I am safe, thanks."

"I *said* . . ." Oliver pawed at Emma's jeans.

"Yes, Oliver. You're right here." She cut off the call and put her hand to her forehead, as if that would somehow slow her whirling thoughts.

"She was drinking flowers, Emma," said Oliver. "Why was she drinking flowers?"

"Quiet, now, Oliver." She paused. "What flowers? I didn't see any flowers." *Or did I?* She pressed her hand against her forehead. *Maybe?*

"I smelled them!" Oliver insisted. "In the tea! She shouldn't have been drinking those flowers!"

"I'm sorry," said Emma over Oliver's grumbling and barking. "What did you say your name was?" she asked the man.

"Parker Taite. And you are . . . ?"

"Emma Reed," said Emma.

"And I'm Genny Knowles." Genny heaved herself up off the bucket. "I run the chip shop just up the way." She pointed over her shoulder. "I think we should all go there, get Emma out of the wet."

"We're supposed to remain on the scene," said Emma.

"We'll be staring at the scene from shouting distance," Genny pointed out. "We'll be able to watch the police arrive from there. Well, Raj Patel. He's our only permanent PC," she added. "And if he's out on the road someplace, it might be a while, and you should sit down and have a cup of tea."

"Well . . . tea does sound like a good idea," agreed Emma.

Except before any of them reached the gate, an engine roar sounded from up the hill, in the direction, Emma realized, of Nancarrow Cottage. All three humans and both dogs watched Jimmy Lambert's red sports car zoom down the road. The car screeched to a halt right outside Victoria's gate.

Jimmy jumped out of the driver's side.

"What the hell is going on?" he demanded as he slammed the car door. "What are all you people doing here? Where's Aunt Victoria?"

They all looked at one another. Jimmy's face flushed.

"Somebody tell me . . ." he began.

"Jimmy," said Genny. "I'm really sorry . . ."

Jimmy stared at her. Then, without another word, he bolted up the garden path and vanished into the cottage.

That was when they heard the siren.

10

....

EMMA, GENNY AND PARKER TAITE ALL TURNED AT ONCE.
Oliver and Percy both charged the open gate. Emma and
Parker lunged, scooping their dogs up into their arms just
as the miniature police cruiser scooted down the road and
pulled up so it was nose to nose with Jimmy's vintage
BMW. A slender young man in a dark blue police constable
uniform climbed out of the tiny car. He had black hair, light
brown skin, and a long, worried face.

"Raj!" Genny exclaimed. "Raj, you have to get in there
after Jimmy. His aunt—"

"Got it!" PC Patel bolted through the cottage door. "All
of you stay right there!" he shouted without stopping.

Emma put Oliver down. Parker kept hold of Percy. Oliver immediately got busy, snuffling the invisible (to Emma)
path of PC Patel's footsteps.

"Did you find her?" Genny asked. "Emma, that's awful!"

"Not as bad as . . ." Emma swallowed and gestured toward the open door. "Poor Jimmy."

"Poor Jimmy," agreed Genny.

"He was here," confirmed Oliver, nose down in the herbaceous border now.

"Any idea what's happened?" asked Parker. "I mean, I . . . she was an old lady . . ."

"Did you know her?" Emma asked him.

"Um. Not as such. We'd had . . . words," he said flatly.

"Oh, you too?" murmured Emma.

Oliver had moved over to the line of sprawling rosebushes that lined the garden wall. "Emma," he said. "Emma, there's something in here. Emma."

"Oliver!" she called. "No digging, Oliver!"

Oliver huffed, annoyed, and kicked out his back leg. "But there's *something*!" He did, however, sit down.

Parker smiled faintly. "Wish Percy listened to me like that."

Genny was looking anxiously toward the cottage door. "Do you suppose—"

Before she could finish, they heard movement inside. In the next second, PC Patel came through the door.

"Come on, Jimmy, mate. Nothing you can do here." PC Patel had his arm wrapped around Jimmy's shoulders and steered him out onto the garden path. Jimmy looked gray and sick with shock.

"I don't understand," Jimmy whispered. "I don't understand."

"Oh, dear." Genny took both his hands. "Jimmy, I'm so very sorry."

"Can you take him . . ." The constable looked at Genny but hesitated.

"How about the King's Rest?" suggested Emma. "There'll be room for all of us." She looked at the sky. The wind was blowing, and the smell of approaching rain mixed with the smell of the sea. Also, her backside was starting to get cold from her little sit-down in the mud.

"Right. Good." PC Patel was looking more than a little shaken himself. "And you all stay put there, yeah? We'll need statements from everybody just as soon as we're finished here."

While PC Patel took everybody's names and contact information, Genny convinced Jimmy he was in no shape to drive, even just to the other side of the village. Jimmy agreed, very reluctantly.

While Genny struggled to get the gate latch open again, Jimmy turned and gripped Raj's shoulder.

"You'll find out what happened, yeah, mate?" he croaked. "*Promise* me."

"I promise, Jim," Raj answered. "I do."

Jimmy went with Genny then, but from the look on his face he did not entirely believe Raj would, or could, do as he said.

Why is he so sure something's wrong? Emma wondered. *She was an old woman. It must just have been a stroke or something.*

Mustn't it?

Emma shook her head hard, as if that could clear her confusion, and looked around automatically for Oliver. Oliver, in the meantime, had crept forward on his belly and managed to get most of his torso under the rosebushes. Percy just wriggled the whole way under.

She exchanged an eye roll with Parker Taite.

"I'll get him," said Parker.

While Parker went after his restless terrier, Emma pulled out her mobile and dialed up the King's Rest.

"Hello, Angelique? It's Emma Reed. There's been . . . there's been an accident."

Lord, I hope that's all it is.

THANKS TO EMMA'S PHONE CALL, ANGELIQUE WAS IN THE B&B's otherwise unoccupied lounge when their motley little parade straggled in. She sailed up to Jimmy Roberts and wrapped her arms around him.

"We're all so very sorry, Jimmy," she said.

Jimmy pulled back, glowering. For a moment, Emma saw his resemblance to his aunt. But he swallowed whatever he'd been about to say.

"Thank you, Angelique," he murmured. "I . . . it's a shock is all. They . . . that is . . . Raj is at the house now, but he says

they have to call out to Truro because they have to treat it
as a suspicious death until they can say for sure it's not, and
the Truro police might not be out for a while, and they're
going to need statements, and I hate leaving her, it's not
right, but—"

Angelique didn't let him get any further. "Pearl is making tea. You come in the private room and sit yourself
down, yeah? All of you, please." She beckoned to Emma,
Parker and Genny. The dogs both darted on ahead.

The private room was a comfortable front room set aside
for use by larger groups of guests, like wedding parties or
coach tours. A table big enough for a dozen people stretched
along the right side under the windows that overlooked the
road and the sea and the steadily falling rain. A sofa and
some plump armchairs were arranged in front of the fireplace. Jimmy dropped down onto the sofa and stared at the
empty hearth.

"I'll go help Pearl with the tea," said Angelique. "I'm
sure you could all use a good strong cup."

"Can I help?" asked Emma.

But Genny was already on her feet. "You sit," she told
Emma. "Angelique and I have got this."

Genny followed Angelique out, leaving Emma and Oliver alone with Jimmy, Parker and Percy.

Emma, uncertain what else to do, sat down beside Jimmy.
Oliver curled up at her feet. Percy wandered the room,
sniffing restlessly and clearly searching for an unguarded
escape route. He wasn't the only one. Parker Taite walked
to the door and peered out into the lounge like he was considering making a break for it.

Unsure what to do, Emma shifted in her seat.

"I'm so sorry about your aunt," she said to Jimmy.

"I don't know what happened!" he whispered. "She was
fine! She should have been . . . It all should have been . . ."
He stopped, and frowned. "Why were there scones?"

"Sorry?"

"Scones. There was this pile of scones spilled out on the

floor. Aunt Victoria couldn't bake. She couldn't even boil an egg."

"Oh, those were mine, sorry." Emma tried to smile, and only sort of managed it. "I was bringing them over to her. As an apology."

"Apology? For what?" Then, slowly, Jimmy's expression shifted. "I'm sorry, but have we even *met*?"

"Erm, no, not really." Emma felt her cheeks heating up. "I'm Emma Reed, and I'm moving to Nancarrow, and Oliver"—she scratched the corgi's ears—"tried to get into Victoria's garden."

"Same thing with Percy," chimed in Parker. Emma started. She'd almost forgotten he was there, but he was, leaning against the threshold with his arms folded.

Jimmy glanced at him, but looked away again immediately. Instead, he put his focus on Oliver. Oliver lifted his head to looked back. Jimmy held out his hand so the corgi could sniff his fingers, which he did, and gave Jimmy a brief lick.

"Flowers," Oliver reported. "And cars and breakfast."

"Good boy," said Jimmy. Percy, sensing Oliver had a good thing going, trotted over as well and also got a rub on his tiny head. "I'm sure it wasn't your fault. Either of you. That garden is . . . was . . . practically Aunt Victoria's entire life."

Parker, who hadn't moved from his post by the door, stepped back then to make room for Angelique and Genny to come through. Angelique carried a loaded tea tray, complete with milk, sugar, spoons and cups for everybody.

"Here now, Jimmy." Genny poured out a steaming mug and put it in his hands. "You drink that."

"We've called Louise," Angelique added. "She's coming right over."

"Thanks, Angelique." Jimmy sipped the steaming tea. "I just . . . I know I keep saying this, but I don't understand it. Aunt Victoria was fine! She'd just been to the doctor's last month. I took her. He said she was in great shape for her age."

Oliver shoved his hard nose against Emma's shin. "It was the flowers."

"It was not the flowers," muttered Emma, exasperated.

"I'm sorry, what flowers?" said Jimmy.

"Oh, did I say that out loud? I'm sorry, I . . ." Emma groped for something that wouldn't sound completely daft. A sudden image rose up out of the maze of her thoughts. "There were some flowers scattered on the floor around the table." *Mixed in with the broken glass and the broken cup.*

"Yeah, I saw that." Jimmy looked down into his tea. "Lilies of the valley, I think." He frowned.

"Lilies of the valley?" said Genny. "Aren't they a spring flower?"

Jimmy shoved his fringe of hair back from his forehead. "Usually, but they'll hold out quite awhile in the shady parts of the garden." He paused, because everybody was looking at him. "I grew up in that garden. I know its seasons. And Aunt Victoria liked having them on the table. She liked the smell."

"Right, yeah," said Emma. "Anyway, I just thought about them and thought that was strange, but they must have fallen off the table when the cloth got pulled off and . . . Sorry, I think I need some of that tea."

Emma filled a mug from the pot. She'd just taken a cautious sip when Louise Craddock hurried in. Louise brushed right past Parker without even looking at him. Jimmy put his mug down and stood. The two of them stared at each other for a split second, and then Louise opened her arms, and she and Jimmy fell into a tearful hug.

Emma looked at Angelique, Genny and Parker. In silent agreement, all of them beat a hasty retreat out of the room, with Oliver trotting beside Emma.

Percy, sensing his chance, zoomed straight for the front door.

"Percy!" Parker chased after him. "For God's sake, not now!" He managed to grab the Yorkie's scruff right before he reached the door.

"Terriers," sniffed Oliver. "No dignity."

Angelique closed the door to the private front room.

"Poor Jimmy," she said as she joined Emma and Genny. "Victoria was all the family he had."

"I can't blame him for being shocked. Victoria always seemed . . . indestructible." Genny grimaced. "I suppose it must have been her heart or something."

"I suppose," said Emma. A heart attack could be very sudden. Even when the doctor said everything was fine.

"Heart conditions are routinely underdiagnosed in women," Angelique went on. "Her doctor . . ."

"It was the flowers," muttered Oliver.

Emma sighed, but at least this time, she bit her tongue before she reflexively answered Oliver.

Then she frowned.

"What is it, Emma?" asked Genny.

"I did . . . I mean . . . it's all a muddle, but I thought . . . there was something strange about her mouth. Victoria's, I mean."

"Strange how?" Parker, still holding a struggling Percy, came over to join them.

"It looked like she had a rash or something." Emma shook her head. "I could be imagining it. Post-traumatic something or the other."

"You're not imagining, Emma." Oliver butted her shin again. "I saw it too. And the flowers were around her mouth, and in the cup and . . ."

"All right, Oliver. All right. Sorry. He knows something's wrong and it makes him antsy."

"I'm not antsy. You're not listening, Emma!"

She crouched down to rub his head, and Oliver subsided onto his belly, but only reluctantly.

"Well, he's not the only one who's antsy," Angelique rubbed her arms. Genny reached out and gave her a hug.

"I'm with you," said Parker. "Listen, there's some calls I've got to make. Do you think—"

Before he finished, the door opened and a big, fit woman entered, shaking the rain off her purple travel umbrella. She had a strong, square face and sandy-gold skin. Her hair had been bleached almost white and cut short enough to stand up in spikes. She wore a dark blue jacket and trousers with a bright green blouse. Oliver probably could have ridden comfortably in the massive handbag slung over her shoulder.

"Sorry to interrupt," the woman said. "Detective Chief Inspector Constance Brent from the Devon and Cornwall police. I understand we have a bit of a situation here?"

11

· · · · · · · · · ·

"NOW, MS. REED, I'M SORRY TO HAVE KEPT YOU WAITING."

The fact was that since DCI Constance Brent had walked into the King's Rest, Emma had had time to drink a full three cups of tea. She'd also persuaded Genny and Angelique she wasn't about to faint a second time, and they let her into Angelique's kitchen to help make sandwiches for all the reluctant guests. Simple, familiar acts like slicing bread, spreading condiments and laying down layers of roast beef and tomato helped steady Emma enormously. So did the half a roast beef sandwich she ate in the lounge. Even after that, she had time to convince a reluctant Oliver, and an even more reluctant Percy, that the only available option for some outside time was the rainy back garden. For once, Oliver didn't go chasing off after Percy, but stayed staunchly at Emma's side, in case she needed him.

Which, she was not ashamed to admit, she did. All that solid, steady corgi loyalty helped her keep her cool even more than keeping busy in the kitchen did.

Now, though, she had to take a seat in front of an actual police detective. All her recently calmed nerves started jangling all over again.

DCI Brent had commandeered Angelique's office for

her questioning. She sat behind the tiny, tidy desk with a little flip notebook in front of her. Oliver had already begun exploring the room and was just now nosing around the filing cabinets and the little table where Angelique kept an electric kettle and a box of tea bags.

"Now. Let's see your hand." DCI Brent gestured with two fingers.

Startled, Emma held her right hand out before she even thought to ask why. DCI Brent turned it over so it was palm up. Oliver came over and stood up on his hind legs, trying to get a look at what was happening.

"Mmm, interesting." Constance squinted. "That's a strong, direct head line."

Head line?

"You're a straightforward person. Very independent and sure of yourself."

What is this?

"Now, your heart line, here"—she touched a crease on Emma hand—"that's more fragmented, especially at the beginning. Not a one-partner woman. But you have a lot of heart."

"What's she doing, Emma?" Oliver backed down to sit on his hindquarters. "She smells good, but like chemicals. What's she doing?"

No idea. Emma rubbed Oliver's head with her free hand.

"Now, what everybody really wants to know about is their life line," the detective went on. "That's right here." She tapped her thumb against the line. It was an impersonal touch. Emma leaned forward in spite of herself. "That's good and strong, also direct, like your head line, and deep. So, it's a long life for you. There." She let go, and Emma found herself staring at her own hand.

Constance smiled. "Learned to do that when I was a girl. I was the chubby, nerdy one nobody would talk to at parties, but they all loved having their palms read. Now." She flipped open her little black notebook. "Feeling up to telling me what happened?"

"Uh. Yes. Yes, I guess so." Oddly, the incongruity of the

palm reading seemed to have calmed Emma's nerves and helped her refocus herself. *Which was probably the point.* She paused.

Unless the point was that DCI Brent had wanted a look at Emma's hands for reasons of her own.

"Right. Here we go, then." Constance clicked her mechanical pencil. "I'm very much afraid that we're having to treat Victoria Roberts's death as suspicious for the moment. Now, I fully expect that what you and the others tell me will show it to be something very sad, but very ordinary." She smiled encouragingly. "So, for the record, you are Emma Phyllis Reed?"

"Yes."

"Let me up, Emma." Oliver pawed at her blue jeans. "I want to see. Please?"

Emma picked Oliver up and set him on her lap. He laid his muzzle on the desk and looked up at the detective.

"And your address is?"

Oliver pricked up his ears. The detective gave him a speculative look. Oliver sneezed.

"Erm." Emma rubbed his head. "I'm sort of between addresses. I . . . I've just rented Nancarrow Cottage here in the village. But I'm still staying here at the B&B, and I've got my flat back in London. My friend Rose Bremer is subletting there, but still—"

"Right. Well, let's have all that, then, and your mobile number."

Emma gave her answers, and Constance wrote them down. Oliver pushed his nose at the detective's pencil. Constance looked at the dog. She gave him her hand to sniff and lick, then rubbed him under the chin.

"Good boy," she said.

"Oooo, that's good, right there," Oliver closed his eyes. "I like her, Emma."

"He likes you," Emma told her.

"Well, I like him too." Constance gave Oliver's head a gentle shake. "You let us get on, Oliver, and I promise Emma here will take you on a good long walk afterward, all right?" She pulled her hand back. "And, Emma, maybe you can tell me what brought you and this little sweetie to Trevena."

"This 'sweetie' is a noble warrior corgi . . ." began Oliver.

Emma petted Oliver's neck firmly. "It's kind of a long story."

DCI Brent raised her brows, just a little. All at once, Emma felt unaccountably nervous, like she'd been called down to the head teacher's office.

"It's okay, Emma. I'm right here." Oliver snuggled closer. Emma hugged him, drawing comfort from his very solid, very familiar presence.

"Well, I am, obviously, moving to Trevena. I hoped—I still hope—to open a tea shop here."

"Oh, like that lovely one that closed. Penhallows, was it?"

"Well, yes."

"Been empty awhile, I understand? Have you looked into it?"

Emma had been ready to have to talk about finding Victoria. This turn of the conversation to her personal business made her uneasy. "I'd love to have the Penhallow's space, but, well, that was always going to be a long shot . . ."

"Because it's located in a building the deceased, Victoria Roberts, owned?"

"Yes, that's right."

How did she find that out so quickly? Emma wondered. Then she wondered, *Why did she think to ask about it?* Her uneasiness intensified.

"So you knew Ms. Roberts?"

"Um, no. Not exactly. I've been working with an estate agent, Maggie Trenwith. But my family used to spend holidays here, and I always loved that shop, and when I found out it had closed down, I thought it would be wonderful to open it again. Maggie said she was sure she could convince Victoria. She wanted . . ."

Just one week.

"She wanted?" prompted Constance.

"When we talked about it, she asked me to give her a week to look into the situation, and if it was a no-go after that, we'd look elsewhere."

Constance nodded and duly noted this down. "I gather Ms. Trenwith and the deceased were not on the best of terms. Did Ms. Trenwith say what she planned to do to convince Ms. Roberts to let you lease the space?"

"Um, no, I didn't get a chance to ask."

"And why should you?" said Constance easily. "Now, how about James Lambert? Did you know him?"

"No. I only met him today. Is he all right?" Emma remembered the blank, sick look on Jimmy's face when he came out of Victoria's cottage with Raj Patel.

Then she remembered him sitting on the sofa in the front room staring at the hearth. *She should have been . . . It all should have been . . .*

Why'd he say that? What did he mean?

Oliver sensed her uneasiness and wriggled closer.

Probably it's all nothing, Emma told herself as she rubbed Oliver's ears. *He's just confused. Who wouldn't be?*

DCI Brent was watching her. Emma felt an unaccountable urge to sit up straighter and stop fidgeting.

"What about Parker Taite? He a friend of yours?" the detective asked.

Emma shook her head. "Never saw him before. As far as I know, he was just passing by and saw me." *Sitting in the mud, having just passed out.*

"But you know Genny Knowles?"

"Just since yesterday."

"All right." DCI Brent flipped through her pages. "So, about this quarrel you and Ms. Roberts had? If you didn't know her, what was that about?"

"Oh, that, yeah." Emma blushed. "My dog tried to get into her garden."

"There was a fox!" Oliver barked.

"Yes, we know, Oliver."

"But, Emma . . ."

Emma put Oliver on the floor. He grumbled and started

snuffling around the room again, just in case anything had changed. "Anyway, I was bringing over some scones as an apology."

"Ah, those were your scones." The detective made another note. "How about the umbrella?"

"Also mine." Emma felt herself blush. "I dropped everything when I saw . . . her."

"You don't remember?"

Emma shook her head. "It's kind of a blur now. Mostly, I remember turning her over and seeing she was . . . well, and then waking up outside."

"No shame," said Constance. "It must have been a really nasty shock." She looked at her notes. "Only homemade scones are a pretty major apology for a bit of a dustup over a dog."

"Well, it was a bit of a bribe too," Emma admitted.

"You wanted to make friends?" suggested Constance. "Smooth the way to getting your shop?"

"Well, yes," Emma admitted. The detective looked at her steadily. Emma suppressed the desire to squirm. "It wasn't just about Penhallow's. It's a small village, and I didn't want to start off on the wrong foot with anybody."

"I see."

But you're not sure you believe me. Emma felt a surge of impatience. "Anyway, when I got up to the door, Oliver started barking, and he wouldn't stop. I thought something might be wrong, but there wasn't any answer when I knocked, and when I tried the door, it was was unlocked, so I went in."

"Sorry, 'scuse me, guv?" Raj Patel knocked and came in. "Got the initials . . ."

He held up some papers.

"Thanks, Raj." Constance took the papers. "Good work today, yeah? You getting what you need?"

"Yes, guv, thanks."

"All right."

Raj left and shut the door after him.

"Good kid," she remarked. "Never ceases to amaze me what the village constable has to deal with, what with lost tourists, and the underworld wannabes who still think they can smuggle a few cigs up the coast, and helping out the life-saving service and what all." Constance laid the pages, facedown, on the desk. "Sorry. Where were we? You were just going into the cottage, and the door was"—she checked her own notebook—"unlocked. You're sure?"

"Yes. I thought it might be because this is such a small village . . ."

"Was it open or closed?"

"Closed. I remember I knocked before I went in."

Constance nodded and made several more notes. "Any windows open you could see? Any signs anything might have been disturbed or forced?"

"No, nothing like that."

"Definitely not," said Oliver. "I would have seen that."

"Thank you. Go on."

"Well, I went in, I was calling her name, and I saw . . ." She swallowed and put her hand on Oliver's head. "Victoria, Ms. Roberts, was in the kitchen."

"On her face, or on her back?"

"On her face, at first. There was a broken cup, and the teapot spilled all over the floor, and I . . . I'm afraid I knelt in the tea and I turned her over. I was trying to see if maybe . . . maybe she was still breathing . . ."

"That's all right. Take your time. This isn't easy."

"I remember thinking, later, she had a rash on her face and her mouth looked swollen. I was wondering if she'd maybe gotten into a patch of nettles or something. But, well, I guess I went back outside and . . ."

"Had a perfectly normal reaction to a sudden and severe shock," said Constance. "But can you tell me anything else about the kitchen? Any other details you do remember?"

"I'm sorry, I don't think . . ."

"Was there another cup set out, for instance? Was there another door into or out of the kitchen?"

Emma frowned.

"One cup," Oliver grumbled. "Emma, there was one broken cup, on the floor, and the flowers. The same kind that she was drinking. Humans don't drink that kind of flower. And there was a door, to the garden, and it was muddy and smelled like green, all fresh and—"

"Oliver," muttered Emma. "I'm trying to think—"

"Tell her about the flowers!" said Oliver.

"What is it with you and those flowers!" said Emma.

"I'm sorry?" remarked Constance. "Flowers?"

"Erm. Sorry. Just . . . something . . ."

"There were flowers in her cup," said Oliver. "The same kind as on the floor. You've got it on your knee."

"Lily of the valley." Emma's mind raced. "I, um, smelled it. I remember. I don't know if it means anything. And there was a bunch of them on the floor, by the sink."

"You're sure?"

"Yes." Emma rubbed Oliver's head. "And the kitchen does have a door to the back garden, but it was closed, but, I think, maybe, there was some mud on the threshold. Maybe Victoria had just come in from the garden or something?"

Constance checked her notes. "I gather Ms. Roberts was a pretty keen gardener?"

"That's what I've heard. Maggie Trenwith says that her roses were prizewinners."

"Excellent." The detective flipped back through her notebook. "Was there anything else? Anything at all? Maybe from the day you met her or . . . ?"

Emma hesitated. "I don't . . . it was probably nothing. Family trouble. But . . ."

"Go on."

"The same day I, well, met her, I saw Victoria arguing with her nephew and Louise Craddock. She was Victoria's best friend. At least, that's what I was told."

"Yes, I heard that too." The detective turned to a fresh page and clicked her pencil again. "Could you tell what they were arguing about?"

"I didn't hear much of it. But Victoria was very upset. She said something about being betrayed, and how could you and . . ." Emma narrowed her eyes, trying to remember.

"'How much did he pay you?' That was it. 'How much did he pay you? How much did it take for you to sell us all out?'"

This earned her another raised eyebrow. "Any idea who 'he' was?"

"None. Sorry."

"And you're sure about this?"

"I'm positive."

"Hmm. Interesting." Constance made a final note. "Well, I think that's everything for now. You go and get yourself a rest. You deserve it. We'll get all this typed up and you can sign it. I am, however, going to have to ask that if you leave town for any length of time in the next couple of days, you let PC Patel know, in case we need to ask any follow-up questions, all right?"

"Yes, of course."

Emma found herself and Oliver being ushered out, politely but efficiently. Emma, lost in thought, returned to the great room with Oliver trotting beside her.

"I told you the flowers were important," he said. "She thought they were. I could smell it."

"You can't smell when someone thinks something is important."

"A noble corgi always knows!"

Emma sighed. She loved Oliver, but sometimes he had an exaggerated sense of his own abilities. "Yes, Oliver."

"You'll see, Emma," he announced as they returned to the great room. "It'll all be okay. Everything will be back where it belongs very soon now."

In the private room, Genny was sitting on the sofa with a cup of tea in one hand, talking on her mobile.

"Yes, no, I'm fine, Martin. I'll be back down just as soon as I can. Tell Becca and Pete . . . Yeah. No. I can't tell you much more. Yeah, I'm sure everybody—" She looked up and saw Emma. Emma waved at her to keep talking. "I'm sure everybody's asking, but we just don't know anything yet . . . Yeah, I promise. Love you too. Gotta go." She hung up and tucked the phone into her apron pocket. "All right, Emma?"

"Yes, fine. Thanks."

"You are not fine, thanks," Genny replied tartly. "That is not a fine face you've got on. What's happened?"

I don't know. Except I do—I just don't want to admit it. "I . . . Genny, I think Victoria Roberts was murdered."

12

. . . .

"MURDERED?" GENNY SET HER TEA MUG DOWN. "GOOD lord, Emma, what makes you think that?"

"I'm sure I'm being overly dramatic, only . . . it's . . ." She dropped onto the couch, defeated. Oliver immediately put his front paws up on the cushions and kicked, trying to scramble up beside her. "The flowers."

"Flowers?"

"Lily of the valley." Emma scooped Oliver up onto her lap and scratched his ears. "On the floor. And Oli . . . I smelled it in the spilled tea. And I think I remember—some lilies are poisonous, aren't they?"

"Well, yes, some are," admitted Genny. "But some are perfectly edible."

"So which is lily of the valley?"

Genny paused. "I don't know, to tell you the truth. But let's think this through. You remember seeing the flowers. Were they actually in the spilled tea? Or near the cup?"

Emma furrowed her brow. "They were mixed with the broken crockery, but Jimmy said Victoria liked to keep some cut lilies in the kitchen."

"Well, that's probably what it was, then," said Genny. "They have a strong scent, after all, and if they were knocked off the table when she fell, that's why you'd smell them mixed with the tea."

"I suppose . . ." said Emma. But she felt strangely reluctant to discount what Oliver was telling her. Her vet, and Oliver, had reminded her more than once what an amazingly precise tool a dog's nose was.

But if there weren't any flowers actually in the tea . . .

Except Oliver said there were.

"Emma," said Genny, firmly but kindly. "You're exhausted and you've had a very bad day. You need to get some rest."

"No, really, I'm . . ." Genny looked down her nose at Emma. Emma suspected it was an expression that her kids saw a lot.

That was when Oliver whined at her and pawed at her ankle.

"You're right," she told Genny. "I do need a rest, but before that, I need to take Oliver for a walk." She attempted to smile brightly, and she must have managed well enough, because Genny nodded.

"And I've got to get back to the shop. According to my husband, we've half the village in there trying to find out what's going on. I strongly suspect DCI Brent knows way more than she's let on so far . . ." Genny stopped. "And that does not mean anything actually suspicious has happened," she added firmly.

"No, of course not," agreed Emma promptly. "I wasn't even thinking it."

Except she was. Even more than that, she was dying to know what the detective was thinking, not to mention what PC Patel was doing. In fact, where Emma should have just felt sad and exhausted, she felt like she had when she was twelve, sneaking down to the dock again, with her spyglass and her notebook.

It was a little disturbing.

"Let me give you my mobile number," Genny was saying. "Just in case you need anything."

They exchanged numbers, Genny gave Oliver a good

scratch along his spine, and Emma promised she'd call first thing in the morning, or sooner if anything happened.

As soon as she left, Oliver nudged Emma's ankle. "Let's go, Emma. You need a walk."

"For once, Oliver," murmured Emma. "I agree with you."

IF THERE WAS A GOOD PLACE FOR A LONG WALK IN THE whole of England, it was Trevena. Emma and Oliver ambled down to the stony beach across from the B&B. Oliver chased waves and shoved his nose into tide pools and was deeply offended by the results of attempting to herd a small crab. Emma climbed over boulders and found the trail leading up the cliffs. They walked along the footpath at the top, following its turn inland and up to the edge of a racing stream that poured through a deep, dramatic split in the cliffs before finally coming to an arching footbridge with wrought iron railings. While Emma stood in the middle of the bridge and watched the rocky cataract race down to the sea, Oliver ran through grass, gorse and heather, nose to the ground.

It felt so good to just be out with her furry best friend and enjoy the open air and beautiful country. With every step, Emma felt the shock and fear ebbing out of her body.

Finally, the sun started to set. Emma and Oliver started back toward the village. The chip shop was closed, and Emma didn't feel like hitting the (very full) pub, but Patel's Royal Indian Takeaway was open, and it smelled divine.

"Are you by any chance related to Raj Patel?" she asked the gray-haired lady at the hostess station who took her order.

"My grandson," she said. "He's following in the family footsteps. His grandfather was a constable in Delhi and joined the force here when we immigrated." She beamed proudly at a black-and-white photo of a tall gentleman looking stern and proud in his old-fashioned helmet and brass-buttoned uniform.

"I can see the resemblance," she said.

"It is very strong, is it not? We are most proud of Raj. He is a credit to the family."

They chatted about Trevena and Cornwall in general, about the weather and how the tourist season was playing out this year, while Emma's order of tikka masala, rice and naan was bundled up.

It smelled fantastic. Emma's stomach rumbled. Oliver kept bumping his nose against the bag like he was trying to hurry her along home.

"What do you think, Oliver?" Emma said as they approached the King's Rest. "It's a lovely evening—should we have our dinner in the garden?"

"Yes! That garden is very interesting. I need to see more of it!" Oliver's tail wagged, and he charged ahead as Emma laughed and followed right behind. "But I think there's a cat. No, I'm sure there's a cat. They get everywhere . . ."

There was a flagstone walkway from the car park to the enclosed back garden. Thick tangles of ivy and trumpet vine draped themselves over the fence pickets.

As soon as Emma unlatched the gate, a black and brown blur streaked past her ankles, causing her to jump back. The startled squeak was purely incidental.

"Percy!" exclaimed Parker Taite.

Oliver barked, pivoted on his hind legs and tore off after the escaping terrier.

"Bad dog!" shouted Parker, and then, "Yes! I'm still here! No, yes, I know I promised I'd call this morning, but something came up . . ."

"We'll get him!" called Emma, although she wasn't sure if Parker heard her. She set the carrier bag with the takeaway by the gate and hurried back down the path.

In the car park, Oliver had already caught up with Percy and was working to herd the smaller dog back toward the garden.

Percy wasn't having any of it. He backed up as Oliver circled, yipping vigorously.

"Don't be rude," Oliver was saying. "Don't be rude. This way. Come on, back we go. This way."

"Yeah, well, as it happens, a lady dropped dead, almost in my lap," Parker was saying back in the garden. "Yeah."

Emma grabbed Percy in both hands. The wiry little creature wriggled so hard, she almost lost her grip.

"Terriers!" said Oliver loftily.

"Yeah, that's pretty much what I said," Parker was telling whoever was on the phone with him as Emma and Oliver came back into the garden. Emma held out Percy. Parker tucked the little dog efficiently under one arm and mouthed, *"Thank you!"*

"No," he said into the phone. "I can't really talk about it now, but I can tell you . . ."

Emma picked up her carrier bag and walked away, making sure to latch the gate behind her.

"No. That's not it!" Parker was shouting. "I . . ."

"Room?" said Oliver.

"Room," agreed Emma.

Which turned out to be for the best anyway. Shortly after they got back upstairs, the same clouds that had produced the dramatic sunset now let loose a fresh rain squall.

To the accompaniment of rain on the roof and a hard wind rattling the windowpanes, Emma and Oliver shared some mild curry. Then Oliver needed to be brushed and get his paws checked and his teeth dealt with. Next, his travel crate, which doubled as a comfy den in whatever room they shared, needed to have its blanket shaken out and refolded. They chatted about their walk. Emma firmly steered away from the subject of finding Victoria. Instead, she let Oliver tell her about all the interesting things he'd found nosing through the grass, which he did with all the energy and enthusiasm that never failed to make Emma laugh.

Finally, Emma changed into her pajamas and boosted Oliver up onto the bed beside her. She also opened her laptop.

"Great British Bake Off?" Oliver laid his chin on her leg. "They show many interesting pictures of ducks and sheep."

"Yes," said Emma. "In a minute. There's something I want to look up first."

"What, Emma?"

"Flowers," she said as she started typing.

"They were important!" Oliver barked excitedly. "I knew it!"

"I don't know," said Emma. "But I can't understand how you could have smelled them in the tea when there weren't any petals or anything . . ."

"A corgi's nose is special," Oliver reminded her.

Emma rubbed his ears, then went straight back to typing.

A search on "lily of the valley" produced thousands of results. A modified search on "lily of the valley toxic" produced rather fewer, but not by much.

Emma clicked, and she read, and she felt her hands growing cold.

"Oliver?" she murmured.

"Yes, Emma? What's wrong? What's it say?

"Oliver, you did smell the flowers, the lilies, in the spilled tea, right? You're sure?"

"Certain and sure," wuffed Oliver. "Is it important?"

"I think it might be."

Because the site from the UK veterinarians association had a stark warning for pet owners about lily of the valley, citing that all parts of the plant were toxic in the extreme.

So toxic, said the site, that pet owners should be careful if they brought cut lilies of the valley in their house to keep in a vase. Because the toxins would leech from the flower stems into the water, and the water itself could become poisonous enough to kill.

13

....

MORNING DAWNED, BRIGHT AND RAIN-FRESHENED. OLIVER, as usual, was up first. After a quick run down to the beach, he and Emma returned to the B&B's public room and Angelique's magnificent buffet breakfast.

Under Oliver's careful supervision, Emma helped herself to muesli and yogurt, fresh fruit, muffins and, everybody's favorite, fresh country sausage. Angelique also kept a bin of doggie kibble available round the clock for her canine guests. Emma had already scooped out a bowlful for Oliver and put it by their table.

Oliver ignored this.

"Did you get enough sausages, Emma?" he asked as he followed her back to the table. "Are you sure? It looks like there are plenty more in that dish thingie . . ."

"You get *one*, Oliver," she told him.

"Yes, of course, one." Emma put the cut-up sausage link down in the kibble bowl and tried not to hear how Oliver mumbled, "To start with."

Emma laughed, shook her head and settled down to her own breakfast.

"Emma." Angelique came in through the garden doors.

"Good to see you up. I'm surprised you're not sleeping in, after yesterday."

"I'm afraid I'm one of those dreadful morning people," Emma told her. "Besides, we both needed the walk." She reached down to scratch Oliver's head.

Angelique nodded. "That's right. Nothing like fresh air to clear your head. Still, no one would blame you . . ."

She didn't finish her sentence. The doors from the car park opened just then, and Louise Craddock walked in.

"Goodness," murmured Angelique. "There's a surprise. Excuse me, Emma."

But Louise had already spotted Angelique and was threading her way between the tables.

"Louise!" Angelique put her hand on the older woman's shoulder. "What are you doing out already? You should be home. How is Jimmy?"

"Oh, well, he's horribly upset, of course, but he'll be all right. With time. It's all been such a shock, and . . ." That was when Louise noticed Emma. "Oh, hello. You're . . . you were . . ."

"Emma Reed," Emma held out her hand. Louise's handshake was rapid, weak and tentative, like her smile. "I'm so sorry for your loss."

"But you were there, yesterday?" pressed Louise.

"Emma helped call the police," said Angelique. "Louise, why don't you sit down? Have some tea, maybe some breakfast. You look exhausted."

"Yes, well. I'm sure Ms. Reed doesn't—"

"No, please," said Emma. "Unless you'd rather be alone, that is?"

"No." Louise knotted her fingers together. "I'd much rather have a little company, thank you."

" 'Scuse me," called a young woman in hiking shorts from beside the bar. "We're out of sausage here."

"Excuse me, won't you?" said Angelique. She fixed a professional smile on her face as she turned to deal with her guest.

Emma faced Louise and tried to smile.

"I'm so sorry to disturb your breakfast . . ." said Louise.

"Not at all," said Emma quickly. "How about that cuppa, hm? Or something to eat? I'm sure you've had a very long night."

"Well, yes, I have, rather."

She looked it too. She had deep circles under her eyes, and her helmet of black curls was badly tousled. The collar on her blouse was rumpled, and her flowered cardigan was buttoned wrong. A crumpled tissue peeked out of her cardigan pocket.

"You stay here," said Emma. "I'll get you something. Oh, and don't mind Oliver."

Emma returned to the buffet and brought back another mug of tea, along with some toast and a fresh muffin, just in case Louise did decide she was hungry. Oliver was snuffling around Louise's ankles. Louise sat frozen and was clearly trying not to flinch.

Not a dog person, then. "Come on, Oliver," Emma said. "Let's let Louise have her breakfast in peace."

Oliver obediently settled back down on Emma's side of the table. "She has cats," he reported. "And smells like the house with all the flowers."

Which probably meant Victoria's cottage. The problem with having a talking dog was that he remained entirely a dog. That meant he experienced the world very differently than Emma, or any other human. That, in turn, meant sometimes it was difficult to understand exactly what he was talking about.

"Good boy," murmured Emma. She set the tea and toast down in front of Louise.

"Thank you." Louise sipped the strong brew gratefully. "Oh, I needed that."

"I'm not surprised. This all has to be dreadful for you."

Louise sighed. "I'm sure I've said this a thousand times by now, but it really was an enormous shock, and then with the police and, well, everything." She shuddered and took another swallow of tea. "That Constance Brent person. So very odd."

Emma smiled. "Did she read your palm?"

"She did!" Louise pursed her mouth tightly. "What kind of police detective engages in amateur theatrics? Completely unprofessional." She lowered her voice. "Did you get any idea of what she was even *thinking*? I couldn't make heads nor tails of the woman. Frankly, I don't like her. Not one bit," Louise added in a harsh whisper. "I'm sorry. I shouldn't have said that. I mean, you don't know me at all, do you? And here I am, interrupting your breakfast." Louise picked up a triangle of toast and tried to give a smile as she munched. Clearly, this was meant to signal that Emma should get on with her own meal. Which she did. At least for a few bites.

Louise's eye flickered up from her toast. "Did Angelique say you helped call the police? Did you . . . were you . . ."

"I found her."

"Oh. Oh, dear. How dreadful for you."

Emma had no idea what to say to that, so she just took another swallow of tea.

"What's going on, Emma?" asked Oliver. "Are we staying?" He also nosed pointedly at his bowl. "If we're staying, I wouldn't mind another sausage. You have another one on your plate, right there. Do you see it?"

Much against her better judgment, Emma put another bit of sausage into his bowl. "This is extortion," she murmured.

"What's 'extortion'?" Oliver mumbled as he snapped down the sausage bit. "Did I do it right?"

Emma grinned and rubbed his head. "Perfectly. As always." She straightened up and faced Louise, who was fiddling with the handle on her tea mug.

"I don't suppose . . . I shouldn't ask this. Positively morbid of me, but after all those *questions* yesterday . . ." Louise was talking to her plate, and her mug of tea, instead of to Emma herself. Her hands moved aimlessly between napkin, mug, plate and back again. "Did you see anything, I mean, *wrong*? When you were in Victoria's house. I mean, I got the feeling that detective thinks something might have *happened* to Victoria."

Like she drank poisoned tea and died? Emma bit her lip.

"They say there's to be an autopsy and everything," Louise went on.

"I guess there'd have to be, wouldn't there?" said Emma. "I mean, she was in good health and alone. As for what I saw . . . I really couldn't say what was normal. She'd fallen, she'd probably pulled the tablecloth off the table trying to catch herself, but beyond that, I can't be sure of anything."

"Oh, yes. That is, no, of course not. Silly of me. After all, you didn't know her either, did you?"

There was an oddly leading tone to that last question. Emma felt her brows drawing together. She couldn't quite make Louise out. The older woman was clearly nervous, but she was also clearly fishing for information, however tentatively. Emma found herself wondering about the history between the two women, and about the argument she'd overheard.

None of my business. None whatsoever.

Except it could be, said a little voice in the back of her head, the one that belonged to the piece of her that had never actually put down the spyglass and notebook.

And that part of her had an idea.

"No, I didn't know her," Emma admitted. "But I had hoped we could at least get acquainted. That's why I went to see her." She paused and made sure she caught Louise's restless gaze. "And, I should probably tell you, I was at the chip shop the other day, and I saw all of you going into Victoria's house."

"Oh," said Louise. "Oh, the chip shop. Yes. Well. That means you probably heard some of our argument too, didn't you?"

"I'm sorry. I didn't mean to."

"No, no, it's not your fault." Louise's self-deprecating smile lasted all of a split second. "We shouldn't have been, well, shouting in the public street like that. My mother would have been appalled. But that was Victoria, you know. She never did care what other people thought. I rather admired that about her," she added softly. "It's such a shame we won't have a chance to patch things up now."

"Money always complicates things, even between good friends," Emma suggested tentatively.

"Money?" Louise blinked. "I'm sorry? What makes you think . . ."

"I thought I'd heard Victoria say something about somebody being . . . erm . . . paid off?"

"Oh! Oh, that." Louisa's relief was palpable. "Oh, no, that was a silly mistake. Victoria, well, she owned a lot of property around here, and there's a developer who's trying to buy up some of it. He wants to put in a new complex, over between St. Marta's and the youth hostel. It's to be quite the thing, very up-to-date, with new detached houses and a posh restaurant and all that. Well, Victoria didn't want to sell. I thought she should, and Jimmy did too. She got angry at us." She paused. "The fact that the developer was working with Maggie Trenwith didn't help any. Victoria never did like Maggie."

"Why not?"

Louisa sighed. "Well, there were a lot of reasons, but mostly I think Victoria felt Maggie didn't really care about Trevena. Maggie is a great booster of change, you know. Very keen on increasing the tourist trade and bringing in new businesses. She even wanted to get the village on one of those reality shows, *Escape to the Country* or *Village of the Year* or something. Victoria hated the very idea."

Emma remembered the blaze of anger in Maggie's eyes and the bitterness in her voice when she talked about Victoria . . . *I was driving Trevena into the dirt by working with any unsavory character who might wander by with a checkbook.*

"Well." Emma hesitated. "I can see Victoria's point. Trevena is so charming just the way it is. If it were my home, I'm not sure I'd want a bunch of strangers tramping all over it." Emma paused and smiled. "Even if I am one of those strangers."

"And I understand too," said Louisa. "I've lived here all my life. We've been through a lot together, Trevena and I, and Victoria and Ruth," she added softly. "But we can't shut ourselves off forever, no matter how much we might want to." Again, Louise tried to speak lightly, but she was clearly too tired to really manage it, and she seemed to realize that. "I'm sorry, I've been nattering on a bit, haven't I? You must find me very shocking."

"Not in the least," said Emma. "This is a difficult time for you, and sometimes it's easier to talk to a stranger."

"Thank you. But you really do have to excuse me. I honestly just meant to stop in and thank Angelique for her kindness yesterday. I'm on my way to see Jimmy. He's working on the . . . arrangements. There's just so much to do. Thank you for the tea, and for listening." She paused. "Speaking of tea, I thought I heard Maggie Trenwith say— she talks a great deal, you know—that you were thinking of opening a tea shop?"

"Yes, that was my plan. I was—"

But Louise wasn't listening. She stared at the passage leading to the upstairs with an expression that looked a lot like panic.

"Yes . . . no . . . yes!" Parker Taite's voice rang through the breakfast room. Which gave Emma an excuse to look over her shoulder and see Parker come into the great room, yet again on his mobile, and with little Percy beside him.

"I swear to God, it's all true. Yes! I'm telling you . . . !"

"No indoor voice," Emma remarked.

"No," breathed Louise. "None at all." She blinked and, with very visible effort, forced her attention back to Emma. "Now. You were saying? About your shop?"

Percy must have scented Oliver, because the Yorkie gave an excited yip and dashed over.

"No dignity whatsoever," grumbled Oliver, but he got to his feet and immediately joined in the snuffling and the nipping that was the canine version of polite small talk.

"No!" snapped Parker. "Please, come on, just one more day . . . Percy?" Parker had been heading toward the buffet, but now he stopped and looked around. He spotted Percy and Oliver, and then Emma and Louise. He flashed them all a bright smile and raised his hand and waved at them.

Louise got abruptly to her feet. "Thank you so much for the tea, and for being kind and, well . . . thank you." She smiled and bobbed her head, but before Emma could say anything, Louise had grabbed her handbag and scurried out the door.

Parker and the rest of the breakfasting guests watched her go.

14

....

EMMA WAS STILL STARING AFTER LOUISE WHEN PARKER strolled over to her table.

"So who was that I scared off?"

"Oh, it wasn't you," said Emma. *Except maybe it was.* "That was Louise Craddock. She's a friend of Victoria Roberts."

"The old lady had one, then? That's not what I heard. Sorry," he added quickly. "Did I mention I'm an obnoxious so-and-so?" He flashed a grin but didn't wait for Emma to reply. "Listen, I was planning on sitting in the back garden. Join me, yeah? No pressure, but you'd be doing me a favor. Percy could use some outside time, and I could use a break from tossing sticks."

"All right, then."

"Great. You get a table. I'm going to raid the buffet."

As Emma gathered up her things, Angelique came out of the back with a fresh tray of sausages. Both Percy and Oliver instantly stopped their busy sniffing of each other and trotted over.

"None for you, you bad boys!" Angelique cried. "Well, Mr. Taite! What a surprise to see you up with the sun."

"I know, I know. You must be thinking I'm completely

nocturnal by now." He chuckled. "But I heard so much
about your breakfast, I decided to check it out for myself."
He grabbed a plate. "Cover me, I'm going in."

Angelique chuckled and shook her head, then came over
to Emma. Percy and Oliver both followed hopefully.

"Louise gone already? How did she sound, poor thing?"

"I think she's really upset." *And worried*.

"Not surprised at all. She always was a nervous one. I'll
ask Nalini Patel to look in on her. They are in the knitting
society together." Then Angelique dropped her voice. "You
maybe take a little care with what you say to Mr. Taite
there. He's an ex-journalist, but that sort never really re-
tires, especially if they can sniff out a fresh headline."

"Oh, bloody marvelous," muttered Emma as she finished gathering her breakfast things. "Come on, boys." She
whistled sharply for the dogs and held open the door to the
garden terrace.

"This way," said Oliver, trotting briskly after her. "Percy,
this way."

The terrier woofed and grumbled, but when he saw the
open door, he was through it like an arrow from a bow. A
very shaggy arrow badly in need of a good brushing.

Oliver looked at her.

"I know." Emma grinned. "Terriers."

"Terriers," agreed Oliver and bounded happily after the
smaller dog.

Emma laughed.

The morning was bright and breezy. The smell of salt
sea and fresh flowers filled the air. Emma settled down in
a sunny corner of the garden. Percy, filled to the brim with
energy, hopped and danced around Oliver, even getting up
on his hind legs. It did not take long for Oliver's remaining
reserve to crack, and soon the pair of them were chasing
each other through the shrubbery.

They were not the only people in the garden this morning, and Emma glanced around for signs her fellow diners
might be annoyed by the dogs, but everyone seemed engrossed in their own conversations, or their mobiles.

Parker came through the French doors and kicked the empty chair back from the table so he could sit down. His raid on the buffet was something Oliver's Viking dog ancestors would have been proud of. Parker's plate was heaped with eggs, sausages, fried bread, baked beans and tomatoes. He'd also brought a mug full of coal-black coffee, which he slurped with gusto.

"So, Ms. Reed," he said as he tucked his napkin in at his neck, "you're looking better. How are you doing? All right?"

"Yes, much better, thanks."

"Good, good. Not part of the summer hols anybody plans, eh? How long have you been in Trevena?"

"Just a few days." Emma split her apple muffin and reached for the pot of fresh butter on the table.

"Wow. You make friends fast." He jerked his head back toward the great room, where Angelique was tidying the buffet and directing a pair of new guests to the tea urn. "Wish I did. Not that kind. Mostly, I irritate people."

"I think I'm supposed to say I'm sure that's not true."

"You wait," he mumbled around a mouthful of beans and tomato. "I'll irritate you too, sooner or later. I'm surprised I didn't irritate your dog when we first met."

Wait. What? "You mean at . . . Victoria's?"

"Oh, no, we met the day before all that. I was walking Percy on the heath"—obviously one of those people who talk with their hands, Parker waved his fork, with a bit of sausage impaled on it, in the general direction of the high street; noting the distinct possibility of flying meat products, both dogs bounced over expectantly—"and there was your fellow, sniffing around. I thought he must have gotten loose from a garden somewhere."

"Oliver!" said Emma sternly.

Oliver tucked his tail. "Sorry, Emma."

"That's no good, you know," said Parker. "Read a book on dogs before I agreed to watch Percy. My brother's overseas for a bit, couldn't take the little guy with. Anyway, this book, it said if you're going to yell at them, it's got to be right away, otherwise they've got no idea what you're on about."

"Well, Oliver's special." Emma popped a piece of muffin into her mouth. Clearly there was a way out of Nancarrow's garden he'd neglected to mention. That meant the first order of business once she took possession of Nancarrow was to find the escape route and block it off. She didn't want Oliver wandering about and getting into fights with the local border collies.

Or the local wildlife. She sighed, remembering his fox fixation.

"So what's brought you to Trevena? Angelique says you're a journalist?"

"I was," Parker answered. "But that was a while ago. Unfortunately."

The last word was soft and bitter. *What happened?* Emma wondered, but before she could work out how to ask, Parker went on, "I'm trying my hand at other kinds of writing. Working on a book."

"A novel?"

"True crime, actually. Unsolved murders of Great Britain." He waved his fork vaguely. "Fluffy bit of pop culture, really, but it should sell. People are always up for a spot of grisly historical homicide." Parker saw her expression and pointed his fork at her. "Know what you're thinking." He flashed another of his grins. "Ex-journo-turned-would-be-true-crime-author stumbles across dead body in peaceful English village. Sounds like a setup for yet another BBC series. If I'm very lucky, of course." He swallowed and grinned again. Emma did not grin back. "And there I go. Irritating."

"Well, I'm sure it'll turn out to be . . . just one of those things."

"Now, you don't really believe that." He used the last of his toast to mop up a bit of runny egg and folded the bite into his mouth. "In fact, I'll bet you've heard a few things already. Who's talking? Not the lady detective, I'm sure. But our good hostess? Or the old biddy you were with just now?" He leaned back, assuming a casual pose Emma didn't for a moment believe. "Anybody said the word 'murder' yet?"

Fortunately, Emma was saved from having to answer immediately by Oliver trotting back up the garden path and flopping onto one side.

"Any sausage left?" he asked. "I'm not begging," he added.

"Of course not," Emma smiled indulgently and set down one last bit on the ground for him. She straightened up to see Parker watching her over the rim of his coffee mug.

"You didn't answer."

"I'm not sure what to say. I mean, nobody knows anything for sure yet, do they?" Somehow, she really did not want to tell him about her search on lily of the valley last night, or the fact that it turned out to be highly poisonous.

Parker narrowed his eyes. There was an edge to his expression that raised the hairs on the back of her neck.

And then it was gone, replaced by a grin.

"Oh, I think you know more than you're admitting, especially since you think I might be trying to get a story out of it. Which is exactly what you should be thinking, by the way."

Now Percy appeared from the shrubbery, damp and tangled. He nosed around the spot where Oliver's sausage had been and came to look hopefully up at Parker.

Parker rubbed the Yorkie's head and tossed him a bit of toast. Percy caught it neatly and settled down to munch.

Emma just shook her head. "I've got too much imagination. My brother's always saying so." She scratched Oliver's spine.

"Imagination's just one facet of instinct," said Parker. "Bet you not only know for sure that the old girl was bumped off, but you've already got someone in mind?" Parker leaned forward. "Who's your pick? The nephew? Sure to inherit. I've heard our Victoria owned half the village, but hadn't a bean in the bank, because property values are so far down right now. Or maybe the old girl who

rushed out of here? Louise? Looked guilty about something, didn't she?"

Which is just about enough, thank you. "How about the
ex-journalist who just happened to be hanging about when
the death was discovered? Oh, he says it was pure coinci-
dence. Maybe he knew something was going to happen and
didn't want to miss out."

Parker froze, staring at her. Then he burst out laughing
so loud Oliver barked, which startled Percy, who yipped.

"All right, all right, you got me there!" Parker leaned
back and stared toward the sea for a long moment. Percy,
bored again, probably, headed off to bark at the bumble-
bees swarming around a host of blue and purple flowers.

Oliver just shook himself and sneezed and settled down,
looking for a comfortable spot on the gravel.

"You know, I've had an idea . . ." said Parker, but then
he shook his head. "No, no, never mind."

Emma resolved not to ask. The resolution lasted all of
three full seconds. "What is it?"

"Probably a terrible idea," he said. "Wouldn't be the first
time I've had one of those, incidentally. Still . . ." he went
on. "What if you and I were to team up? See what we can
find out from the village grapevine. Impossible to really keep
secrets in a place like this." He waved a hand to indicate the
whole of Trevena.

Emma sighed. "Listen, Parker. This is enough. It's just
one of those everyday tragedies. There's no need to go wandering around playing . . . I don't know, Hercule Poirot or
something." *Who are you trying to convince, Emma?
Parker, or yourself?*

"Always fancied myself a bit more the Sam Spade type."
He grinned and took another enormous swallow of coffee.

"I'm sure the police can handle everything," she said,
but even she could hear there was no conviction behind her
words.

"Sure, sure, sure," said Parker. "Eventually. Maybe. Unless
the village decides to take a dislike to that lady detective out-
sider and shut up. I've seen it happen before now, believe me."

"Why would you even ask me to help you? We don't know each other."

"Instinct again, Emma. Pure instinct." Parker touched the side of his nose. "I know people, and I've got a feeling about you. Besides, I've already seen for myself that people talk to you. They like you. They don't like me, and I don't improve on further acquaintance." He grinned. "But I know a thing or two about research, and even little Trevena has a library and an Internet connection."

"Why would you want to do something like this?"

Parker didn't answer right away. Instead, he gazed across the garden, a whole set of expressions chasing one another across his face.

"Maybe it's payback," he said finally.

"I don't understand."

"I've . . . well, done some things in my life that did not turn out so well," he said softly. "Some people got hurt. Maybe this is my chance to make up for some of that." He turned back toward her. "What do you say? Will you help me?"

Emma reached down and scratched Oliver's ears. He made a low, happy growl and rolled over for a belly rub.

This is daft. I shouldn't even be considering this, Emma thought as she petted her corgi. Just then, her phone vibrated.

"Sorry," she said to Parker and checked her texts. There was a fresh one from Maggie:

Talked with Nancarrow owner last night. Swing by office today to see lease details. Free here between 10 and 12.

Parker watched Emma as she texted back. Be there at 10.

Even as she did, Emma remembered Maggie's face filled with anger about Victoria's refusal to sell her properties to the new developer. *How much did he pay you? How much did it take for you to sell us all out?*

And then there was Jimmy talking in Angelique's par-

lor. *She should have been . . . It all should have been . . .*
What did that even mean?

How much did he pay you?

At the same time, Emma remembered Louise and how
fidgety she had gotten when Emma asked about Penhallows, as well as how her hasty retreat from the King's Rest
coincided with Parker coming downstairs.

After everything I've done! All these years!

She was frowning and was distracted enough that it took
her two tries to get her phone back into her pocket.

"Thinking about it, aren't you?" asked Parker.

"I don't know," answered Emma. "I—"

Before she got any further, Percy came galloping back.
He butted his head against Oliver a few times, but the corgi
was having none of it and just rolled over on his other side.
Percy shook, disappointed, and flopped down next to him.

Which gave Emma time to gather herself. "Look," she
said, striving for a cool and reasonable tone, "I really don't
think . . ."

"Give it a little time." Parker got to his feet. "Enjoy your
day. See what happens."

Emma frowned at him. She remembered him talking on
the phone about the dead body that practically fell into
his lap.

What is it you're really up to? she wondered as Parker
got to his feet.

"Well, must be getting on. No rest for the wicked. Come
on, Percy." He hoisted the wriggling terrier up under his
arm and left her there with his empty plate and yet another
knowing wink.

"Do you like him?" asked Oliver. "Are we friends?"

"I don't know," Emma breathed. "I really don't know."

15

· · · · · · · · · · ·

EMMA'S CONVERSATION WITH PARKER WAS STILL ECHOING through her thoughts as she walked into Maggie Trenwith's office at ten o'clock.

The Trenwith Estate Agency was located about halfway down a narrow, sloping cobbled side street in the oldest section of Trevena. The front reception area had been furnished as a cozy sitting room. Brochures featuring properties for sale and lease covered the tea table. The receptionist's desk was empty, but there was a bell and a sign that read **RING FOR SERVICE**.

Emma rang. Oliver barked.

"Sorry, Emma," he mumbled, tucking his curly tail between his legs. "Reflex."

"It's okay, Oliver."

"I'm coming!" shouted Maggie from the back. "Oh! Emma! I thought it must be you. Come on back. You too, Oliver." Oliver wagged and barked again. Emma gave him a look.

"Ahem, yes." He dipped his muzzle and followed Emma into Maggie's office quietly.

"First things first," Maggie said as Emma sat down. Oliver laid at her feet, his chin on her toes. "How *are* you, Emma?"

Clearly, word of Victoria's death, and the fact that Emma found the body, had flown ahead.

"I'm fine," Emma said. "It was a shock but, well . . ."

"Poor Victoria." Maggie shook her head before Emma had to say anything more. "Not my favorite person by any means, but still, you don't wish anyone dead, do you? I mean, not *really*."

"I guess it'll make for a lot of changes."

"Oh, you have no idea. We might *finally* be able to make some actual progress around here." Considering they were talking about a sudden and suspicious death, Maggie's tone was oddly cheerful. She seemed to realize this a split second later. "Don't get me wrong. I'm truly sorry for what happened to Victoria. And it's not as if I thought she was entirely wrong. We all love being part of a quaint Cornish village with the close ties of a vibrant community, et cet, et cet, but we can't pretend we're still living in the nineteen fifties. Things are changing, and if Trevena doesn't change with them, there's going to be nothing left of us. With Victoria hanging on to half the land around here like grim death . . ." She stopped, belatedly realizing what she'd said, and smiled again. The expression, however, was strained. "But you didn't come to listen to me raving about local politics. You want to hear about your lovely new home." Maggie pulled a manila folder out from the stack on her desk. "Like I said in my text, I talked with the owners last night, and they are fine with your bringing in your own furniture. You can call them and work out the details for moving, storage and so on. Also, they're willing to take on improvements to the kitchen and garden, but if you have specific updates you want, you'll have to provide a list. It's all written down here." She passed Emma the list. "If you're good with that, we can go over the rest of the lease."

She flipped the folder open, but the sharp ping of the reception bell cut her off.

"Back in a tick." Maggie hurried into the front room. Oliver, ever curious, trotted out behind her.

"What can I . . . Oh, for heaven's sake!" Maggie's exasperated exclamation was followed by a flurry of forceful whispering.

You will stay right where you are, Emma Reed, Emma told herself sternly. *Whatever's going on in there is none of your business. At all. Full stop. Never mind what you said to Parker over breakfast, or what he said to you.*

Oliver trotted back in and plunked down on his hind-quarters.

And all her virtuous resolve melted like buttercream in the heat. "Who's out there, Oliver?"

He scratched his ear. "The man with the pale hair and the round face. The one who smells like the shouty flower lady."

Emma frowned, trying to translate from the corgi.

"Jimmy?" As wonderful as it was to have a talking dog, for Oliver, smells and behaviors were infinitely more important than names, and he had never gotten around his habit of identifying people by their scents or their actions.

Oliver scratched harder and sneezed. "He's angry about something. The shouty lady made a lot of people angry."

Out in the reception area, the whispering was still going on. Emma reached down and scratched Oliver's neck.

I will stay right here. It's none of my . . . Oh, to heck with it. She got up and stood beside the partially open door.

"Jimmy," Maggie was saying. "I know you're scared. I'm scared, but you start telling lies, and you are going to make everything worse."

"But if they find out about the money . . ." That was definitely Jimmy Lambert out there.

"Then they find out," Maggie said. "It's not like we've done anything wrong. In fact, you probably should have told them when they interviewed you."

Jimmy didn't answer. Maggie blew out a sigh. "Oh, for heaven's sake. Look, just let me finish up here. I'll call you in—half an hour, all right?"

Realizing Maggie was about to come back into the office, Emma hurried to her chair, so she missed Jimmy's reply. To complete the picture of perfect innocence, she gathered Oliver up into her lap, scratching him right at the base of his neck. A couple of seconds later, Maggie strolled in, her smile and chipper professional manner firmly in place.

"Sorry about that," she said as she settled back behind her desk. "Some late paperwork on another property."

"It's always something," said Emma.

"Too right. Now. Where were we?"

Maggie Trenwith while showing a property was warm and confidential. Maggie Trenwith behind a desk and a pile of papers was brisk, efficient and businesslike. Emma almost felt like she was back in the London office dealing with a high-powered attorney.

So what's going on between you and Jimmy? Because from that little snippet she had overheard, it was clear that something was.

Emma remembered sitting across from Maggie at Nancarrow. *Can you give me a couple of days?* Maggie had said. *I may be able to work out a deal for you.*

What, exactly, had she been expecting to work out? Was it possible she had been planning to use Jimmy Lambert to get through to his aunt?

How would that work?

Eventually the last page on the lease was read over, the last dotted line was signed, and Emma had handed over the check for the deposit and the first month's rent. Maggie produced a small brown envelope and shook out two keys.

"Front door; kitchen door." She laid them one at a time on the desk in front of Emma and then held out her hand. "And welcome to Trevena!"

"Thank you!" Emma shook Maggie's hand. She also grabbed the keys, as if she thought someone might snatch them away.

"Is there anything else I can help you with today?"

Leave it, Emma, she counseled herself, but she also didn't move. On her lap, Oliver craned his neck and licked the bottom of her chin. "You want to talk about Pale Jimmy, Emma. Go on. You do."

So much for one's better angels. "Actually, yes. Given everything that's happened, I think I'd like that list of possible sites for my tea shop for us to go over."

"Ah! Yes. Well that's some good news for you, actually. As soon as the paperwork is sorted, Jimmy Lambert, obviously, will be in charge of Victoria's property, and we will stand a much better chance at getting you into Penhallow's."

"Really?" said Emma, a little startled. "Well, yes, that would be lovely, I mean, if he'd be interested in having me, and obviously, I'll need to see the shop. But it'll take a while to get the probate sorted, won't it?"

"Not necessarily," said Maggie, her tone turning warm and confidential. "Not if one knows who to talk to, which I do. I'd be happy to sound him out for you," she said.

"Oh, yes, that'd be great," said Emma. "I suppose he is going to . . . well, I mean, everybody says he's Victoria's only family . . ."

Maggie looked at her, a sharp, knowing light gleaming in her eyes.

"Oh yes, he's it. Victoria only had the one sister; that was Jimmy's mother. She died with her husband in a car accident about fifteen years ago now. That was when Jimmy came to live in Trevena. Her parents are long gone. She looked after them too." Maggie paused. "Strange that such an unpleasant woman should end up taking care of so many people, isn't it?"

The only reason someone walks around carrying that much bitterness is that something bad happened to them. Angelique's words played back inside Emma's head.

"Anyway, ever since he came back, Victoria had been training Jimmy up in property management."

"Oh, that's right. I'd heard he was working for a games company out in San Francisco."

"Right. Some fairly famous outfit called BlastSys. But it collapsed rather suddenly, I understand."

"That happens with tech firms. A lot more than people think, actually."

"So I hear. Not really my field." Maggie shuffled some

of the pages on her desk. Clearly, she was ready for this part of their conversation to be finished. "Now, about your shop? Did you want me to talk with Jimmy about getting a move on Penhallows for you?"

"Well, yes, but I still think I'd better see the whole list of potential shops," said Emma. "Just in case. I mean, setting up the new shop is going to take some time, and I really do want to get the ball rolling as soon as possible."

"Oh, of course. Of course," said Maggie, but there was no mistaking her disappointment. Emma wondered about that. After all, Maggie would get her commission on any property she helped lease. Why should there be a difference with Penhallows?

And why was Jimmy coming to Maggie now, of all times? And what was Maggie worried he was going to lie about?

"Are we going soon, Emma?" Oliver wriggled uneasily.

"Soon, Oliver." Emma patted his back. "I wonder . . ."

"Wonder what?" asked Maggie.

"Nothing. Stupid. Sorry. Shouldn't have said it."

"No, no, go on. I won't tell anybody, whatever it is. Wonder away."

Emma looked at her. Maggie returned a direct, not to mention open and fully trustworthy, gaze. It was, Emma thought, the sort cultivated by bankers, used car salesmen, and, of course, estate agents.

"I was wondering if Jimmy might be having . . . well, money trouble."

"What makes you ask that?" asked Maggie, a little more sharply than she had before.

"Oh, well, it's just that on the day you showed me Nancarrow, I wound up with a front-row seat for an argument between Victoria, Louise and Jimmy. Victoria was accusing Jimmy of being ungrateful and untrustworthy, and of having sold her out to somebody."

"Really?" Maggie's carefully plucked brows shot up. "That's strange. I wonder what that could have been about? Jimmy's always been devoted to her, despite everything."

"Everything?"

Maggie waved this away. "Just . . . how she was, you know? Always so angry and closed off."

Maggie was still smiling, but her expression was brittle.

"Emma . . ." Oliver slithered off her lap and down onto the floor. "I need to be outside now."

Come on, Emma, time to get your head back in the game.

"I'm sorry. I do need to get going. If I could have that list? I'll look it over and let you know which properties I'm interested in seeing." She held out her hand.

"Right you are, then." Maggie pulled a fresh set of pages out of the folder and handed them over. "Call anytime. I'm sure we can find you the perfect spot."

Emma collected her papers and her brand-new keys and said goodbye. Out in the narrow street, Oliver went to investigate the signpost on the corner, and Emma hesitated.

Oliver came back and wagged expectantly. "Where are we going, Emma?"

"To heck with it," she said.

Emma turned and strode purposefully toward the high street.

"With what? Where's heck?" whined Oliver as he raced to catch up.

"We're both about to find out."

It wasn't going to take long, either. When Emma reached the high street and rounded the sharp bow in its middle, she saw a cluster of people gathered in front of the Towne Fryer. She spotted Genny on her steps, but Genny didn't seem to notice Emma or Oliver as they hurried up to join the tiny crowd. She was too busy staring,

Emma didn't blame her. She was staring too. Because a dozen meters away, DCI Brent was keeping stern watch while PC Patel unspooled yellow crime scene tape all around Victoria Roberts's garden wall.

16

....

HUMANS, OLIVER KNEW FROM LONG EXPERIENCE, SPENT A lot of time talking to one another. It wasn't their fault, of course. Without anything even approaching a proper sense of smell, they had to do *something* to find out what was going on.

Some days, though, even a noble warrior corgi dog could get a little impatient with it.

Still, he was a corgi, and he was Emma's friend as well as her protector. If she wanted to find out what was happening, it was his job to help.

So, while Emma talked to the fish lady and the other humans, he started investigating the nooks and crannies in the cobbled street.

This was a busy place, and there were all kinds of smells—human, animal and lots of dogs. All kinds of dogs, in fact, around the streetlamps and right on the cobbles, ranging from good old dogs to a brand-new puppy and—

Concentrate, Oliver. Good dog.

A new scent reached him on the winding breeze. Oliver lifted his head and raised his ears. Upwind, beside the garden wall where the fox had been, he saw the lady with the pale spiky hair that Emma had talked to before. Maybe she could tell him something useful.

Oliver trotted over to snuffle around her shoes (green and gasoline, linoleum and indoors and bleach, and dogs—two dogs).

Spiky Lady lifted one foot and looked down.

"Well, hello there. Don't I know you from someplace?" She crouched and opened her hands for Oliver to sniff and lick. *A very polite and interesting human.* She still smelled like chemicals and those dogs and coffee (lots of coffee) and worry (lots of worry too) and old, bad things that had been lying around for a while, and perfume and soap and . . .

"Oh, Oliver!"

Oliver's ears lifted. Emma, exasperated and worried, had come up to them.

"I know, I know," she was saying to the Spiky Lady. *Spiky Lady has a name . . . a name. Brent! Spiky Lady Brent!* "He should be on his lead. I've got it right here."

Oh, crumbs. "I was just trying to help, Emma!"

"It's all right." Spiky Brent gave his ears another rub. "Everybody else is here—it'd be a surprise if you weren't. But as you can see, we've got ourselves a crime scene." She straightened up with a grunt. "Can't have the civilians wandering about—not even corgi civilians."

"Yes, I know, good boy," Emma murmured. But Oliver heard, and felt, the unmistakable *snap!* of the Lead clipping onto the Collar. "You're sure it was—well, murder, then?"

"Oh, yes, we're sure," answered Spiky Brent.

Oliver nosed the cobbles. There might still be something interesting here. He was getting hints, he was sure of it, but he didn't know what they were hints of, exactly. Maybe he could find one of the other dogs and maybe . . .

No, not maybe. That fox had been back. Definitely. He barked.

"Gosh," Emma breathed. "I thought . . . I mean, don't

these things usually take a while, with, you know, labs and stuff?" Emma was saying.

"Emma . . ." began Oliver urgently.

She bent down and scratched his ears, which was very nice, but it was also a little frustrating. It meant Emma felt she was too busy with human things to pay proper attention to what was really important.

"Usually it does take several days, but we got lucky again," Spiky Brent was saying. "Seems one of the pathologists at the hospital—grand old girl, retiring next year and moving to the city to get away from all the village weirdos—her words, not mine. Anyway. She's worked here through several of the 'back to the land' and 'natural living' phases we tend to go through. As a result, she's seen just about every variant of plant-based poisoning Cornwall has to offer."

"Are there that many?"

This was clearly going to take a while. Oliver resolved to wait patiently. He returned to his close examinations of the cobbles. Of course the pale man—Jimmy?—had been here. He was the shouty lady's family, after all, so that made sense. And the nervous Louise had been here, and not just yesterday, but a lot of times before that. There were whole layers of her scent built up. The other lady—the one in the office that they'd just spent so much time talking to this morning, she'd been here a lot too. What was her name? Oliver couldn't remember. But she must have been friends with the shouty lady, because friends played together. At least, they ate food together, which seemed to be humans' idea of playing a lot of the time.

"Turns out, too many people think 'natural and organic' means perfectly safe," Brent was telling Emma. "They forget that cyanide and arsenic are also natural, so they drink all kinds of concoctions. Even lily of the valley. Supposedly, in small doses, it's good for the heart. Like foxglove."

Oliver stuck his nose in another complicated crevice between the stones. That was when he realized what hints he'd been getting.

Percy had been here. Oliver turned around, nosing at more of the stones, following the trails as far as the Lead would let him. Percy had been here. In fact . . .

Oliver snuffled farther. He followed the trails to the house, and back again, and to the left, and to the left some more, and . . .

"Oliver!" Emma called. "Sorry!"

That was when he realized the Lead was pulling hard, and that was because it was wrapped right around Spiky Brent's ankles. She laughed. Emma did not laugh. Emma unclipped the Lead and got it unwound and said she was sorry a lot.

Oliver sat down, right on a particularly interesting patch of stones.

"Emma? Percy and his human have been here."

"Yes, Oliver, all right." She ruffled his ears. "Almost done here. Promise."

"He's been here a lot, Emma. Lots of times on lots of days."

Emma froze. She stared at him, her face all bunched and wrinkled.

Oliver nosed at her hands. "Lots of days," he confirmed.

"Okay, good boy." She rubbed his head and stood up, but she didn't clip the Lead back on.

"Erm, so, your pathologist recognized that rash around Ms. Roberts's mouth?" Emma said to Brent. "She thinks Victoria was taking some kind of herbal remedy?"

"No, that's exactly what she does not think." Brent sighed. "Because we knew what we were looking for, we were able to target the test. The quantities of toxins found in Victoria Roberts were far too high to have been self-administered." Brent was looking straight at Emma. Oliver did not like that look. It made his ears twitch and his hackles stand up. "So I can now say what I'm sure you and the other citizens of Trevena have already guessed." She was wrinkling her mouth at the big bunch of humans standing around with the fish lady. That distinct smell of worry around her got a little worse. "Victoria Roberts was poisoned, and we now have to begin our inquiry into her murder."

17

"VICTORIA WAS *POISONED*?" EXCLAIMED GENNY. "YOU CAN'T be serious."

"It turns out that lily of the valley is not one of the edible types of lily," Emma told her. "And DCI Brent certainly sounded serious."

Emma and Genny stood on the steps of the Towne Fryer with what seemed like half the village spread out along the cobbles. Most everybody was texting away on their mobiles or standing in knots talking or both. Every few seconds, Emma caught some variant of "I can't believe it!"

"Who could have hated Victoria enough to kill her?" Emma murmured.

"That's the problem, isn't it?" murmured Genny. "I could think of a dozen people right off the top of my head."

"But . . . *why*? I mean, she wasn't a nice woman, but . . ."

Genny bit her lip. Over at Victoria's house, DCI Brent was slipping blue paper covers onto her shoes and zipping up a pair of white overalls. "Tell you later," said Genny. "I imagine you'd rather be somewhere else right now."

The problem, Emma reflected, was that she didn't actually have anywhere she'd rather be. Curiosity was burning a hole straight through her. She even found herself wondering what Parker was up to and whether he'd found out anything today.

She also wondered whether Jimmy really was having money trouble of some kind, and how bad it was and if Victoria had known. She wondered how Maggie Trenwith's situation had changed, now that Victoria was no longer around to obstruct her plans for Trevena's future.

Oliver was wandering away, nose to the cobbles, hindquarters wagging happily.

Oliver said Parker and Percy had been to Victoria's house a lot. Parker hadn't mentioned that. In fact, hadn't he said he didn't know Victoria at all? Emma's brow wrinkled.

"Emma?" Genny waved a hand in front of Emma's face. She blinked, hard, and blushed. "You okay? You were a long way away there."

"Yes, yes, fine. Sorry. Just . . . it's all such a lot. And, yes, I probably should get going." Those words came out a lot more reluctantly than they should have. "I was just over with Maggie signing the lease and picking up the keys to Nancarrow, and I was headed back to the King's Rest to check out."

"Oh, fantastic! Tell you what, I'll pop round to the cottage during our afternoon lull. We can have a good talk then."

Emma agreed that this was a great idea, and she headed back up the high street and through the village.

"Is heck this way?" asked Oliver.

"Oh, definitely," said Emma. "Right this way, step up, step up. See the city woman turn into a nosy old lady in designer running shoes."

"I don't understand, Emma."

"Neither do I, Oliver," Emma sighed. "And I really wish I did."

THERE WAS NOBODY STAFFING THE RECEPTION DESK AT THE King's Rest when Emma and Oliver got there, but as soon as Emma rang the bell, Pearl appeared.

"Ms. Reed, what can we do for you?" Unlike her mother's Caribbean-tinged diction, Pearl's accent was pure Cornwall. She was a tall, broad young woman with deep midnight skin and long, braided hair streaked with navy blue. Angelique had told Emma that Pearl took after her father for looks and her mother for brains. Pearl had overheard and rolled her eyes.

"Ma's on the phone just now," Pearl said. "I guess there's been some news about poor old Ms. Roberts."

"Yeah." Emma forced herself to shut her mouth after that. Pearl would hear all the gory (*Oh, good word choice there, Emma!*) details soon enough. "I'm just here to say I'm going to be checking out this afternoon."

"You got Nancarrow, then? Ma said you were going to talk to Maggie. That's terrific. We can settle the bill now if you like, and you can just leave your key in your room when you go."

Pearl worked the keyboard, asked a few questions and ran Emma's credit card through the machine.

"All set," Pearl said, handing the card back. "If you check that sheet of local numbers in your room, you'll find Trevena taxi. You probably don't want to wrestle those suitcases all the way up that hill, and I think I remember you don't have a car."

"Nope. Not worth it in London." This was another one of her brother's arguments against Emma moving out to a village. "The buses aren't near as good out there," Henry had reminded her. "You'll spend half your life waiting around at the station."

"Yes, because that's so different from the Tube at rush hour," she'd shot back.

"Oh, and before you go, I wanted to thank you for that look at your business plan," said Pearl.

"Oh, you're welcome. Anytime."

"Actually, I was hoping we could set up a time to get together? I have an idea I wanted to talk with you about."

"Oh? Well, sure. Just give me a couple of days to get settled, all right? You've got my number."

This is exactly what I should be doing, Emma told herself. *Making friends, minding my own business and moving forward with my life.*

She scooped Oliver into her arms and headed up to her room. The B&B's steep stairs were a bit much for his stumpy legs.

And I should not be worrying about who might have killed Victoria Roberts. I should especially not be worrying that it might be a choice between Maggie Trenwith and Jimmy Lambert.

The King's Rest still used actual keys on the doors to the guest rooms instead of electronic cards. While Emma fumbled in her bag and Oliver scratched his ear, she heard a voice come rumbling through the door across the hall.

Emma was somehow unsurprised to realize it was Parker Taite.

". . . Yes! Yes! I keep telling you, I have the proof . . . No! Listen, I just got a call from my guy at the hospital! It's all right *there*! Did you even read what I sent you, you great . . . No, no, Mark, I'm sorry, I'm sorry, please don't hang up. Yes, yes, I know how much is on the line. What do you think's been keeping me up nights? But I'm telling you, it's all *there*."

"He's a very shouty kind of human," Oliver remarked pensively. "There are a lot of shouty humans here."

"He is. There are. And eavesdropping is impolite." Emma finally got her door open and went inside.

"I wasn't eavesdropping," said Oliver.

"No. Good boy."

When Emma had packed for Cornwall, she'd brought a suitcase for herself and another one for Oliver, as well as his travel crate, of course. It wasn't that she spoiled him, although she did, but being the human companion of a Welsh Pembroke corgi required traveling with a variety of chew toys and treats, not to mention a full range of dog combs and brushes. When Emma had first acquired Oliver, she had also acquired a deep familiarity with the details of "overcoat" and "undercoat," and the fact that corgis tended to shed (or "blow out," as the term was) everything at once, like low-riding canine ginkgo trees.

And, of course, Oliver couldn't stay overnight anywhere without his pillow, blankie and Mr. Squeaky the Moose, but Emma tactfully did not mention these things. The reminder tended to bruise Oliver's well-developed sense of dignity.

Never mind that Oliver immediately snatched up Mr. Squeaky and ducked into his crate for some quality chew time.

Emma packed up their things, amazed, as always, about the fact that the same stuff never fit as easily when you were repacking as when you packed the first time. In her head, she started creating lists of things she'd need to buy and calls she'd need to make.

Or, at least, that was what she wanted to be doing. Instead, she kept replaying all the conversations she'd had recently with Maggie and Louise and Parker and DCI Brent.

Oliver poked his long nose out of the crate. "What's the matter, Emma?"

She smiled. Of course he'd picked up on her change of mood. He always did. "Oh, I don't know, Oliver. It's what happened to Victoria and, just, everything. I keep asking questions, even when I know I shouldn't. It's not my business. The police are on it. Why am I even thinking about trying to get involved?"

Oliver came trotting out and plopped down beside her. "Are we staying here?"

"Here in the B&B?"

"Here, this place, this town, *here*." Oliver woofed. "You like it here?"

"Yes, I do. I like it a lot."

"Then that's why." Oliver poked her gently with his nose. "You care about this place, and your humans, and you want to keep it safe. You want to be a . . . a . . . *guard* human."

"But what if I make things worse?"

"What if you make things better?"

Emma stared at him. Then she bent down and gathered him into a big hug.

"You're the best, Oliver."

"So are you, Emma."

She kissed the top of his head, and he gave her a very sloppy lick in response.

As Pearl had told her, the directory pages on the desk listed a Trevena Taxi. Emma put in a call and was told there'd be a car round for her in ten to twenty minutes. Emma heaved her suitcase off the bed and opened the door.

Percy zoomed straight in, yipping at Oliver.

Emma squeaked, which was perfectly normal and not at all undignified.

"No, no, no!" Oliver emerged from his crate and immediately started trying to herd the Yorkie toward the door. "No, Percy, this way! *This* way!"

"Percy!" groaned Parker. He was shoving his mobile into his trouser pocket. He had the door of his room open. "I'm sorry. I swear, I just turned around for a second."

"It's all right," Emma snatched the Yorkie up and crossed the hall to hand him back.

"Kyle should have named you Houdini," Parker muttered, tucking the dog back under his arm, a gesture that seemed to have become pure reflex. "Leaving us, Emma?" He gestured to the suitcases. "That's my keenly honed journalistic instincts coming into play, there."

Emma laughed. "Yes. I'm moving into my new cottage."

"Well, congratulations to you. Whereas I am condemned to continue my rootless bachelor existence." He chuckled. "I know, such a trial when all I have to live off of is Angelique's breakfasts and Genny's fish."

Now that she was standing in the doorway to his room, Emma couldn't help noticing that Parker was not exactly a tidy person. His suitcase was open on the luggage stand. Assorted clothing items hung out over the sides. A pile of towels on the floor looked suspiciously like Percy had been using them for a doggie bed. But what really caught her attention was the desk, because it held something she hadn't actually seen since she'd played in her grandfather's study back when she was a little girl—a portable typewriter, flanked by a thick stack of paper.

"I see you've noticed the anomaly," Parker said.

"My keenly honed office-worker experience at play, I guess. Do you really work on that?" she asked.

"I really do." He looked at it with a kind of rueful pride. "I'll admit, once upon a time, it was merely the affectation of a pretentious young man, but now"—he grinned sheepishly—"now it's the affectation of a pretentious middle-aged man. Maybe it's just that I got used to it, but sometimes I just find it easier to work if I don't have to think about who, or what, might be spying on my files." He shrugged. "Speaking of, mind if I shut the door? Nothing nefarious, I swear, it's just . . . the Houdini hound here." He gave Percy a little shake.

"Oh, sure."

Emma closed the door and Parker put Percy down. The Yorkie and Oliver exchanged the usual snuffling greetings, and then Percy hopped up onto the windowsill—a complicated maneuver that involved going from a stack of books on the floor to the seat of the room's armchair to the heating unit to the window.

Oliver tried to follow and immediately toppled the entire stack of books and magazines, rolled over and came up on his hindquarters, looking thoroughly confused and indignant.

"Oh, Oliver!" Emma sighed and immediately started gathering the books up. There were a thesaurus and a dictionary and several guidebooks and a battered hardback book with a red-splashed cover and the title *Death and Pasties*.

Emma held the book up and raised her eyebrows.

"Research." Parker took it out of her hand and set it on the desk. "Want to get a feel for the local crime-scape. Some very interesting stuff there. Speaking of which, have you had a chance to think about my proposal from this morning?"

"Well. Yes. Sort of. Erm." Emma shook her head and tried again. "Did you hear what the police found?"

"Lily of the valley in the tea? Yes, as a matter of fact, I did. She's a quick one, is our DCI Brent. I've got a feeling about her. I think she's actually a still water running very deep."

"Are you going to write about it?"

"Maybe. I've been talking with my editor, as you no doubt heard." He gave a self-deprecatory grimace. "But it hasn't all been shouting at the world of publishing. I've been looking into our late lamented Ms. Roberts's background."

"Oh?"

Parker nodded. "Yes. Have you heard about her little run-in with the Tesco manager over the car park?"

"Actually, I have. But didn't he move to Canada?"

"Meaning he's a bit far off to be putting poison in the old lady's tea, yes. That's not the point. The point is Victoria wasn't just unpleasant; she was determined to keep her hold over Trevena, and she was willing to fight dirty to do it. She might have gotten herself in over her head. What?" he said abruptly.

Emma bit her lip and made up her mind. "When I told Genny Knowles, at the chip shop, that Victoria was murdered, she said she wasn't surprised."

"Did she now? Did she say why?"

"She said she'd tell me later."

Percy jumped off the windowsill and headed for the door, whining all the way.

"He needs out," Oliver said helpfully. "Or there's going to be an accident."

"I think I'd better get Percy out of here," said Parker. "So can I take it you've decided we'd make a good team? I can maybe stop by your new digs later and we can talk?"

"That depends," said Emma.

"On what?" said Parker.

"Am I remembering right that you said you didn't know Victoria?"

He glanced at her sideways. "Strictly speaking, I didn't know her. But I'd been to the house. Several times, actually."

"What for?"

"Mostly to get the door slammed in my face." He waved his hand. "It's all right, I'm used to it. But like I said, I was checking out the local crime-scape for my book, and it can be a real help to interview long-time residents, for background color and so on. Victoria was not interested in talking. Now, Jimmy, he was a little more forthcoming."

How much did it take for you to sell us all out? screamed Victoria in my memory. "Did you offer to pay him?"

That startled Parker. "Good lord, no. Don't have anything like that kind of budget."

Emma frowned.

"You know something," said Parker.

"Nothing certain. But I did overhear Jimmy and Maggie Trenwith talking, and Maggie lied to me about it."

Slowly, Parker's expression shifted from interest to intense, delighted greed. It was a little unsettling.

"Now, that is very interesting," he said softly. "The nephew and the best enemy. All kinds of possibilities there."

"What do you mean?"

Parker shook his head. "Nothing. At least not yet. So I take it you're in?"

Emma hesitated, and then Emma decided.

"I'm in. I may regret it later, but I'm in."

"Wonderful!" Parker stuck out his hand, and he and Emma shook, just a little too firmly. "Now, you go get yourself settled in your new home. I am going to be putting in some time at the library tomorrow. How about you and I meet up there? Around eleven? We can talk. I might have one or two more things to share." Without waiting for an answer, Parker scooped up the Yorkie and opened the door. "And thank you, Emma. You don't know how much it means to have you on my side in this."

Emma stared after Parker as he carried Percy down the

stairs, whistling, or trying to whistle, "Rule Britannia" the whole way down.

But Emma kept seeing that greedy, hungry look on Parker's face.

"What was that about?" murmured Emma.

"Humans are very confusing," grumbled Oliver.

"You are so very right, Oliver."

18

WHATEVER EMMA EXPECTED FROM TREVENA TAXI, IT WAS not a black cab with a massive silver grill that looked like it had just driven out of a black-and-white film.

"Austin FX4," said the driver as he got out to help load her cases into the boot and caught her staring. "Picked it up at auction about five years ago."

"It's amazing." Emma scooped up Oliver and climbed into the broad back seat. "I've never seen anything like it."

"Not a lot of them running," the driver climbed in front. "I'm Brian Prowse, by the way, garage and taxi."

"Emma Reed. Would-be tea shop lady."

"Oh, right, you're Maggie's Londoner. Welcome to Cornwall." Brian smiled at her over his shoulder. It was a nice smile. In fact, it was a nice face, rugged and tanned, with cheerful blue eyes. He also possessed broad shoulders and had rich black hair just beginning to turn gray about the edges. Brian had clearly settled comfortably into his middle age.

She watched over his shoulder while he worked the surprising array of knobs on the old car's dash, all of which doubtlessly had names like "throttle" and "choke" and possibly "gear shift thingie."

Oliver, of course, put his paws up on the window so he could see out. When Emma tried to urge him to sit down, Brian laughed and told her it was fine. "Need to wash the windows today anyway. Nancarrow, isn't it?" he asked, as they pulled smoothly onto the road.

"A sensible human," woofed Oliver. "Do we like him?"

Yes, I think we do. Emma felt herself smile.

Brian navigated the twisting route between the village and the shoreline smoothly but with care, like a man who knew you couldn't tell when a tourist or a sheep might wander into the road. It felt somehow wasteful to be taking a taxi a distance she could have walked in a half hour. A Londoner born and bred, Emma was used to walking everywhere. But, as she had never been one of those people who traveled light, Pearl had been entirely correct. She simply couldn't wrestle her suitcases and Oliver's travel crate, not to mention her briefcase and laptop case and tote bag-of-possibly-useful-stuff-that-wouldn't-fit-back-in-the-suitcase up the hill.

Brian helped carry her luggage to the doorstep. Oliver took the opportunity to have a good snuffle around the man's shoes and ankles. "Gasoline, oil, green, and a dog . . . a collie? Definitely a collie . . ."

"Good luck, Emma," Brian said with a smile that, Emma was prepared to swear, did make those blue eyes twinkle. "Call if you need a lift anywhere." He held out his hand for her to shake, and she did, and at the same time she noticed there was no wedding ring on his left hand.

Emma! she scolded herself. *What are you doing? First you're playing Nancy Drew and now you're scouting the local talent?*

Emma turned her thoughts firmly back to the matter at hand.

"This is it, Oliver!" Standing on a small stoop, surrounded by her luggage, Emma unlocked the door to her own house with her own key. "We're home!"

Oliver, who had zero sense of ceremony, barged right past her.

"All ours?" Oliver began nosing everywhere, sniffling, snuffling, and diving under things, not to mention trying to open the kitchen cupboards with nose and paws so he could see what was in there.

"All ours. No tenants' association, no thundering herds and disapproving gits upstairs, downstairs or anywhere else. Just us." Emma knelt on the (still hideous) couch and leaned over the back to wrestle with the latch on the diamond-paned windows. The latch gave, and she pushed open the window to let in the fresh air.

"It's going to rain," said Oliver.

"I know." Emma rested her chin in her hands and looked at the clouds rolling in across the sea. "And I don't care, because it's going to be beautiful!"

THE REST OF THAT DAY WAS ALL ABOUT NANCARROW. Emma took a raft of pictures to share with her brother and his family and, of course, to text to Rose. She opened every closet and cupboard to investigate their contents. She even went down into the tiny cellar while Oliver stood at the top of the ladder and barked encouragingly.

OMG! AMAZING! When am I coming over??!!! Rose texted.

As soon as I get rid of this. Emma texted back with a shot of the sofa.

Oh, lord, yeah, no, replied Rose.

Eventually, however, Emma's triumphant exploration and texting did give way to practicality.

She pulled out the three-ring binder she'd labeled *Cornwall* and started making lists. The cottage was stocked with blankets and linens, as well as a lot of other basics. Unfortunately, they were all about the same quality level as the furnishings. But she had enough to make the bed, and there were fresh towels to hang in the bathroom.

She did have to wonder who had ever thought the fuchsia shower curtain was a good idea.

"That's the first thing to go," she told Oliver.

Oliver stood up on his hind paws and put his nose over the edge of the tub. "Spiders," he remarked.

"Oh, thanks loads, sunshine."

"You need to know these things, Emma," he replied loftily.

"Yes, Oliver."

But even as she bustled and organized and took yet more snaps with her phone, parts of her mind would not stop turning over everything she'd heard and seen. It was as if she was trying to turn all the recent conversations about Victoria's death into entries in a spreadsheet that could be made to add up neatly.

Thankfully, she had Oliver to help her keep her priorities straight.

"Dinner?" He bumped her shin hopefully with his nose. "It's almost dinnertime. You have been very busy. You must be very hungry. Maybe we could get some fish? The fish was very good yesterday. I think we should get fish . . ."

The ancient refrigerator was, of course, as bare as Mother Hubbard's cupboard. She did have a bag of kibble and some treats in Oliver's suitcase, but she'd completely neglected the fact that she was going to need some human food.

Emma sighed. "All right, yes. I'm hungry too. We can—"

She was interrupted by a knock at the door. She opened it to see Genny standing on the other side.

"It's the welcome committee!" Genny lifted up two carrier bags. "And your housewarming present!"

"Oh, gosh, Genny, come in! We were actually just thinking about heading down to the shop. Oliver's hungry."

"Emma's hungry," said Oliver. "She doesn't look out for herself properly when she gets excited. What's in the bag?" he added, shoving his nose at the bags as Emma helped Genny carry them into the kitchen. "Ooo . . . ham!"

Oliver was, of course, correct. Along with a selection of cold cuts, there were a bag of dog kibble, a couple of take-away containers of salad, a loaf of sliced bread, milk, eggs, a pot of raspberry jam and a jar of mustard Genny insisted should be used sparingly.

Emma opened the jar and took a cautious sniff. "Wow!"

"It's possible there are articles in the Geneva convention about the stuff," Genny said with a laugh. "They make it at Wolsted Farm up the road. The jam's theirs as well."

"Let me put the kettle on," said Emma. "Have you got time to sit? Or do you need to get back to the shop?"

"I'll stay for a cuppa. Martin and Becca are handling the teatime rush, so I can be a little lazy."

Of course there was a box of tea in the bags as well. While Emma found and filled the kettle (with Oliver's able assistance) and swore a little as the burner on the ancient cooker proved reluctant to light, Genny found some plates and set them out on the table. Emma loaded hers up with salad and a ham sandwich with cheese and a cautious dollop of the local mustard. Genny agreed to have a half sandwich as well, to be companionable.

Emma found a chipped bowl under the sink and poured out some kibble for Oliver. That she may also have slipped him a half slice of the ham, and a bit of tomato and cucumber, was purely beside the point.

They all settled down at—or, in Oliver's case, under—the kitchen table. The clouds were well and truly gathering overhead, so Emma propped open the kitchen door to let Oliver get outside while he could do it without getting soaked.

"So," began Genny, "do you want to talk about it, or avoid it altogether?"

There was no question what "it" was. Emma sighed. "I don't expect there's going to be any way to avoid it. Do you know, I even had Parker Taite ask me to turn amateur sleuth."

Genny started to laugh, but then she stopped when she saw Emma's face. "Are you serious?"

"Angelique says he's an ex-journalist. Writing a book about the history of British crime."

"And he wants you to help him find out what happened to Victoria?"

Emma sipped her tea. "Apparently. He thinks he stands, well, we stand a chance of being able to find out something the police can't."

Genny considered this. "Well, it's not as daft as it sounds. Trevena's a pretty typical village, you know. Like to keep themselves to themselves, and might not want to be what they call wholly forthcoming about the local dirty laundry with the police."

"Especially the kind of laundry Victoria was so good at digging out," said Emma.

"Especially that," Genny agreed. "At the same time, we are all more than ready to engage in a spot of gossip over a pint."

"Or a cuppa." Emma raised her mug again.

"Exactly," agreed Genny. "Are you going to do it?"

"I wasn't. The problem is, he seems to have gotten in my head." She plucked a lettuce leaf out of her salad and chewed thoughtfully.

"And you're going to share the details with your new village friend, right?"

Emma smiled. "Right."

"Emma?" Oliver pawed at her jeans leg. "I'm going out, Emma."

"Go on, good boy." Emma scratched his head, and he loped away happily. Emma stared at the garden. She was forgetting something. Something that should go on the lists. *Well, it'll come to me later.*

Emma took a swallow of tea. "You remember that argument we overheard with Victoria, Jimmy and Louise . . ."

"Not likely to forget anytime soon, considering."

"Too right. Well, this morning, Louise came to the B&B and we talked a little."

"She talked to you? What did she want?"

"Surprised me too. I think she wanted to sound me out. She was trying to find out if I knew what DCI Brent was doing, or thinking, which I didn't. But what was weird was that as soon as Parker Taite came down the stairs, Louise practically jumped out of her seat and ran."

"That is weird," Genny said. "Even for Louise. She's always been nervous, but . . . does she even know who Parker *is*? I mean, I only know him because he's the chatty sort and a steady customer. Let me tell you, the man likes his deep-fried foods."

"How long has he been here?"

"I'm trying to think." Genny swirled her tea gently. "Three weeks, maybe?"

"Well, it turns out he'd been visiting Victoria, or at least trying to."

"He told you that?"

"Not right away. That's the problem. I . . . found out, and when I asked him about it, he said he was trying to get some local background for his book, but that she shut the door in his face."

"That sounds like Victoria."

"Yeah, it does, but then he said . . ." Emma stopped. "Okay, this is none of my business . . ."

Genny waved this away. "None of mine either, but I'm not letting it stop me."

"I knew I liked you. Anyway. Parker told me he couldn't get anything out of Victoria, but he had talked to Jimmy."

"Jimmy? That doesn't sound likely. He'd never go against Victoria."

"Are you sure? Because I'll tell you something else about Jimmy." Emma leaned forward. "When I was signing my lease with Maggie, Jimmy came in and she went to talk with him. Now, I wasn't eavesdropping—"

"Why on earth not?" exclaimed Genny. "I would have had a glass to the door."

"Remind me to double-check behind doors when I'm having personal conversations."

"Smart move around here. I'm not even the worst gossip in Trevena by a long chalk. You wait until you meet David and Charles."

"Anyway. He told Maggie he was worried about how the police weren't letting him back in the house, and Maggie warned him not to tell lies." *I know you're scared. I'm scared, but you start telling lies, and you are going to make everything worse.* "But then Jimmy said, 'But if they find out about the money?'"

Genny set her mug down. "Money?"

Emma nodded. "Jimmy was worried about money. Maggie wasn't. In fact, she said that Jimmy should have told the police about it when they interviewed him, but I don't think he did."

"That is definitely weird. I mean, as far as I know, Jimmy never had anything to do with Maggie, let alone with Maggie and money."

"Well, if he's been out of work for a year, he's probably pretty broke by now."

"I'd imagine so. I supposed Victoria had him on salary, but still, having to move home to be supported by your cranky aunt has got to be a comedown for a young man."

"Why didn't he get a new job in his field? I mean, I don't know a whole lot about it, but I do know video games are a huge business. I wouldn't think jobs could be that hard to find, especially for a single man willing to move abroad."

But Genny just shook her head. "I don't know. He never talked about it."

"Well, we do know one thing," Emma said. "Jimmy did want Victoria to sell some of her property, right? What if he was trying to work out some kind of deal with with Maggie Trenwith?"

"But Victoria hates—hated—Maggie down to her socks. I never knew Jimmy to have anything to do with her." She paused. "What could have changed, I wonder?"

"How did Maggie feel about Victoria?"

"No love lost there. Maggie's spent years blaming Victoria for blocking her plans for the village." Genny stared into the distance with narrowed eyes. "No. Wait. Whatever was behind that argument, it can't be Maggie. Remember, you heard Victoria shouting that Louise and Jimmy had sold her out to 'him.' Now, Maggie Trenwith is a lot of things, but she's definitely not a 'him.'"

"I thought of that. 'Him' could be the land developer, the one who wants to build this fancy new set of shops and things." She paused. "Or 'him' could be Parker Taite, I suppose. But how does that work? What could Jimmy know that would interest Parker?"

Genny's eyes went wide. "Oh. My. God."

"What is it?"

"Parker Taite. I know what he's up to." Genny pressed her hand over her mouth. "He's got hold of the Penhallow rumors!"

Emma pulled back. "Penhallow rumors?"

"Oh, Emma," Genny sighed. "I hate to be the one to tell you this, but your future tea shop is supposed to have been used to dispose of a corpse."

19

· · · · · · · · · · ·

EMMA BLINKED SEVERAL TIMES. RAPIDLY. "I'M SORRY. Genny. What did you say?"

"It's an old rumor, from before I was born, actually, and nothing ever proved. But you know how it is. Nothing ever really gets forgotten in a place like this." She nodded toward the front window and the garden and the road beyond. "People still talk about it. I thought about telling you when we first met, but"—she shrugged—"I was worried it might scare you off."

"And you need to make up for that. Right now." Emma stabbed her finger at the tabletop.

"Okay. Honestly, there's not that much to it. Before Penhallows was a tea shop, it was a bakery run by Nicholas Penhallow, Ruth Penhallow's dad. One night, old Nick up and vanished. My mum said he was not a nice man, and that was putting it mildly. So nobody really missed him."

Emma frowned. "That's it?"

"Well," Genny drawled and reached for the teapot, "the problem was 'nobody' included his wife and daughter."

"Oh."

"Right, oh." Genny topped off her mug from the teapot and took a swallow. "Anyway. Like I said, nobody ever proved anything, but back in the eighties sometime some-body decided to write an exposé of village life. Something nasty in the woodshed always sells, doesn't it? So they basi-cally ranged over the whole southwest digging up all the local dirt they could find. One of the things they found was the Penhallow disappearance. They mixed in all kinds of gossip about love triangles and late-night meetings for rolls in hay and . . . stuff. There was a real tempest in the Trev-ena teapot when it came out, let me tell you. I remember because it was the first time I'd ever heard about any of it.

"Anyway, the gossip back then was that old Mrs. Pen-hallow had finally gotten sick and tired of Mr. Penhallow's little ways, hit him over the head and shoved him into one the big old wall ovens, Hansel-and-Gretel style."

Silence fell between them while both women contem-plated this old and gruesome rumor.

"Sounds like exactly the kind of story that would get an ex-tabloid reporter all worked up," said Emma.

"And since Victoria owns Penhallows, which is where the body was supposed to have been disposed of . . ." added Genny.

"He might have been badgering her for a look round inside."

"Which Victoria would probably not have appreciated." A cold gust of air blew through the open back door and snaked around Emma's ankles.

"I'd say definitely not." Genny nodded.

"Is the old kitchen still there, even?"

"Oh, yes. Haven't you had your look yet?"

Emma shook her head. "Not yet. First there was Victo-ria, and she wasn't likely to rent to me, and now they're going to have to wait on the will and all that."

"I'd be surprised if Maggie let that stop her. She's got to be over the moon now that Victoria's out of the way . . ." Genny stopped. "That doesn't sound very good, does it?"

"No, it doesn't," admitted Emma. "Do you think . . . maybe Jimmy might have done something like let Parker into Penhallows . . . ?"

"He might, although I don't know. I mean, the Penhallow disappearance is—that is, was—a real sore spot with Victoria."

"Because she was friends with Ruth?"

Emma nodded. "And, of course, since the rumor was that Mrs. Penhallow killed Mr. Penhallow, the rumor *also* was that Ruth must have known about it. Maybe even helped. Victoria did *not* like people telling tales about her friends." She paused. "But I don't see what that would have to do with anything. I mean, if Victoria did know anything, she kept the secret. Mrs. Penhallow's long gone. Ruth's all but gone. There's nobody left to care."

Outside, rain began tapping at the windows. Emma set her mug down and went over to kneel on the sofa so she could wrestle the window shut. "Unless . . ." she said, through gritted teeth.

"What?"

Emma slumped onto the sofa, facing Genny. "Victoria kept the secret, but Victoria kept a lot of secrets, didn't she? And she also used them when she needed to."

Genny narrowed her eyes. "So what you mean is that if Parker was coming around digging up the past, and Jimmy was seen talking to Parker, somebody might have gotten nervous that Victoria was ready to let something spill?"

"Something like that. Yeah. The only problem is this is all absolutely daft, isn't it?" Emma rubbed her hands together and went over to the garden door. "I mean, we really have no idea what we're talking about."

Genny sighed. "I suppose you're right. But still, it's all very weird."

"In fact, it is all so weird that there's probably something completely obvious that we're not seeing."

"Oh, yes, I'm sure that's right," Genny agreed.

Emma meant to whistle for Oliver, but the corgi had evidently had enough of the Cornish weather and was already trotting back inside. He stopped right in front of Emma and shook himself, hard, spraying droplets everywhere.

"Oh, Oliver!" Emma cried with fond exasperation.

"What?" Then, he noticed the muddy footprints, and muddy belly, and he dropped his head. "Sorry, Emma."

She found an old towel and rubbed his paws, and his belly, as best she could.

"So, how was it out there? Meet the neighbors?" she asked softly, rubbing his ears.

"The fox has been here," he reported. "And there are hedgehogs. Their matron is very rude. She told me to shove off. Just like that!"

"Dear me." Emma sat back on her heels. Her corgi still had half of Cornwall clinging to his coat. "And what on earth did you find to roll around in?"

"Nothing," said Oliver. "I mean, not much, really, it was just an old—"

"Never mind," said Emma quickly. "I don't need to know. But it's bath time for you tonight, laddie me boy."

"Oh, crumbs."

Genny laughed at them both. She also checked her watch. "Gosh, stayed longer than I meant to. Are you set for tonight, Emma? Do you need anything?"

"No, I'm great, thanks. And thanks for coming by, and for bringing the groceries."

"You're welcome. Glad I can help." She beamed. "Oh, by the way, I assume you're going to want to refurnish Nancarrow?"

"What!" Emma laid her hand on her heart. "And destroy this lovely retro-chic feel?"

Genny laughed. "Well, I'm sure you've got plenty of your own stuff, but just in case, you should check out Vintage Style. They've got lots of brilliant furniture and things." She paused. "It also just happens to be run by David and Charles, who are not only the worst gossips in Trevena—they have lived here for absolutely ages. Just mentioning this in case there was something you might want to know."

20

....

THE RAIN SETTLED IN FOR THE WHOLE NEXT DAY. THANKS TO Genny's groceries, Emma was able to stay snugly inside the cottage, snacking on leftovers at random intervals, making lists and phone calls, and generally enjoying herself in her new home. Of course, her idea of enjoying herself included things like looking up the Trevena bus routes and creating lists of the licenses and permissions she'd need when she did actually find a space for her tea shop, as well as talking with her new landlords about options for getting the old furniture moved to storage once she started finding her own things.

She also spent time with Maggie's list of potential sites for her shop. Two in particular looked really promising— one was a former lunchroom, and one was a former wine bar. The first would need a lot of remodeling; the second was just a bit out of her budget, but might be made to work.

A fried egg sandwich for dinner was spiced up nicely with that powerful local mustard. She added a note in her binder that a visit up to Wolsted Farm was definitely in order. She wanted to make as much use of local produce in her shop as she could.

It was, in short, a lovely, busy day. But some things about the cottage were becoming clear.

First thing, it was cold. The wind off the ocean wrapped right around the house, and when the windows were shut tight, all kinds of sneaky little drafts still wound across the floorboards, over her toes and around her ankles.

Which led to the second thing. There was enough wood in the bin by the stove to tempt Emma into resurrecting her ancient Girl Guide skills and lighting a fire in the hearth stove. Unfortunately, a half hour's futile searching showed there were no matches in the cottage. That might have ended the matter, but Emma decided to get clever. She used the cooker to light a twist of paper and used that as a taper to light the stove.

The result of all this effort was a great cloud of smoke pouring into the living room.

Coughing and cursing, Emma finally found the flue damper and wrestled that open. This fresh burst of self-sufficiency was promptly rewarded by a shower of black soot fountaining down on top of her fire, smothering the whole thing and sending both her and Oliver reeling out to stand under the pathetic little overhang above the front door until the dust literally settled.

Which led to the third thing—Emma needed a chimney sweep.

"Who on earth needs a chimney sweep?" she demanded of the cottage at large.

"You just said we do," Oliver reminded her.

"Yes, yes, I did." Emma sighed and went to get the broom and dustpan.

After that, she abandoned plans for a fire and instead piled the vast majority of the quilts in the house on her new bed and bundled herself underneath them with a cup of tea and her laptop.

"*Great British Bake Off*?" asked Oliver, snuggling up next to her.

"Not yet." She opened her search engine. She should

have done this before, and she knew it. In her defense, the situation had been a little, well, fluid.

"What are we doing, Emma?" Oliver poked his nose at the screen.

"Well, to start with, we are going to look up Jimmy Lambert and see what we find."

"Why are we doing that?"

"Because I want to see if there's any reason he is sitting here in Trevena instead of getting back out there in the great wide world of video games." Of course, he might be working remotely or have picked up some freelance gigs, or both.

Finding out about his background probably wouldn't explain what he had been doing whispering in Maggie Trenwith's reception room, but it would eliminate some possibilities.

A search on "James Lambert, game design" turned up an online résumé and even a couple of industry awards for teams he'd been part of.

Then there was a blog post on the website for the Silicon Valley company BlastSys from three years ago welcoming James Lambert from the UK as their newest senior coding associate.

That was, however, the last bit of connection she found between Jimmy and BlastSys. But it certainly was not the last the Internet had to say about the company itself.

A new search, this time on BlastSys, got a whole lot of hits, all about the rapid collapse of a company that had been hailed as a massive success. Venture capitalists had been pouring money into the firm to try to cash in on the reputation of its boy genius CEO. Emma's fingers itched. She had watched too many of her clients learn the hard way not to put their trust in someone with a dream and a brilliant line of patter.

BlastSys's investors had learned that same lesson. The promised products failed to appear, and the company faltered and flamed out. The boy genius did himself a moonlight flit, vanishing into the ether and taking a significant percentage of his investors' cash with him.

Poor Jimmy. Emma shook her head. Being out of work was bad enough. Being out of work because your boss turned out to be a total fraud was even worse.

Which made her think of something else. Emma opened a new tab.

"What are we doing now, Emma?" Oliver rolled over onto his back.

Emma gave him a one-handed belly rub. "Now we are looking up Parker Taite." She hit SEARCH.

"Why are we doing that?"

"Because I'm not sure about him, or what he's actually doing here. And I'm not sure he's telling me the whole story."

"Good." Oliver settled himself more comfortably. "You need to know these things, Emma."

Yes. Yes, I do.

Her search just on Parker Taite turned up a lot of entries for an artist who painted idealized still lives, mostly of flowers. "Parker Taite Journalist" got her a travel writer, first name Tara; a "lifestyle coach"; and an entry from a nineteenth-century directory of journalism in Great Britain.

"Okay, this is getting strange," Emma murmured.

"Parker Taite tabloid" got a graphic artist and an author of lesbian fiction. "Parker Taite author" turned up more of the same.

She bit her lip and kept typing. She tried all the London tabloids by name and looked up their publishers' employee/ contributor directories. She tried everything she could think of.

In the end, Emma let her hands drop to her sides and stared at her screen.

"Oliver?"

Oliver shook himself out of his doze. "Yes, Emma?" he yawned.

"Oliver, we have ourselves a situation."

"Why?"

"Because, according to the Internet, Parker Taite— ex-journalist, current true crime author, would-be Sam Spade type—does not exist."

21

. . . .

THE NEXT DAY DAWNED SUNNY AND BRIGHT. TO EMMA'S way of thinking, the obvious thing to do with such a gorgeous day was go shopping. With maybe one or two stops on the way.

"Besides," she said to Oliver, "you need the walk."

"So do you," said Oliver.

"Absolutely. We'll go to that shop Genny recommended. What'd she call it? Vintage Style."

"A shop?" Oliver looked downcast. "What about the hills? Or the beach? You like the beach." He wagged hopefully.

"The beach is in the same direction," said Emma. "Maybe we can get fish on the way back."

"Oh, well, that is a very sensible plan. When do we leave?"

After enjoying a leisurely breakfast and catching up on her emails, Emma called Maggie Trenwith's number and left a message about the properties she wanted to see. Then she and Oliver set off down the road toward Trevena.

That the route into town took them right past Victoria's cottage was, perhaps, not entirely coincidental.

The question is, how do I get Jimmy to talk to me?

Because something was clearly going on between Jimmy and Maggie, and it involved money. On the long list of things Emma had learned during her years in London's financial trenches, it was that money brought out the best and the worst in people, and families, and companies.

As Victoria's cottage came into view around the bend, Emma saw that the crime scene tape had been taken down from around the garden wall. The police must have gotten what they wanted from Victoria's house, despite yesterday's rain.

It seemed like her luck was in—a little, anyway. Jimmy was out in the front garden, raking.

Emma pictured herself walking up to him. What would she even say? "Hi, how are you? All right? Listen, I wanted to ask you, did you lose any money when your games company went under? Only I was wondering because apparently you've got something going with Maggie, and maybe it was the same thing your aunt was yelling at you about?"

She could just imagine how *that* would go over.

Time for plan B. Emma crouched down and unclipped Oliver's lead. "Oliver?"

"Yes, Emma?"

"You know how I'm always telling you not to get into people's gardens?"

"Yes, Emma. Only sometimes it's absolutely necessary."

She rubbed his chin. "Well, this is one of those times."

Oliver's ears went up. "It is?"

"Yes. I need you to get into Victoria's garden."

Oliver cocked his head at her. "Really?"

"Really. I might have to scold you a little afterward, but I won't mean it. Do you understand?"

Oliver scratched his ear. "This is one of those human things, isn't it? You're going to stand around talking when it's done, aren't you?"

"Yes, it's a very human thing, and yes, I hope we are going to stand around and do a whole lot of talking." If, that is, she was right that Jimmy was less dog-hostile than his aunt had been.

If she was wrong, she might be about to blow her one chance to get him to talk to her.

Oliver finished his thoughtful scratch. "Should I go now?"

"Yes, please." She gave his ears an extra rub.

Oliver barked once, whisked around, stuck his nose out and ran, barking at the top of his lungs.

Emma straightened up. "Oh, Oliver!" she cried, putting as much exasperation as she could manage into the shout.

In the garden, Jimmy whipped around just in time to see Oliver slide under the gate and make a beeline for the rose-bushes.

"Oh!" Emma ran up to the gate. "Oh, I am so, so sorry. I don't know what happened. The lead must have slipped."

"It's okay." Jimmy pushed the gate open. "Only get him before he can start digging, yeah?"

"Yes, yes, of course. Oliver!" she called. "Oliver, bad dog! Come back here!"

Oliver appeared from under the roses. He shook the damp off his coat and trotted over.

"Bad dog," she whispered softly, rubbing his wet ears. "Such a very bad dog."

She straightened up and turned around. Jimmy was standing behind her with the rake in his hand. He was dressed for gardening work—a tartan shirt over a gray T-shirt, old jeans and worn boots. His blond hair was uncombed, and sparse gold stubble fuzzed his jawline.

"Sorry," she said again. "He just gets the zoomies sometimes."

"No worries. Um, it's Emma, right?"

"That's right."

She couldn't help noticing how all the recent police activity had marred the formerly immaculate front garden. Boot prints made muddy gouges in the grass and the borders. The broken branches on the rosebushes drooped sadly.

Oliver was busying himself with snuffling the tops of Jimmy's muddy trainers.

"Flowers, flowers, flowers," said Oliver. "And mud and tarmac and . . ."

Memory sparked inside Emma. Jimmy and flowers and Oliver. He'd said Jimmy smelled like flowers before. When was that?

Jimmy stared down at the busy corgi. Oliver looked up and wagged. A tiny smile flickered across the young man's face, and he reached down and scratched Oliver's ears. Oliver flopped down happily on the flagstone path and leaned in.

"Who's a good boy, then?" murmured Jimmy. He glanced up at Emma. "You said his name's Oliver?"

"That's right, and he's a complete attention hound."

"Complete warrior corgi," Oliver corrected her.

Jimmy scratched Oliver until Oliver rolled over for a belly rub. The young man obliged, and Oliver wriggled in appreciation. Emma watched the tension in Jimmy's face slowly drain away.

She counted to ten. "Well, we should probably go," she said finally. "Sorry to have disturbed."

"Nah, it's all right." Jimmy straightened up. Now he was looking at her in a speculative, and not unfriendly, fashion. Oliver gave a soft "Woof!" and scrambled to his feet. "It's not like you're . . . well, some people," he finished lamely. "Listen, I was just putting the kettle on. Would you like a cuppa?"

And that, ladies and gentlemen, is the power of the friendly corgi. Emma smiled. "That'd be great, ta."

"Did I do that right, Emma?" asked Oliver as they followed Jimmy inside.

"You were perfect," breathed Emma. "Good boy."

THE KITCHEN WAS VERY MUCH AS EMMA REMEMBERED IT, minus a few crucial details—like the broken crockery, the spilled tea and Victoria's body. This time, however, she was able to look around and see the details she'd missed before, like how the oilcloth on the table was ragged at the edges and the linoleum floor was cracked and starting to curl in places. The cooker was at least as old as Emma's at Nancarrow. So was the fridge. One of chairs had been mended with electrical tape. In fact, the entire kitchen was quite down-at-the-heels. The only new thing Emma saw in the whole place was the gleaming white laptop on the kitchen table.

This is the home of the woman who owns half of Trevena?

Oliver snuffled across the floor, following a scent trail that only he could navigate. Through the open windows, Emma could see the beautiful back garden. The summer scents of herbs and flowers filled the kitchen. At the same time, it was plain the police had been there too. The poles for the tomatoes tilted in every direction, and muddy footprints made wandering paths through the beds and across the grass.

Jimmy saw her looking at the garden.

"I was trying to clean it up, but . . ." He shook his head. "It's like I suddenly don't even know where to start."

"I don't know much about gardening," said Emma. "But maybe it'd be better if you waited until things dried out a little. You might have better luck."

"Yeah, well, I do know a bit about gardening, and I should have. I just couldn't stand sitting around taking condolence calls or waiting for . . . news."

Before he got any further, an electronica riff cut abruptly through the kitchen. Jimmy swore and yanked his phone out of his pocket. He looked at the number and swore again, then shut the call off.

"Listen, if you need me to go . . ." Emma said.

"Nah, nah, it's nobody I want to talk to." Jimmy tossed the phone onto the table and got busy filling the electric kettle and getting the pot down from the cupboard.

The electronica riff sounded again, and again.

Jimmy swore harshly, slammed the mug he was getting out onto the counter and snatched his phone up instead. His face flushed bright red, and for a second, Emma thought he might throw the phone against the wall.

Instead, he turned the ringer off, pulled the lid off one

of the canisters on the counter and dropped the phone inside. Then he went back to making the tea.

Who is it? she wondered. *Parker? Maggie? Louise? An old girlfriend? Who?*

There was no way to ask, so Emma settled on small talk. For certain values of small, at least.

"So. You're in video games, right?"

"Kind of. You know." Jimmy shrugged. The kettle pinged at the same time, and he poured the steaming water into the pot.

"That's big business. Lot of instability though."

Oh, very subtle, Emma. She suppressed a grimace.

Jimmy glanced over his shoulder at her. "What do you know about it?"

"I used to be in finance before I came out here. You see software companies come up and go down like yo-yos." She paused. "Not just games. All kinds." Jimmy was setting the cups and the pot onto a tray with the milk bottle and the sugar bowl. "It can get really bad. You get some CEOs who decide they can make anything happen just by talking big, but that only works for so long, and eventually the money stops rolling in, and they can even turn to shaking down their employees and . . ."

Emma stopped. Jimmy's face had twisted tight, and for a second, Emma thought he looked like he wanted to throw up.

"Anyway," she went on hastily. "It can get really messy."

Jimmy's shoulders slumped. "Yeah, 's the truth, innit?"

There was a weird metallic clatter. Oliver's nose shot up and his ears went back. He trotted over to the counter and barked.

It was Jimmy's phone, vibrating inside the canister. Jimmy's face went beet red. Emma got up, grabbed the canister, carried it out the back door, set it on the path and shut the door.

Jimmy was staring at her. "Thanks."

"You're welcome." She sat back down. "Reporters?" she guessed.

He paused long enough before he nodded that Emma was almost entirely sure that whoever was on the phone, it was not the *Cornish Times*.

"Well, it won't last," she said as Jimmy poured out the tea. "The police will have it all figured out soon. I read somewhere most crimes are actually solved in the first forty-eight hours."

"Wish I could be so sure." Jimmy collapsed gracelessly into the other chair. "It's like, I don't know who anybody is all of a sudden. Not even Raj, and we've been mates for years. Everybody keeps coming around with all this fake concern." He picked his mug up, but set it right back down again without drinking. "'How *are* you, Jimmy?'" His voice rose to an affected squeak. "'Guess that was some surprise, Jimmy.' 'Well, never mind, Jimmy, you'll make out all right.' 'We all knew what she was like.'" His face twisted tight, and he eyed Emma uneasily. "But all they really want to hear is something they can all gossip about."

"Was that what Parker Taite's been after?" Emma asked, and she hoped that he didn't hear how stiff she sounded. "Gossip?"

Jimmy looked at her sharply. "Who told you that?"

Emma shrugged, a little startled at the sudden anger in Jimmy's voice. "He's working on a book about old murders and so on, and I heard he thought Victoria might have known about some old scandals or crimes or what have you he could add in for local color."

"Yeah, well, there was nothing like that," Jimmy snapped. "I don't care what anybody's told you. I mean, yeah, there was some stuff maybe forty years ago or something, but that's got nothing to do with anything. At all. Got it?"

Emma drew back. "No offense."

But that is an awful lot of protest about something that's got nothing to do with anything.

Jimmy ran his hand through his hair again. "No, I'm sorry. It's not you, really. It's me and, well, everything."

"You must miss her."

Jimmy's face twisted tight again, and Emma wasn't sure

he was going to answer. Oliver trotted over to his side and lay down with his chin on Jimmy's shoe.

The young man smiled, just a little.

"Yeah, I do miss her. She wasn't like everybody thinks. When I first got here after my parents died . . . I couldn't sleep, like, at all." He filled both mugs and pushed one toward her. He sat with the other, both elbows planted on the table and the mug held in front of him. He didn't drink; he just looked hard into his own memory. "I think I was afraid that if I shut my eyes something or somebody else would disappear. Anyway, she never tried to tell me I was silly or I needed to get over it or even that it was natural. She just sat up with me. Every night. And she had these big gardening books, really horribly dull stuff, about pH balance in soil and bone meal fertilizer and, oh lord, *The Complete History of the English Rose*. That was the big guns. We'd be in the front room, and she'd put on her reading glasses and say, 'Well, if you're going to sit up, Jimmy, you might as well learn something.' And she'd start reading, just droning on and on until I'd fall asleep without realizing it. Went on for months like that, until I could make it through the night again. And never said one word about it afterward." He stopped. "Nobody knew that side of her, did they?"

"You knew," said Emma. "That's what's important."

"Yeah, I knew. For all the good it did either one of us."

Before Emma could ask what he meant, Jimmy looked up at the old chrome-trimmed clock on the wall. "Oh, sh . . . sugar. It's later than I thought. Listen, I've got an appointment and I gotta get cleaned up. Lawyers, you know?"

"Yeah, I do know," said Emma sympathetically. "I'll let you get on. But if you ever need to just get out for a bit, you can always come up the hill, all right? Throw sticks for Oliver or something."

Jimmy scratched Oliver's head. "Might just. Thanks."

They said goodbye and Emma headed back out with Oliver at her heels.

"Did it work, Emma? The human thing? Did it work?"

"Yes, Oliver, it did."

She'd seen and heard more than enough to confirm one of the suspicions on her growing list.

She was ready to bet an entire chocolate layer cake that Jimmy Lambert had lost much more than a job when Blast-Sys collapsed. He'd lost money as well.

The question now was how much did he lose, and did any of that money belong to Victoria?

The other question was, why was he so adamant that forty-year-old gossip had nothing to do with what happened to Victoria?

And had he told Parker that too?

22

· · · · · · · · · · ·

"WHERE ARE WE GOING, EMMA?" ASKED OLIVER AS EMMA wrestled with the front-gate latch.

"Library," she said. "I'm supposed to be meeting Parker." *Which is good, because I've got a few questions for him.*

Trevena's library was a relatively new building, wedged between a bric-a-brac shop and an outdoor clothier, across the street from the sprawl of King Arthur's Castle. It was immediately obvious that Parker had gotten there before them. A disconsolate Percy lay flat on the pavement, his lead tethered to the bike rack.

The library's front desk was commanded by a tiny Pakistani woman named Mrs. Shah, who looked to be about ninety years old. Mrs. Shah explained to Emma, very politely and very firmly, that dogs were not permitted in the library, not even if she was just nicking in to try to find another patron, who had, by the way, been stationed at the microfilm machine for the past hour, and would she please remind her friend that, like Mrs. Shah herself, that machine was not as young as it used to be and to please take some care not to let it overheat, because they had the very devil of a time, excuse her language, finding the parts.

Now, understanding how the residents of Trevena and visitors felt about their dogs, the library kept a bowl that could be filled with water and some treats right by the door if she would care to help herself. Thank you very much.

"That is a highly unreasonable human," muttered Oliver as Emma knotted his lead loosely to the bike rack.

"You'll be all right, Oliver. I'll just be a minute. And Percy's right here." Emma gave the slouching Yorkie a thorough petting. She also put down some fresh water and biscuits, and left the dogs exchanging their greeting sniffs and snuffles

Just like Mrs. Shah had said, Parker was stationed in the back corner of the library's basement at an ancient microfilm machine that hummed like an army of discontented bees. The film reels clicked and clacked as he flicked through what looked to be back issues of a newspaper.

This was the moment where Emma had hoped a plan would come to her. On the one hand, she was supposed to be working with Parker to look into Victoria's death. On the other, she knew he was keeping secrets from her. So how to get him to tell her the truth?

Right. We play it by ear. Heaven knew she'd faced down bigger, more canny players a hundred times in a hundred different boardrooms. Usually there were two approaches: You found out what the other person really wanted out of the meeting, and you worked that angle. Or, if you were in the mood to play a straighter line, you found out where their vulnerability was, and you worked that.

"Oh, hullo!" Parker said as she came into his line of sight. He also shut the machine off, which would be welcome news for Mrs. Shah, but it did also keep Emma from seeing exactly what he was reading. "Welcome to the depths of the twentieth century!"

Emma arched her brows. "Bit much coming from the man who's writing his book on a typewriter, isn't it?"

"Well, I'm hoping for a new career as a pretentious artist. What's their excuse?" He leaned back in the chair and laced his fingers together across his stomach. He eyed her stance and the way she kept her distance. "Was it something I said?"

Right. Emma squared her shoulders. *How about start with the direct approach?*

"Actually, it was more something you didn't say."

"Which doesn't sound at all portentous."

"I did an Internet search on Parker Taite last night."

"Ah." Parker's easy grin slowly melted away. "I was wondering when you'd get around to that. Didn't find much, did you?"

"No."

He sighed. "I guess I should explain."

He glanced at her to see how she was taking his show of sheepishness. Emma folded her arms and waited.

"Okay. Here it goes." He took a deep breath. "Remember when I said I'd done some bad things and people got hurt? The truth is that somebody nearly got killed. Because of words I'd written, because I wanted a headline. There." He spread his hands. "That's the long and the short of it. You want to walk away, I don't blame you."

"Why didn't you tell me before?"

Parker's face flushed with anger. "You think this is easy?" he demanded. "That I should have just come right out and said, 'Hey, Emma, know what happened to me? I screwed up, massively. My paper threw me under the bus. I spent a year drowning my sorrows and another year trying to climb out of the bottle I'd dived into. The year after that I spent sponging off my brother because none of my former colleagues would even talk to me anymore, let alone help me find work. I finally cashed in some favors with an old friend who was a true crime editor. He said if I produced a manuscript, he'd smooth the way to getting it published. My brother said he'd pay for me to travel to do the research, and so I changed my name and here I am." He spread his hands wide. "A worthless ex-drunk leech praying that he might, maybe, be able to make his own way again, if he's a very good boy and eats his veg and says his prayers. You will forgive me if it's not something I'm particularly eager to take up over a cup of tea in the garden!"

He turned back toward the microfilm reader. Emma could hear him breathing harshly.

"I'm sorry," said Emma.

Parker shook his head, but he also didn't look at her. "Not your fault. I knew this would come out eventually. I should have . . ." He heaved another sigh. "Let's just skip it, okay? I've found some stuff out about our dead woman, and about Maggie Trenwith. You want to hear it?"

"If you want to tell me."

"I do, actually. I want to know what you think." He paused, and she could see how his forehead glistened in the dim light. "Because if I'm right, I may have done it again."

Emma felt herself go cold. "What do you mean?"

"Victoria's death," he whispered. "It might be my fault."

"How on earth could it be your fault?"

Finally Parker turned back to face her. Emma noticed how tightly he gripped the chair arms, like he was trying to hold himself in place.

"I told you I've been doing research into the local crime-scape, right?"

"Did that include Nicholas Penhallow's disappearance back in the seventies?"

"You've heard about that? Well, of course you have. You're looking to set up shop in the property where the body is supposed to have been hidden."

"That's a long way from certain." Either about Nicholas Penhallow's body or about setting up shop in his old building.

"Probably for the best. Anyway, I started going back through the old newspaper reports, and there's a bunch of articles that quote a young Ms. Victoria Roberts as a close friend of the vanished man's daughter."

"Really?"

He shrugged. "Yeah, well, when you're hard up for quotes, you'll take what you can get. Anyway, when I saw that, I thought I might go round and ask her about it. I got shouted at for my troubles. First by her, and then by the nephew."

Emma remembered Genny sitting at her kitchen table, tea mug in hands and eyes narrowed.

. . . if Parker was coming around digging up the past, and Jimmy was seen talking to Parker, somebody might have gotten nervous that Victoria was ready to let something spill . . .

"Anyway, I got to thinking. Usually, people get angry at questions when they don't want to answer. I thought maybe Victoria knew more about the missing Mr. Penhallow than she wanted to let on. So that's what I've been doing down here." He reached out and tapped the stack of microfilm cases. "Going through old newspapers about Penhallow's disappearance. It was fairly well covered locally. Pretty much everyone not on the police force agreed he was an unpleasant bloke, and not one to go away quietly without some help."

"Wait. You're saying Victoria Roberts had something to do with Nicholas Penhallow's disappearance?" Emma didn't wait for an answer. "I mean, she was friends with Ruth Penhallow back then, but that's an awfully loose connection," said Emma. *Never mind that Genny and I were thinking the same thing.* "What makes you think it has anything to do with what happened to Victoria?"

"I'm getting there. Now, Victoria had enemies. We know that, right?"

"Yes." Because Victoria collected people's secrets and was not afraid to use them to get what she wanted.

"One of them is Maggie Trenwith, because Maggie is in the business of selling property, and Victoria is in the habit of buying it up and sitting on it."

"Right."

"In fact, it's possible Victoria's been *deliberately* buying up land to keep Maggie from getting it."

"Do you know that for sure?" Emma tried to put some skepticism behind her words, and failed.

"Not yet, but I'm getting closer. Anyway, along with the old newspapers, I've been going through the local estate records. Trevena hasn't had a lot of sales or new leases or anything much in the past couple of years. The Trenwith Agency has got to be hurting. Then this development deal comes along. Big opportunity, by local standards. But it all hinges on Victoria being willing to sell a particular parcel of land. Our Maggie is at her wit's end. She threatens to revive old rumors about Nick Penhallow's disappearance if Victoria doesn't sell."

"What rumors?" asked Emma skeptically. "I thought it was Mrs. Penhallow who was supposed to have killed her husband."

"Yeah, but Victoria bought the building, didn't she? Maybe she knew for sure who killed old Penhallow and used that to force Mrs. and Ms. Penhallow to sell."

Emma stood there without answering. It would certainly fit with what she'd heard about Victoria. If she wouldn't hesitate to threaten an embezzling supermarket manager, why would she hesitate to threaten a murderous baker's wife?

Except Ruth was her friend. And Victoria was said to be protective of her friends.

Although clearly she had her limits. *After everything I've done! All these years!* Emma remembered Victoria shouting. *You have the nerve to try to defend him now!*

Emma frowned. "But if Maggie was threatening Victoria, why is Victoria dead? You'd think Victoria would have—"

"Killed Maggie?" Parker finished for her. "Maybe. Or maybe Victoria had something juicy on our Maggie. Maybe Maggie's been taking payments under the table or kickbacks or helping get some building codes bypassed. There's a thousand ways to make a little extra in property development."

Emma swallowed. "Or maybe it was closer to home."

Parker leaned forward. "What have you got?"

"I was talking to Jimmy."

"Really?" he sounded genuinely surprised, and impressed. "What'd the nephew have to say?"

"Not a lot, really, but . . . it's possible he lost more than his job when the games company he worked for collapsed."

"You think he lost some money as well?"

"Maybe, and it's possible he was trying to work out some kind of deal with Maggie Trenwith."

"Why not go to his aunt if he needed money? The old lady was loaded."

"That's just it," said Emma, remembering Victoria's shabby kitchen. "I'm not sure she was."

"But she owns . . ."

"Half the village, yes. I know. And land is supposed to be the ultimate investment, and usually that's right. But what if it's like this? What if she put everything she had into her properties, and then when the bottom dropped out of the market and the businesses closed, she was left living on a shoestring?" Her father had seen it happen; back during the collapse of the Thatcher years, some of his clients had been forced to take huge losses on property they'd been planning on using for retirement income. "Property poor," he had called it.

"But then why not sell?"

Emma shrugged. "Maybe she was waiting for things to recover, or maybe she just didn't want the village to see she'd failed."

Parker pursed his lips, staring into the distance. "That's possible. When you hate everybody and you're convinced everybody hates you, you might not want to give them the satisfaction of seeing you have to sell up." His eyes gleamed thoughtfully, but Emma very much got the impression they were not nice thoughts.

"So maybe Jimmy knows he can't talk Victoria round on his own, so he enlists Louise Craddock. He tells her that Victoria is at the end of her funds and that something has to happen."

"Okay, so that could explain the fight you heard." He nodded thoughtfully. "So we're thinking, what? Jimmy can't get his aunt to see reason, and he has to tell Maggie, and she decides that there's only one answer left?" He shook his head. "Won't wash. All Jimmy has to do is tell the police and it's all over."

Emma bit her lip. "There's another wrinkle."

"I'm all ears."

"That money he lost, what if it wasn't all his?"

"You think maybe he stole from his auntie?"

"Or asked her for a loan he couldn't pay back."

Parker was silent for a minute. "Do you think Jimmy could have killed her?"

Did she think that? She didn't want to. She liked Jimmy. *Oliver* liked Jimmy. She didn't really believe all that stuff about dogs being great judges of character. She'd asked her vet about it once. The woman had laughed and said, "Give him a pound of calf's liver and a dog will become best friends with anybody at all."

But Oliver was special. And Jimmy had loved his aunt. Emma was sure of that.

"I'm not going to accuse anybody without proof," said Emma. "Besides, it doesn't matter what either of us thinks. It matters what the police can prove."

"But if Jimmy's involved, it also matters what Jimmy thinks the police are *going* to think," said Parker. "And if he thinks *they* think that he had a motive to kill his aunt *and* he thinks Maggie might be ready to point this out, *that* might be reason enough for him to keep his mouth shut about any dealings he's had with Maggie. And Maggie might have known that." Parker grinned, thoroughly satisfied with himself. "Neat. Very neat. Could be either one of them, couldn't it? No need to bring the past into it at all. I knew I was right about having you in on this."

Emma felt her stomach curdle. Suddenly, this investigation business didn't seem like such a good idea. The slick, sly smile spreading across Parker's face didn't make it any better. He looked happy, and greedy. Again.

What have I gotten myself into?

Emma shivered so hard that, for a minute, she didn't realize that the tremor under her palm was her phone vibrating in her handbag.

She pulled it out and saw it was Maggie Trenwith. She felt the blood drain from her face. Parker saw and raised his brows. She turned the screen toward him, and he saw the name shining on the screen. He pulled his round chin back and gestured for her to get a move on.

Emma swallowed hard and hit the ACCEPT button.

"Hello, Maggie?"

"Hello, Emma. Sorry to bother, but I've got your dog."

23

LATER. OLIVER WOULD EXPLAIN TO EMMA THAT IT WAS NOT his fault. Which was absolutely true. It wasn't. It was Percy's.

"This is boring." Percy had slumped down onto the pavement, chin on his tiny paws.

Oliver crunched on another biscuit and nosed the pile toward Percy. "They'll be back."

"You're boring." The Yorkie jumped to his feet and backed away to the very limit of the leash, straining against the collar. He wriggled and stretched and yipped. "Don't you want to play?" He scratched at his collar and strained again.

"Have a biscuit. They'll be back."

Percy's next yip was rude. And dismissive. Then he went back to scratching at his collar. And wriggling. And pulling.

Oliver nosed the pavement. Whole layers and worlds of smells greeted him. He'd need to get used to all these smells, and learn their human names from Emma, so she could talk properly about them. There were even more smells on the fresh breeze. Some of them were just starting to get familiar. There was the fish shop. Maybe he could convince Emma that the fish shop would still be a good idea once she was done with . . . whatever human thing she was doing right now.

"Why don't you like your human?" he asked Percy.

"He's not my human," the Yorkie snapped. "He's my human's brother. My human went away." Percy's whole body drooped. "I miss him."

Oliver nosed him under his belly to comfort him. "Your human will be back soon. Humans always come back."

Percy yipped and grumbled. He also started scrabbling at his collar with his front legs.

"What are you doing?"

"I told you," growled Percy. "I'm bored. I'm bored with this boring old human and his boring old rooms and his boring old 'Here, Percy; now, Percy; no, Percy,' and I'm bored with always being carried around . . ."

That collar must have been loose, because with each grumble and growl, Percy managed to shove his paws a bit farther under it and wriggle his head a bit farther out of it until, at last, the collar was on the ground and Percy was on his feet and shaking his head, hard.

"Free at last!" he barked. "Come on! Come on! You wanna play?"

Oliver scrambled to his feet. "You can't!" He barked. Some humans turned to look, but nobody stopped. Oliver barked again. "Emma! Emma!"

"Suit yourself!" Percy raced off down the street. "Free! Free! Oooo . . . hey! What's that?"

"Stop!" Oliver threw himself forward, still barking. Maybe Emma would hear. The knot at the end of the lead gave way, and he plunged forward, almost landing on his nose. He jumped up and started after Percy.

He couldn't let Percy race around on his own. He'd only get in trouble. Somebody had to bring him back home.

Oliver charged around the corner and down an alleyway. Percy was right there, standing on his hind legs beside a pair of wheelie bins.

A big orange cat sat on top of one, washing its front paw.

"Hello." The cat blinked at Oliver. "Is he with you?"

"Come down here!" barked Percy. "You think you're so great? Come on down!"

The cat tucked all four legs under her. "No, thanks. I like it up here just fine."

"It's no good, Percy." Oliver tried to nudge the Yorkie away from the wheelie bin. "It's just a cat. No need to make a fuss."

"That's right. Live and let live. You explain it to him." The cat yawned hugely. "I'll wait."

"Scaredy cat!" barked Percy.

Slowly, the cat unfolded herself and stood. "What did you say?"

"Percy!" barked Oliver. "Leave it! Let's go!"

Right then, the door flew open and a waft of familiar human scent reached Oliver just before the voice did.

"What in heaven's name is . . . Oh, goodness." It was the office lady, the one Emma had gone to see to get the keys and things from. Maggie? Yes! Office Maggie.

"Oliver?" she said. "Oliver! Where's Emma?"

Oliver looked around. Emma definitely was not there. He barked.

"Oh, for heaven's sake." Office Maggie bent down.

"Oh, no," said Percy. "I'm free! I'm not going back inside! I'm not!" He turned to run, but only succeeded in smashing into Oliver's very solid side.

Office Maggie grabbed Percy and hoisted him into her arms.

"Traitor," he grumbled at Oliver.

"You shouldn't run off so much," Oliver huffed back. Maggie wrapped his trailing lead around her free hand and tugged him toward the door. The truth was, he didn't much want to go inside either, especially without Emma, but just now, there wasn't much he could do about it.

Maggie took them into the same room he'd been in before. Just as she nudged the door open, Oliver knew something else: Nervous Lady was in there too.

"Oh!" Nervous Lady got slowly to her feet. It was almost like she was scared of them all. "Oh, dear."

"Sorry, Louise. As you can see, we've got some unexpected guests." Office Maggie set Percy down and shut the door behind them. The Yorkie immediately started scrabbling at the space between the door and the floor.

"When are you going to stop that?" Oliver nosed him away. "It doesn't work!"

"Shows what you know," grumbled Percy. "Works all the time. They all open eventually."

"Oh, ah, yes, I see," Nervous Lady—Louise—was saying. "I . . . this is not my best day, Maggie."

"I know, I know, and I really appreciate your coming to see me." Maggie went and sat down in her chair. Slowly and reluctantly, Nervous Louise sat back down too.

"Just give me one quick second." Maggie picked up her phone and dialed. Oliver heard her say Emma's name, and he jumped up to look around, but Emma was nowhere to be seen, or smelled.

"Hello, Emma. Sorry to bother, but I've got your dog."

Maggie put the phone back down. "I'm sorry. Now. Let me just say that I'm not surprised you've been having a difficult time."

"It's all been rather a lot to get used to," Nervous Louise said. "Victoria being gone, and, well, everything. Oh, what on earth am I going to do without her?" Louise pulled a tissue out of her handbag and blotted her nose. Oliver nosed at her shoe tips. Definitely cats. Two. But neither was the very rude animal outside. "She always knew what to do! Always!"

"You're going to do what you need to," said Maggie firmly. "You're going to be there for Jimmy, just like Victoria would have wanted."

"Maggie, forgive me, but you really have no idea what Victoria really wanted, or . . . well, anything."

Nervous Louise was starting to be less nervous and get a little angry. Oliver didn't like angry humans. But at the same time, if Office Lady made her nervous, she should stand up to Office Lady. He put his chin on her shoes and gazed up at her.

"Oh, I, oh." She looked down at him. He wiggled his bottom hopefully. "Oh, he's a good boy!" she murmured.

Oliver rolled over onto his back.

Percy sneezed and yipped. Not quite as rude as the cat, but close. Oliver ignored him.

"Look, Louise," said Maggie. "I'm trying to put the past behind us. What I do know is that you care a great deal about Jimmy, just like Victoria did. And I know that he's about to be saddled with a whole new set of responsibilities. And I know, and you know, that Victoria would have wanted Jimmy's friends to help protect him."

"What are you talking about, Margaret?"

Maggie sighed. She smelled like perfume and cars and coffee and breakfast. "Jimmy has made some very bad money decisions, and he was trying to keep Victoria from finding out."

"Maggie, I'm sorry, I can't—"

"Louise," said Office Maggie firmly. "Like it or not, you've got a responsibility now. With Victoria gone, Jimmy is going to be looking to you for guidance. You are going to need a plan that takes into account Jimmy's long-term interests. I just want you to know that I am ready right here to help you both sort everything out."

When Louise answered, her voice was low and intense. "You're here for me, but where were you when Victoria needed help?"

"Louise, I wanted to help Victoria, believe me. And I did try. But you know how stubborn and suspicious she was."

"Maybe she had reason to be." Louise was getting all tense, putting her tissue away into her handbag, gathering herself together. Oliver jumped up. He knew these signs. She'd be leaving soon. "I'm sorry. I made a mistake coming here."

He had to get Percy away from the door.

"Louise, whatever disagreements I had with Victoria, they've got nothing to do with you and me."

"I very much want that to be true, Maggie. Jimmy has been speaking very strongly on behalf of you and your plans. That's why I came here at all. He seems to think Victoria was entirely wrong about you."

"And what do you think?"

"Come on, Percy, over here." Oliver nosed at the terrier. "She'll step on you."

"Nope, nope, nope," yipped the smaller dog. "Not moving. Nope."

Nervous Louise got to her feet. Oliver nudged Percy harder. "I just came to tell you that any understanding you may have with Jimmy has nothing to do with me, and I thought you should know that sooner rather than later."

Somewhere outside of the office, a different door opened and a breeze cut through the room, bringing new smells with it.

Emma! Oliver whisked around and barked. "I'm here, Emma!"

The bell rang in the next room. Office Lady opened the door, and Oliver shot through it, with Percy following right behind.

24

"EMMA!" OLIVER RACED DOWN THE SHORT HALL FROM Maggie's office.

"Oliver! For heaven's sake!" Emma went down on her knees and took his face between her hands so he had to look at her. She gave him a gentle shake. "What on earth were you thinking? I'm so sorry!" she added to Maggie. "He never used to be like this! Bad dog!" Emma gave Oliver just one more gentle shake to let him know he was in disgrace.

"I wish I could say the same about Percy." Parker held up Percy's empty collar on its lead.

"I'm just glad I found them." Maggie's brittle tone made Emma glance up.

As she did, she saw Louise Craddock come out of Maggie's office and close the door carefully behind herself. Maggie met Louise's eyes. Louise stiffened, and an expression Emma had never seen on her before flickered across the older woman's face.

Pure, unfiltered anger.

Parker noticed it too, and that shining greed Emma had seen so briefly before lit up his eyes.

Emma stood up slowly. Oliver picked up on her uneasiness and pressed close.

"Well, all right, I'm on my way," Parker said to the world at large. "Thanks again, Maggie. Emma, we'll talk more soon, yeah?"

Louise started at this, badly. If Parker noticed, he ignored it. "Come on, Houdini, let's leave the civilized folks to their work." He strolled back out, whistling.

"Yes, well, I must be going as well," said Louise primly.

"Louise . . ." Maggie began, but Louise marched straight past her without stopping.

The door banged shut behind her. Oliver barked.

What on earth was that *about?*

Maggie sighed. "Well. That's that, then." Without bothering to elaborate, she turned to Emma. "How's Nancarrow treating you?"

"It's been wonderful, thanks." Emma mustered a smile for the woman she'd just been speculating might have murdered Victoria Roberts. "Except I'm going to have to call the owners about the chimney being blocked."

"Right. Hang on." Maggie went out and came back with a card. "If they don't have someone they like, have them call these guys and say I recommended them. Best contractors for miles."

"Thanks."

They said goodbye and Emma took Oliver outside.

"What has gotten into you!" she whispered sternly as they headed for the high street. "Just because we're not in London anymore doesn't mean you can go running off in all directions. There are still cars around here, Oliver! You could get hurt!"

"I'm sorry, Emma!" he whined. "Percy slipped his collar and I had to go after him. I meant to bring him back, but there was the rude cat on a wheelie bin, and that was when Office Lady found us, and I would have come right back, but she shut the door while she talked to Nervous Lady and—"

"Wait. Stop." Emma did stop. Right in the middle of the

pavement. So, of course, Oliver stopped too and sat down. "Nervous Lady? You mean Louise?"

"Yes. Louise. The nervous lady."

"You heard what they were talking about? What was it?" He scratched his ear. "Human stuff."

"Were they happy? Sad? What did it sound like?"

He shook himself and scratched his side. "They were getting angry. Office Lady—Maggie—was trying to be nice, but she wasn't doing a good job of it. She wanted Louise to believe they were friends, but I don't think they are friends. Something's changed. Louise is mad at Maggie for not being nice to the shouty . . . Victoria! The shouty Victoria lady, and there was a lot about Jimmy too, but I didn't understand that part."

Emma sighed. This wasn't the first time she'd regretted not being fluent in Oliver's language of smells, but usually their conversations didn't matter this much. Probably he'd actually witnessed a lot more than he was able to tell her.

What could Louise have that Maggie Trenwith wanted? And did Louise know there was something going on between Maggie and Jimmy? And . . .

What if Parker's right? His story's still pretty sketchy, but he could be onto something. What if Maggie really did kill Victoria? She had a motive. It didn't even have to be blackmail, or anything to do with Penhallows. If Jimmy inherited Victoria's property, he'd be more likely to sell than Victoria would, especially if she had some kind of hold over him because she'd already been loaning him money—

That was when Emma was nearly yanked off her feet. She spun round.

Oliver had charged toward a shop window, taking his lead, and her right arm, with him.

"Oliver!" she cried as she staggered after him, trying to catch her balance.

Oliver paid no attention. He had both front paws up on the window of a small shop.

"There!" Oliver pressed his nose against the glass. "There! That's the cat!"

Of course it is.

Like the Towne Fryer, this shop had a pub-style shingle over the door. On it, someone had painted a motorcycle with a Fedora hanging off the handlebar. The gold lettering read VINTAGE STYLE.

Well, I did want to go shopping . . . Maybe the pause would give her a chance to let everything she'd learned and seen this morning settle down.

Emma pushed the door open. Oliver plunged in ahead of her.

The shop was an old one. It still had the long wooden counter where dry goods would have been measured, cut and wrapped. Drawers and cubbyholes lined the wall behind it. Each cubby held a single antique: a glass-shaded lamp, a graceful vase, a record player or vintage radio. A large sign on the counter read SEE SOMETHING YOU LIKE? JUST ASK FOR ASSISTANCE! WE ARE HERE TO HELP.

Oliver, of course, zeroed in on the huge marmalade cat sitting on the counter with all four feet tucked under herself in the classic cat-yoga position known as "resting bread loaf."

Oliver looked up at the cat. The cat looked down at Oliver.

"Hello, cat," muttered Oliver. He gave a couple of perfunctory tail wags to show he was willing to play nice.

The cat yawned and began to wash its whiskers.

"She's the cat we met earlier," Oliver explained. "She's very rude, but that can't be helped. Cats simply don't know any better. This is an *interesting* place." He turned his back on the cat, showing his own perfect unconcern at the cat's unconcern, and began nosing about the shop.

Most of the floor was filled with furniture, grouped roughly by era, from the white and gilt table and chairs that looked like they'd been looted from Versailles to the Formica dining table and vinyl chairs that had survived from the fifties. There was plenty of in-between as well, including an entire Victorian drawing room suite.

With a chaise lounge.

Oh, dear.

Almost against her will, Emma walked over to the lounge. It was a red velveteen and dark wood affair, carved all over with curlicues, fruits and flowers. It looked like a Brontë heroine should be collapsed on it wailing about her beloved Heathcliff. Or something.

Emma instantly imagined it in place of the hideously flowered couch in Nancarrow, right under the windows. She could lie back and stare out at her amazing view and dream of new cakes for her shop . . . which would all be infinitely more reliable and satisfactory than a Heathcliff.

"Good afternoon!" sang out a man's cheery voice. "Can I help at all?"

Emma's father would have described the man as "dapper." He wore a dark jacket, with a square in the pocket and an actual waistcoat, with a chain across the front. His dress shirt was pristine white and was decked out with cuff links and an old-school tie. His snowy hair was brushed straight back across a mottled scalp.

"Erm, hello. Is it all right for me to have my dog here?" She gestured toward where Oliver was nosing around a nineteen fifties living room set, complete with television.

"Yes, he's fine, as long as he doesn't mind the Cream Tangerine."

Emma decided "the Cream Tangerine" must be the official designation for the cat, who picked her way delicately along the counter, leapt down and disappeared into the back. Thankfully, Oliver was too engrossed in whatever mysterious and informative odors lurked in the shop's front corners to try to follow.

Emma turned her attention back to the shopkeeper— and the chaise lounge.

"Lovely piece, isn't it?" he said. "Not practical, but oh, the old-school drama of it. Charles—he's my husband—he said we'd never sell it, but I couldn't resist."

Emma found herself looking at the gilded table and chairs in the front window. The man sighed. "What can I say? My resistance is *terribly* low. David Kemp." He held out his hand. "This is my shop, in case you hadn't worked that out already."

"Good to meet you. Genny Knowles suggested I stop by. I'm Emma Reed, and—"

"Don't tell me you're Maggie Trenwith's mysterious Londoner? The one opening the new tea shop?"

Now it was Emma's turn to blink. "Well, I don't know about 'mysterious' . . . "

"And, goodness, you're the one who found Victoria! Oh, lord, how awful for you!"

"Erm, I guess that's pretty much the news around here."

"I'm afraid you're quite the local celebrity now. I must have had half a dozen people stop in asking if we've gotten a glimpse of you yet. Now, where are my manners? You must meet Charles. He's the brains of the outfit. Charles!" David called toward the back room. "Charles, love, come and meet Maggie's Londoner!"

"All right, all right, keep your shirt on," rumbled a voice from the back office.

Charles was a tall, bald man with olive skin and a long, rather horsey face. He wore a classic cream linen jacket over a yellow shirt that had somehow remained crisp despite the fact that the shop was quite stuffy. He also wore black-framed reading glasses low on his long nose, and he peered at Emma over the rims.

"Charles, this is Emma Reed. She's just leased . . . Nancarrow, isn't it?"

Emma laughed. "Well, I've heard about how fast word spreads in a village. Now I see it wasn't an exaggeration!"

"Not with David about," growled Charles. "Man's a menace. If you've got any secrets left, I advise you to give them up quietly and don't struggle."

"This is why we don't let him interact with the customers." David shoved at his husband's shoulder. "Go away, you'll scare her off."

"You're the one who brought me out here. I've got Rudy waiting on Skype, and he's got a line on a stash of suits from an estate in Cumberland. So *if* you don't mind, love, I'll get back to doing actual work." He reached out and solemnly shook Emma's hand. "Welcome to Trevena, Ms. Reed. So nice to meet you. I hope we can talk again soon."

David sighed happily after Charles as he headed back toward the office. "We're a mixed marriage, you know. I was a mod; he was a rocker. He kidnapped me on his motorbike, whisked me off into the sunset and all." He chuckled fondly. "Now. Enough of that. You did not come in here to get my life story. How *can* I help you?"

"Oh, well, I'm really just looking. I'm going to have to refurnish Nancarrow, you see—"

"I should hope so! The place is overflowing with a sea of cheapness! Now, if you're renting to the summer tourists, that's fine. You want something that's going to take hard use and be easy to replace. But for the lady who is going to live there, we can do much, much better."

Emma was looking at the gilded French chairs again. Oliver noticed and trotted over to nose around the curlicued legs.

"Oh, no, no, no, of course not *that*." David waved away all consideration of the gilded furniture. "I was thinking much more the arts and crafts movement for Nancarrow. Simple. Functional. Comfortable. Made to be used and cared for by a family, not an army of servants. That"—he gestured toward the gilded, curlicued dining set—"is for the pickers and the trippers. Although." He laid his hand on the chaise. "Perhaps there'd be room for just one statement piece?"

Oliver gave up on the chairs and came over to investigate the chaise.

Emma thought about her bank account. She thought about Nancarrow's clogged chimney and its ancient cooker. She thought about how of all the things she should bring back from her first day of shopping for her new home, a "statement piece" should definitely not be it.

She looked at the chaise and pictured it under the window, beside the hearth with its woodstove. Oliver ducked underneath, flopped down and panted happily.

"Traitor," Emma muttered.

"What?" Oliver grumbled back. "What'd I do?"

"Well, well, well."

They all turned. Well, Emma and David turned; Oliver slid out from under the chaise. But it amounted to the same thing.

Charles came out of the office.

"What is it? Is there a problem with Rudy?" asked David.

"No, no, that's all fine. But I just had a call from Angelique with some *terribly* interesting news. Seems they've just had the reading of Victoria Roberts's will, or whatever they're calling that particular little ceremony these days."

"And . . . ?" David made a "hurry up" gesture.

"Seems the old baggage has gone and disinherited poor Jimmy."

"You can't be serious!" cried David.

"I can. Angelique says Victoria left every last one of her properties to Louise Craddock."

25

....

"EMMA!" EXCLAIMED GENNY AS EMMA EDGED HER WAY INTO the Towne Fryer. "You look exhausted."

Genny was behind the counter working the fry baskets. Most of the shop was taken up by a family—two harassed-looking parents and three kids, all under ten, with a fourth in a sling on the father's chest.

"It's been a long morning," said Emma.

That was when the red-headed toddler saw Oliver and shouted. "Doggie!"

Oliver obligingly wriggled his entire bottom and opened his mouth to laugh. The toddler giggled and plopped down right in front of the corgi.

"It's all right," said Emma as the father lunged forward. "He's really good with kids."

She crouched down and took hold of Oliver's collar, more to reassure the parents than because she needed to. "His name's Oliver," she told the toddler.

Oliver sniffed the toddler all over. "A very healthy infant," he announced. "Very well-fed." He licked the child's cheek, and the toddler laughed.

"Just let me finish up. Won't be a moment," Genny said, both to her customers and to Emma.

"Mum!" The oldest girl tugged at her mother's arm. She looked about seven and was flushed from the sun, despite her floppy hat. Her voice had that dangerous note Emma recognized from taking care of her nieces—a little too hungry and a little too tired. "I want ice cream!"

"Lunch first," said the mother with forced patience. Then she turned pleading eyes to Genny. "Do you sell sweets at all?"

"Not us, sorry," said Genny as she lined three baskets up on the counter. "But just two streets over, there's Holman's Icery."

"Thank you. Come on, let's go outside." A basket in each hand, Mum shooed the girl out the front door. "Steve . . ."

"Doggie!"

Oliver was giving the toddler's hands a thorough lick and the child was obviously delighted. The father paid, took the third basket in one hand and hoisted the toddler up with the other. "Come on, Paulie, say goodbye to the doggie."

Emma stood up and immediately slumped against the counter.

Oliver wagged his tail at her. "You look hungry, Emma. The fish smells very good today."

"Yes, of course." She rubbed her eyes.

"What's wrong?" asked Genny.

"Oh, nothing really," Emma told her. "I was just realizing I've been in my new home for two days, and I have yet to cook an actual meal in my kitchen."

"Moving is always harder than we think it's going to be."

"Too right."

"And then somebody goes and dies in the middle of it."

Emma sighed hard. "And I don't have enough sense to stay out of it."

"Emma Reed," said Genny sternly. "What have you been doing?"

"Well, for one thing, I *think* I just agreed to let David Kemp furnish Nancarrow for me."

"Oh, lord. I should have warned you. The man could sell salmon to a Scotsman."

Emma shook her head. "It'll be fine. I think. Anyway, it's not just that. I've been . . . I don't even know what I've been doing, really." She pushed some stray strands of hair back from her cheek. "I know what I'm *supposed* to be doing. I'm supposed to be finding a space where I can open my shop; I'm supposed to be gauging the local market and developing my menu and sourcing suppliers and *baking* things . . ."

"But?"

"But I seem to have started trying to work out what actually happened to Victoria Roberts."

Genny looked at her blankly for a minute.

"Oooooh, dear," she breathed. "This is going to take a very strong cuppa, isn't it?"

IT DID IN FACT TAKE A VERY STRONG CUPPA. IT ALSO TOOK about a half hour before Genny could join Emma, because she was on her own at the fryer and she had a mini-rush of day trippers as well as local patrons. Emma couldn't help thinking Genny should get a commission from the ice cream shop, given the number of times she sent people looking for sweets over there.

Genny did manage to hand Emma a basket of fish and chips in the interim so she could go outside with Oliver and sit at the table and eat and think, and feed Oliver more fried fish than was good for him.

"We have to get you back on your proper diet," she said, popping a chip into her mouth.

"Yes, Emma," he answered. "And there need to be more walks. Lots more walks."

"Yes, Oliver," she sighed and scratched his ears. "More walks for both of us."

At long last, the crowds cleared away, and Genny came out, bringing two mugs of tea. She plunked one down in front of Emma, and then plunked herself in the other chair.

"Now, Emma Reed. Are you sure about Jimmy? That Victoria disinherited him?"

Emma's mouth twisted into a wry smile. "I was in Vintage Style when Charles got a call from Angelique. He sounded pretty certain about it."

"I can't believe it," said Genny. "I mean, I didn't like Victoria, but she was devoted to Jimmy."

"And he loved her. I mean, everybody talks about her like she's the equivalent of the monster under the bed, but Jimmy says she was always good to him, and she took care of her parents too. I mean, is it possible people were wrong about her?"

Genny considered this. "People can be different with their families." Then she stopped. "When were you talking to Jimmy?"

"This morning. After Oliver got into her—that is, his— that is, *the* cottage garden."

Genny eyed Emma over the rim of her tea mug. "Well. That was a piece of luck, wasn't it?"

Emma ignored this. "Anyway, I think he's been having money trouble. The game company he was working for collapsed and the CEO took off with a bunch of the money. I think he's broke, and I think he might be having trouble finding work in his industry again." She frowned at the street, thinking hard. "So if he had a history of bad money decisions, it could be that Victoria was trying to protect him from himself. He might even have known what she was planning, which would mean mean he wouldn't have any reason to kill Victoria . . ." She stopped. "But that brings us back to Maggie."

"Maggie?" exclaimed Genny. "Wait. Stop. Am I hearing this right? You really do think Maggie Trenwith killed Victoria?"

"Parker does, but I'm not sure I trust him. He's got a lot to hide."

"And you know this because . . . Oh, bother." Genny set her mug down and stared past Emma's shoulder. Emma twisted around and saw an entire party of students with rucksacks and walking sticks striding determinedly toward the shop. "We are *not* done, Emma," she said quickly as she got to her feet. "But I may be some time."

Genny was right. The whole village and its visitors suddenly seemed to be starved for fish and chips. Emma, tired and more than a little bewildered by the whole strange day, felt certain catching up with Genny could wait until tomorrow.

She cleared her table, waved to her friend, and set out with Oliver back to Nancarrow. They did make a brief detour to a small shop where Emma was able to pick up a small bag of flour and one of sugar, as well as a quart of milk and some sweet butter.

They passed Victoria's cottage on the way up the hill, but even though Jimmy's car was parked out front, the windows were dark. Emma tried not to slow down as she passed, but she couldn't help it.

This time, though, nothing happened. No open doors, no strange arguments or police arrivals. Not even a fox.

For the best, she told herself. *Maybe he's finally catching some kind of break.*

When they got home, Emma propped open the garden door for Oliver and got to work. Her ideas were bouncing every which way. She couldn't settle on what she thought or what she wanted to do. She needed something to focus on.

She needed to *bake*.

She settled on shortbread. It's one of those things that in its simplest form needs very few ingredients—sugar, flour, butter, and a pinch of salt. Then an hour in the oven, and there it is, warm and inviting.

As she used her fingers to rub the butter into the sugar and flour mix, Emma felt her scattered thoughts begin to come back together.

I need to remember what I came here to do. I may want to be Trevena's "guard human," but I am still supposed to be working on starting my new life.

Just as she was shutting the oven door, Oliver came back in, shook himself and sneezed.

"Whatcha doing, Emma?"

"Making us snacks," she said.

"Hurray! Snacks!" He bounded over to the oven and plopped down in front of it. "When?"

Emma laughed and rubbed the top of his head. "Not for another hour, greedy guts. You've got a bowl full of kibble, in case you haven't noticed."

"Oh." Oliver slumped, and Emma laughed again.

She made herself a sandwich. If nothing else, tomorrow she was going to have to do some serious shopping. They were about down to the last of the groceries Genny had brought.

After her light supper, Emma boosted Oliver up on the (still really hideous) flowered sofa so he could snuggle up next to her while she opened one of her idea binders. She'd added in the descriptions and floor plans of the alternate spaces Maggie had sent her, and she picked up a pencil, adding some lines here and there to try to start plotting out seating arrangements.

At the same time, her mind kept straying back to Parker's theories about who might have killed Victoria.

They're your theories too, said an annoying little voice in the back of her head. *You stood there and you listened and you told him about Jimmy.*

And you really do think Maggie could have done it.

Emma sighed.

"What's wrong, Emma?" Oliver put his chin on her knee.

"What's wrong is when I talked to Parker at the library about who might have killed Victoria, he had some ideas about who might have done it, but no proof at all. He also said some very strange things about his past, but I don't know if I can trust him, but I can't stop thinking about . . ." She stopped. "Oliver, when we were in Victoria's kitchen, did you say Maggie Trenwith had been there?"

"Yes. And Nervous Louise and Parker and Percy."

"Do you know when Maggie was there?"

Oliver scratched his chin. "Not long, not short. Some days ago, and then again, maybe a day before?"

Well, it was worth a try. She ruffled his ears. At the same time, the oven timer pinged.

The shortbread was perfect—rich and buttery and melt-in-the mouth, just like it should be. Emma dunked her bit in her mug of tea, and then stopped.

And stared.

"Bakes! That's what I can do!"

Oliver immediately rolled over and sat up. "Bakes? Like cake? Are we getting more cake!"

Emma scrabbled at her binders. "Yes! While I'm figuring out what we do about Maggie and Victoria"—*and Jimmy and Parker*—"we are going to start getting our foot in the local market!"

"Oh, good. I like cake."

She had a plan. It wasn't a whole plan or a good plan, and it wouldn't cover everything, but it would be enough.

That is if—and it was a pretty big if—she could get Genny to go along.

But in the meantime, she had lists to make.

26

IT STARTED WITH GINGER BISCUITS.

Well, actually it started with an early-morning bus ride out to the Tesco so Emma could be there as soon as it opened, and then running into Angelique and meeting Raj Patel's mother, Indira, and working her way through a shopping list that felt like it must be a meter and a half long, followed by a call to Trevena Taxi, because there was simply no way she was going to get everything she'd bought onto the bus.

"Well, you certainly look set to open a shop," remarked Brian as they unloaded the boot and piled the bags on her doorstep.

Emma laughed. "Very soon now!"

Brian raised his eyebrows in surprise. "Tea, wasn't it?"

"Tea. And cakes. And biscuits."

"Well." He sighed. "Goodbye, waistline. We hardly knew ye."

He also winked. Which was somehow more charming than it should have been.

Which you have no business noticing, Emma told herself firmly.

As soon as she'd hauled the bags into the kitchen, Emma

propped the kitchen door open so Oliver could get out if he wanted to, which he did, at top speed. Once again, Emma considered the possibility of putting in a doggie door, and once again she remembered she'd forgotten something important.

Emma brought her recipe binder down from the bedroom. Included among the clippings and printouts was her collection of Nana Phyllis's recipes. She'd carefully copied them from the box of index cards her grandmother had kept in her kitchen for years. She had hoped they'd be inspiration for her as she was finding her feet.

Now, they'd be a bit more than that.

Then, it really was ginger biscuits.

Emma had never been in her grandmother's kitchen without a tin of her biscuits waiting in the cupboard. The recipe was classic Phyllis—just butter, brown sugar, treacle, baking soda, salt and powdered ginger, with some candied ginger chopped up in the mix. Emma's own additions were lemon zest and toasted hazelnuts.

Oliver came back in and plopped himself down by his kibble bowl in high dudgeon. The hedgehog matron apparently did not appreciate being disturbed during the day.

"She is really very rude," muttered Oliver.

After the ginger biscuits (and soothing wounded corgi dignity), it was on to the chocolate-orange shortbread. This was one of Emma's party bakes. It had the same base as the shortbread she'd baked last night, but what made it special was the addition of good cocoa powder and fresh orange zest. She'd brought these into the office more times than she could count. They were perfect for celebrating promotions or leave-takings or any other occasion when you might suddenly need a sweet.

Like asking a favor from a new friend.

Thankfully, Nancarrow cottage came equipped with an ancient, but functional, mixer that she and Oliver had found stuffed into the absolute darkest back corner of one of the lower cupboards. Otherwise her arm would have fallen off trying to cream butter and whip egg whites into stiff peaks.

Last came the vanilla layer cake with dark chocolate icing. No delicate, fussy sponge here. This was a sturdy and flavorful creation that (touch wood!) could last all day on a cake stand without going dry or slumping or getting soggy.

Simple. Lovely. Crowd-pleasers. All of it perfect for kids who might otherwise be begging to go to Holman's Icery.

Emma looked up at the clock.

"And bang on time!" she announced.

"What is?" asked Oliver, who had just come back in from the garden.

"Afternoon tea." She surveyed her spread and adjusted the cake plate, considering the best angle. "What am I forgetting?" she asked Oliver. "And how on earth did you get so muddy? Again?"

"It's different out here," he said. "Much more mud than London. I like it. Are you going out?" He put his paws up on the seat of the chair and craned to see up on the table. "You've been inside all day. It's not good for you."

"Not yet. I'm expecting company."

A knock on the front door announced that company had arrived. Emma wiped her hands on the tea towel and went to answer the door.

"Genny, hi!" Emma let her friend in. "So glad you could come. I know this is your busy time."

"Becca's got the counter today—I was doing books and inventory. Believe me, I'm glad for the break . . . Good lord!"

This last came as she saw the spread of biscuits and cake on the dining table.

"You did all this?"

"I did all this," Emma affirmed. "Tea?" She lifted the fat old Brown Betty pot. "You take milk, right?"

"Right," murmured Genny, sliding into the chair. "What on earth is the occasion?"

Emma set the cup down in front of her. "Try a biscuit. I'll cut us some cake."

Genny eyed her. "I feel like I'm being fattened up. You haven't decided to go all Sweeney Todd on us, have you?"

"No, I swear. Oliver!" Emma exclaimed.

Because Oliver was struggling mightily to try to scramble up onto the chair seat.

"But I want to see!" he whined. He also dropped straight down to the floor. Genny caught the chair before it dropped down with him.

"You want a biscuit," said Emma. "I just filled your bowl!"

"It's not as good as your biscuits!" He whined and wagged. "Your biscuits are always the best!"

Genny was eyeing her with intense amusement. Emma blushed.

"He's hopeless." Emma gave Oliver a ginger biscuit, which he carried under the chair he'd just been trying to climb so he could munch in peace. "And so am I."

"You're wonderful, and are my new best friend." Genny mumbled around a mouthful of chocolate-orange shortbread. "This is divine!"

"Try some cake," Emma set a slice down in front of her.

Genny responded by looking down her nose at Emma. "As soon as you tell me what's going on. I've got two kids, missy. I know when I'm being set up."

"All right, all right, I'm nicked." Emma held up her hands. "You are being set up. I've got a proposal for you. It's in the rough stages. I'll need to do a proper write-up—"

"You really were a banker, weren't you?"

"Yes, I really was. Now I really want to be a baker. Remove one letter, add some sugar. Shouldn't be a problem. Only it's going to take some time, even without . . . well, the spanner in the works."

"You mean Victoria's murder?"

"Yes. Anyway," she said quickly, before Genny could get another word in. "I'd always meant to try what the Yanks call a 'soft open' on the shop and try out a whole range of bakes. I wanted to see what sold best so I'd know what I should make sure to keep on the menu. But then I was watching those kids in your place begging for pudding with their chips, and it came to me that while I'm working on getting the storefront going, I could jump-start things . . ."

"And you thought about a plate of biscuits on the counter . . ."

"Or cake. Yes."

"Emma, that is brilliant!" cried Genny. "Martin and I have been talking for months about doing something like that! Our business is all takeaway, and we get so many trippers in with kids, we've been thinking a rack of sweets or something . . . but homemade bakes would be so much better!"

"I'll have to look up all the codes and stuff for packaging and all that . . ."

Genny waved this away with her fork. "I know just who to call. We'll have it sorted in no time. Well, in what counts for no time when dealing with the county bureaucracy. Now, the one thing they may give you grief about is the kitchen . . ." She pointed her fork in the general direction of the hearth.

"I know. Besides, there's no way I'm going to turn out anything but tiny batches with that oven."

"Well, we'll figure something out." Genny poured herself another cup of tea. "Now, I will say that my agreement with this grand plan depends on one thing."

"What's that?" asked Emma uneasily.

"You finish telling me what happened to you yesterday and why Victoria's death is a problem for you opening your shop. I thought you weren't even looking seriously at Penhallows anymore."

"Well, no, it's not really about Penhallows itself. It's . . . where do I even start?"

"The beginning is good." Genny reached for a shortbread.

As she tried to marshal her thoughts, Emma became aware of a soft rumbling near her toes. Oliver was stretched out on the flagstone floor, muddy belly turned toward the sunbeams filtering through the window above the sink. He was also sound asleep.

"Don't mind him," she told Genny. "Solar corgi is recharging."

Genny laughed. "Now. Spill."

Emma sighed. "All right. I'll try. You remember I told you that Parker Taite said he wanted to look into Victoria's death, and he wanted my help?"

"Right."

"Well, it all seemed a little off, so I went and did a search on him."

"What did you find?"

"Not a sausage. No articles, no bios, no news, nothing. So I went and told him what I'd found—"

"Or hadn't found."

"Right. And he told me this story about how when he was a journo, something had gone very wrong with a story he'd worked on, and somebody almost got killed because of it, and the paper threw him under the bus, and he was still trying to find a way back from the disaster."

"So what's his name?" asked Genny.

Emma drew back. "Sorry?"

"What's his real name? If nothing comes up under Parker Taite, it's not his real name. Or he maybe wrote under a . . . a . . . whatchamacallit . . . a pseudonym. What was it?"

Emma opened her mouth and closed it again. "I forgot to ask," she said, and felt her cheeks begin to burn. "Good lord. Some detective I make!"

"Well, never mind that for now. You can ask later. It doesn't seem like he's going away any time soon."

"No, especially not now."

"What makes you say that?"

"He's got hold of the idea that Maggie Trenwith might be the one who murdered Victoria."

"I thought that was your idea?" exclaimed Genny. Oliver snorted, and his paw waved, but he didn't wake up.

"Well, we're sort of sharing custody. He thinks Maggie finally had enough of Victoria refusing to sell her land and that it'd be easier to get what she wanted out of Jimmy."

"But Jimmy didn't inherit. Louise did. Well," Genny went on. "Six of one, isn't it? Louise wouldn't stand a chance against Maggie if Maggie decided to put the pressure on."

Emma remembered the anger she'd seen on Louise's face and realized she wasn't so sure about that.

"So what's Maggie's story?" asked Emma. "Is her family from Trevena?"

"No, actually. They're from over Devon way. She and her husband moved here, I guess twenty years ago now, when he got hired on as a manager up at the Grand Hotel."

"Which probably makes them newcomers by village standards?"

"Oh, definitely. Which did not win her any points with Victoria, that's for certain."

"Outlanders coming in and trying to tell people what's best?"

"Something like that, yeah," Genny agreed. "Plus, I don't think Maggie was actually cut out for village life. She's the kind who always needs to have something on the go. I think she had visions of herself as the woman who remade Trevena into some thriving, dynamic hub of business and tourism. I mean, there were all the times she tried to get the council to apply to get the village onto one of those reality shows and things—"

"While Victoria wanted to pull up the drawbridge?"

"And lock the gates. Victoria thought we had enough tourists and that Trevena needed to look after its own."

"But there must have been plenty of people who agreed with Maggie that the village needed to grow."

"There were, and there are. But there are also a surprising number who agreed with Victoria, whether they liked her or not. The Cornish can be a very stubborn lot."

"Did you have a side?"

Genny shook her head and dunked the remains of her biscuit in her tea. "Me and my shop are strictly neutral. Haddock, cod and plaice served equally to all comers." She took a thoughtful bite. "But I will say, when they put the new development plans up, it did look impressive. They talked about taking advantage of the new British foods movement *and* the escape to the country movement. There was going to be a posh restaurant, a range of luxury holiday flats and new detached houses. It could all be a very big deal."

"What, exactly, is standing in the way?"

"A half acre of coastline occupied by one rather surprisingly nice and much in demand holiday cottage, which happens to be part of the National Trust, so it can't be seized by the usual means, and also just happens to be owned by one Victoria Roberts."

"Then, she didn't just buy property to hold on to it . . . ?"

"Oh, no. Victoria was a sharp businesswoman. Had a management degree and all. Ran her properties herself, with some help from Jimmy now, of course."

"I wonder if that's where the disagreement came in? Maybe Jimmy thought he could take some initiative, and Victoria got angry?"

"It could be, but I haven't heard anything for certain."

"So." Emma gazed toward the front room, thinking hard. "Here's Maggie, her dreams of changing the face of Trevena forever finally in reach. She tries to sweet-talk Jimmy over to her side. Jimmy lets himself be persuaded, but Victoria finds out, and that whole scheme blows up, and Maggie decides she has only one option left."

They both sat quietly for a moment, letting the full import of that idea settle in.

Genny topped off her mug from the pot and added some more milk from the little pitcher. Then she said quietly. "Do you really think Maggie could have gone that far?"

"I think grudges can make normally intelligent people do surprisingly stupid things." Emma poked her fork at her cake crumbs. "And I think that, from where I'm sitting now, the best alternative is Jimmy himself."

"Oh, now you've got to be kidding me."

Emma shook her head slowly. "The company Jimmy worked for collapsed. He may have lost money when it went down. He comes home. He's defeated. His aunt is trying to slot him into the family business, but when he tries to take some initiative—"

"If that's what he was doing," Genny reminded her.

"—he gets her so upset that she actually changes her will."

"So maybe he thinks it'd be easier to talk round Louise than his aunt?"

"Maybe. Or maybe he didn't intend to kill her." Emma took another swallow of tea. Her throat felt suddenly tight. "He knows about the garden; he knows the lily of the valley is poisonous . . ."

"He maybe means to make her sick for a while, just so he can handle things with Maggie and the developer without Victoria getting in the way. But he mucks up the dose," Genny finishes. "Ouch. I'm not sure I like that idea at all."

"Me neither. But there's a limited number of people who were in and out of that kitchen recently—Louise, Jimmy, Maggie, Parker and Victoria herself."

"And you."

"And me," agreed Emma.

Genny frowned again. "Hang on. How do you know who's been in the kitchen?"

"Oh. Erm. Jimmy told me."

"Oh. Would have liked to see how you got that out of him in the course of casual conversation."

"It wasn't easy," Emma mumbled. "Anyway. Victoria was poisoned and died inside her house. It's got to be one of them."

"Are you including Mr. Pseudonym Taite on the list?"

Emma nodded.

"What's his motive?"

"I don't know yet. But we know that he's got secrets, and we know that Victoria considered finding out secrets a business strategy."

"So, what are you thinking? If Parker killed her, it was because she was going to expose him?"

"Maybe." Emma prodded her cake crumbs again.

"I'm not sure I'd buy that," said Genny. "I mean, he told you about his past pretty easily." She paused. "Unless you think he was lying?"

"If I was going to lie about my past, it wouldn't involve

saying I'd almost gotten somebody else killed." Emma drummed her fingers against the side of her mug.

"So how about this?" said Genny. "He didn't do it, but he touched it off. Here's Parker, researching his book. He's read about the Penhallow disappearance, he starts poking around, and he finds something—something suspicious enough to send him to try to talk to Victoria."

"And somebody found out and got scared?" Genny finished for her. "It's possible. Everybody in town knew how she operated."

"So, here's a question." Emma rested both elbows on the table. "How did Victoria come to own Penhallows? And why did Ruth and her mother sell it to her?"

Genny considered. "Do you know, I have no idea."

"But you do think Nick Penhallow really was murdered?" she asked.

"As in, do I think Mrs. Penhallow and/or Ruth really killed old Nick and got rid of the body by burning him up in his own ovens?"

"Erm, yeah," said Emma.

"I know Cornwall's got a Gothic reputation and all, but honestly? I knew Ruth Penhallow for years. We were shop neighbors, if not house neighbors. It's not possible she could have done anything like that."

"And her mum?"

"Wouldn't say boo to a goose. Tiny little thing too. It's very hard to picture her actually taking a frying pan to the back of her husband's skull, let alone shoving him into the ovens."

"What about Victoria?" said Emma quietly. "Could she have done it herself?"

"Phew!" Genny blew out a sigh. "I don't know . . . From what I heard, every woman and girl in the village was a suspect in the disappearance at one time or another. Penhallow was what my mother used to call a horrible old goat."

"So you never heard anything about Victoria in particular?"

Genny drummed her fingers against her tea mug. "Well, I've *heard* things, but are they accurate? Victoria had a tendency to get blamed for every missing cat and closing shop." She shook her head. "But that doesn't make any sense at all. If somebody found out Victoria had killed Nick Penhallow, Victoria would be the one in danger of being exposed, wouldn't she?"

"Which means her death might not be a murder," said Emma. "I mean, one thing we haven't considered yet is that maybe poor Victoria killed herself."

27

....

THERE WASN'T MUCH TIME FOR TALK AFTER THAT. BECAUSE Genny had to get back to the shop. She did, however, leave Emma with one important piece of news.

"Victoria's funeral is tomorrow," she said, giving Emma a particularly knowing look. "See you there?"

Emma agreed that she probably would.

While Emma was still waiting for the majority of her clothes and personal items to arrive from London (yet another favor she owed Rose), she always traveled with her black suit. After all, one never knew what might be coming around the corner. Now, admittedly, what came around Emma's corners was usually something like an emergency client meeting, rather than an unexpected funeral, but it was always good to be prepared.

Unfortunately, when she unearthed it the next morning, the suit proved to be horrendously wrinkled from being in the bottom of her overfilled suitcase. So she'd needed to find Nancarrow's iron, which the cottage thankfully had, although, like the rest of the furnishings, it also looked to be a refugee from the nineteen seventies. Then she had to find an ironing board, which Nancarrow apparently did not have. That left her with only the kitchen table to work on, where she barely remembered she should probably put down a towel instead of using the hot iron on the oilcloth.

During all this, she'd had to shoo Oliver out of doors, because, as it turned out, corgi commentary on the ironing process was spectacularly unhelpful.

With all the delays about irons and brushes and extra treats and ginger biscuits to stuff into her handbag to ensure corgi silence during the ceremony and to stave off her own hunger if the ceremony turned out to be a long one, Emma and Oliver were almost late to church.

ST. MARTA'S OF THE HILLSIDE, WHERE THE FUNERAL WAS TO be held, proved to be an old-school country church, and like Trevena itself, it came with all the frills. Outside, there was an overgrown churchyard dotted with elaborate Celtic crosses. Inside, there was a beautiful stained-glass window and oak pews that had gone dark with age.

Much to Emma's shock, by the time she and Oliver got there, those pews were filled to overflowing with mourners. Emma squeezed herself into the very last pew in the back, next to a slender young man with a white rose pinned to his lapel. Oliver went down on his belly, slunk under the pew and poked his muzzle out beside her ankles.

"You okay under there?" Emma patted him.

"Are you okay up there?"

"Just about." Emma craned her neck to see through the forest of heads and shoulders. "Wow."

Quite literally every seat was filled. The people filing in behind Emma had to stand against the walls. Emma spotted a scattering of villagers she recognized—Louise and Jimmy were right up front, of course. Angelique and Pearl sat toward the middle with a tall man Emma guessed to be Angelique's husband. They shared a pew with Genny; her husband, Martin; and their two kids. David and Charles sat across the aisle. Raj Patel was there too, although not in uniform, sitting beside his parents and his grandmother.

But the rest of the congregation were strangers to Emma. Many of them carried roses in their hands or had roses pinned to their lapels. Wreaths and bouquets and vases of roses of all colors filled the altar.

They must be gardeners.

It turned out she was right. After the opening hymns and prayers, the vicar gave a brief, bare-bones biography of Victoria, praising her as a loving aunt and longtime Trevena villager who was always involved in local affairs. Emma thought she heard one or two coughs of the less-than-polite variety at this.

Then the vicar asked if any friend of Victoria's would like to come up and offer a remembrance.

A line formed.

There was the little white-haired woman who described Victoria's patience in helping preserve and transcribe a series of letters between her grandmother and an obviously famous-to-rose-enthusiasts horticulturist from the nineteen twenties.

There was the thin Bangladeshi man who spoke about his lengthy exchanges with Victoria while he struggled to resurrect a particular lost variety of tea rose known for its delicate fragrance.

A young Welsh woman credited Victoria with her second-place win at the Chelsea Flower Show and drew decorous murmurs when she announced that she was naming her new varietal "the Victoria Roberts Grand."

It was all Emma could do not to let her jaw drop open. Even with Jimmy's description of how Victoria took care of him, Emma had not expected anything like this outpouring of warmth.

And from the looks on the faces of the other villagers as they turned to one another, neither had anybody else.

So much for the idea you can't keep a secret in a village, she thought. *I wonder what else she was keeping secret?*

"Is something wrong, Emma?" Oliver laid his muzzle on her toes and looked up at her. "You're all tensed up. Are you okay?"

"Yeah," she breathed. "At least, I will be. I think."

"The spiky lady's here," growled Oliver.

Emma turned. He was right. DCI Brent, wearing a black trouser suit and carrying a black bucket-sized handbag, stood in the church doorway. Her cutting gaze swept across the congregation. Either she saw what she was looking for, or she didn't, because she very quickly backed away out of Emma's line of sight.

Emma bit her lip. She also made her decision.

I'm going to talk to Constance, she told herself firmly. *I'm going to tell her what I know about Maggie and Victoria and Jimmy and Parker. If she laughs at me, I'll know for sure I'm being ridiculous and I should just leave it all to the professionals.*

At last, the final hymn finished, the vicar intoned his blessing, and the congregants filed slowly out of the church. Emma collected her handbag and Oliver's lead.

But by the time Emma was able to make her way out of the church, DCI Brent was nowhere in sight. Emma frowned and scanned the knots of visitors and villagers spread out across the church green, all talking or making their way to their cars. Louise Craddock stood beside a white-haired woman in a wheelchair.

But there was no detective. Somebody else was missing as well. Emma couldn't see Jimmy anywhere. He should have been in the receiving line with the vicar.

Probably he's just taking a moment to collect himself. You were looking for Constance, remember?

"Oliver." Emma bent down and rubbed his ears. "Can you find Constance . . . the spiky lady for me?"

Oliver snuffled at the gravel walk and the unkempt lawn for a moment. "This way!" he barked, and trotted off toward the car park. Now Emma could see DCI Brent standing beside a battered blue compact car, talking with Raj Patel. Emma started toward them, but fresh movement caught her eye. Maggie Trenwith, in a full-skirted black dress and high black boots, strode across the church green, away from the parked cars.

Where's she off to? Emma bit her lip. Probably nothing. Probably just going to get her car.

Except there were still all those questions and possibilities surrounding Maggie and Victoria's death.

Should I follow her? Emma looked around at the wide-open landscape of the churchyard. *And how would I do that without getting spotted in ten seconds?*

"Emma!" a voice called. Emma froze, startled. Then she saw Genny waving at her. Genny stood beside Louise and the older woman in a wheelchair Emma had noticed earlier. Another, much younger woman in a nurse's scrubs stood off to the side, giving the friends a bit of privacy.

"Emma!" Genny waved again.

Emma waved, but hesitated. Then an idea hit. It was probably borderline mental, but . . .

Before she could have second thoughts, Emma crouched down next to Oliver.

"Oliver," she whispered and rubbed his ears. "I need you to follow Maggie, the office lady."

Oliver shook his ears. "Why, Emma?"

"I need to know where she goes and if she meets anybody."

"Why, Emma?"

"Because she might have had something to do with Victoria dying, and I want to find out."

"That's important?"

"It's important," Emma agreed. "And you come right back, okay? And stay out of the way of the cars!"

"A noble warrior corgi is always watchful!"

Oliver whisked around and dove through the grass. Emma watched and tried not to worry when he vanished from sight.

He'll be fine. Emma tried to silence her misgivings as she turned away from Oliver and toward the car park. *Really. He will.*

Emma fixed a smile on her face and headed over to join Genny, Louise and the woman in the chair. When she got closer, Emma recognized the woman as Ruth Penhallow.

Her curling hair had gone snow white, but she had the same round face, Coke-bottle glasses and air of gentle cheerfulness that Emma remembered so fondly. She wore a basic black dress and black stockings, complete with a single strand of white pearls and a wide-brimmed black hat.

"Hello, everybody," said Emma. "Louise." She held out her hands. "I'm very sorry."

"Yes, thank you." Louise gripped her hands briefly and attempted a smile. "Still. Wonderful to see so many friends."

"I wanted Emma to get a chance to meet Ruth Penhallow," Genny said. "Ruth, this is Emma Reed."

"Hello, Ruth." Emma shook the tea lady's plump hand. "So very nice to see you again. I don't expect you'd remember me, but I used to come to your shop every summer when my family was in Trevena."

"Oh, dear, how nice!" Ruth's hands were still strong from all her years as a baker. "So lovely to meet you . . ." She paused. "Oh, no, now, wait. There was an Emma, or was it Emily? A regular tomboy, with a notebook and a spyglass. Always at the windows, looking for dangerous types."

Emma laughed. "That was me."

"Well, how lovely to see you again!" Ruth squeezed her hands.

"I'm sorry it's under these circumstances."

"Poor Victoria," Ruth breathed. "She hated being the center of attention. Hated it," she repeated softly. "She'd be relieved it was over, I'm sure. Want to get straight back to her garden." She blinked, thinking of something else for a moment. "But there. Now. Did Genny tell me you're going to open a tea shop?"

"I hope to."

"I think it's marvelous," said Ruth. "You must come down to visit. It's very quiet where I am now. We can have a nice chat, all about tea and cakes. People around here have very strong preferences, you know."

"Emma wants to reopen your shop, Ruth," said Louise quietly.

Ruth's coffee-brown eyes widened behind the magnifying lenses. "My shop? Oh. Well. That would be lovely, of course, but that's all up to Victoria and . . ." She stopped for a moment, realizing what she'd just said. "Yes, well, but Victoria really did know best about these things, didn't she, Louise? It was what she was good at. Managing things."

"Is that why you sold her the shop to begin with?" asked Emma.

"Sold her the shop?" Ruth drew her chin back, surprised. "I *sold* her? No, dear. You've got that wrong. We never owned the building. That was Arthur Cleary. He's been gone . . . oh, lord, it must be ten years ago now. Or twelve? In any case, he was a hard man. He and Da were friends, and, well, once Da was gone, Arthur was going to turf us out. It was Victoria put a stop to that. Got him to sell her the premises. I'm not exactly sure how that happened, but Victoria did have her little ways." She smiled again, as if Victoria's little ways involved gentle hints and bouquets of flowers. "Anyway, she made sure we never had to worry about the roof over our heads again. That's just the kind of person she was, wasn't it, Louise?"

But Louise was looking away, out across the road toward the distant spread of the sea, and not saying a word.

"People misunderstood her, you see," said Ruth stoutly. "Because she wasn't ever *nice*. Not like Louise." She beamed at Louise. "But Louise will manage everything just as Victoria would wish. I know she will. Louise always sees to things. Ever since we were girls." Ruth patted Louise's hands. Louise smiled down at her, but the expression was forced. "Now, can I get your help, dear?" She shifted in her chair. "It's very hot, isn't it? We should go inside. I'm sure it's not good for me. I'm sure—"

"Yes, of course, Ruth," said Louise quickly. "We've got a car and we'll get you right back to your hotel." She signaled to the attendant, who came over and took the handles on Ruth's chair.

"Thank you so much for coming." Louise gave Emma and Genny another weak, fake smile and immediately got busy helping Ruth with her handbag and her cane, and directing the attendant toward the car, and generally making it clear the conversation was now over.

"Phew!" whistled Genny as Louise and Ruth moved out of earshot. "All right. I know we just spent a whole morning hearing people talking about what a wonderful person Victoria really was, but honestly, you'd think she'd've known how awkward she was making things for poor Louise by cutting Jimmy out of the will."

"But Victoria wasn't nice," murmured Emma. "What she wanted was for the people she cared about to be safe."

Genny considered this. "I suppose that's one way of looking at it."

"Did you get a chance to see how Louise and Jimmy are doing?"

"You mean around each other?" asked Genny. "Well, if they're putting on a show for the neighbors, it's a good one. From where I sat, it looked like mostly Jimmy was trying to be stoic and keep Louise supplied with tissue. Held her hand during the recessional too."

"That doesn't sound like they're nursing hard feelings."

"No. It doesn't," said Genny thoughtfully. "You don't suppose they *knew*, do you? About the will?"

Emma shrugged. "Maybe. The more I hear about Victoria, the more I start to think we shouldn't be underestimating her."

Genny smoothed her sleeves down. "I'm starting to agree with you. But I'll tell you who else we shouldn't be underestimating: Maggie."

Emma turned to her, brows raised. Genny leaned closer.

"After we closed up the shop last night, I went round to the pub and had a bit of a chat with Shelly Lucas. Have you met her yet?" Emma shook her head. "Maggie is one of her regulars. She brings in clients or comes in for a glass of wine herself after a long day. Well, Shelly said about a week after he got to town, Parker Taite came in looking for Maggie specifically. Said they sat together for quite some time, and looked very cozy, she thought."

"Did she hear what they talked about?"

"I asked, but the place was full that night. She did say they left separately."

So Maggie had met Parker. Well. That was something else he hadn't remembered to tell her. What had they talked about? What had she told him? Emma puffed out a sigh. She looked toward the car park. DCI Brent was still there, standing with Raj. Emma had a sudden vision of the detective driving off before Emma got a chance to talk to her.

"Can you give me a second, Genny. I, erm . . ." She gestured toward the car park.

Genny looked and saw Constance. "Oh. Yeah. Of course. I need to round up Martin and the boys anyway. Call me later?"

Emma agreed she would and headed for the car park. She wondered where Oliver was. She wondered where Jimmy was.

And Maggie and Parker.

And I wonder what on earth I've gotten myself into.

28

THE GRASS TICKLED AT OLIVER'S EARS AND NOSE AS HE ran. Dozens of fascinating smells filled the air, but he ignored them. He was a noble corgi on a mission. There was a human to find. He dropped his nose toward the ground. So many humans had been walking this way, it took a moment to sort them all out. But there was the office lady.

Oliver zipped around the church corner into the shadows beside the building. There was a little paved area for the rubbish and recycling bins. Oliver stopped short.

He'd lost it. The human's trail. It was gone. How could it be gone? He snuffled at the ground, turning tight circles.

She was here. She was here. She was just here . . .

The breeze shifted and Oliver smelled the distinct odor of cat. He whirled around. There, beside the recycling bin, sat the big orange cat from the village, and the shop.

"Looking for something?" the cat inquired.

"It is none of your business," said Oliver. *She was here, she was here, she was just here . . .*

But mostly he smelled the rubbish and the grass and all the many, many humans and a bunch of dogs and . . .

"Try in here. I saw her go through." The cat strolled over to the three stone steps that led down to a small door in the side of the building. The door, Oliver now saw, was slightly ajar.

"You're helping?"

The cat shrugged. "I'm bored. You're amusing. I'd hurry if I were you." She began to wash her paws.

Noble warrior corgis did not take instructions from cats. On the other hand, noble corgis on a special errand from their best humans did not ignore vital information.

Oliver carefully eased himself down to the door. The cat snickered as his bottom bumped on the edges of the steps. Oliver firmly resisted the urge to bark.

I'm on a mission.

He thrust his nose through the door, and then his head and his shoulders. This room was full of closets and chairs, and a table and cabinets. The window by the table was open to bring in all the fresh smells from outside.

It was a place for humans to sit and talk, and maybe change clothes. The floor was stone and he could smell Office Maggie clearly. But she wasn't in here. There was another door. This one was closed, but there was a big gap between the floor and the bottom of the door. Almost big enough for him to get his nose through. Oliver settled down on his belly and lowered his ears, straining to hear.

Office Maggie was definitely on the other side of the door. Her scent was clear as could be. There was somebody with her. A man. He had it. That was Pale Jimmy, the one who was family to Shouty Victoria.

Jimmy was talking. "I haven't got long. Somebody's going to come looking for me."

"I just wanted to make sure you're all right," said Maggie.

"You know, I'm really not." Pale Jimmy sounded angry, and worried. Oliver could hear the echo of his hard shoes against the stone floor as he paced back and forth. "Not only was my aunt murdered, but I've got the police showing up at her funeral."

"Oh, you saw that?"

"Yes, Maggie. I saw that."

"I'm sure it was just . . . routine."

"And how would you know?"

Maggie sighed sharply. "Look, Jimmy, I didn't come here to fight, okay? I just wanted to let you know you need to talk to Louise."

"Louise? What about?" There was a long pause, and his footsteps stopped. "Oh, no, Maggie, seriously? We're doing this now?"

"I don't have a choice! I've got a meeting with the developers today, and I've got to have something to tell them!"

"How about you tell them your schemes and your payoff didn't work? How about you tell them they can just forget the whole thing?"

"Is that all you think I was doing?" demanded Maggie. "Paying you off? You came to me, remember? You were the one sitting in the pub and wailing about how your aunt was bankrupting herself trying to pay for Ruth Penhallow's care home, which, purely incidentally, didn't leave her with any extra money to help you pay off all the credit card debt you got into while you were off swanning around America!"

"I didn't ask you for money!"

"But you took it when I offered, and you agreed to work on her about the development. That wasn't me, Jimmy, that was all you. Oh, and by the way, you didn't remember to tell me you weren't in line to inherit a damn thing! Or are you going to tell me you didn't know?"

"Why would I have told you anything about Aunt Victoria's will, Maggie?" he demanded. "It's not like killing her was actually part of the plan, was it?"

There was silence, and then the sound of Office Maggie's footsteps stomping away from him. Oliver pressed his nose closer to the door. A distant, familiar scent reached him—a combination of soap, beer, sweat, and Yorkshire terrier.

"Oh, hullo, Maggie!" It was Percy's human, Parker. "Thought I heard voices. Just getting out of the sun. Getting hot out there already, isn't it?"

"Right." Pale Jimmy was moving now, in the direction

of the other voices. He did not sound happy. "I'd better get out there. Everybody's going to think I've had a breakdown or something."

Oliver sniffed. Percy wasn't there. *Where is Percy?* Maybe his human left him back in his room so he wouldn't have to worry about him getting away again . . .

Pay attention, Oliver. Good dog.

"Jimmy, wait," said Office Maggie. But Jimmy didn't wait. Oliver heard his footsteps walking away.

"Sorry," said Parker. "Was I interrupting?"

"As if you didn't do it on purpose. You've got a hell of a lot of nerve, haven't you?" snapped Maggie. "But not enough to be here when your girlfriend came looking."

"My . . . ?" Parker sounded puzzled.

"DCI Brent," said Maggie. "She was here earlier, looking for you."

"Oh." Suddenly, Parker didn't sound quite so cheerful. "She was?"

"I can tell you where she went if you want to catch up with her."

"Maggie, I don't like that look on your face. You don't really think I've been talking to the cops, do you?"

"I don't know. Have you?"

"Of course not! The last thing I want is the cops paying any kind of attention to me."

Maggie hesitated, and something rustled.

"You all right, Maggie?" Parker asked. "You having trouble with the nephew?"

"That's my business." Oliver heard some more rustling, then footsteps pacing away. "How's the book coming?"

"Oh, you know, pretty well."

"And the chapter about Victoria?"

"Almost done."

"Good. Look, Parker," Maggie's voice had changed. It was softer now, coaxing, like she wanted Parker to get into his crate or take his medicine. "It's been a bad few days, but nothing has really changed. Your book is going to expose the person Victoria really was and how she tried to rule the village as her personal fiefdom for years, when she was nothing but a criminal."

"So that's still the story? That she was killed because of her connection to the Penhallow disappearance?"

"Of course it is. Why wouldn't it be?"

There was more rustling. Maybe Parker shrugged. "Just wanted to be sure we're all still on the same page."

"Same page," said Maggie firmly. "I want Victoria buried and my deal signed. After that, we'll take care of everything else."

Then, he heard a shuffling noise and the sound of Maggie's footsteps getting closer.

"Back here!"

Oliver had been so intent on what was going on with the humans, he hadn't noticed the cat had come in behind him. The Cream Tangerine crouched in the shadows under the table.

Oliver hesitated. The footsteps were getting closer.

Oliver jumped up and darted under the table, squeezing into the shadows beside the cat. Office Maggie marched through the inside door and slammed it. Oliver winced. She stormed through the outside door too, and slammed it.

Uh-oh. Oliver slid out from under the table. He nosed at the outside door.

"Problem?" The cat came up beside him. "Oh, I see. Hmm. I guess the window's out of the question?" She batted at Oliver's paws.

"It doesn't matter," said Oliver stoutly. "Emma will find me."

"Will she?" The cat sounded skeptical. But cats never did understand the special bond between humans and corgis.

"She will." Oliver lifted his muzzle and started to bark. "Emma! Emma!"

"I should have known," muttered the cat. "I do not have to listen to this!"

The cat leapt onto the chair, then the table, and out the window. Oliver ignored her and kept on barking.

"Emma! Emma! I found them! *Emma!*"

29

BY THE TIME EMMA REACHED CONSTANCE, RAJ WAS LONG gone. The detective stood on her own, leafing through her notebook. Whatever she saw engrossed her so much that she didn't even look up as Emma approached.

"Hello, Detective."

Constance started. "Oh! Oh, Emma. Hello."

"All right? You look a bit grim."

Constance tucked away her notebook. "Personal remarks this early in our relationship?"

"Sorry."

Constance smiled apologetically. "No, no, I'm sorry. No, I just didn't get breakfast." A quick, and not entirely sincere, smile flickered across Constance's features. "Makes me cranky."

"Oh. Erm." Emma dug into her own bag. "Ginger biscuit?" She held out the little baggie she'd brought.

Constance peered at it for a moment before taking one. "Ta." She bit into it. "Wow! This is great. Did you make these?"

"My nan's recipe, but I added the nuts and the lemon zest. I try to keep some with me when I go to weddings and things. There's always a restless kid around."

"Or a restless detective?" Constance cocked an eyebrow at her. "Got another?"

Emma held out the bag. "Help yourself."

Constance did. When she finished it, she folded her arms. "So was that Ruth Penhallow you were talking to?"

"Just now. Oh. Erm. Yes?"

"Hear anything interesting?"

"Oh. Erm."

Constance sighed and folded her arms. "I wish I had," she said. "That lady is tougher than she looks. Got very shirty about a police detective coming round asking questions at the funeral. I thought you might have had better luck."

"Oh," said Emma again. "Well. No. Not really. It was just about the shop. I was curious, you know, how Victoria came to own the building. I thought she must have got it from the Penhallows. But Ruth said her family never owned it. Victoria bought it from someone named Arthur Cleary. Cleary was a friend of Ruth's father, and he threatened to throw her and her mother out after Mr. Penhallow vanished. She said Victoria kept hold of it to make sure the Penhallows didn't have to worry about losing their livelihood."

"Well, well." Constance shook her head. "I keep feeling like I'm hearing the tale of two Victorias. One's a scheming old baggage, and one's practically a saint. How do you reckon that is?"

"People are complicated?" ventured Emma.

Constance chuckled. "Too right."

"Erm," began Emma. "There's something, I think, maybe, you ought to know."

"I'm listening," said Constance, with the barest undertone of *and I'm waiting*.

Emma swallowed. "I was talking with Jimmy Lambert, and . . . I think he's having money trouble. And I think Maggie Trenwith was trying to take advantage of it."

Constance pursed her lips. "That's interesting. What got you thinking that?"

Emma told Constance about the conversations she'd had

with Jimmy and with Parker. The detective huffed out an exasperated sigh. "Just what we need. A potentially corrupted works project. The local media's already jumped all over this business with Victoria. They do love a poisoning. Somebody must have called in some favors to keep the cameras out of the church. But then again, our Ms. Roberts did have some friends in pretty high places. I'm sure I saw the Earl of Ambrosund in there among the rose crowd. He's a regular at Downing Street." She paused. "Now, I'm pretty sure our Mr. Taite said he's an ex-journalist. Did he give you any hint who he was working for?"

"Well, that's just it," said Emma. "He told me that he was working on a book about historic murders, and one of the things he was looking into was the disappearance of Nicholas Penhallow. He seemed to think Victoria's death might have some connection to what happened back then."

"Well, it's a theory," said Constance. "But I have to say, if it's a choice between rumors swirling around the disappearance of one man decades ago and current evidence of money changing hands and a property deal about to go south, I know where I'd put my focus."

"And you're sure it was murder?"

Constance looked surprised. "Why do you ask?"

"Well, I was thinking. We know that Parker was looking into the Penhallow disappearance, and we know that Victoria was friends with Ruth at the time, and there's all the rumors about Nick Penhallow being killed, and I just found out from Genny Knowels that Maggie was talking to Parker as well."

"Maggie Trenwith who thinks Victoria was Trevena's own private ogress?"

"Erm, yes. What if Parker found something out? What if Victoria was about to be exposed as something worse than a blackmailer?"

"As a murderer, you mean?"

"Yes. And so she decided she'd rather die than face arrest."

Constance was silent for a long moment. *At least she's not laughing.*

"Is that your theory?" she asked finally.

"I . . . to be honest, I don't know. Maybe?"

"Well, at least you admit it." Constance smiled patiently. "Look, I understand you're trying to help, and heaven knows, with something like this, we need all the cooperation from the public we can get. And I really do appreciate you telling me about Parker and Maggie, and Jimmy. And I will admit that having an ancient murder come back to haunt the participants is satisfyingly dramatic. But if there's one thing I know, it's that coming up with a story when you've only got some of the facts is a dangerous business." Her voice was tight.

She's remembering something, thought Emma. But there was no way to ask what that might be.

"For instance," Constance went on, "you told me there was lily of the valley in Victoria Roberts's tea. Turns out you were right about that. And you told me you found the body just a few minutes before Parker Taite turned up, although nobody saw either of you arrive."

Emma felt the hairs on the back of her neck stand up.

"But somebody did see Parker Taite walking up the hill right by your new home the day before Victoria died," said Constance.

"He was walking his dog . . ."

"You were also seen talking to him over breakfast at your B&B."

"But that wasn't anything. He was just trying to"—*get me to help him dig up something about the murder*—"get some background information about the village. For his book."

Constance gave Emma another patient smile.

"We also know you had a grievance with the deceased, as she owned a building you would like to set up shop in and she would not go along with the plan, *and* when we were searching Victoria's back garden, we found several animal tracks that could very well have been paw prints from a small dog. A corgi, say."

Emma stared. "You can't be serious. Are you actually

saying that I stalked and killed a woman to get my tea shop?"

Constance met Emma's shocked gaze directly. She also waited one single second before she spoke. "No," she said. "I'm not. But I am saying is it's very easy to take a few facts and fit them together into patterns that don't actually match reality."

"Oh." Emma felt herself blush. "And you're also saying I should mind my own business?"

"No, you should continue to mind the business of all your new neighbors, like a good villager, but"—she raised one finger—"you tell me if you hear anything, and you save piecing it all together for the professionals, all right?"

Emma met Constance's gaze. The detective didn't even blink, but there was a hint of a nod, so slight that Emma might even have imagined it.

"Yes," said Emma. "All right."

"Good." Constance smiled, a firm, reassuring smile that reminded Emma of her favorite grammar school teacher. "Now, I've got to get back to the station. A policewoman's lot is not a happy one, and it involves endless amounts of paperwork." She glanced to Emma's side. "By the way, didn't I see you with your dog earlier?"

30

EMMA STROLLED ACROSS THE CHURCH LAWN, TRYING NOT
to look like she was in any way worried. Oliver was around
somewhere, *and* he was fine.

The knots of mourners had thinned out, except the ones
clustered around the vicar by the church entrance. Jimmy
was there now, shaking hands and talking with people.

She hesitated. Should she go say something? It felt rude
not to, and yet she needed to find Oliver . . .

Then she heard the barking. Very faint, but still clear
enough.

"Emma! Emma! I found them! Emma!"

"Oh, lord." Emma tried to run, but almost turned an
ankle. Cursing softly, she hobbled toward the sound.

She came round the church to the side door that probably
lead to the office or the vestry. As she passed the rubbish
bins, a large marmalade cat, probably the Cream Tangerine,
ran out from the other side. Emma didn't pause for a second
glance. She just hustled down the steps to the church door.

"Oliver?" She tried the latch. Thankfully, it was open.
She pushed the door open and Oliver bounded out.

"Oh, Oliver!" She crouched down, and to heck with her
stockings. "How'd you manage that!"

"It was Office Maggie! She didn't see us and she shut the door and the cat went out the window but I knew you'd be here and—"

"Yes, yes, all right," she murmured, patting his back to help him calm down. "But you did find Maggie? And Jimmy?"

"I did what you said," Oliver told her as he licked at her hands. "I followed Office Maggie, and she went in the church, and Pale Man Jimmy was there too, and they talked, and Jimmy left, but then Percy's Parker came in, and *they* talked."

"What did they say?"

Oliver scratched his chin and shook his ears, clearly thinking hard. "Pale Jimmy and Office Maggie were angry at each other. Maggie wanted Jimmy to talk to Louise about . . . about something. I didn't understand . . ."

"Never mind, just keep going." Oliver's memory for human-related matters was a short one, and he got easily distracted.

"Jimmy was angry at her. He wanted to know if she was paying him off. What does that mean?"

"It's about money," said Emma quickly. So there had definitely been money changing hands between them. How much? And what for? Was Jimmy taking a bribe, or was Maggie, against the odds, really trying to help? Maybe trying to put an end to the feud, or—Emma's thoughts lurched to a halt. Maybe she was trying to make it *look* like she was. Maybe she'd decided it was time to try playing good cop.

Emma felt her pulse speed up.

"Then what?" she asked Oliver

"Maggie wanted to know why Jimmy didn't tell her Louise would inherit a damn thing and then he wanted to know why should he say that because . . . something . . ." Oliver scratched his chin again. "You said it was important, about, I know! He said killing Victoria wasn't part of the plan!" He wagged triumphantly. "And *then* Parker came in and Jimmy left, and Maggie and Parker talked."

"About what?"

Oliver dropped his muzzle and his ears. "It was hard to understand. It was very human. I tried. I did . . ."

"I know, Oliver." Emma gave him a quick kiss. "Just tell me."

"First, Maggie wanted to know if Parker was talking to the police. He said he wasn't. Then he wanted to know if she was angry at Jimmy, and she didn't want to talk about that. Maggie wanted to know if Parker was still working on his book, and he said he was, and he wanted to know if the story—this was the hard part—if the story was still that Shouty Victoria died because somebody else . . . Nick!" he barked. "Nick died."

Emma sucked in a breath. "What did Maggie say then?"

"She said of course. And they were polite and all those things, but Emma, I don't think they're really friends anymore. I think they're doing that human thing where you pretend to be friends because nobody wants to start a fight in front of other humans."

"But you think they were friends? For real, not just pretend?"

"Friends play together. Maggie was in his room."

Emma froze. "Emma was in Parker's room? You're sure?"

"Certain and sure. I smelled her when we were in there before. A corgi's nose—"

"Once? Or more than that?"

Oliver wriggled his bottom and scratched his chin again. He got up and nosed around in a circle. Emma sat back on her heels, trying to be patient.

"Yes," he said finally. "And yes. Lots. She was in the corners and all over the rug and . . . there a lot."

Meaning her scent was there. Meaning Maggie Trenwith had been in Parker's room more than once. Meaning that there had been more than just a drinks meeting. They knew each other well enough to be on visiting terms, and to want to get together in private.

She remembered her conversation with Parker in the library.

Neat. Very neat. Could be either one of them, couldn't it?

Either Maggie or Jimmy.

Emma remembered that happy, greedy smile on his face and felt her mouth go dry.

"Emma?" Oliver pushed his nose against her leg. "Emma? What's wrong?"

"I'm not sure," she whispered.

Because she wasn't sure what was going on. Was Parker trying to find out who had really killed Victoria? Or was he just trying to find a story that would make a sensation? Because on the one hand, he was telling Maggie he was going to implicate Victoria in Nick Penhallow's disappearance-slash-death.

On the other, he was looking to pin Victoria's murder on Maggie.

And he had tried to get Emma to help.

31

EMMA'S FIRST INSTINCT AFTER TALKING WITH CONSTANCE, Genny and Oliver had been to find Parker Taite immediately and confront him with his two-faced behavior. It took every ounce of experience she had to hold back. It was always a mistake to go into a hostile meeting without plenty of background research. She needed to know more about Parker before she confronted him again, *and* she needed to know more about what he might have found out.

Because if he had found out something damaging or dangerous about Victoria's past and she'd killed herself because of it, that was one thing. If he'd found out something damaging or dangerous about Victoria, she'd been murdered, and he knew who did it, that was something else again.

She also needed to know more about Maggie Trenwith and this developer she was courting.

So, after the funeral, Emma had spent the night online. The developer was a firm out of London, Apex Properties. With Oliver snuggled (and occasionally snoring) beside her, Emma took a deep dive into partner CVs, firm history, plans and prospectuses, and even made a few phone calls to old friends about funding and finances.

The results almost had her snoring along with Oliver. As far as Emma could tell, Apex Properties was exactly what it looked like: a specialist in high-end land development, all tidy, aboveboard, and well-funded.

She also looked up the plans for the Trevena development. She had to agree with Genny. It was impressive. Impressive enough that she could see it driving an ambitious, frustrated estate agent to extremes.

So which is it? she wondered. *Is Maggie using Parker? Is Parker using Maggie? Both? Does Jimmy know about the two of them? Does Jimmy know what Parker found out?*

Does Jimmy know Parker might be trying to set Maggie up?

Does Parker know Maggie actually did kill Victoria? Or . . .

Emma shook her head. "Too many pieces," she muttered to her screen.

Oliver snorted and his head jerked up. "Pizzas?" he barked.

Emma laughed and ruffled his ears. "*Pieces*, Oliver. This puzzle has too many pieces and I can't see how things fit."

"Oh." Oliver yawned and licked his muzzle. "Then you should move them out of the way."

Emma stared at him. "You're right," she said. "That's exactly what I should do. First thing in the morning."

EMMA ALWAYS SLEPT WELL WHEN SHE HAD A PLAN. UNFORtunately, today she also slept in, and she only woke up when she heard the hammering on the front door. Well, actually, Oliver heard the hammering on the front door, and he started barking. *That* Emma definitely heard.

The source of the disturbance turned out to be the postman with a whole set of boxes Rose, as promised, had posted down from London with Emma's clothes and her personal items.

More on the way! said the cheerful note in the first box. *When am I invited down?*

Soon, Emma promised her friend silently. *Right after I figure out what really happened to Victoria.*

Oliver had been right. She needed to move some of the pieces out of the way, and Emma planned to start back at the beginning. Emma needed to know about Nick Penhallow and what had or hadn't happened to him. If Victoria had been involved, she needed to know how.

Fortunately, she had a direct source of information, along with an excuse to contact them.

"Vintage Style," David answered cheerfully when Emma phoned the shop. "How can I help you?"

"David, this is Emma Reed up at Nancarrow."

"Oh, yes, my dear, how *are* you?"

"Well, it's been an eventful couple of days, that's for sure, but I want to set all that aside for now." Emma crossed her fingers behind her back. Oliver responded by licking them. "I wanted to set up a time to take delivery of the chaise. And maybe we could talk about some of those other possibilities you mentioned?" This was not entirely an excuse. Having her own things around just emphasized the tackiness of the rented furnishings.

"Wonderful." David paused, and she heard turning pages. "I don't suppose you might be free later this afternoon? The shop's closed today, so I could bring Charles and we could look the house over, take some measurements and so on."

"That sounds perfect. I'll tell you what, I'll even make tea."

"We shall be there with bells on."

"Don't laugh!" shouted Charles from the background. "He really might!"

Emma did laugh, and she also rang off.

After that, Emma was able to spend a delightful and relaxing morning unpacking her clothes, her photos, her favorite cookbooks and, most important of all, her good baking tins. It was like looking at old friends.

Oliver, of course, officiated over all the unpacking. After that, there were kibble and water bowls to be refilled, and after that, Emma determined nothing was going to stop her from fixing herself a lovely ham sandwich with cheese and mustard and a fried egg, and feeding Oliver some tomato and carrot and ham.

After that, she had to get ready for her guests, and of course, that meant baking. Fortunately, Emma's recent supermarket run had filled her pantry and refrigerator to the point where she could serve something besides leftovers to her guests. She decided on a ham and cheese quiche. Oliver attempted to point out it was unfair for humans to get all that marvelous ham when they couldn't properly appreciate it. This once, Emma stood firm, which earned her a lot of corgi grumbles.

But in the end, she had a glorious golden-brown and fragrant quiche to put out on the battered dining table alongside the remaining layer cake and biscuits from her tea with Genny, ready for when Charles and David knocked on her door, promptly at three.

"My dear Emma!" breathed David when he saw the spread. "You shouldn't have!"

"Don't listen to him." Charles immediately drew up a chair. "You absolutely should."

"She should have left some ham." Oliver settled down by the sofa, his muzzle resting on his paws and his eyes turned accusingly on Emma.

"Don't mind the corgi," she told her guests. "He's sulking."

"Looks exactly like David when I won't let him have a second slice of cake."

"And for pretty much the same reason." Emma laughed and poured them all fresh cups of tea while the men served each other (and her) the quiche.

For a while, they—quite literally—talked shop. Charles and David were a font of knowledge and advice about running a business in Trevena. They talked about the importance of billing systems, inventory control, working websites—all sorts of behind-the-curtain details. Emma listened avidly and kept pouring the tea and passing around the food. Even Oliver eventually had to give up his sulks and come over to search for crumbs and enjoy the presence of the lively pair.

"So tell me," said Emma when they'd all moved on from quiche to cake and biscuits, "when did you two come to the village?"

"Oh, let's see." David sighed. "That must have been in seventy-two. Maybe seventy-three?"

"Seventy-three," said Charles. "The London scene was getting old by then. Bit of a risk in those days, coming out to a little place like this. David wasn't too keen."

David looked shocked. "I thought it was a marvelous idea. You were the one who wasn't so keen."

"Pay no attention to him. Senility setting in, I'm afraid. Anyway. A lot of our friends said we had lost our minds, but we did it, and we've been here ever since."

"So you must have known Victoria Roberts when she was still a young woman?"

David eyed Emma, then eyed the remains of the tea spread out across the table.

"Emma, you'll forgive me for saying, but as a bribe, this is not exactly subtle."

"I guess not. But I did deprive my corgi of his ham to make you that quiche."

"So we owe you?" David looked at her owlishly. "What is it exactly that you want to know?"

"Just about Victoria back in the day. You did say you knew her."

"Oh yes," said Charles. "We knew the whole trio."

"Trio?"

"Yes." He poured David a fresh cup of tea, then topped off his own. "Victoria Roberts, Louise Gaines—Louise Craddock now—and Ruth Penhallow."

"I didn't know Louise had been married."

"Oh, yes. And quite happily for a number of years. He was from Penzance, as I recall. Taught reading at the grammar school, where she was a secretary—an administrative assistant, as we'd say now."

A reminder not to jump to conclusions about people. Emma poked at her quiche crumbs. *I would have thought she was a lifelong single.* "How did they seem then, Victoria, Louise and Ruth?"

"Oh, lovely girls, and thick as thieves, all of them," said David.

"We used to throw parties, which had a tendency to shock the neighbors," Charles added. "Not that anything really shocking went on, mind. We'd come here to get away from all that. But we were who we were, so by definition, anything we did was shocking. Anyway, the three of them would always show up as a mob—come together, leave together and no man shall put asunder."

Emma pictured Victoria waving her trowel and screaming, at her, at Louise and at her nephew. David must have guessed at her thoughts, because he looked at her knowingly.

"Yes, hard to believe, isn't it? I don't know what happened. I truly don't. But somehow that lovely, vivacious girl turned into . . . well, I hate to say it, but an old crab."

"It was very sad." Charles sighed and helped himself to another ginger biscuit. "I tried to talk to her once, when I saw the change taking hold. But she thanked me very kindly to keep my nose out of it. There may have been a few other things added, and well, that was very much the end of that." He shook his head. "Now I feel like I should have tried harder. Maybe I could have helped."

David took Charles's hand and held it. "You can't help someone who doesn't want it. Vicky was determined to keep her secrets to herself. "

"So you don't know what happened to cause the change?"

"No idea," David took a biscuit and promptly dunked it in his tea. "But something did. If anyone knows, I suppose it would be Louise."

"Not that she'd talk," said Charles. "Loyalty to Victoria was her watchword. Victoria took her secrets to the grave, and Louise will do the same."

"What about Ruth?" Emma asked as she poured herself more tea.

The men looked at each other, clearly trying to decide where to start.

"The Penhallows were not a happy family," said David, carefully. "I always thought there was more going on in that house than met the eye."

"You did not," said Charles.

"I did."

"You never said."

"You never listened."

Emma decided it was time to break this up. "What did you think was happening?"

Charles was silent for a moment. "I remember noticing Mrs. Penhallow had a fondness for long-sleeved blouses," he said softly. "Even in summertime. And she wore a lot of very thick makeup."

Emma felt herself go cold. "Like she was trying to hide something?" *Bruises?*

Charles nodded solemnly. "It was not the sort of thing that anybody talked about back then. Not out loud."

Emma put her cup down. "I hadn't heard about that. I'd just heard Nick Penhallow was . . . maybe having an affair? Maybe more than one?"

David waved his napkin dismissively. "Oh, he chased the counter help around the bakery, but I'd hardly call it an affair. More like gross bullying."

"Oh."

"Yes," said Charles solemnly. "Oh."

Emma watched them both. They were suddenly tense and choosing their words cautiously. "So what actually happened to him?"

"Well, that's the question, isn't it?" David sighed. "All I remember is walking out to get a loaf of bread one morning and finding the shop shuttered and everybody in the pub talking about how Penhallow must have done a moonlight flit."

"Do you think he was killed?"

The two men exchanged a long, careful glance.

"I think it is a distinct possibility," said Charles.

"But, I mean . . . if he was, what happened to the body?"

"Well, the usual theory is that it was either burnt up in the ovens—"

"But there was also the fact that the floor was being torn up," said David. "Don't forget that."

"Then there was the possibility of his having been dragged to the cliffs and tossed over," put in Charles. "There's a bad undertow around here. We still lose swimmers to it."

"Wait, dragged?" said Emma. "By a woman, or women, through a small village?"

Charles shrugged. "I believe the tossed-off-a-cliff partisans theorize they used the wheelbarrow the bakery kept to haul the flour sacks."

A shiver ran down Emma's spine. Victoria was a manager. Victoria arranged everything. What if the first thing Victoria had done for Ruth was arrange for the disposal of Nick Penhallow's corpse?

"News, or at least gossip, started trickling out over the next couple of days about a pile of debts and unpaid rent," Charles said. "Whole thing was an utter mess."

"It was, it was," David agreed. "Ruth and her mother almost lost everything. It was Victoria who saved them."

"And Louise," added Charles.

"Yes, yes, Louise too."

"I'm afraid I don't understand that," said Emma. "I mean, why couldn't Ruth and her mum just carry on for themselves?"

David sipped his tea and considered how to answer. "Well, part of it was that old Nick was a *very* traditional man, very controlling. He took care of all the money—if 'care' is what you can call it. His wife and daughter were supposed to stick to serving the customers and baking the buns. After years of that kind of treatment, Mrs. Penhallow really had no idea how to manage the business side of things, especially with a whole financial mess dumped into her lap and a landlord who wanted her gone. She hadn't the strength, and Ruth hadn't the experience." Charles was visibly relaxing into the memories now. "I can only imagine how hard it was for them. This wasn't that long ago, if you think about it, but everybody forgets how different it all was, especially for women." He shook his head. "I don't know what Ruth would have done without Louise and Vicky, truly I don't."

"What did Victoria do?"

"She had a nest egg from her grandparents and got Cleary to sell. I expect the fact that she knew about his second wife and two kids down in Truro might have helped grease those particular wheels. As did the fact that the bank manager at the time had a boyfriend in Swansea."

"Oh."

"Yes. Oh. Again." David frowned. "Victoria had limited tools in her box, but if the people she cared about were threatened, she'd use them all."

"So do you think—"

But before she could get any further, Charles abruptly set his cup down. "Emma," he said. "I understand natural curiosity, believe me, and I'm sure that whatever's behind this little trip into the past is from the very best of motives, but you really need to take care."

"That's in no way ominous." Emma tried to smile.

"I mean it. When you've had to live with your own secrets, you develop a sixth sense for them in other people. There's a lot unsaid and unseen rolling around our peaceful little village right now, especially around people who knew Victoria."

Emma was about to make some joking remark, but then she got a look at how Charles's facial expression had gone closed and cold.

And she wasn't the only one who noticed the change.

"Well, now," said David briskly. "Maybe we should get onto those measurements? Emma, would you give us the tour?"

"Yes, of course."

The next couple of hours were a welcome distraction. Charles and David wielded their rulers and tape measures with practiced efficiency, despite Oliver's earnest and repeated efforts to help. David showed her some catalogues and printouts of arts and crafts style furniture, mostly good modern reproductions that could be had for "really quite reasonable prices."

"Can you leave these with me?" Emma asked.

"Of course," said David. "Sit with them for a while. Get used to the ideas. See what's going to match your budget. I wouldn't take too long, though; some of these are unique pieces, and we'll have to stake our claim before they're snapped up by somebody else."

"Of course."

They agreed to a delivery time for the chaise as well, and all said their goodbyes. As they were leaving, Charles turned to her and took her hand. "You will remember what I said, won't you? You will take care."

"I will," she promised.

Emma closed the door. Charles was right. She should take care. She should remember that it was entirely possible Victoria had been murdered and that the murderer was still out there. They might not appreciate an extra nosey parker stirring things up.

32

"WELL, SO MUCH FOR *THAT* IDEA," EMMA MUTTERED TO HER-self after David and Charles left.

"What idea, Emma?" asked Oliver.

"I'd wanted to eliminate some possibilities around Victoria's death." She started carrying the remains of the tea into the kitchen. "Instead, I've got a new one."

Victoria might have killed Nick Penhallow. Victoria might have known a secret that got Nick Penhallow to leave town. Victoria might have helped dispose of the body, which would mean she'd also have concealed evidence and lied to the police, and those were all actual crimes. They weren't the same as murder, but still, it'd be pretty bad.

Emma drummed her fingers on the counter. Bad enough to kill herself over? Her fingers stilled. "And leave Ruth to face the music alone?"

That did not fit with anything she'd heard about Victoria.

"And we are right back to the beginning." She clenched her teeth. She also started wrapping up leftovers and stowing them in the fridge.

"Where is the beginning, Emma?" Oliver asked, nosing about for crumbs.

Emma closed the fridge and made a decision. "Parker Taite," she said. "He got us into this. He's going to get us out."

Such a momentous decision required a fresh cup of tea. Emma brought Oliver's doggie bed down from upstairs so he could sit beside her if he felt like it, settled herself onto the sofa and opened her laptop.

Oliver, of course, ignored the doggie bed. He put his paws up on the sofa and tried to see around the screen.

"Whatcha doin', Emma?"

"What I should have done before," she told him. "I gave up on finding out about Parker too early. I should have tried . . . something."

"Like what?"

"Like . . . like . . ."

An idea hit. Emma snatched up her phone and dialed the King's Rest. Pearl answered.

"Hello, Emma. All right?"

"Yes, at least mostly. Pearl, I need a favor. You've got no reason to do this, but—"

"Well, let's hear it."

"Do you know what Parker Taite's middle name is?" Hotels and B&Bs asked for identification, or passports, to confirm their guests. Pearl might have seen Parker's.

"Why do you ask?"

Emma took a deep breath. This was either going to work or she was about to convince Pearl she was either a raving loony or a creepy stalker. "He's writing a book about crime in Cornwall—well, Great Britain, really . . ."

"Yes?" prompted Pearl.

"But I think, since Victoria died, he might be trying to make trouble for Jimmy or Maggie." Which was true. Well, mostly true. Well, true enough.

Pearl was silent. Emma waited. She also scratched Oliver's neck.

"I know how it sounds . . ." Emma tried tentatively.

"No, actually, it makes sense," said Pearl. "He's been trying to get me to talk about Jimmy. Did we know each other as kids? What was he like? How did he and his aunt get on? All that. And Parker is his middle name, by the way. His first name is Paul. We joked about it. Paul Parker meets Pearl Prudence."

"Your middle name is Prudence? Your mother did that to you?"

Pearl laughed. "Actually, it was my nan's fault. She insisted all of us kids get a family name. Could be worse. My brother Francis got stuck with Fortinbras."

"Wow. And thank you, Pearl."

"You're welcome. Oh, and have you had a chance to talk with Genny yet?"

"Um . . . no. Should I?"

"She told us you were going to be partnering up to provide baked goods for the Town Fryer and you were looking for a better kitchen to work out of."

"Well, it was an idea . . ."

"I think I've got a way we can help each other out, if you want to hear about it."

"I do, but now's not the best time. Can I call you back?"

"Anytime. And good luck."

"Thanks," said Emma. *I'm going to need it.*

She rang off and started typing.

"Walk?" Oliver suggested, putting his chin on her knee. "You've been inside all day. It's not good for you. You need some healthy exercise. With me."

Emma laughed and kissed his furry head. "You are incorrigible."

"I am a corgi."

"Just give me a few minutes. There're some things I need to look up. But I'll prop the door."

Thank goodness it's summer, thought Emma as she wedged the dishcloth in place. *We're definitely going to have to put in a doggie door.*

Oliver shrugged in his extremely eloquent, full-bodied way to indicate that if his human was going to be foolish and stubborn, he, as the noble and reasonable member of the group, was willing to resign himself to it. For now.

He also trotted outside. Emma watched him nosing around the bare garden for a minute.

She was still forgetting something. She shrugged. If it was important, it would come back to her.

Just a quick look round the web, she promised herself as she settled back down on the couch.

"Now, then, Mr. Paul Taite. Let's see what kind of trouble you really got yourself into."

She typed in *"Paul Taite journalist."* As an afterthought, she added: *"Murder."*

A half hour later, Emma was on the phone to Genny.

"Emma! What's up?"

"I've finally tracked down Parker Taite online."

"You did?" exclaimed Genny. Cloth rustled. Emma pictured her leaning forward. "What did you find?"

"Seems he was fired from his tabloid three years ago for making stuff up."

Genny snorted. "Is that all? Making stuff up is standard operating procedure for a London tabloid."

"He really did almost get somebody killed. And he got the paper involved in a libel suit."

"Oh, well, there's your trouble."

"Yeah, that's what I thought. But, listen, he'd basically written this series of articles about an Irish family, saying they had ties to some stuff that happened during the Troubles, and . . . well, most of it turned out to be untrue, but the family had to move, because after the article was printed, somebody threw a petrol bomb through their window."

"That's horrible!" Genny and Emma were both silent for a long moment. "But it does mean he was telling you the truth about why he's here writing a book instead of in London chasing down MPs and minor royals."

"But what he left out is the part that after he got here, he started spending a lot of quality time with Maggie Trenwith."

She could picture Genny sitting up straighter. "Are you sure? I mean, I know Shelly says they met, but she only saw them the once."

"Maggie was in his room. More than once."

"How did you find that out?"

"Erm. I talked to one of the cleaners at the B&B."

"Emma Reed," said Genny sternly. "Why didn't you tell me you'd started interrogating the help?"

"Sorry. There's been a lot going on."

"What's got you onto Parker? I thought you suspected Maggie. Or Jimmy."

"Maggie and Parker were talking in the church. I, um, lost track of Oliver"—she crossed her fingers behind her back—"and when I went to look for him, I overheard them. "

"So what are you thinking, exactly?"

"What if it went like this? Parker comes into town to do research. He stumbles across the Penhallow disappearance, and maybe he finds something that leads him to believe Victoria was more involved than the police could prove at the time. He's also heard enough local gossip to know Maggie and Victoria are rivals, so he figures Maggie would be willing to dish the dirt."

"So he goes and finds her at the pub."

"They realize they've got a good thing going. Maggie can get Victoria's reputation destroyed and get Trevena talked up at the same time."

"Because there's no such thing as bad publicity," put in Genny.

"Right," said Emma. "And Parker gets a sensation. Hidden murder uncovered after forty years, and all that.

"But then Victoria actually up and dies. Now Parker's got a problem. He suspects Maggie might be responsible, but if he makes too much noise about it, Maggie might be willing to frame him instead."

"But if he can stay out of the frame and prove who actually did it, that'd be quite the feather in his cap, wouldn't it?" said Genny. "'Journalist unearths killer who baffled cops' is yet another great headline."

No need to bring the past into it at all . . .

"It'd probably be fantastic for book sales. Lord." Emma stopped. "You don't think . . ."

"No," said Genny firmly. "I'd believe Maggie would do a dirty trick or two over a land deal, but I do not think anybody would kill to sell books."

"But just imagine being him. There you are, used to being in the thick of the news world in London. Now you're disgraced and stuck wandering around villages, reading old newspapers and listening to pensioners tell stories about dead people nobody cares about. Then, suddenly, an actual murder case lands right at your feet, and you just might be able to solve it yourself." *With a little help from your friends.* "You start thinking about BBC specials and bestseller lists and maybe getting your old job back and, as a bonus, having people say they were wrong about you."

"It certainly would explain why he wanted your help," said Genny. "Maggie's got to be watching Parker. He couldn't let her see him going around asking questions about her."

"Exactly." *But I'd be a really convenient distraction.* Emma felt anger surge through her. *And because of my blasted curiosity I walked straight into it.*

"So you don't think Victoria killed herself?"

Emma rubbed her eyes. "Actually, I don't. Because if Maggie and Parker were bringing the Penhallow rumors back into the spotlight, I cannot picture Victoria leaving Ruth, and Louise, to face that alone. Not when she's spent so many years protecting them." She told Genny what she'd learned from David and Charles.

Genny was quiet for a long moment. "You know, a few days ago I would have laughed at the idea of Victoria protecting anybody. But now, I think you're right, about her anyway. Not about Parker."

"Why not about Parker?"

"Because of the two of them, Maggie's got much more reason to kill Victoria than Parker." Genny stopped. "Besides— and this is going to sound morbid—but if he was going to kill somebody, I wouldn't expect him to use poison. I mean, that takes patience, and planning. Parker doesn't strike me as the patient type."

"Maybe," said Emma slowly.

"What are you thinking?" asked Genny.

"I'm thinking that murder for career purposes requires a nasty turn of mind. What could be nastier than poisoning a gardener with her own flowers?"

33

....

OLIVER MEANT TO BEHAVE.

Emma was clearly distracted by all the human things that had been happening. Some of them were very dangerous. More dangerous than cars or strange dogs, foxes or even train tracks.

Oliver was confident Emma would find her way. She was very good with her fellow humans, and hadn't she brought them to this excellent new home? In the meantime, if there was a dangerous human, or a dangerous anything else out there, it was his job to keep Emma safe.

So Oliver decided that as long as he was already outside, it would be a good time to patrol the garden and check the gate.

Oliver circled the weedy enclosure. Wind gusted over the walls, bringing clouds of shifting scents. Instinct urged him to follow them all. Any one of them might be important. But the gate was closed and Emma was still inside looking at her computer. Whatever she saw there, it must have all seemed really important, because she didn't even glance up when he came to the open kitchen door.

He could have barked to get her attention. Maybe she really wanted to be done with her screen. Sometimes that happened. She'd be all busy at her table or with her screens, but when he came over with a toy or his blanket, she'd remember what was actually important and come to play. He could have just gone in and sat with her too, but the truth was, he didn't really want to be inside. What he really wanted was to run right across all these excellent hills. What was the point of being home otherwise? The garden was so small, it was almost like indoors.

Except there was the hole.

No. That would be bad. I have to be here to protect Emma.

Except what if something got in through that hole? That wouldn't be any good either. Oliver huffed and scratched and made his decision.

Just a quick check. Just to make sure nothing's wrong.

Oliver wriggled under the yew bushes. The hole was right in front of his muzzle. The wind gusted. A world of damp, salty, musty, musky, earthy smells swirled right through him. The wind gusted again, and Oliver's hesitation vanished. Whatever his brain was thinking, his body flattened itself against the ground—paddling, wriggling and shoving its way through the hole.

He tumbled out on the other side and pressed his nose against the dirt. There. There it was. A fox, and not just any fox. *The* fox.

I knew it. I knew he'd be back.

The scents were gushing full force now. Oliver turned into the wind and trotted down the broad hillside.

Just a little ways. Not far.

But the fox scent was getting stronger and fresher. It was nearly sundown, and the world was filled with hard edges and unfamiliar rustlings. But Oliver wasn't frightened. His nose took the lead and told him everything he needed to know.

He's here. Oliver delved down under a rocky outcropping, sniffing the crevices. *He's here . . .*

"Oh, it's you."

Oliver's ears went up, and the rest of his head followed.

The fox stood on top of the tumbled boulders, looking down. He smelled like dinner and green and salt, and he was laughing at Oliver.

"Let you off the lead, did she?" The fox scratched one ear. "Can't think why. Little thing like you's just going to get into all kinds of trouble out here."

"You want trouble!" Oliver barked. "Come on down here! You'll get trouble!"

He could feel his self-control slipping badly. He should back away, but he couldn't make himself move.

"Oh, you mean me?" The fox picked his way down the rocks until he stood directly over Oliver. Oliver jumped and snapped and missed.

"Oh, good one, mate!" laughed the fox. "Come on, try, try again!"

Oliver did. He couldn't help it. He barked. *Fox, fox, fox! Emma! Fox!*

"Oh, deary, deary me, you're not even going to try to make it interesting, are you?" The fox swished his tail. "Up to me, I guess. Come on, then. Follow the leader!"

The fox jumped, right over top of Oliver's head, and landed downwind. Oliver swung around, but the fox was already bounding away into the dark.

Oliver raced after him.

34

· · · · · · · · · · · ·

WHEN EMMA RANG OFF WITH GENNY, SHE SAT FOR A LONG moment, frowning at her laptop screen. The sky outside was darkening, so she reached up and switched on the pole lamp.

Murder for career purposes requires a nasty turn of mind . . .

Genny's words sat heavily in Emma's thoughts, but so did Parker's sly, greedy grin.

Could be either one of them . . . No need to bring the past in at all . . .

Emma shook her head. *The question is what does Parker really know? And when did he find it out?*

On the one hand, everybody around Victoria's death could be acting (relatively) honestly. Maggie might really believe that Victoria had been a criminal. But the police were not likely to help look into a minor disappearance from years ago, so why not talk to the crime writer instead?

Then Parker might actually have found something that made him believe that Nick Penhallow had been killed and that Victoria Roberts was closely involved. Maybe he even thought Victoria had committed the murder.

Now Parker, with those famous trained journalistic instincts, might really believe that either Maggie or Jimmy had killed Victoria. Maggie for land and a future. Jimmy for money.

And Mr. Journo just has a funny way with words.

On the other hand . . .

Maggie might simply have been trying to ruin Victoria using whatever came to hand. She could have been planning it for a long time, first by trying to undermine her relationship with her nephew and then by using Parker to revive the most damaging rumors she could find, all at a safe remove.

Parker, intent on reestablishing a career and an independent existence, might not care what was true. He might just care what would make the best story.

But Emma remembered Genny's skepticism. She was right. Did anybody really kill for book sales? Even nasty, blackmailing . . .

Emma's thoughts froze and backtracked.

Victoria was used to finding out secrets. Maybe when she heard Parker was snooping around, she smelled a rat. Maybe she talked to Shelly Lucas too. Maybe she talked to Mrs. Shah at the library and found out that Parker was digging into old newspapers from around the time of the disappearance.

Maybe she got worried that he'd find something that would hurt her old friend Ruth.

Constance said Victoria has friends in high places. Could Victoria have threatened to make trouble for Parker or Maggie? English libel laws were fierce. Victoria could have promised legal action.

If that was true, which one of them could actually have been worried enough to kill her?

But none of this explained the fight she'd overheard with Genny.

Well, maybe while she was trying to figure out what was happening to Parker, she found out Jimmy was talking to Maggie.

Or maybe that fight had nothing to do with her death at all. Maybe it was just one of those things.

Emma sighed and rubbed her eyes.

Constance was right. This is a dangerous game. I should give it up and get back to worrying about moving and how I'm going to bake a decent number of cakes and biscuits for Genny to sell.

Except right then an idea occurred to her, and she started typing another search into her computer.

35

"COME ON, MATE, KEEP UP!" SHOUTED THE FOX.

Some small part of Oliver still knew this was bad.

He was a noble corgi, and he was Emma's protector, and he should *not* be distracted by a fox, no matter how smart-alecky he was. But his legs kept running and his nose stayed thrust out front.

Just a little farther. Almost got him . . .

The fox jumped and Oliver jumped, but the ground wasn't there when he came down, and he yipped as he tumbled nose over tail down into the hollow.

Oliver scrambled to his feet and shook himself all over. The fox was nowhere in sight. He nosed the ground in every direction.

Where are you? Where are you?

He caught the scent and scrambled down a scree of stones, skidding and sliding straight into the wind, toward the sea and the cliffs. The fox thought he could use the damp and the mud between the stones to confuse his scent, but he was out of luck. A corgi's nose was better than that.

Just a little farther . . .

The fox had splashed through a set of puddles. Oliver

could just make out the tracks on the stones. He struggled over the loose rocks, nose down.

Just a little farther . . .

They'd come to one of the heath's rises, and the fox started climbing. Oliver followed, shoving himself hard up the slope. He got to the top and . . .

Nothing.

Oliver circled, his nose practically plowing up the ground. But there was nothing at all. It was like the fox had vanished into thin air.

No. No. No. He circled wider. *He's here somewhere. I know he is. He has to be . . .*

But there was nothing. Or rather, there was something. Oliver froze, his nose twitching.

What's he *doing here?*

That was when Oliver realized he wasn't sure where "here" actually was.

36

......

EMMA STRAIGHTENED UP AND STRETCHED HER ARMS OVER-
head. She glanced at the old railroad clock on the wall. Past
seven. Outside, the summer sky was darkening toward evening. She'd been so busy reading and researching Parker
Taite and his colorful history that she'd lost track of time.
Her latest cup of tea had gone stone-cold.

And she still had no idea what had actually happened in
the time leading up to Victoria's death. So much hinged on
motivations that had all been kept close to the heart.

*So what do I do? Do I tell DCI Brent about Parker and
Maggie? Do I wait until I find out more? How do I find out
more? Can I get either of them to talk to me? How?*

And speaking of finding things . . .

Emma looked around her. Oliver was nowhere in sight.
Emma frowned. She hadn't heard him bark or scratch
in . . . a while. She heaved herself off the sofa, groaning a
little at how her knees popped, and went round to the
kitchen.

The towel she used as a doorstop was still wedged in
place, holding the door open to corgi width. She peered into
the twilight garden, but she didn't see anything.

"All right, Oliver," she called. "Come on in!"

A crow cawed in the distance. In response, a nightjar chugged. But there was no movement under the yew bushes, or anywhere else. Emma scanned the empty, weedy square of her back garden uneasily.

"Oliver!" she called. "Here, Oliver!" She stuck her fingers into her teeth and whistled.

There was no answering movement, no flash of white fur and no sound of Oliver's distinctive voice or bark.

"Oliver!" Emma shouted. "No games tonight! Oliver!"

But there was no answer.

OLIVER WASN'T ACTUALLY WORRIED. EVEN THOUGH THE daylight was fading and the wind was picking up, which made it harder to distinguish one scent from another. It would still be easy enough to follow his own trail back home through the grass and bracken, just as soon as he found it again.

But Emma would be worried. Emma didn't like it when he was gone for too long. He needed to get back to her.

Oliver nosed his way along the hillock. There. He picked up the slightly wobbling trail of his own scent, and he wagged in satisfaction.

But he found something else, something he'd scented in passing.

Percy. The Yorkie's scent was strong and unmistakable. There was something else, though . . .

"I'm here! I'm here!"

Before Oliver had had time to start more than an exploratory snuffle, Percy charged up out of the grass. He bonked straight into Oliver's side, as if a little terrier could topple a well-grown corgi. All that happened was Percy toppled over, which did not seem to bother him at all.

"Let's go!" Percy scrambled to his feet. "Come on, Oliver! Bet you can't catch me!" He stretched out his front paws, wagging his tail furiously.

"What are you doing here!" Oliver yipped as he nosed the smaller dog. Percy had plainly been outside for a good long while. He smelled like salt water and green, and his fur was drenched. "Where's your human?" There was no fresh trace of the human on Percy's fur, or anywhere else.

"I keep telling you, he's not my human!" Percy snapped back and charged at Oliver's paws. "Don't you want to play? Come on! You can't catch me!"

But Oliver ducked Percy's play-nipping and instead bounded around him in a wide circle. "You need to get home! Home!" He charged, bumping his muzzle against the Yorkie's side. The terrier teetered, but then bounded out of reach. "I need to get home. Emma needs me!"

"Okay, you want a human so much?" Percy wagged. "There's a human out here. Come on! I'll show you!" The Yorkie darted away. "Come on!"

Oliver plopped down on his hindquarters, panting. This was not good. Emma would be worried. He was getting tired. He wasn't sure where he was, but it was a long way from home. He couldn't smell any of the cottage smells from here.

And Percy was already out of sight.

"Come on!" he heard the Yorkie bark. "Come on! There's a human!"

Oliver grunted and jumped to his feet and raced after him.

"Which human!"

"OLIVER!"

Emma circled the back garden. She checked the gate, which was latched, and there was no sign of fresh digging under it.

Emma hurried to the front of the cottage and snapped on the light. She scanned the front garden and the path and the road. Nothing.

Oh, no. No. Come on, Oliver, you can't do this to me.

She made her way around the outside of the walled garden, whistling and calling. The only answers were the distant noises of sheep and cars.

"Oliver!" she shouted again. "Oliver!"

Nothing moved on the hillside out back of her garden; nothing she could see, anyway.

He's fine, she told herself. *He's fine. Just . . . wandered off. Again.*

She turned back toward the house, and that was when she saw what she'd missed before: the gap between the wall's stones, right at the base.

No.

She saw the fresh scratching in the dirt and the tiny clump of fur caught on the edge of the hole.

Oh, no.

And then she remembered. Emma straightened up slowly and stared out across the empty hillside. Parker had told her about finding Oliver outside the garden. She'd scolded him. She'd promised herself she'd find the hole and block it.

She'd gotten so wrapped up in everything else, the repair had completely slipped her mind.

Oh, Oliver!

Just then, her phone buzzed in her pocket. Emma yanked it out and hit the CALL button.

"Emma?" It was Genny. "I had another idea—"

"Genny!" To Emma's shame, her exclamation sounded a lot like a sob—a fact that Genny did not miss.

"Good lord, Emma! What's happened?"

"It's Oliver! He got out of the garden. I can't find him anywhere!"

"Okay, okay, calm down. I'm sure he's fine."

"He could have been hit by a car! He doesn't . . . he . . ."

"It's okay, Emma. People drive a lot more slowly out here. Nobody wants to hit a sheep or something. How long has he been gone?"

"I don't know! Maybe an hour!"

"All right, he can't have gotten that far."

"Yes, he can! You don't know him! When I first found him, he was out in the middle of nowhere in Canada trying to argue with a moose!"

"I'm . . . wait, what?"

"Never mind." Emma waved her hand in front of her face like she could shoo her panic away. "I just, I have to find him!"

The idea of Oliver lost in the dark, maybe hurt, maybe . . . No, she wasn't going to think about that.

"Okay," said Genny again. "Listen, maybe he just got confused. Maybe he went back to the King's Rest."

"I hadn't thought about that." Relief started to clear some of the cold fear out of Emma's thoughts. "I'll call Angelique, ask her to keep an eye out for him. Genny . . . could you . . ."

"What do you need, luv?"

"Go over to the King's Rest, and keep an eye out for Oliver on the way? I'll head down the hill, see if I can find him."

"I will, but are you sure, Emma? That ground out there's not as smooth as it looks, and it's getting dark."

Emma squinted at the dimming sky. "There's still plenty of light. I'll be fine."

"Okay, but you keep your phone on, yeah?"

"Yes, I will. Thank you, Genny."

They hung up, and Emma set off down the hill toward the village.

"Oliver!" she shouted. "Oliver! Come home!"

37

"COME ON!" BARKED PERCY.

They were still heading down the hill. Oliver could smell fresh water as well as salt now, and he heard the sound of a rushing stream. They must be coming up on the rift and its broad, cascading brook.

Percy showed no sign of slowing down. Oliver felt a surge of frustration and worry. He was out of breath. His paws hurt. The ground was ragged with stones and dirt clods. His whole body itched, especially his tummy.

I should stop. I should go back. Emma will be worried. Emma needs me.

"You're so slow!" yipped the terrier.

But he couldn't just leave Percy. The terrier was alone, and he was reckless, and he didn't know where he needed to be or even how to behave with his human.

"Come on!" Percy scampered up another small rise, huffing and laughing the whole way.

"Terriers!" Oliver barked, then gathered his hindquarters under him and charged up the slope.

"Here!" shouted Percy as Oliver came up next to him. "Right here! I told you!"

The wind and its wealth of smells hit him and directed

his attention. Far down the slope, Oliver could see the ragged edge of the cliffs. All the smells of the sea rose up, threatening to overwhelm every other trace of scent.

A woman stood right at the edge of the cliff, staring out across the rushing ocean.

Oliver was almost sure he knew her, but she was too far away, and the salt scents were too powerful for him to make out anything more than a vague human scent.

"Can't catch me!" Percy careened down the slope, barking the entire way. Oliver followed, more slowly. He'd taken enough spills today.

Percy reached the cliff's edge.

"What on earth!" exclaimed the woman. She drew her arms tight against her, clearly startled by the little dog hopping around near her feet.

Now Oliver was close enough to recognize her scent. It was Nervous Louise, the one who had been in the kitchen and the office and all the other places.

"Percy!" Louise exclaimed, turning around as the terrier circled her. "Oh, Percy! What are you doing here!"

The terrier was barking and charging at her toes, eager to play, not seeming to notice how close he was coming to going right over the edge.

"Oh, oh, goodness. No, no." Louise steeled herself and snatched the Yorkie up with both hands.

Good human! Oliver barked and wagged. Louise's head jerked up.

"*And* Oliver! What on earth!" She turned around, looking up the hill and all around her. "Where's Emma? Did you get out?"

"Yes," Oliver whined. "But it wasn't my fault."

But Louise wasn't Emma, and she didn't understand him. Oliver flopped down on the grass, panting hard. He was tired, but he still felt much better. Here was a human— maybe not the right human, but a human—who had hold of Percy. His work was done. He could go home now.

He put his nose back down and sniffed hard. Home was that way.

No, wait . . .

"Oh, oh, dear," murmured Louise. "I can't . . . I just can't . . ."

Home is this way . . .

Louise was holding Percy out at arm's length.

"Lemme go!" whined the terrier. "Lemme go!"

"But I can't leave you both out here on your own," she whispered. "You might . . . you might go over the edge. I just can't do that. Can I?"

She slowly put Percy down and patted his back. Surprisingly, the Yorkie stayed put, at least for the moment.

"Come on, come on, Oliver. Oh, dear, I wish I had . . . Oh, heavens, I *do* have something." She was patting her pockets. "Oh, this is ridiculous."

She pulled out a packet and tore it open. "Here, would you like a treat, Oliver?"

Oliver sniffed at the little bar she held out. Louise smelled like coffee and chimneys and cats. The bar smelled of sweet and salt and flour . . . It was a biscuit. A human biscuit, the kind Emma never let him have. Well, almost never. Well, not often enough.

Oliver wolfed it down.

"Oh. There. Ah, good dog." She patted the top of his head too quickly. Oliver forgave her. She smelled of cats, but she was trying, and she thought to keep a biscuit in her pocket. She might not ever be a favorite human, but she was not too bad.

She gave a second biscuit to Percy, who crunched and wagged happily and promptly rolled over, belly exposed, begging for another.

Louise straightened up. "Yes. Now, come along. We'll get you home." She scooped Percy up before the terrier could made a dash for it.

"Darn it," muttered Percy.

"You shouldn't beg," said Oliver.

"I'll get out of it."

"Yes." Louise squared her shoulders. "We'll get you home. That's what we'll do. All for the best. Yes. I'm sure it is."

She tucked Percy under her arm, just like Percy's regular human did, and started walking up the slope toward the cottage.

There was something bad in the wind now. It was hard to make out, because the night had gone still and damp, and there was all the water spray from the cascade below. But it was still there, and he didn't like it.

He should get back to Emma, but . . . he was having a hard time finding the trail. It wouldn't do. But Emma knew this lady, and this lady knew Emma, and she said they were going home.

Oliver shivered along with his whole body and sneezed in the bargain, then trotted after her.

38

"STUPID, STUPID CITY GIRL!" MUTTERED EMMA, AS SHE STUM-
bled over (yet another) unseen stone.

Unfortunately, Genny had been right. The hillside down
to Trevena looked fairly smooth, and it was certainly easy
to see where she meant to go. Trevena's handful of streetlights had flickered on and now shone like beacons against
the deepening backdrop of the twilight sea. But that same
twilight made it surprisingly difficult to see the hillside's
rocks and divets, not to mention the full-grown holes and
hollows.

And even as she thought this, Emma's toe caught the
next stone, sending her reeling. This time, she couldn't
catch herself and she fell down onto her hands and knees,
jarring her arms up to her shoulders.

"Stupid, stupid city . . . woman," she muttered as she
picked herself up and wiped her hands off on her jeans.

"Oliver!" Emma shouted. She wished she could calm
down and be sensible but she just couldn't. This was *Oliver*
that was missing—her best friend, her furry little footstool,
her blasted, blessed, bloody talking dog who would face
down a moose without a second thought . . .

"Oliver!"

Away off in the distance, Emma heard something bark.

"OLIVER!" THE VOICE WAS CARRIED DOWN THE WIND. DIStant and echoey, without any scent to it. But Oliver would know it anywhere.

Emma! He whipped around and started barking. "I'm here, Emma! I'm here!"

"What!" Louise started so badly, she lost hold of Percy. The terrier tumbled to the ground and instantly bounced up again. He ran up beside Oliver and started barking too.

"What are we barking about?" he asked.

"Emma!" shouted Oliver. "She's lost!"

EMMA STUMBLED UP THE RISE AND LOOKED DOWN THE long slope toward the rift bridge. There, she saw a woman waving frantically. Beside her, Oliver stood out as a pale blob against the darker hillside. Emma's flood of relief momentarily blinded her to the fact that the woman was Louise and that the wriggly little lump next to Oliver was Percy the Yorkie.

What on earth . . . ? she thought as she hurried down the slope as quickly as she dared. *What are you all doing out here together?*

As soon as she reached the rift, she fell to her knees. Oliver immediately bounded into her arms.

"Emma!" he shouted, licking her face all over. "It's okay! You're found."

Emma laughed and hugged him. "Don't tell me, you bad, bad corgi, let me guess. There was a fox."

"How did you know? You can't smell that well. Did you see him? Was he rude?"

Emma rubbed his ears hard and laughed. "Thank you, Louise! I've been looking for him everywhere."

"Yes, well." Louise gave a sharp sigh, as if she was trying to bring herself back from being lost in other thoughts.

"I just happened to be out for a walk by the rift and . . . well, they found me." She took a little sideways step back from Percy, who was sniffing hard at her ankles. The little dog yipped at Oliver.

"Percy says something's wrong. Percy says she smells like the stuff his human drinks. She does, and coffee and chimney smoke."

Emma frowned.

"Where's Parker?" she asked Louise.

"He's not out here," said Louise. "Not that I've seen."

"Percy said he got out." Percy had backed away from Louise now and was barking at her, hard and fast. His tail wasn't wagging at all. Oliver started in barking at the little dog. Louise went pale and stared down at the dogs in genuine alarm.

"Quiet, Oliver. Percy." Emma picked up the wiry little terrier and rubbed him under the chin. "It's all right. Percy probably just got out again. I've never met such an escape artist." Emma gave Louise a smile that, hopefully, had more assurance in it than she actually felt. "I'll tell you what, I'll take Percy back to the King's Rest. If Parker's not there, Angelique should have his mobile number."

"Would you? Oh, thank you." Louise fidgeted with the hem of her flowered jumper. "I really don't think I can face Mr. Taite just now. We . . . well, we're not exactly on speaking terms."

"Oh. I'm sorry." Emma really wanted to ask what had happened, but now was probably not the best time. "And it's no problem. Percy shouldn't be out by himself, and whatever else, Parker does try to take care of his dog."

"Yes," she murmured. "I suppose that's true."

"Are you okay, Louise?"

"She's not," said Oliver. "She's all worry and smoke and cats . . ."

"Oh, yes," said Louise, but even without Oliver's commentary, Emma would have known she was lying. "I'm fine. It's just been . . . a lot lately, with Victoria's funeral and everything, you understand."

And you've been saddled with an inheritance that was supposed to go to somebody else, and now you're responsible for all that property and for what happens to your best friend's nephew, and you're having to deal with people she never liked, all while you're still grieving.

"I do understand," was what Emma said out loud. "Listen, why don't you come with me? I mean, maybe being alone right now isn't the best idea for you. You can wait downstairs while I return Percy, and we can get a drink afterward." When Emma saw Louise's look at the mention of "drink," she added quickly, "Or maybe a coffee?"

"Oh, no, no, I'm fine. Although, I admit, a glass of wine would be very nice right now." She looked down toward the village lights. "But no. I think I'd rather have some time to myself."

"Are you sure? I mean, it's getting dark."

The smile Louise gave her was genuine. It was also full of patient indulgence for the city slicker (slickeress?). "I'll be fine, Emma. I grew up on these hills, remember. They're old friends. Nothing makes me feel better than an evening walk. You go take care of Percy."

"Yes, Percy. And okay, if you're sure?"

"I'm sure," Louise said, and for the first time she sounded fully confident. "In fact, if you're all right, I'll be going now." But she hesitated. Then, awkwardly, she bent down and patted Oliver on the head. "Thank you, Oliver. Ah, good boy." She smiled, then turned and strode briskly across the rift bridge and up over the heath.

"What was that for?" asked Emma.

Oliver scratched his ear. "I don't know. Cat humans are harder to understand than normal humans." He wagged his tail. "But she had biscuits."

"Greedy guts." Emma chuckled. "Well." She rubbed Percy's head but kept watching as Louise's silhouetted receded in the distance.

Emma shook herself. Standing here in the dark was no good. She had to get Percy home. What she hadn't told Louise, of course, was that returning the Yorkie would provide the perfect chance for her to let Parker know what she'd found out about him. She could confront him with his omissions and find out exactly what he was doing.

And maybe what he really knows about Maggie, and Jimmy.

But there was one small matter to be taken care of first. "Oliver? Can you find the road?"

39

....

"ROAD!" OLIVER IMMEDIATELY PUT HIS NOSE TO THE ground and started casting about. "Of course! Road, road, road," he murmured. "Road is . . ."

Percy barked and wriggled. Oliver huffed. But his head and his ears went up, and he sneezed. Percy yipped again, and Oliver shrugged.

"Emma," he said gravely. "Release the terrier."

"Are you sure?"

"I'm sure." But Oliver did not sound happy about it.

"Okay." Emma put the Yorkie down. "But you're catching him if he takes . . ."

Percy, however, had already zoomed away.

"That way," muttered Oliver, and he loped off after the vanishing Yorkie.

Emma followed them both. They all topped the next rise together. From here, Emma could make out the winding ribbon of country road snaking down the hillside between the steep dirt and stone embankments. She breathed a sigh of relief and lengthened her stride. And stubbed her toe.

Just as Emma and the dogs made it to the narrow shoulder of the (barely) two-lane road into Trevena, a pair of headlights came toward them from the direction of the village.

The car pulled over to the shoulder and stopped. The driver put the window down.

"Emma!" Maggie Trenwith poked her head out the window. "What are you doing out here?"

"Oh, hi, Maggie!" Emma scooped Percy up to be on the safe side as she came up to the car door. "It's a long story. Well, actually, no, it isn't. Oliver got out of the garden, and I went looking for him, and we found Percy on the way."

"Wow." Maggie squinted up the hill, mentally measuring the distance to Nancarrow. "I wouldn't have thought he could have gotten this far."

"Corgis are herding dogs. They're faster than they look."

"I guess. Well. Would you like a lift back?"

Emma met Maggie's gaze and felt like she was seeing double. One part of her saw the savvy, friendly estate agent who helped her get her lovely little cottage. Another part saw the woman she'd begun to suspect of murder.

"I was headed down to the King's Rest," Emma croaked. "I need to get Percy home."

A flash of anger crossed Maggie's face. "Yes, well, I suppose. I mean, can't leave anybody worrying about their dog." The "anybody" had a poisonous undertone. "I can still drive you."

"I don't want to be any trouble . . ."

"No trouble," said Maggie. "You can load the dogs in the back."

Emma swallowed. Did she really want to get into the car with a woman she thought might be a killer?

On the other hand, did she really want to pass up this chance to talk to Maggie and maybe get some of her looming questions answered?

Emma steeled her nerve. "Thanks," she said, and hoped Maggie didn't hear the (very slight) tremor in her voice.

Emma lifted the dogs into the back seat of Maggie's BMW and then climbed in after them. As soon as Emma was buckled in, Maggie expertly backed her car down to a spot where she had room to turn around and headed back to town.

"Hope we're not making you late for anything," Emma said.

Maggie laughed, a little too loudly, Emma thought. "Oh, no. I was finally done for the day. Just back from having some drinks with a developer. He had some concerns and I had to head them off at the pass."

"Is this the representative from Apex Properties?"

"That's the one." Maggie was keeping her eyes rigidly ahead.

"Well, I hope it went all right."

"Nothing we can't handle," said Maggie. Which was a strange sort of nonanswer. Emma rubbed Oliver's back. Percy was standing up on the back seat, paws pressed against the window. Emma hoped Maggie wouldn't mind the smudges. This was a nice car. Clean as a whistle, and even on the hill it ran smooth and quiet. Either Maggie had splashed out on a gift for herself or her realty business was doing very well.

Except, according to Parker, it couldn't be.

One thought followed another, and before she knew it Emma had leaned forward.

"So have you gotten Louise to agree to sell up some of the land?"

Now Maggie did glance in the rearview, and she frowned. "Been doing your homework?"

"Pure curiosity. Also, I ran into her while I was looking for Oliver. She seemed . . . conflicted."

"Emma." Oliver pawed her thigh. "Percy smells wrong."

Looking in the mirror, Emma could see Maggie's mouth moving, but she couldn't hear what the other woman was saying. Then, as if aware she was being watched, the real estate agent smiled tiredly. "Oh, well, Louise is just getting used to the idea of dealing with the person her best friend considered the local version of the Wicked Witch of the West," she said, but her tone was too bright and too brittle.

"Emma." Oliver nudged her again. "There's something bad. It's all over Percy."

Emma looked at him sharply. Oliver licked at her hand.

"I couldn't smell it before, because there was too much wind and mud, but now I can."

"So do you think she'll be interested in letting us have a look at Penhallows after all?"

"I think that's very much on the table," said Maggie. "I'll see if I can get permission tomorrow if you want."

"Yes, that'd be wonderful, thanks."

"Emma?" Oliver bumped her hard with his nose. "Are you listening? Percy doesn't want to go home," Oliver whined. "Not like he usually doesn't. This time he really, really doesn't."

"I'm listening," she breathed. "Really, I'm listening."

"Sorry?" Maggie glanced at her in the mirror again. "Did you say something?"

"No, sorry." Emma raised her voice. "Just trying to settle Oliver down. He doesn't actually like car rides very much."

"Is that the human thing where you're telling them what they need to hear?" asked Oliver.

"Shhh, yes, yes." She rubbed his back.

"Humans are very strange."

"I know. We'll be home soon."

"So you said you ran into Louise?" said Maggie, but her tone of casual curiosity was strained. "Where was that?"

"Out by the rift bridge."

"Well, that's Louise. She loves her country walks. They help her think, she says."

"She seemed depressed. Tired, maybe."

"Probably worried she's going to be haunted by the ghost of Victoria Roberts now that she's actually decided to part with some property. I swear, that woman browbeat Louise for years. Actually, she browbeat everyone," Maggie went on fiercely. "Even her poor nephew. There was nothing she wouldn't do to get her way."

Emma held Maggie's gaze in the mirror, and for a moment neither of them said anything more. "Does that include getting involved in a murder?"

Maggie's hands jerked on the steering wheel, and the car

wobbled. Percy squeaked and toppled sideways. Emma
gathered him up onto her lap.

"What are you talking . . . Oh, you're talking about Nick
Penhallow, aren't you?"

"Parker Taite told me he was sure that Victoria knew
something about that."

"Oh, I think she knew," said Maggie. "In fact, I think
she knew a great deal more than anyone ever let on."

Emma frowned. "You don't think . . ."

"You mean do I think Victoria Roberts helped murder
Nicholas Penhallow? Oh, yes," said Maggie. "I do. I always
have. I just couldn't ever prove it."

"Until now?"

They were back in Trevena proper, passing the turreted
sprawl of King Arthur's Castle. Maggie carefully navigated
the minuscule roundabout and then took them up the zig-
zag slope of the high street and started down the other side.
Out in front, the King's Rest lights shone a mellow gold
against the looming bulk of the cliffs.

"Here we are!" Maggie sang out. She eased the car into
the B&B's little dirt and gravel parking lot. "You all right
from here, Emma? I've got some paperwork I need to get
to, and Gwyn's keeping my tea warm for me."

You didn't answer me, Emma thought. What she said
was, "Yes, I'm fine. Come on, boys."

"Out." Oliver shoved his muzzle at the terrier. "Come
on. Out, Percy."

Percy barked and whined, but Oliver kept shoving and
nipping to urge the terrier along ahead of him. Emma remembered what he had said about Percy really not wanting
to go home. A shiver crawled down her spine.

Genny and Angelique were both in the great room. Of
course, they both had cups of tea, with a plate of biscuits
between them.

"Emma!" Genny jumped to her feet as Emma and the
dogs came in. "I was starting to get worried."

"Return of the prodigal corgi!" Angelique laughed as
Oliver trotted up to snuffle her ankles. "No, no sausages,

you bad, bad boy! You should not go worrying your mum like that." She rubbed his ears.

"But I found her," barked Oliver.

Emma laughed. "He thinks he found me wandering around in the dark."

"What's Percy doing with you?" asked Genny.

Instead of charging forward like usual, Percy was hanging back by the door. Shivering.

"Oliver found him out on the heath, and then Louise found them both. I wanted to get him back to Parker."

Percy yipped. "I think he's chilled," Emma said. "Have you got an old towel or anything?"

"Sure, I'll get you one." Angelique got to her feet. "But I don't know if Parker's here. I haven't seen him since right after breakfast."

The three women looked at each other and then down at the shivering terrier.

"I'm sure it's fine," said Emma.

"We're being overly dramatic," said Genny.

Angelique shook her head. "I want to check his room. I don't like this."

"Oliver," breathed Emma. Oliver barked once and darted up the stairs. Angelique, frowning, followed the corgi, and Genny and Emma followed Angelique.

At the top of the stairs, Oliver froze so abruptly that Angelique almost tripped over him.

"Emma . . ." he growled. "Emma, it's that smell again."

"Oh no." Emma shoved her way past her friends and banged against Parker's door with the flat of her hand. "Parker! Parker!"

"It's bad! It's bad!" Oliver barked.

"Here, let me." Angelique brought a key ring out of her pocket. "Mr. Taite? Mr. Taite, it's Angelique! We're coming in, Mr. Taite!"

Finally, she got the recalcitrant door open, and Oliver charged in. Emma just barely managed to catch him by the scruff and haul him backward.

Because, like Victoria Robert's kitchen, Parker Taite's

bedroom was now very clearly a crime scene. The chairs were overturned; the suitcase and its contents had spilled out on top of scattered books and magazines. Drawers had been pulled out. The typewriter lay on the floor, its side stained and splotched dark red.

That same sticky red spread across the side of Parker Taite's skull. He lay on his back in the middle of the room, his eyes wide open and staring motionless at the ceiling.

40

"WELL, HERE WE ALL ARE AGAIN," SAID CONSTANCE.

She was right. Emma, once again, faced the detective across Angelique's tidy desk. Oliver was on high alert beside Emma's chair. Percy, looking more like an unraveled skein of yarn than usual, snuggled up tight against him.

Constance Brent sat with her little notebook and mechanical pencil in front of her.

It was just like when Victoria had died. Except this time, the detective's air of brisk efficiency carried a sharp edge, and that sympathy she had been so careful to express during their previous interview and their conversation at the funeral was nowhere to be seen.

The other difference was that this time, she asked for Emma immediately.

"I'm not sure what to say," murmured Emma. Reflexively she put her hand down to rub Oliver's ears. She needed the reassurance.

"Well, if it's any consolation, I'm not either." Constance's smile and her tone were grim. "So let's begin at the beginning." The detective made a "come here" gesture with two fingers.

"I'm sorry?" said Emma.

"The hand," said Constance. "Let's see it."

Emma met the detective's gaze and held it. A slow realization crept into her mind. She extended her hand across the desk, palm up.

Constance did not even look at her hand. She kept her eyes on Emma's face. "You were having second thoughts."

"Wouldn't you?"

"Depends on what I thought was going on."

"I think you're looking for a reaction," Emma told her. "Everybody's so sure they know what the police are about. We all watch television. We all think we know the script. But if you present people with something off the script, you get to watch what they do when they're caught off guard."

"There now," said Constance, with an air of satisfaction that did nothing to relax Emma. "I told you, strong head line. Very direct. Very sure. Not always right, but you do get there." The detective opened her notebook.

"Was that why you wanted me to let you know if I found out anything about Victoria?" Emma asked.

"That, and the fact that what you hear and what I hear might be two different things. Now. Perhaps you could tell me how you got to be the one to find our unfortunate Mr. Taite?"

Emma pulled her hand back and tried to pull her nerve together at the same time. She only sort of succeeded.

She hadn't had a long time to look around Parker's room when they had found him, but even from that short glimpse, she saw that this time there was no possibility of some kind of accident. There'd been an enormous bruise across the side of Parker's head. Blood had dried to a dark crust on his temple and his cheeks. The typewriter lay overturned on the floor beside him, with more dried blood spattered along the edge.

She was going to be a long time getting the image out of her mind.

Who could have done it? Maggie? Jimmy? Somebody else? Had the same person killed Victoria? Or were there two murderers now?

But even while she thought this, Emma had the feeling

something was missing. She frowned at her memories. Something else should have been there and wasn't.

Sensing her discomfort, Oliver whined up at her and wagged his bottom. Percy grumbled and pressed against the corgi's side.

"Emma?" prompted Constance.

"Yes. Sorry. It's just a long story . . ."

"I have literally nowhere else to be at this time."

"Yes. Right. Sorry." *And we can stop apologizing now.* Emma took a deep breath. "Oliver got out of my garden, and I went looking for him." Fortunately, Oliver seemed to have picked up on the change of tone in the room and didn't try to explain the perfectly sensible (from his perspective) reasons he had gone out onto the heath. "I found him down by the rift with Percy—that's Parker's dog." She frowned. "Well, actually, I found Louise Craddock, and she'd found both the dogs, or they'd found her . . ."

"Louise Craddock?" said Constance. "What was she doing out at the rift?"

"She said she was taking a walk to clear her head. Victoria's funeral, and everything . . . it's all been pretty hard on her."

"Unexpected inheritances are difficult to absorb," remarked Constance.

"Well, I'm sure that hasn't helped. Genny Knowles said she still seemed to be on pretty good terms with Jimmy, but it can't be easy."

Constance made a note. "So Mrs. Craddock was at the rift. She found the dogs, and you found them all together, but Mr. Taite wasn't there?"

"No. Percy gets out a lot, so I didn't think that much about it. Although"—she paused—"he looked like he'd been outside for kind of a long time."

Constance raised her eyebrows. Emma picked up the snoozing Percy. "His coat's all tangled, and he was really damp from running around in the weather."

"Yes, I can see," murmured Constance. "Poor little guy. Then what happened?"

"I offered to take Percy back to Parker. Louise isn't really a dog person. So I left her—"

"Just like that?"

"I did ask if she was all right. She said she was fine and that she just needed some space after everything that had happened. So I let her go and we walked down to the road. When we got there, we met Maggie Trenwith. She was driving up from the village, and she offered to give us a lift down to the King's Rest."

"Did Ms. Trenwith say what she was doing out?"

"Yes, she said she'd been meeting with the developer, the one who is supposed to be putting in the new shops and all."

"And needs land that Louise Craddock now owns, thanks to Victoria Roberts."

"Erm. Yes."

"How did Ms. Trenwith seem?"

Emma tried to think. "I . . . as usual, I guess. Worried about her deal, I think. Trying to act more confident than she felt."

Like someone who just committed another murder? Emma felt cold. Beside her, Oliver whined and put his chin on her shoes. Emma tried to draw some of that that loyal corgi warmth into herself.

"Genny had called me right about the time I found out Oliver was missing, and she had the idea he might have gotten confused and come back here instead of going to the cottage—"

Oliver sat up, ears raised. "Corgis do not get confused," he protested. "I knew exactly where I was going."

Percy gave a tiny growl. Oliver managed to put on a look of gravely wounded dignity.

Focus, Emma. Priorities. She forced her attention back to the detective. "Anyway, I'd asked Genny to come here and watch for Oliver on the way over, while I walked down the hill . . . And anyway, when we all got here, I asked about Parker, and Angelique said she hadn't seen him all day, and we went up to check on him, and the dogs started barking, and Angelique unlocked the door, and . . ."

And the room was a disaster area, with everything overturned. And there was Parker Taite in the middle of it. And something else. Something she'd seen, or hadn't seen, or . . .

"The manuscript!" Emma exclaimed, so loudly that Percy woke up and rolled over, yipping.

"It's okay, it's okay." Oliver nosed him reassuringly. "Just humans."

"You lost me there," said Constance.

"Parker was writing a book, but he was doing it on the typewriter. He said he'd got into the habit of working on one when he was younger, and pretentious."

Constance laughed, once.

"Anyway, the last time I was in his room, he had this big, thick stack of pages on his desk. I didn't see any of them when . . . when we found him." *I saw the drawers pulled out, and the suitcase turned over, and the covers messed up on the bed . . .*

"Right." Constance stabbed her pencil into her page, making a full stop. "Ms. Reed, why don't you tell me what you'd been doing visiting Mr. Taite in his room?"

Emma's thoughts froze in their tracks. The detective turned over a page in her book and waited expectantly. There was a fresh light in her eye, and Emma remembered thinking when she first met this woman how careful and thorough the detective seemed, and how she would not like to get on Constance's bad side.

Emma swallowed to clear the knot that had suddenly formed in her throat.

"My room was right across the hall, and I ran into him while I was getting ready to move up to Nancarrow. He . . ." She stopped. Constance tapped her pencil, very obviously and very patiently waiting for Emma's explanation.

Right. "Parker told me he'd been trying to talk to Victoria about the Nicholas Penhallow disappearance."

"Ah. We're back to that."

"Yes, and to the idea that Penhallow might have been killed, and that Victoria might have been involved."

Constance leaned back. She was looking at Emma with a new, thoughtful expression. Emma did not like it. It made the hairs on the back of her neck stand up. "New death brings all sorts of old rumors to the surface."

"But it makes no *sense*," said Emma.

"What doesn't?"

"People"—*Maggie*—"keep talking like Victoria might have killed Nicholas Penhallow herself. But how does that work? Victoria murders the old goat of a baker, then turns around and buys the building so the family doesn't get evicted and makes sure they've got a home for as long as they need it and stays friends with the daughter to the point where she's straining her own budget to pay for her care home?"

Constance blinked. "Have you considered Victoria did all that so Mrs. and Ms. Penhallow would keep quiet about her involvement with old Nick's disappearance?"

Emma opened her mouth. And closed it.

Percy gave one of his yipping little barks and scrabbled at the door.

"Emma, Percy says he needs an out," Oliver told her.

"Seriously? He's been out all day!"

"Ms. Reed?" began Constance. Percy barked. Oliver went over and tried to nose him away from the door.

Before Constance could continue with her questioning, the sound of footsteps running down the hall vibrated through the door. Emma turned in her chair just as the door flew open and Maggie Trenwith burst into the room.

Two things happened at once: Constance shot to her feet, and Percy gave a triumphant yip and bolted through the open door.

"Oh . . . crumbs!" groaned Emma. "Oliver!"

"I'll get him!" Oliver charged out after him.

Maggie entirely ignored the dogs. "Is it true?" she gasped. She was breathless and more disheveled than Emma had ever seen her.

"Ms. Trenwith," snapped Constance. "I am conducting an interview."

"I can see that." Maggie strode up to the desk. "What I want to know is is it true? Is Parker Taite dead?"

"Ms. Trenwith, I am neither going to confirm nor deny—"

Maggie cut her off. "He is, then. That . . . that . . . *idiot!* What about the book?"

"I'm sorry?" said the detective.

"The book he was writing, that mess of lies about Trevena and . . . well, about Trevena. Have you got that?"

Constance drew herself up to her full height. The office suddenly felt very crowded. "I'm not prepared to discuss anything we may or may not have found at this time. Neither am I prepared to discuss Mr. Taite's personal characteristics. You will please close the door on your way out."

Maggie would probably not have liked knowing how much her step backward looked like a retreat, but it very clearly was.

"Look, please, this is important . . ."

Constance didn't let her get any further. "Ms. Trenwith, I understand you are upset, and frankly, I don't blame you. We will be speaking to members of the public as soon as that can be arranged, but at this time I am going to have to ask you to leave."

Maggie looked at Emma, hoping, maybe, for help or at least sympathy. Emma spread her hands, and Maggie turned on her heel and marched out. The door swung shut behind her.

Constance sighed and dropped back into her chair. Whatever she muttered under her breath, it sounded a lot to Emma like "Spare me from eternal villagers."

"Um, Detective?" said Emma carefully. "Can I . . . that is . . . my dog? I don't want him running off again."

Constance ran one hand through her spiked hair. "Yes, all right. I think we're done here for the moment. But I can say it is highly likely there will be follow-up questions. And, Emma?"

"Yes?"

The look Constance turned on her was an odd mix of pleading and close-held anger.

"I know this is probably trying to lock the barn door after the horse has gotten out, but will you please not talk to anyone else about this matter until we've made an official public announcement, all right?"

"Yes. That is, I won't."

"Thank you. Please close the door."

Emma did. And she walked away, and did not look back, even when she heard what sounded very much like someone throwing a mechanical pencil at the wall.

41

WHEN EMMA GOT BACK TO THE GREAT ROOM, MAGGIE Trenwith was nowhere to be seen. Perhaps half a dozen other guests were scattered around the place, talking uneasily to one another or texting on their phones. Pearl stood near the front door talking with a young couple in hiking shorts and boots.

"I'm so sorry, but one of the other guests has had an accident," she was saying. "The ambulance has been, and the police are just doing some follow-up. They've asked us to have all guests wait in the public room for now. They assure me that everyone will be able to return to their rooms within an hour. We are terribly sorry for the inconvenience. Can I get you something? Tea or coffee? Or something stronger, maybe?" She gestured to the bar that had been set up with a full drinks station.

Emma also saw that the French doors to the garden had been opened. Genny was outside lighting candles on the tables, setting up an inviting atmosphere so people who were shut out of their rooms could still have a place to relax.

Oliver and—oh, thank heavens—Percy followed hopefully at her heels, in case she dropped anything interesting.

Which gave Emma an idea. She hurried out to Genny.

"Genny? Can you keep an eye on the boys for me for a minute?"

"Yeah, sure," she answered softly. "At least until it's my turn in the barrel. How did our DCI Brent seem tonight?"

"Shaken, like the rest of us."

"Too right." Genny blew out her match. "Poor Angelique."

"Where is she?"

"On the radio. Daniel's out on the boat, and I'm sure she's trying to persuade him she's fine, she's got Pearl right here with her, and he doesn't need to abandon his campers and come back right this instant. In the meantime," Genny said, sighing, "she's got a whole set of worried and increasingly annoyed guests out here."

"Yeah, I was thinking I could help with that. I'm going to the kitchen."

"Good luck."

The guests Pearl had been talking to were helping themselves at the coffee bar. Pearl herself was heading toward the passage to the kitchen and offices. Emma caught up with her.

"Hullo, Pearl. All right?" she asked softly

"It's holding together anyway," Pearl murmured. "Do you need something? Only I want to check on Mum."

"No, I'm fine. I thought maybe I could help. Maybe throw together some snacks for the guests while they wait? Angelique let me use the kitchen the other day, so I kind of know my way around."

Pearl chuckled. "Timing is everything."

"Sorry?" Emma blinked.

Pearl huffed out a sigh and glanced toward the back room. "I *was* going to ask you about putting together a plan for you to come in maybe once or twice a week and do cream teas for us, and as part of the deal, you'd have access to the kitchen for your baking for the Towne Fryer."

Emma stared, stunned. It was a great idea. A fantastic one, in fact. It solved all sorts of problems and would provide multiple opportunities for getting her established in Trevena even while she was working on the storefront. Of course, there would be a lot of details to sort out, especially . . .

Especially now that we've got not one murder in town, but two.

"Um. Well. Thank you, Pearl. It really does sound like a great idea. We'll talk later?"

"Hope so," agreed Pearl blandly. "I'll go check on Mum and come help you in the kitchen, all right?"

They split up, and Emma hurried to the kitchen.

The King's Rest kitchen boasted the biggest stand-alone refrigerator Emma had ever seen. She pulled out bags of carrots, peppers and celery. She could slice these up quickly to make a snack tray. There were some wheels and blocks of cheese too, which would be good to make into cubes, and . . .

And then she spotted a container of shredded Parmesan cheese.

"Even better!" Emma pulled it out and turned the oven on high. She found a sheet pan and a silicon liner, and started putting down generous heaps of the fragrant cheese. Just a few minutes in a hot oven, and the cheese would melt and crisp up into tasty little crackers called "frico."

But even as she felt the familiar calm that slicing and baking and arranging brought, Emma couldn't help wondering what Constance was doing upstairs, and what she was thinking.

What could have happened to Parker? Did Maggie find out he suspected she killed Victoria? What if Maggie really *had* killed Victoria, and Parker had proof? Maybe he'd written it into his manuscript, and she stole it after she killed him? Maybe that scene in front of Constance was to throw off suspicion?

Or was Maggie just *afraid* of what Parker was writing, and she had come back to try to get hold of it before the police did?

Or maybe it was Jimmy. Maybe he had killed his aunt, accidentally or on purpose, and Parker found out, and in a panic, Jimmy killed him.

Or maybe Louise. Emma's hands shook. No one thought about Louise, but she had been out and about tonight too. Maybe she'd had enough of Victoria's bullying and manipulation. Maybe Parker had cornered her with . . . something . . . and *she'd* panicked.

Or maybe Parker had killed Victoria because she was going to ruin his chance at a comeback, and Jimmy had killed Parker for revenge.

Way, way too many maybes. Emma sighed and tried to focus on the solid facts of cheese and bread.

In just a few minutes, Emma had a platter of sliced veg and another of baguette rounds with crocks of butter and jam. She was just pulling the first tray of frico out of the oven when Angelique came into the kitchen.

"Oh, Emma, Pearl said you were in here. This all looks wonderful!"

"I just wanted to do something to help." She stripped the oven mitts off her hands. "Angelique, I'm so sorry about this."

"It's hardly your fault." Angelique shook her head. She looked tired and worried, and Emma could hardly blame her. "I knew that man was making trouble for himself, but I never imagined there would be anything like this."

"What did Daniel say?"

Angelique smiled. "He wants to be here, of course, but I told him to stay with his tourists. He listened, eventually."

Emma pulled a spatula out of the utensil drawer and started loosening the frico from the pan. Angelique opened the overhead cupboard and brought down another serving platter.

"Angelique?" said Emma, laying the frico out in a neat circle. "Can I say something that is going to sound absolutely horrible?"

"I expect you can." Angelique went to the fridge and pulled out some large bottles of mineral water. "But I don't mind hearing it. I don't think." She was trying to joke and mostly succeeding.

"I'm just thinking about how badly Parker's room was turned over."

"Looked like there was a fight, didn't it?" Angelique set the bottles on the counter. "I know what you're going to say, and I expect our good detective is going to ask the same question. How come nobody heard anything?"

"Yeah." The fact that Angelique was expecting the question didn't make Emma feel any better about asking it.

"If it had happened in the evening, or first thing in the morning, everybody and their uncle would have heard. But the middle of the day?" She shrugged and spread her hands to take in the whole of the B&B. "This place is usually deserted. The guests are all gone. The girls we have in to do the rooms usually have earbuds in while they're cleaning, and they leave straight after they're done. Pearl was out at Wolsted Farm picking up some provisions, and today was laundry day, so I was in the utility room for most of the morning. You couldn't hear a bomb go off when the machines are running. Now," she said. "My turn."

Emma laid the last frico on the platter. "What?"

"What did Maggie Trenwith want with DCI Brent? She ran through here like something was on fire."

Emma realized she probably shouldn't be talking about what she'd heard, but despite her promise to Constance, she didn't have it in her to keep secrets from Angelique right now.

"Maggie'd heard from . . . somewhere that Parker was dead, and she wanted to know what happened to his book."

"His book?" echoed Angelique. "That would still be in the room."

"Except I don't think it was," Emma said. "Last time I was in there, it was a stack of pages on the desk. I didn't see it when we were in there . . . just now."

Angelique frowned. "Now that you mention it, I didn't either. Maybe he finished it and mailed it to his publisher already." Angelique's eyes narrowed as she took in Emma's expression. "But you don't think so?"

"I don't know," said Emma. "I mean, it's possible. But I think he was still working on it."

"What makes you think that?"

"Because he was trying to find out more about the Nick Penhallow disappearance."

Angelique rolled her eyes, clearly appealing to Heaven for patience. "Oh, good lord. Not that again. That thing. I hope he didn't tell Maggie that's what he was after."

"*Really?*" Emma choked on nothing but air. "But, I mean . . . I'd heard that Maggie was *encouraging* Parker to write about the murder."

"Well, Maggie might have been," said Angelique. "But I can tell you for a fact, her developer was not happy about it. Shelly Lucas's brother, William, is on the council, and he says the fellow's been getting cold feet, looking for an excuse to pull out, maybe take his deal to a bigger town. Maggie's been working overtime trying to convince him that Trevena is on the cusp of a huge comeback. Knowing Maggie, she's maybe been a bit generous with her estimations."

"Yeah, because estate agents never do that."

"No, indeed they do not," agreed Angelique with a perfectly straight face. "But from what I hear, this sad business with Victoria was starting to make the man nervous enough."

Having some drinks with a developer, Maggie had said when Emma asked where she'd been. *He had some concerns and I had to head them off at the pass.*

"So maybe she got the message that if there was some kind of tell-all about murder in our lovely, scenic village . . ."

"The developer might just head for the hills?" suggested Emma.

"He might, at that," agreed Angelique. "Which would not be good for Trevena—or at least it would not be good for Maggie Trenwith."

42

IT WAS PEARL WHO DROVE EMMA BACK HOME.

It was astonishing to Emma how quickly she'd come to thinking of Nancarrow as home, but the thought, and the feeling, were very real.

Since it was home, Emma had no problem accommodating a guest.

Percy, well supervised by Oliver, scampered all around the front room, snuffling every corner and baseboard and, knowing the Yorkie, probably looking for all the exits.

"Can you take him?" Angelique had asked as Emma got ready to leave. "Genny would, but she's got her setter, Derry, and he's not always good at sharing his space."

"Yes, of course. I'd be glad to."

Emma meant it too. Of course, she couldn't exactly tell anybody the real reason she was glad. Her new friends and neighbors were broad-minded people, but she was not about to tell them that as soon as she had a quiet moment, she planned to have her corgi interrogate the Yorkie about what had happened when the ex–tabloid writer got murdered.

Emma went into the kitchen and got out extra bowls for food and water for Percy, then watched both dogs dig in with gusto, despite the fact that they'd both had kibble and snacks at the King's Rest. She looked at the clock. It had already gone on ten. She was exhausted. She wanted nothing more than to crawl straight into bed.

But there were a couple of things that she had to do before she could collapse.

As she'd left the B&B, Emma had gotten Louise's phone number from Angelique.

"I just want to check on her," she had said. "She was looking worried when I ran into her. I want to make sure everything's okay."

"Except it isn't exactly," Angelique pointed out.

"Too right," agreed Emma.

Emma fished her phone out of her handbag, dialed Louise's number and waited while it rang.

"Hello, Louise? It's Emma Reed," she said as soon as Louise answered. "I hope I'm not calling too late."

"Oh, no, that's fine, Emma. I've never been the early-to-bed sort."

"I just wanted to make sure you were all right. I had Angelique give me your number. I hope that was okay."

"Oh, dear. Yes, yes. Fine. And I'm fine. Really. Thank you for calling. I had my lovely walk and a hot bath, and after a good night's rest, I'm sure I'll be ready to take on the the world."

"Oh, good. That's great." Even as she said it, Emma watched Percy resume his exploration of the front room, with Oliver's able assistance. The fact of Parker's death seemed to suddenly be sitting much more heavily on her than it had earlier when she had so many things to keep her busy.

"Are *you* all right, Emma?" asked Louise. "You don't sound very well."

"I'm not, actually. It's . . . turned out to be a long night."
I should just ring off, because this is getting awkward . . .

"I can't imagine there was any sort of problem when you took Mr. Taite's dog back?"

"Um, yes, there was."

"Emma." Louise spoke her name with a surprisingly stern note. "What's happened?"

Emma decided honesty was not only the best policy—it was her only available refuge. "It's not something I can talk about, Louise."

"Oh, dear."

"Louise?"

Louise's tone changed. Emma pictured her straightening her shoulders. "I think I have an idea what you can't talk about. Raj Patel has just pulled up in front of my flat."

"Oh."

"Can I ring you back?"

"Yes, yes, of course."

"And would you please make sure someone checks on Jimmy? In case I need to be a while?"

"Yes, yes, of course. Um, take care, Louise."

"Oh, I shall," Louise answered with tense cheerfulness. "Never fear."

Louise rang off. Emma put her phone down and stared at it for a while. Louise had sounded . . . resigned, as if she'd expected what was coming.

Oh, Louise. Emma felt her jaw tighten. She did not like not knowing what was really going on. She wanted to help. But what could she do?

"Emma?" Oliver trotted over, Percy trailing in his wake. "Are you okay, Emma?"

Emma stared at the dogs, who were both looking up with that particular expression of canine concern.

I can do something, Emma reminded herself. *I can question the witness.*

"All right, boys," she said briskly to both dogs. "Everybody in this house needs a good going-over. Oliver! Fetch the brush!"

Oliver, being a good dog, immediately went to the basket by the kitchen door and dug out his favorite brush. Percy, being, well, Percy, responded with a panicked yip and a very serious attempt to shove his entire tiny self under the couch.

"Oh, no, you don't." Emma grabbed the wriggly escape artist and sat on the floor with him in her lap. Oliver dropped the brush, and himself, next to them.

"Don't worry," he told the Yorkie. "Emma's really good at brushing."

"Thanks, Oliver." Emma gripped both terrier and brush firmly and got to work. "Good lord, you've got half of Cornwall tangled in here. And you've probably got the other half," she added to her corgi.

"But it was for a good cause?" Oliver suggested with a hopeful wag.

"This once I'm going to agree with you." She paused over a particularly twisted knot in the Yorkie's long brown fur. She might end up needing scissors. She wondered if Parker had even owned a dog comb. "Oliver, can you ask Percy about the times he and his human were at Victoria's house?"

"I'll try, Emma."

Emma had decided years ago that if she was going to own a dog she could talk to, she had a responsibility to try to understand him as best she could. So she'd gotten several books on dog nature and behavior. Among other things, she read that, unlike humans, who got most of their information through their eyes and their ears, dogs got most of their information about the world through their noses and their mouths. That meant Oliver's idea of a "conversation" with another dog was a very different, well, animal, than Emma's conversations with her fellow humans. The corgi got all up in Percy's face, literally. Oliver nosed at him and rubbed his cheeks and wagged and wriggled while he grumbled and whined. Percy yipped and wagged and growled in answer.

"Percy says they were boring. Percy says a lot of times his human would go out and leave him in the room, or he would tie him up outside the wall while he talked with Victoria."

"Wait. Stop. Parker *talked* to Victoria?" But Parker had told her Victoria shut the door in his face.

"He says they'd go in the evenings sometimes, and sometimes his human would come back smelling like stuff, strong stuff, not beer, the other stuff . . ."

"Scotch? Gin?"

"Scotch!" Oliver waggled his bum.

So, Parker had lied. Parker was visiting Victoria in the evenings, and she was giving him scotch. Possibly lots of scotch.

Why would he lie about that?

Because he didn't want anyone to know what he was telling her. Because he was supposed to be helping out Maggie, not Victoria.

Parker was playing both *sides?*

And lying about it?

Parker was after a story. No, Parker was after a sensation, something big enough to cement his comeback. Emma knew for a fact he was ready to use her, Emma, as a partner, and a smoke screen for his game. Why would she think he'd hesitate to play both sides with Maggie and Victoria?

"Does Percy know what they talked about?" Emma ran the brush briskly across Percy's neck.

Oliver growled and nipped gently. Percy yipped in return.

"Percy says it was boring and he remembers wanting to go home."

Emma sighed. *So much for the star witness.* "Okay, let's try this. What happened to Percy today? How did he get out onto the heath?"

"Percy says it was after they got back from here," Oliver informed her. "He was stuck in the room and he was bored. His human . . ."

"Parker?"

"Parker, he was sitting at his desk all afternoon, like you do sometimes." This last had the air of an accusation. Emma sighed.

"Yes, go on."

"Then the phone rang, and Parker talked for a while, and he went downstairs, and Percy went with him, and while he was talking to another human, Percy snuck out into the garden." Oliver bopped Percy with his muzzle. Probably this indicated deep corgi disapproval. The Yorkie grumbled back in defiance. "He says that was fun for a while. He found a—"

This Emma did not need to know. "Who was Parker talking to?"

"Percy says they smelled like coffee and anger, and like the shouty . . . Victoria."

"Oliver, I need to know their name."

More growling and snuffling. Oliver flopped backward. "This is hard," he said.

"I know." Emma rubbed his belly. "But I need you to try. It's important."

"Percy says the human smelled a lot like Victoria, like all those flowers."

Emma froze. "Like family?" *Like Jimmy?* "Or just like somebody who'd been in the house a lot?" *Like Louise?*

Oliver wriggled himself up across Emma's lap until he was nose to nose with Percy. The two of them huffed and protested, and Percy waggled his tiny bum.

"Family," said Oliver. Emma bit her lip. Victoria's only family was Jimmy. "So what happened then?"

"Percy says there's no way out of the breakfast lady's garden. He looked, hard, and he was kind of surprised when his human, Parker, didn't come get him, but he also got hungry and he went upstairs. He smelled all kinds of bad smells and he didn't want to go in the room. He went back downstairs and somebody was opening the front door, so he ran out, and he was outside until I found him."

Percy was down in the B&B's garden. Parker was in his room, talking to Jimmy. Percy was gone long enough to get tired and hungry and actually try to find his way back to Parker. And by then, Parker was dead.

Emma pressed the heel of her hand against her forehead like she was trying to hold it in place. *It doesn't mean Jimmy killed him. There might have been time for Jimmy to leave and for somebody else to arrive.*

For one searing, comic instant, Emma pictured herself

trying to take this revelation to Constance. *No, Detective, I'm trying to explain. I can't talk to Yorkies. I had to ask my corgi to translate* . . .

But what she did know was that Parker had been working with Maggie and then been drinking with Victoria. She also knew that the day he died, he met somebody, possibly multiple somebodies. And that meeting, or those meetings, had been so important, or distracting, that he hadn't bothered to go after Percy after Percy escaped yet again.

Then, he died.

43

IT TOOK ANOTHER HOUR TO FINISH BRUSHING BOTH DOGS and check their paws and fix up a bed for Percy next to Oliver's. By the end of it, Emma was barely able to keep her eyes open long enough to crawl into her own bed.

Emma woke late to a beautiful day. She reflexively rolled over to see how the boys were doing and found both of them snoring in Oliver's bed, with the corgi curled protectively around the restless Yorkie.

Grinning, she kicked back the covers, washed and dressed, opened all the cottage windows to let in the summertime, and then, of course, she let the dogs out.

This time, though, she remembered to keep a close eye on them to prevent jailbreaks. She also mentally added items to her list of tools and repairs she was going to need.

But first, breakfast.

"Cake is a breakfast item," she informed both dogs as she rummaged in the fridge. "Right?"

"Percy wants to know if cake has sausage," said Oliver.

"Tell Percy he needs some good food." Emma pulled out the quarter section of cake David and Charles had failed to eat the other day.

"Is cake good food?" asked Oliver.

"Touché," she muttered, and she also got out the muesli and the last of the ham.

Nothing had changed. Everything that had happened yesterday was still waiting out there, but for a moment, she had some breathing space. She could think and she could plan.

But plan for what? What more could she actually do?

"Percy wants to know if we're going on a walk," said Oliver. "I've told him you are a diligent walker."

"Well, we can't make you out to be a liar," said Emma.

And besides, that was something she could do. As Louise asked, she could check on Jimmy.

JIMMY WAS ALREADY OUT IN THE GARDEN WHEN EMMA AND the dogs reached the cottage. Despite the warmth of the day, he wore a long-sleeved shirt and gloves, and was currently engaged in trimming back the broken branches of the rosebushes with wickedly curved shears. He still hadn't shaved, and the young beard seemed to suit him. The sun and the work had brought some of the color back into his cheeks. In fact, he seemed more at ease than she had seen him yet.

That's got to be a good sign, right?

"Good morning, Jimmy!" she called as she reached the gate. "All right?"

"Just about," he said as he pulled a branch away from the bush and dropped it into the bin beside him.

"Mind if I come through?"

"Not if you don't mind if I keep working." He snipped off another branch and pulled it away. "I've left all this too long as it is."

"No, no, keep on. Erm, do you mind if the dogs . . ."

"Them? Ah, no, I'm sure they'll be fine."

"Thanks." Emma pushed open the garden gate. Both dogs, of course, raced through, eager to explore the previously forbidden territory. Emma stepped through more gingerly.

Jimmy wiped his sleeve across his forehead. The day was already warming up.

"Almost as good as a holiday, being out here." He waved his shears at the garden.

"I can see how you'd feel that way. It's all so beautiful." Emma breathed in the scents of roses and herbs. The inside of Victoria's house might be a little shabby, but her garden was a place of color and luxury.

"Emma!" Oliver barked. "Percy says there's something under the bush!"

"Well, tell Percy no digging!" Emma shot back without thinking.

Jimmy looked at her sideways.

"Sorry." She felt herself blush. "It's been just me and Oliver up at the cottage. I'm starting to treat him like he can really talk."

"You should hear me with the ramblers." Jimmy gestured to the great spray of red flowers that sprawled along the ancient wall.

Emma smiled, and Jimmy smiled, and somewhere under the roses, Percy barked and Oliver grumbled.

Not awkward at all, this. Emma took a deep breath. "Jimmy, have you heard from Louise this morning?"

The minute she asked the question, she regretted it. Jimmy's proud, contented expression drained away, and he turned back to the bush he was working on.

"Should I have?" He snipped off a dying blossom.

"I was just wondering, because we talked last night and she asked me to check in on you."

"What for?"

"The police were coming to ask her some questions."

Jimmy froze, shears pointed toward the sky. "What possible reason could the police have for hassling Louise? She's harmless!"

What do I tell you? Emma asked herself. *When in doubt, go for the truth,* she answered herself. Fortunately, there was a lot to choose from.

Emma made herself shrug. "Maybe because she's suddenly inherited all Victoria's property. Or"—she was tiptoe-ing up to the line of Constance's prohibition, and she knew it—"maybe because she might know something about old Nick Penhallow's disappearance from back in the day."

Jimmy's face tightened in sudden anger. "Oh, Christ! They cannot possibly be bringing that up again!" He stopped. "Well, why wouldn't they?" he muttered. "God knows Taite was."

"Parker was talking to your aunt about Nick Penhallow?"

"Wouldn't shut up about it," Jimmy snapped. "I can't believe she let him in the house. Normally, she shut any-body who mentioned it down before they could draw a sec-ond breath." He shrugged irritably. "Look, what's all this about?"

Emma selected another truth. Despite the legendary speed of the village gossip network, it was pretty clear Jimmy hadn't yet heard Parker was dead. "He's been trying to make something out of the Penhallow disappearance and your aunt's death for his book, and he was trying to get me to help him."

Jimmy pulled back, looking remarkably like Oliver did when he smelled something nasty. "Don't tell me you said yes."

"I'm sorry," said Emma. "It was a mistake. My only ex-cuse is that I wanted to help, and I thought that maybe I could find out what he was really up to."

Jimmy stared at her. Then he stared out across the lovely, fragrant space of roses that was his aunt's garden.

"Right." He shoved the shears, point down, into the bucket of tools. "Cuppa?"

"Ta."

Oliver slid out from under a rosebush. "Are we going, Emma?"

"Inside, boys!" she answered. "I've got treats."

"Hurray!" Oliver barked. "Percy! Treats!"

Jimmy took them all into the kitchen. Percy grumbled and whined about it and had to be gently herded inside by Oliver. Emma pulled out the packet of doggie treats she kept in her handbag and scattered a few by the kitchen door. Both dogs flopped down on the mat, crunching away happily, while Jimmy put the kettle on and pulled the box of tea bags down from the cupboard.

"Sorry to be bringing this all up again." Emma sat down at the kitchen table. Jimmy didn't turn around; he just got out the pot and the mugs.

"I just can't see what it'd have to do with her murder," he said. "I mean, she wasn't ever involved in the Penhallow disappearance. Not really."

"What did she tell you?"

"She only talked about it once. I don't even remember how it came up." The kettle whistled abruptly, and both dogs sat up, ears and noses at full attention.

Jimmy turned the fire down and poured the water into the pot.

"Anyway, what she told me was old Penhallow ran the bakery where the tea shop is—was. Louise worked for him and—"

"Louise did?"

"Yeah. Ruth got her the job, because they were friends."

"Oh, right. So what happened?"

"All Aunt Victoria ever said was that he was a right bastard and one day he disappeared. She reckoned he'd just run off and maybe had an accident, fell off the cliff or something. He drank, so you know . . ." Jimmy shrugged again and brought the tea things over to the table. "Anyway, when he didn't come home, people started asking questions."

"Including the police," Emma prompted.

Jimmy nodded. "Aunt Victoria was hauled all the way up to the station at Middlemore and questioned."

"Victoria was?" asked Emma, surprised. "Why?"

"She'd had some kind of row with Penhallow, and people blew it out of proportion, so they questioned her. But she'd spent the whole night with Ruth and Louise, and they both backed her up, so the police had to let her go."

"Gosh. It must have been hard for her after that."

"Oh, it was." Jimmy sat down. "People sort of . . . they turned their backs on her. At least, that's how it seemed to her. That was what started her, well, war with the rest of Trevena."

So, Angelique was right. Something bad had happened to Victoria Roberts, and she'd reacted to it by building herself a fortress of anger.

"Was that what you were talking to Parker about when you went to see him yesterday?"

Jimmy froze. "How did you know . . . ?"

"You were seen," said Emma quietly.

Jimmy swore and ran his hands through his hair. "Yeah, okay. I went to see him. Louise told me that he was getting set to make something big out of the old rumors. I tried to explain what had really happened. I didn't want her reputation to get trashed any worse, you know? Trying to make amends. Not that it helped. He just told me not to worry. Said Aunt Victoria would get exactly what she deserved and so would everybody else."

Which doesn't sound portentous at all. "Did you know he was working with Maggie Trenwith?"

His jaw hardened. "Turned out Aunt Victoria was right about her, didn't it? Only good there is it looks like her developer isn't too happy with this idea of a new tell-all. At least, that's what Louise said. Serves Maggie right too," he added bitterly.

The tea was ready and Jimmy poured. Percy shifted and curled up on Emma's lap.

"He's asleep," remarked Oliver, settling under her chair. "I didn't know terriers slept. They're too nervous. Are we going soon?"

Emma took a cautious sip of tea and tried to decide what she should say next. "Jimmy, what really happened between you and Maggie?"

"Look, Emma, you're nice and all. I like your dog. But that's not really something I feel like sharing, all right?"

Emma set her mug down and looked him in the eye. "Jimmy, you are going to have to tell somebody eventually.

Tell me and I can tell DCI Brent, and maybe she'll stop looking at you as a suspect in your aunt's murder."

Silence stretched out between them for a long time, and it didn't get any less awkward.

Part of her was aware that she should back off. This was none of her business. But it was so very obvious that Jimmy was hurting, and it was something more than his natural grief over Victoria's death.

Emma ruffled Percy's ears, and she thought about Victoria, and about Parker, and about her new home. She thought about the bitter note in Jimmy's voice.

She thought about Maggie realizing she'd made a ghastly mistake by encouraging Parker to write about Victoria and the Penhallow disappearance. She thought about Parker working both sides of the game.

She thought about Maggie giving Jimmy money. She thought about him coming home broke and staying in Trevena.

"Jimmy," said Emma finally. "What really happened with BlastSys?"

Jimmy watched the steam curling over his tea for a moment. "The CEO was a mate of mine from uni. He said if I came to work for them, I could take most of my salary in stock options. They let you do that kind of thing in America, you know? He said live off the credit cards for a few years, and then cash in big. Become one of those instant millionaires."

Emma sighed. "Oh, Jimmy. I'm sorry."

"Well, he was developing the next big thing, wasn't he? One of those mobile games? Nobody thinks about them, but they bring in millions every year." His jaw worked back and forth. "Anyway, he sets himself up in a massive office, hired all kinds of fancy developers and a big PR team, and threw all these parties and kind of never got around to finishing the game."

"Harsh."

"My own fekkin' fault, wasn't it? I knew he was a wanker

at heart." He turned his tea mug around. "So Jimmy comes home with his tail between his legs." Oliver perked up his ears. "No offense," he added to the corgi. Oliver decided now was the time to come over and give Jimmy a good tail waggle to see if he could get some attention. It worked, as it usually did. Jimmy scratched his ears. "And Aunt Victoria, she tried not to be mad. She really did. But, you know, she said she was going to change her will. Just in case she died before I got things squared away. That way, none of the properties could get confiscated for debts or taxes. If everything cleared after a few years, she'd change it back."

"So you knew?"

"I knew she was trying to protect me the only way she knew how. And she was trying to teach me how to run the properties, but . . . it became really clear that she was having a hard time trusting me."

"So if you were working for Victoria, why were you taking money from Maggie?"

Jimmy gave her a grim smile. "You mean why would Maggie Trenwith give a loan to a total loser?"

"You're not a loser."

"Don't be too sure about that." Jimmy leaned across the table. "See, I might not have told Aunt Victoria just how much I owed. Especially not after I found out she was so short on cash herself. I thought I could string things along, play for time. But I couldn't, and the phone calls started and . . ." He swallowed. "I knew I was running out of time. And, well, I went out and I had a few too many pints, and Maggie ran into me, and while she was helping me get cleaned up, I kind of told her what was going on with me.

"And she made me an offer I couldn't refuse."

Emma set her mug down carefully.

"I never would have done it if I didn't think the development was a good idea," he insisted. "Never. But Aunt Victoria had gotten so set in her ways, and she couldn't get over her grudges to see that maybe selling wasn't the same as giving in." He paused, and when he did speak again, his voice shook. "Only I messed it all up, didn't I? Aunt Victoria found out I was getting money from somewhere. I should have known she would." He choked. "She thought it was the developer paying me off."

I never thought I'd see the day when you'd be so ungrateful.

"She thought Louise was in on it too. I *tried* to explain, but she wouldn't listen. She said she was going to change her will again, leave everything to the government land trust. We could all go to hell." For a minute, Emma thought he was going to be sick. "After everything she did for me, the last thing I did for her is make her think she's lost her only friend." He propped his elbows up on the table and shoved his fingers into his hair. "I don't know how I got this messed up. I really don't."

Oliver, sensing Jimmy's distress, put his paws up on the young man's knee. "It'll be okay."

Jimmy rubbed the corgi's ears. "Good boy."

"Is he really sorry?" murmured Emma.

Oliver sniffed all around Jimmy's shoe tops. "He really is."

"The dog always knows, eh?" Jimmy actually chuckled.

"That's what he says," said Emma. "The jury's still out on the question though."

They sat in silence again, drinking their tea. The silence was a little less strained this time, but Emma's thoughts were spinning. So, Jimmy came home from the states, in debt and defeated. Victoria changed her will to protect him and tried to help get him back on his feet. But he was lying to her and taking money to pay his debts from Maggie. Maggie, at the same time, was working with Parker to destroy Victoria's reputation.

And Jimmy found out.

So what if there are two murderers after all? What if Maggie killed Victoria to get her out of the way for the development. And Jimmy killed Parker because he was going to destroy Victoria all over again?

Oh, Jimmy . . .

Jimmy drained his tea mug and set it down again. He leaned forward, mouth open.

He never got the chance to speak. A firm knock sounded on the front door. Percy jerked awake, tumbled off Emma's lap and came up barking, which set Oliver off as well.

Jimmy frowned and got to his feet.

"Half a mo'!" he called as the knocking started up again.

Emma tried to hush the dogs. She also got to her feet so she could see down the hall as Jimmy opened the door.

On the other side stood Raj Patel in his blue uniform. Constance waited a bit behind him on the garden path.

Emma felt herself go cold. Oliver pressed instinctively against her shins. Even Percy failed to charge the door.

"Raj," croaked Jimmy. "Good to see you, mate."

Raj just shook his head. "I'm so sorry about this, Jim."

"Sorry about . . . ?"

Raj cleared his throat. "James Robert Lambert, I am arresting you on suspicion of the murders of Victoria Roberts and Parker Taite . . ."

"What!" shouted Jimmy. "No! I . . ." He choked. "Taite's *dead*?" He turned to stare at Emma. She tried to look surprised, and failed. Jimmy's face twisted up into a mask of anger and disappointment.

Raj plunged ahead with the caution, liked he hoped it would hurt less if he just blurted it out. "You do not have to say anything. But, it may harm your defense if you do not mention when questioned something which you later rely on in court. Anything you do say may be given in evidence."

"Don't say anything, Jimmy," called Emma.

Raj's hand closed around his friend's arm. "You've got to come with me now, mate."

Jimmy was too stunned to resist as Raj tugged him forward. Jimmy staggered down the garden path.

Emma's power of motion returned in a rush.

"Detective!" She ran down the hall, dogs barking and galloping behind her, and out onto the garden path. Constance turned, putting herself squarely between Emma and her constable and Jimmy. "You can't be serious!"

Constance didn't even blink. "Constable Patel," she said crisply. "You have charge of the prisoner. I am going to have a little word with our Ms. Reed."

44

....

IT FELT COMPLETELY INCONGRUOUS TO BE FACING DOWN
a police detective in the middle of a rose-filled garden, but
Emma could not let herself stop and think about it.

"Detective, you have to listen to me," she said. "Jimmy
did not kill Parker Taite. He didn't even know the man was
dead."

Constance raised both brows. "And you know this
because . . . ?"

"Because I've been talking to him for the better part of
an hour, about Parker Taite." *And a few other things.* "Nobody's poker face is that good."

"So, let me ask you this, Ms. Reed." Constance folded
her arms. "Just why were you talking to Mr. Lambert about
Mr. Taite?"

Emma opened her mouth and closed it again. "You told
me I should keep talking to people," she said lamely.

"Yes, I did, didn't I?" Constance was clearly now questioning whether this had ever been a good idea.

That, of course, was when Emma's phone rang.

"Erm." Emma fumbled with her handbag. "Just a second."

"No, no, you go ahead and take that. I'll wait." Constance crouched down and held out her hands for the dogs. "Here, boys!"

Percy and Oliver came over to sniff and, not coincidently, get their ears scratched. Emma watched them snuffling around the detective with decidedly mixed feelings.

"Yeah?" she said into the phone.

"Emma?" It was Genny. "I'm at the chip shop. Is everything okay? Do you need anything?"

"Yeah, no. Just not the best time. Can I ring you back?"

Percy circled the detective, sniffing her ankles and yipping. Oliver just rolled over for a belly rub.

Fickle corgi.

"Only I saw Jimmy being driven off with Raj in the police car . . ." Genny was saying.

"Yes, that's right."

"It's bad, isn't it?"

"You could say that, yeah. But I will ring, I promise." Constance was laughing and giving Oliver his rub. Percy responded by going up on his hind legs and barking for attention. It was competitive cuteness at its very worst, and it left Emma feeling stubbornly gloomy. Just now she did not want the detective to be one of the good guys.

Because that would make it easier to believe she was right about Jimmy.

"I've got Martin and Becca at the shop," Genny told her. "I was heading down to the King's Rest to see Angelique. You will come straight over and meet me there when you're done."

"Yes. Promise. Absolutely. Tatty-byes!" Emma rang off and stuffed her phone back into her handbag. "Sorry, Detective. You were saying?"

Constance straightened up so she could look Emma in the eye. Oliver and Percy both whined a little at the sudden shift of attention.

"She's a good lady," barked Oliver. "Did you know she has dogs? Two of them. I think they're mutts. And she's got treats in that bag."

"Sorry, boys." The detective smiled down at them. "Business first."

"Constance," said Emma. "I know the situation does not look good. And I know Jimmy was having money trouble, and I know he was taking money from Maggie, and I know that Victoria found out and that she was threatening to change her will . . ."

"Again," said Constance calmly.

"And I know that all looks very bad, but he didn't do it. Jimmy loved his aunt. He just wanted her to be proud of him."

Constance sighed. "Let me show you something, Emma."

Constance started around the corner of the cottage, following the flagstone path to the back garden.

Emma followed, her brain swimming with worry and confusion. It suddenly felt like very small comfort to see Oliver and Percy playing in Victoria's magnificent back garden, peacefully chasing after the honeybees and investigating fallen rose petals.

"This whole case has been one for the books." A combination of frustration and something that sounded a lot like admiration underscored the words. "For a while there, we weren't even sure how Victoria was killed."

"She was poisoned . . ."

"But how did the poisoner get to her? That was the question. Now." Constance picked her way carefully through the kitchen garden's rows of tomatoes and runner beans. "We found some footprints that tell us our murderer stood about . . . here." She stopped and held up her thumb, like an artist taking a sighting on their subject.

"It's an interesting spot, because you can *just* see into the kitchen, but with the beans and all, you're mostly screened away from anybody casually going about their business inside." She lowered her thumb and stood gazing at the window, clearly painting her own kind of pictures in her mind. "It speaks to a certain familiarity with the house and the gardens. It also tells us our murderer has already decided on their method. They just need their opportunity. But they weren't leaving things to chance. At some point—perhaps when they observed Ms. Roberts putting the kettle on—they made a call from a disposable mobile to her landline. Phone records," she added, before Emma could ask how she knew. "Which means they had to have her number ready, which, again, speaks to both familiarity and planning.

"So, when Ms. Roberts left the kitchen to answer the phone, the murderer came in through the unlocked kitchen door and administered the poison, probably by pouring it straight into the water in the kettle."

"So Victoria poured poison water into her tea and drank it," breathed Emma.

"While the murderer walked calmly out the back gate and around to the high street. We think, anyway. We lose the trail in the muck."

"I could loan you Oliver," Emma murmured.

"Thank you," replied Constance, her voice bland and polite. "But I don't think that will be necessary at this time."

"So let me get this straight. You think Jimmy killed his aunt . . . why?"

"Because he was young and in over his head, and he couldn't see a way out anymore. Because she'd threatened to turf him out altogether when she found out he was working with Maggie Trenwith."

"But if that's true . . . why would he kill Parker?"

"Because Parker knew he'd killed Victoria. The man was a reporter. A slimy one, but not a sloppy one."

"But . . . what about Maggie Trenwith?"

"She was working with Parker on the book."

"But she found out her developer was getting cold feet, and the murder and the possibility of a tell-all were only making it worse. What if she tried to get Parker to rewrite the book, or hold off on publishing it altogether, and he wouldn't? Or!" she added before Constance could cut in. "What if Parker killed Victoria because she was going to threaten a libel suit? He'd gotten in trouble that way before. And then Maggie killed him because of the book and—"

"Emma," said Constance firmly. "I need you to focus here. It is a sad truth that when things like this happen, it's usually a family member. The rest is . . . fog of life." She touched Emma's arm. "I understand that you like Jimmy. *I* like him. But that doesn't change facts. And when you've had a chance to think about it, you'll remember that he needs to face up to what he's done."

Emma met Constance's gaze, pleading for her to relent, just a little. Constance's expression didn't shift at all.

"I understand," Emma said.

Constance smiled, but there was uncertainty in the expression. "In light of what we've said here, is there anything else you can tell me?"

Emma dredged up the expressionless mask she used for business meetings, and she did not speak until she was absolutely sure she had her voice under control.

"No, Detective," she said. "Nothing I can think of."

"Well, then, I'll just say thank you for your time." Constance's tone was just as casually bland as Emma's, and her face just as expressionless. "Without public cooperation we cannot do our jobs."

"I'm glad I could help you."

"And since you have been so very cooperative, I'm going to give you an added extra. Just in case you think we haven't been as thorough as we should. We have examined the case file on the Penhallow disappearance, and our experts agree with the conclusion of the police at the time—Nick Penhallow did a runner to get out of an unhappy domestic situation."

"Can I ask why?"

"No body."

"Nobody what?"

Constance stared blankly at her for a moment, and then, to Emma's surprise, she laughed. "No, Ms. Reed. Not 'nobody.' No *body*. It's been forty years and no body was ever found. People simply do not realize how difficult it is to actually dispose of a corpse, especially in a small town."

"I'd heard they maybe threw it off the cliffs . . . ?"

Constance shook her head. "Not a chance. I've read the file from the time." Emma must have looked surprised, because Constance rolled her eyes. "Yes, Emma, we poor plodders did look into it. They watched the shore. No body matching Penhallow's description came up anywhere within a hundred miles of Trevena."

"I'd also heard they were remodeling, and the floor—"

Constance cut her off. "First place the boys looked at the time. They dug up the whole place, much to the landlord Arthur Cleary's annoyance."

"The ovens?" she tried.

"Ah! I wondered when we'd get there. I'm afraid the burnt-to-ash theory makes for a dramatic story, but unfortunately, it's not possible. To completely carbonize a human body, your heat source needs to be a minimum of seven hundred and sixty degrees centigrade. Even a modern baker's oven is only capable of reaching two sixty or two seventy. A point I made sure to have PC Patel verify," she added. "Just in case."

"Oh."

Brent glanced at her watch. "Now, I'm afraid I have to get back to the station. Take care of yourself, Ms. Reed."

EMMA SAID GOODBYE TO THE DETECTIVE. CONSTANCE LEFT via the garden path, but Emma stayed where she was, among the roses, the bees and the beans.

"Emma?" Oliver gave her a gentle push with his muzzle. "You okay, Emma?"

"No. I'm not."

Because I don't want it to be Jimmy who did this. I don't want it to be anybody.

But it was somebody. Somebody, maybe two somebodies, had murdered Victoria and Parker. If she really didn't think it was Jimmy, then who could it be?

Emma squared her shoulders and started for the front of the house.

"Where are we going, Emma?" asked Oliver as he fell into step beside her.

"We're finding out what really happened to Victoria and Parker."

"Will there be walks?" Oliver wanted to know.

"Yes. Lots of walks."

"Oh, good. Where to?"

"The King's Rest."

"Hurray!" Oliver bounced happily. "Sausages!"

45

IT WAS A BUSY DAY IN TREVENA. THE STREETS WERE FULL of hikers and day-trippers. Kids raced back and forth up the cobbled streets. Half the people seemed to be traveling with dogs, all of whom wanted to come say hello to Oliver and Percy.

Everybody was having a good time and enjoying their summer day. Emma wished she could feel like part of it, but she had too many questions ringing around her head.

And if I think I'm having a tough time, what about poor Jimmy?

Because as much as Emma might hate to admit it, Constance had some quite good reasons to suspect Jimmy of killing both his aunt and Parker Taite. Money. Family arguments. Lies. A young man's devastated pride.

Heaven knows I've seen enough of what that can do. Especially when money's involved, she thought glumly.

And this whole time, there was Parker Taite looking for something he could use to turn his book into a bestseller. If it was possible for Parker to have suspected Maggie, it was equally possible he had suspected Jimmy. After all, Emma had been going back and forth between the two of them for days.

Jimmy could have gone to his room to steal the manuscript. Parker could have surprised him, and Jimmy could
have killed him in the fight.

Could have. Maybe.

But what Emma knew for certain was that Maggie Trenwith had a definite reason for trying to stop Parker from
publishing, never mind that she was responsible for at least
some of what was in that book in the first place. That might
even have increased Maggie's desperation, because when
people saw their carefully laid plans come crashing down,
they did get very desperate.

Which made Maggie very much worth talking to.

"Emma?" Oliver poked at her calf with his nose.
"Emma, this isn't the way to the sausages."

"Sorry, we've got one stop to make first. Although she
might not be in," she added, mostly to herself.

"Oh." Oliver's ears drooped. "Are we going to see the
cat? She was actually helpful, for a cat."

They were passing Vintage Style. Through the window,
Emma saw David standing beside his gilt-trimmed dining
set, talking to a well-dressed silver haired couple. He spotted her and waved through the window. Emma waved back
and silently wished him luck.

"Emma . . ." began Oliver.

But he didn't have to finish. Emma heard the raised
voices coming through the door.

Maggie Trenwith was in her office after all, and she was
arguing with somebody.

Emma didn't even bother to think about how eavesdropping was rude, or ill-advised at this time. She just scooped
up Percy, opened the door as softly as possible and tiptoed
into the reception area.

"It is your fault he's in this position at all and—"

Louise. Louise was in Maggie's office, and from the
sound of things, the meeting was not going well.

"My fault!" Maggie shouted back. "It's Victoria's fault
for trying to use everybody to keep control over this village, and your fault for not standing up to her!"

"You have no idea what you're talking about!" Emma could hear the tears in Louise's voice.

"Yeah, well, I could say the same about you."

The next thing Emma knew, the office door flew open and Louise ran out, a handkerchief pressed against her face.

"Louise," said Emma, but Louise just shook her head hard and dodged past her.

"Louise, please wait!" exclaimed Emma. "It's Jimmy!"

Louise stopped just before she reached the door and pivoted. Maggie stormed down the hallway.

"What's going on?" she demanded.

"Jimmy's been arrested," she told them both. "For murder."

Louise went dead white. For a moment Emma thought she was going to faint. Maggie pushed past Emma, took Louise by both shoulders and steered her to the couch.

"Sit," she ordered. Then she straightened and faced Emma. "Say it again. What's happened and how do you know?"

"I was there," she said. "I was talking with Jimmy when the police came. He's been arrested for Parker's murder." She swallowed. "And Victoria's."

"That's impossible," said Louise, her voice soft but remarkably steady. "Jimmy is innocent." She looked pleadingly at Maggie. "You know he is."

But Maggie's face was grim, and she didn't answer, not directly. "Wait here. I'm getting my handbag. I'll drive you out to the station."

"Oh, no," said Louise. "I can—"

"No, you can't," snapped Maggie. "Sit there. I'll be back in a tick." She glared at Emma. "You can wait too."

"Of course."

Maggie marched down the hall toward her office, and Emma turned to sit by Louise. Percy wriggled and yipped. Louise didn't even notice. She just sat staring at her hands.

Emma put the terrier down, trusting Oliver to keep an eye on him. She laid her hand over Louise's.

"I'm sure it'll be okay," she said. "If he didn't do anything . . ."

"Yes, of course," said Louise. "And he didn't. He's done some very wrong things, but not that." She shook her head slowly. "Not that."

"Well, you can tell the police what you know."

"Yes." Louise looked up and watched Maggie coming down the hall. "Yes. I can do that much."

Louise stood. Her color had returned. In fact, if anything, she looked a little flushed.

"Ready?" said Maggie briskly. She put her hand under Louise's elbow and helped her to stand.

"I am perfectly fine, thank you." Louise shook her off. "I would rather you didn't fuss."

"I'm just trying to help, Louise," said Maggie. "That's all I've ever done."

The women stared at each other, the tension so thick in the air between them that even the restless dogs went quite still.

"Yes," said Louise finally. "That's all either of us has ever done, and now look where we are."

Louise turned and walked out into the street.

46

WHEN EMMA REACHED THE KING'S REST, SHE FOUND PEARL and Daniel working the front desk.

"Things are settling down," Pearl reported. "We've only had one cancellation, so that's a good sign."

"All due to our girl's hard work," put in Daniel. He was a tall man with midnight-dark skin and the kind of build that came from a life of working boats and leading hiking parties. He was dressed in a plain work shirt and trousers. Like Angelique, his Cornish accent was blended with traces of Jamaican. "Pearl's been a one-woman charm offensive."

"Daaaad . . ." groaned Pearl with exaggerated daughterly outrage. "You're embarrassing me!"

Daniel just smiled and kissed his daughter's cheek. Pearl rolled her eyes and then said, "Oh, Emma, did you have a chance to think about doing the teas for us?"

"Erm, I think it's a great idea, but things have been a little bit busy just now," said Emma. "But I will call. All right?"

"Fantastic," she answered cheerfully. "I suppose you're looking for Mum and Genny. They're in the garden."

"With tea," added Daniel.

"Do the English do anything without tea?" asked Emma.

"Not where anyone can see them."

AS SOON AS EMMA AND THE DOGS WALKED OUT INTO THE back garden, Genny jumped to her feet.

"Emma! We've been worried about you!"

"I'm fine, I'm fine," Emma assured them both. "I'm not the one in trouble." *Yet.* "Have you heard anything more about Jimmy?"

"We were going to ask you the same thing," said Angelique. "Genny said DCI Brent was talking to you." She paused. "I hope you don't mind my saying, but you look awful."

Emma wasn't surprised, actually. She sat down at the table and shoved her hair back from her face with both hands.

Angelique pushed a cup of tea toward her. "What did Brent have to say?"

Emma shook her head and took a grateful swallow of tea. "She really does think Jimmy killed both Victoria and Parker. She says it's got nothing to do with the Penhallow disappearance. It's all about money and property in the here and now."

"Well, she could be right," said Angelique reluctantly. "The connection with Penhallow was always pretty tenuous."

Genny frowned. "Was it really, though? I mean, Parker was bothering the entire village about it. You know, I talked to Mrs. Shah at the library. She says he wouldn't stop bothering her about it, and she didn't even move to Trevena until ten years after Nick vanished."

"Have the police found the manuscript?" Angelique asked Emma. "That would be the biggest clue of all."

"DCI Brent didn't say, but from the way she didn't say it, I don't think so."

"So that's a no?" asked Genny.

"Yes, that's a no," said Angelique.

"It's a no," agreed Emma. "She doesn't even think Nick Penhallow died all those years ago."

"Why not?" Angelique asked, surprised. "Everybody else does."

"Because they never found a body. She says bodies are a lot harder to hide than people think."

"Well, I supposed she'd know," said Genny.

"And the ovens?" put in Angelique.

"She had some very technical details about how you can't actually cremate a human in a commercial bakery oven."

"I think I will ask that you please not share," said Angelique.

"I would be happy not to share." Emma took another swallow of tea. "But I cannot believe Jimmy killed Victoria. He loved her. I'd stake everything on that."

"If not Jimmy, then who?"

Jimmy is innocent. Louise's flat, firm statement rose up in Emma's mind. So did the pleading way she looked at Maggie when she said it. *You know he is.*

"I hate to say this," she told her friends. "But it keeps coming back round to Maggie. She's the one who got Parker digging into the Penhallow disappearance at all. She wanted to end Victoria's influence in Trevena."

Silence fell between them, thick and cold. Somewhere up among the flower beds, Oliver and Percy were barking and chasing each other. Right here, very unpleasant thoughts were rising with the scents of tea and summertime.

"Because Victoria won't sell, of course, because Victoria hates change." Emma stared out at the peaceful green hills, trying to put her jumble of thoughts together in a straight line. "And then Victoria becomes convinced that Jimmy is sneaking behind her back."

"Yeah, it'd be good to know what that was about," muttered Genny.

"Maggie was loaning him money."

"What!" Genny choked.

Angelique raised her eyebrows. "You have been a busy woman, Emma Reed."

"Yeah, well, I was motivated. Anyway, he was telling me about it when the police came. He'd run into debt while he was in the States, and he was taking money from Maggie to help pay it off."

Genny and Angelique were silent for a long time. Emma could not blame them.

It was Genny who broke the silence. "That is not going to look good when our DCI Brent finds out."

"No, indeed, it is not," said Angelique. "Do you think Victoria found out?"

"I do," said Emma. "I think she did it by chatting up Parker Taite."

"Okay." Genny rapped her knuckles against the table sharply. "I want to know where you got that idea."

"Parker was visiting her house, and she was feeding him drinks. He drank too much as it was. Probably she was getting information out of him."

"You can't believe Victoria would need to go to Parker Taite about anything happening with Jimmy," said Angelique. "Wouldn't she have just asked Louise?"

"Not if she thought Louise was taking Jimmy's side. Did Genny tell you about that argument we heard?" Angelique nodded. "So maybe she was already suspicious when Parker came poking around, and whatever he told her just confirmed it."

"I suppose that could be," said Angelique.

"Suppose this too," said Emma. "That Victoria was using Parker's interest in the Penhallow disappearance to get him talking. Jimmy said he couldn't understand why she was letting him into the house at all. But I think that's why."

"Right. So Victoria finds out about Jimmy and Maggie, and she moves in to sabotage the whole thing, and for Maggie, it's the final straw."

"So Maggie kills Victoria," said Angelique slowly. "And

it doesn't particularly matter to her who inherits. Whoever it is has got to be easier to deal with."

"But Parker Taite finds out and writes the proof into his book, or at least says he's going to. So, Maggie kills him too and takes the manuscript."

"We know she was out that night," added Angelique. "Do you remember which way she was going when you met her, Emma?"

"I do. She was coming from the village. I remember she said she was having drinks with the developer, and her tea was waiting." She looked down into her own empty mug. "That scene with DCI Brent could have been all for show, to make it look like she had no idea what was happening."

"So she steals the manuscript and does what with it?" asked Genny.

"Destroys it as quick as she can, if she's smart," said Emma flatly.

"All very neat and aboveboard. So why isn't DCI Brent arresting Maggie?"

"Maybe Maggie has an alibi for one death or the other."

"Do you know," said Angelique, "there's nothing that says the same person had to kill both Victoria and Parker."

"I keep thinking about that," Emma told them. "I mean, what if it went like this?" she said. "Victoria hears that Parker got hold of the old story that Nick Penhallow was murdered. She worries it might make life difficult for her—"

"Or for Ruth and Louise," put in Angelique. "Victoria was protective, even if she wasn't nice about it."

Emma nodded. "She decides she needs to find out what he's up to, so she pretends she's ready to talk about Nick Penhallow. He drinks, so maybe she starts pouring the whiskey into him."

"She finds out what he knows, and also finds out who he is. She threatens to bring his past back up . . ." added Angelique.

"Or call down a libel suit," said Genny.

"Or just call in a favor from a friend to interfere with the publication or something," Emma said slowly. "Some of those people at the funeral looked pretty upper-crust."

Angelique nodded. "I talked to a countess, and an actual Earl of Somewhere, and this Russian fellow who smelled very rich to me."

"You never know who's a rose fancier, do you?" murmured Genny.

Angelique nodded. "And instead of slinking away quietly, Parker decides to do something about it."

"And poison Victoria with her own flowers," murmured Emma.

"So that's done," Angelique went on. "And Parker thinks he's gotten away with it and can finish his book in peace. He throws out some red herrings—"

"By pretending he's hunting Victoria's killer," said Emma.

"Right, and by enlisting someone who's keen but a little inexperienced—"

"You mean me?"

"Sorry, Emma," said Angelique.

"No, no, go on."

"So he's laying a false trail. In the meantime, somebody else—"

"Maggie," said Genny.

"Or Louise," added Angelique.

"Or Jimmy," said Emma gloomily. "But somebody figures out Parker did it."

"Maybe because Parker dropped one too many hints about his upcoming bestseller," suggested Angelique. "Or got a little overenthusiastic at the pub."

"And that person shows up, planning to steal the manuscript, because they know that this place empties out during the afternoon," added Emma. "But they get their timing wrong. Parker confronts them, and they get in an actual fight, and Parker dies. The killer steals the book and skedaddles and that's where we come in. Literally."

"I can believe it." Genny wrapped her hands more tightly around her tea mug. "But the question is, how would we even start to prove it?"

"It all depends on who stole the manuscript," said Emma. "That's the person with the most to hide."

"So find the manuscript and we find the killer."

"But they'd have destroyed it right away, wouldn't they?" said Genny. "If they were smart. You just said so."

"Probably," said Emma.

"Definitely," said Angelique.

"Which puts us at a dead end." Genny looked into the teapot, which must have been empty, because she put the lid down with a sigh.

"Not that we'd know where to look anyway," Emma said. "I mean, if for some reason the killer didn't just toss it off the cliff right away, they'd still have a whole village to hide it in."

"Yeah." Genny sighed. "All right. So there goes the easy answer. I've only got one more question."

"Only one?" Emma raised her brows.

"What I want to know is"—Genny leaned across the table and looked Emma right in the eye—"did you really find Oliver while he was arguing with a moose?"

Angelique snarfed her mouthful of tea. She coughed and stared at Emma. "A moose? Where on earth did the little fellow find a moose?"

"Oh, that." Emma felt herself blush for no good reason. "Yeah. That did happen. I'd gone out to visit some of my mother's family in Canada, and they took me camping. Anyway, we were way out in the woods, and I . . . heard something strange." *A really tiny, high-pitched voice.* "I suppose I should have just ignored it. I'm not exactly an expert on woods noises, especially not in the Canadian bush, or whatever they call it, but I didn't." *Because it sounded like a lost child.* "I followed it and there was this little bundle of fur barking at this full-grown moose. I didn't know what to do. I just grabbed the puppy and I ran.

"Anyway, turned out I ran in exactly the wrong direction. By the time I stopped to catch my breath, I had no idea where the cabin or the trail was, or where I was.

"Well, the puppy knew. He got us right back to the cabin, and, well, that was how I got Oliver."

"But . . . how'd he get all the way out there?" asked Genny.

"I don't know," said Emma blandly. "He never told me."

"Speaking of which," said Angelique, "where is Oliver?"

47

OLIVER DID NOT ALWAYS UNDERSTAND WHAT EMMA WAS doing. Her human world was a large and mysterious place. It was filled with all kinds of wonderful things, but a lot of other things in it were simply bewildering.

What he did understand was that all the questions about the shouty Victoria and Percy's Parker were making Emma sad, and angry, and she wasn't going to feel any better until she got her answers. So he had to try to help.

While Percy charged through the flower beds and under the bushes and then bounced back to tell Oliver about all the interesting things he'd found, Oliver started snuffling around the stony garden paths.

Percy had said his human had met the other human out here. But there were so many smells overlapping and blending, Oliver was having difficulty sorting them all out. Percy's human had in fact been here, a lot, but so had every human Oliver had met since they came to this new place.

There was only one thing to do. Oliver was going to have to go up into the Room.

He didn't want to go. The smells in there got down into the back of his brain and made it difficult not to bark or run. But this was important. Emma was looking for answers, but she was doing it in her inefficient human way by talking to all her friends. She might get to the truth eventually, but it would take a lot longer than simply using his nose.

Emma and her friends were all drinking their tea. She'd be fine without him for just a little bit.

Oliver slipped quietly into the great room and headed for the stairs.

The big room where the sausages were was empty. Oliver resisted the urge to see if anything interesting (or tasty) had been left behind. He had an important job to do. A noble corgi warrior did not let himself get distracted when he was working.

He certainly did not hesitate at the bottom of the stairs because there was a bad smell. He was used to that smell. He knew that smell was getting old. The events that left those traces were over and done. It, and they, couldn't hurt him.

Oliver put one paw on the stair. The smells here were so strong, he was missing the most important one.

"What're you doing, Oliver?"

Percy's yip came out of nowhere. Oliver jumped and tried to spin at the same time and wound up toppled over on his back.

"You okay, Oliver?" the Yorkie whined, and wagged.

"I'm fine, I'm fine." Oliver scrambled to his feet. "You should be in the garden."

"So should you," the terrier laughed. "What are you doing in here?"

"Looking," answered Oliver sharply. To prove it, he pointed his muzzle up the stairs.

"Looking for what?" Percy started nosing around with him. "Sausages? I think those are over this way . . ."

But Oliver had already scrambled up the first step and had his front paws on the second.

"Where you going?" Percy barked. "Don't you want to play?"

Oliver pushed himself up the second stair, and the third.

"Oh, no," whined Percy. "I don't want to go up there."

"Then don't," puffed Oliver. Before, he'd had Emma to help him up these steep old stairs if he needed it. But he didn't want to bother Emma right now. She had been upset enough today. She didn't need to go back in with the bad smells. If he bent his back just like *this* and pushed just like *that*, he could do it. The next two stairs were easy, and the one after that.

"You're boring!" snapped Percy.

The terrier's nails clicked loudly on the floor as he retreated.

Oliver shoved himself up the next two stairs.

The truth was he couldn't blame Percy. The air was only getting worse with each step he climbed. He couldn't get away from the nasty, hurting, coppery smells. Oliver shuddered and whined. Every part of him wanted to run away.

But Oliver thought of Emma. She didn't want to come up here either, he was sure of that. He was her friend and protector. This was for him to do so she wouldn't have to.

All the doors in the hall were closed. The bad scent trail told him exactly which one he needed though. That, and the fact that some human had helpfully taped a big yellow X over it.

But they'd also shut it as firmly as every other door on the hallway.

Oliver growled, frustrated, and scrabbled at the door. To his surprise, the door shifted under his paws. He shook himself and backed away a little. He listened and he sniffed carefully. No humans were coming. He scrabbled at the door again. It drifted open a little farther.

He wanted to bark. He wanted to tell Percy he'd been right after all and the doors always did open, eventually. But he remembered at the last second he should keep quiet.

I can tell Percy later.

Oliver shoved his muzzle against the door so it opened to corgi width. Then he crouched down under the slanting stretch of tape and slipped inside.

Oliver suspected Emma would say the room was a mess. It wasn't the same mess as the last time he'd been in here.

Some things had been piled up, on the bed and on the desk. Other things had been taken away. Spiky Brent had been here, and Pale Jimmy and Office Maggie, and a bunch of other humans Oliver didn't know.

Oliver woofed and put his nose down. He had to find an answer—he had to. It was important. Emma wanted to know who had been in the room. Emma wanted to know about the papers and the books and the human things.

Oliver put his nose down and got to work. He zigged and he zagged around the room. He got under everything he could; he plunged into every corner. He snuffled at the piles of books that had been knocked over and scattered every which way. He stuck his nose into the turned-over desk drawers. He put his front paws up on the bed and sniffed at the covers that had been yanked half off. Then he crawled under the bed and found it surprisingly clean, especially compared to under the bed at home. He let the whole world of smells fill him up to the brim.

"Oliver!"

"Oh, crumbs." *Emma*.

48

· · · · · · · · · · · · ·

OF ALL THE THINGS EMMA HAD WANTED TO SEE WHEN SHE ran up the stairs, her corgi nosing about the middle of a crime scene was not on the list.

"Oliver!" she shouted. "What are you doing?"

"Helping," he answered with a hopeful waggle. "You wanted to know who took the papers."

Emma opened her mouth, and closed it. And swallowed.

"Yeah, right. Now I want you to come out of there. Right now." *Because somebody's already going to be in for it for not locking that door.* Emma hoped it wasn't Raj or Angelique. *It'll only be worse if our detective finds paw prints.*

Oliver, unconcerned with these little human details, trotted out and plopped down on his belly at her feet, paws over his nose. "Sorry, Emma."

Emma, suddenly very tired, slid down to sit next to him. "It's okay." She rubbed his ears and stared at the open door. *Well, as long as we're here . . .*

"So do you know who's been in the room?" she asked. "I mean, besides Parker and Percy?" *And you and me.*

Oliver's ears perked up and he raised his head. "Lots of humans," he said. Emma remembered to take a breath before she answered.

"What about Jimmy?"

Oliver cocked his head. He also scratched his ear vigorously. "No, he wasn't there."

Emma scooped up Oliver's front paws and lifted him up so they were eye level. "Oliver, this is important. Are you sure?"

"I'm certain and sure!"

Relief flooded Emma and she hugged her corgi tight. Oliver wriggled happily and licked her face. "Was that the right answer, Emma? Was that what you were looking for?"

"Yes, Oliver." She kissed the top of his head and scritched his ears. "That's exactly it."

"I did a good job?"

"Yes. Yes, you did."

"Oh, good. Um, Emma? What did I do?"

"You told me Jimmy, the pale man, couldn't have killed Percy's human." Because Parker had been killed in his room, and if Jimmy had never been in there, he couldn't possibly have killed Parker or stolen the manuscript.

"Is that a good thing?" Oliver asked her.

"Yes."

"Will there be sausage?"

She laughed and hugged him again. "Yes, Oliver. Lots and lots of sausage."

Emma looked over Oliver's head at the turned-over room. Her delighted relief drained away in the space of a couple of heartbeats. "Now, we just have to find a way to convince everybody else."

"You'll tell them!" Oliver dropped down and nosed at Emma's bum, as if trying to lift her bodily off the floor. "You'll go now."

"I wish it was that easy." Emma pulled her knees up to her chest, like she had when she was little and afraid. "Listen, Oliver . . . who else was in there? Do you know?"

"I told you," he huffed. "Lots of humans—the sausage lady, Spiky Brent, the man in blue, Office Maggie . . ."

Emma straightened up slowly. She stared into the room. It was as if she thought she'd miss something vital if she so much as blinked. A heavy, morbid anticipation rose up in her.

"Was Maggie in there recently? Like yesterday?"

"Her scent's fresh," said Oliver. He scratched his other ear and kicked his back leg out, like he did when he was particularly agitated. "Just not as fresh as the nervous lady."

That morbid anticipation froze, and shattered.

"Who?" Emma croaked. She'd just helped down a whole pot of tea, but right now, her throat had gone bone-dry.

"Nervous Louise," Oliver said patiently. "But it must have been before she had trouble with her chimney. She's having trouble with her chimneys, did you know that?"

"Emma?" Angelique's voice drifted up the stairs. "Did you find him?"

"Uh, yeah, yeah, I did. Everything's fine," she added. "I just . . . I'll be there in a tick."

She stared at Oliver. She was remembering something, something that had gotten lost in the whirlpool of events around Parker's death.

Chimneys. Oliver had said something about chimneys that night too.

"How do you know Louise is having trouble with her chimney?" Emma breathed.

"Emma?" called Genny. "What's going on?"

"One second!" she called brightly and then turned back to her dog. "Quick, Oliver. How did you know?"

"Because she smelled like the chimney did when that big black cloud came down."

"She smelled like smoke?"

"Yes, like that. Smoke."

"You're sure?"

Oliver sniffed indignantly "Corgis are never wrong."

Louise smelled like smoke when she found Oliver, but she didn't smell like smoke when she was in Parker's room. "Okay," Emma murmured. "Okay. That's good, Oliver. That's very good."

"You don't sound like you think it's good."

There were footsteps on the stairs. Emma didn't bother

to stand up. She wasn't sure she would have been able to just then anyway.

Angelique and Genny appeared on the staircase, and both hurried over to where she was sitting with Oliver.

"Are you okay?" Angelique crouched down so they were eye level.

"You didn't faint again, did you?" added Genny.

"No, no, I'm fine." Emma took the hand Angelique held out and let herself be heaved to her feet.

"Well, that's good," said Angelique. "Because, girl, you look like you've seen a ghost."

Genny eyed the taped-off door uneasily. "Um. You haven't, have you?"

"No, but . . ." Emma swallowed. How to explain? What could she possibly tell them? "You know how we've been saying that you can't burn a body in a baker's oven?"

"Yeeeessss . . ." said Genny slowly.

"Oh, Mary and Joseph," breathed Angelique. "I think I see what you're getting at."

" 'Scuse me!" Genny waved her hand like she was trying to get the teacher's attention. "Once more for the people in the balcony?"

"A baker's oven is a bad place to dispose of a body," said Emma. "But it'd be an amazingly good place to dispose of a stack of paper."

49

IT WAS DECIDED THEY SHOULD WAIT UNTIL TWILIGHT.

"I read it somewhere," said Genny. "People actually pay less attention to their surroundings at twilight than at full dark."

"And after all," murmured Emma, "I'd hate for my bit of breaking and entering to keep me up past bedtime."

It was further decided that Percy should stay at the King's Rest. The Yorkie protested vociferously, until Angelique pulled out some of the sausages leftover from breakfast, at which point Emma was not sure she'd be able to get Oliver out of the kitchen. Angelique, of course, said he'd be welcome to stay too, but Emma needed Oliver. She told her friends it was for protection, but the truth was, she needed to make certain of the suspicions boiling inside her, and for that, she needed Oliver's nose.

Genny, of course, offered to come along, but Emma asked her to stay and help Angelique taking charge of the phones, keeping tabs on the news and the gossip.

What she didn't say was that if they got caught breaking into Penhallows, she didn't want anyone else to get into trouble.

"Besides," she added, "you never know—the way things have gone, I might end up needing an alibi."

Perhaps she shouldn't have been so surprised that this was the argument that carried the day.

Regardless, at seven thirty, as the shadows from the hills stretched out across Trevena, Emma and Oliver left the King's Rest and headed up into the village.

"Act casual," Emma said to her dog.

"What's 'casual'?" asked Oliver. "Am I doing it right?"

I really hope so.

Around them, Trevena was settling down for the night. The streetlights were coming on, but the streets themselves were clearing out. The villagers were all going home to their tea, while the tourists were settling into their rooms after a long day of sunning and hiking. She and Oliver practically had the place to themselves.

That was good. It meant there was no one around to hear her heart thundering like the bass drum in a brass band.

Penhallows stood on the high street. This close up, Emma could see how dirty the windows had become. She peered inside, but she saw nothing but darkness. There wasn't even a light over the door.

Oliver sniffed around the doorjamb.

"Anything?" whispered Emma.

"The fox," he reported. "And cats, lots of cats, and dogs. There's a setter, and Percy, of course, and . . ."

"Okay," said Emma quickly. "Let's . . . try round the side."

The half-timbered building had less than a meter between itself and its neighbor. Oliver slid easily into the narrow space. Emma had to turn sideways.

But she did find what she was hoping for—a set of old windows, right at street level, looking into the basement space that should be the old kitchen.

Oliver was snuffling around all of them, of course. Inspiration struck suddenly. "Oliver," she whispered. "Are any of the windows loose?"

Oliver sniffed. He also pressed gingerly at the frames with his muzzle. "This one." He bopped up against the one dead center in the middle of the wall.

Emma knelt, carefully because of the small space, and because she didn't want a sudden movement to attract attention from anybody who might glance out a window or pass by on the street.

I cannot believe I'm actually doing this. A totally inappropriate sense of excitement threaded through her.

Emma's youthful obsession with the Gothic side of Cornwall had led her to attempt to acquire some of what her younger self was sure would be useful skills, just in case she was kidnapped by smugglers. In addition to getting Henry to tie her to a kitchen chair so she could practice wriggling out of the ropes—an exercise that got them both in trouble when their parents got home—she'd spent a couple of holidays trying to jimmy the window locks on their rented cottage.

She'd actually gotten pretty good at it. And, fortunately, the tool she'd used was not hard to come by.

Emma pulled a butter knife out of her handbag. She also pulled out a pair of latex food service gloves she'd borrowed from Angelique and snapped them on.

"Keep watch, Oliver," she whispered. She was in deep shadow, and unlike London, Trevena did not have closed-circuit TV on every corner. But as she slipped her knife into the crack between the window sashes, she felt like she might as well be dancing naked down the high street.

Oliver plopped down beside her, facing said high street, and panted softly. Emma grit her teeth. She wriggled the knife. She closed her eyes, concentrating, trying to call up the memories of her childhood. She had done this; she could do this; she would do this.

She couldn't.

She wouldn't.

Oliver whined. Emma's eyes flew open. She heard a car rumble past. Startled, her hands jerked.

Something clicked, then shifted.

Emma held her breath. She drew the knife back slowly,

and with one—very cold, very shaky hand—she dug her fingers under the sill and pushed.

Slowly, and with extreme reluctance, the window shifted upward, just a little. Emma dropped the knife and dug all her fingers into the space. She clenched her teeth, and she heaved.

The window shot up and banged against the top sill. Emma screeched and fell backward. She stayed there, heart hammering, until the thought hit her that if anyone did see her, they might snap a photo, and she'd be all over the Internet like this.

Emma straightened.

In front of her, the window was open.

"I did it!" she whispered triumphantly.

"Of course you did. You can do anything." Oliver nosed the knife toward her. "Don't forget your toy."

EMMA DID NOT FORGET HER TOY. NOR DID SHE FORGET TO turn around so she could ease herself through the window and drop feetfirst down the last half meter into the deserted kitchen. Oliver took a little persuading to follow her, but in the end, he slithered over the sill and let himself fall so she could catch him.

Emma also remembered to close the window. Then she took a deep breath and turned around to get her first proper look at Penhallows.

The kitchen was almost entirely dark. Only a little light trickled in from the outside. Emma stood where she was and let her eyes finish adjusting.

"Mice," announced Oliver, nosing the dirt-streaked tiles. "All kinds of mice and cats and the fox, Emma." He froze and growled low in his throat. "And *rats*."

Emma nodded slowly. The local kids had clearly been here as well. Graffiti covered the walls. There were gaps in the ceiling tiles, and in the floor tiles as well.

"Why didn't Victoria take better care of it?" Emma asked furiously. "Why'd she let it get like this?"

Because she was angry. Because she was sad. She couldn't stand one more change, one more loss. Not after everything. So she locked it up and decided not to look at it anymore.

Or maybe . . . Emma looked uneasily at the floor. Maybe there was another reason, despite what Constance said.

"Emma?" Oliver pressed against her shins. "Emma, I don't like it here."

"I don't either, Oliver," she murmured. "Come on, let's find the ovens. The chimney," she amended.

Oliver sniffed, and then he dropped his muzzle and started nosing around the floor. "Here, here, here," he muttered to himself as he trotted confidently into the darkest end of the kitchen. "They're here."

Emma moved forward more cautiously. *Do not think about bones buried under the floor,* she ordered herself. *There are no bones. There never were any bones.*

Which did not stop her from tiptoeing like she was walking over hot coals.

Emma saw Oliver's white patches before she saw the glimmer of light on the oven door. She stopped in front of it. Her toes curled and her arches tensed.

There are no bones under this floor.

"Oliver, do you smell smoke?"

"Of course I do," said Oliver. "This is the chimney. And here." He nudged a black sliver of debris on the floor. Emma knelt and cautiously picked it up in her gloved fingers. It was a burnt match, one of four scattered on the floor.

She set it back down carefully and straightened up.

The wall oven was an ancient cast-iron creation. Unlike an oven in a modern bakery, which would have a series of long, narrow slots, each just tall enough to admit a tray of bread, this had one door, doubtlessly opening onto a whole series of racks. But what Emma noticed most was that it was more than big enough to get a human body through.

Right before she left London, Emma had been to see a

revival of *Sweeney Todd*. Just now, she found herself rather wishing she hadn't.

She rested her gloved fingers on the oven door's handle. Oliver whined.

Emma gritted her teeth and pulled hard, like yanking off a Band-Aid all in one go.

That turned out to be a mistake.

A cloud of soot whirled out of the oven and straight into Emma's face. She reeled back, blind and coughing. Oliver barked.

"There! There! I told you!"

"Yes, Oliver." Emma coughed again and knuckled her eyes. "You did tell me."

When she got her stinging eyes cleared, she looked again. There was a huge heap of ashes in the bottom of the oven. Whatever had been burned, there had been a lot of it.

"Oh, lord," breathed Emma.

She stepped forward and peered inside the dark oven, wishing for the umpteenth time that she had a torch with her. But the light was good enough for her to see flashes of white in the black soot. She reached in and gently poked at one with her finger.

It was a scrap of paper. Emma shivered.

"Oliver," she breathed. "Was the nervous lady here?"

Oliver nosed around. It took him all of three seconds. "Yes. Right here. You're standing on her."

Oh, Louise. "Nobody else?" Because Maggie could have gotten a key, or Jimmy could have.

Or anybody could have. I just proved it's not exactly hard.

Oliver snuffled in a wider circle. "Just us. I mean, that's fresh. There's lots of old stuff. There's mice and cats and some dogs and old human . . ."

"Okay." Emma pushed the oven door carefully shut. Fresh ash swirled and settled on the floor at her feet. "Okay."

"Where are we going now, Emma?"

Maybe she didn't kill him. Maybe she found him after he

*was dead and just took the manuscript to protect . . .
someone. Ruth. Herself. Victoria's memory. Jimmy. Of
course, Jimmy.*

Jimmy is innocent, Louise had said to Maggie. Maybe
she knew Maggie had done it.

Or maybe it was a confession.

"Oliver, we have to find Louise."

50

LOUISE WASN'T ANSWERING HER PHONE. EMMA CALLED AN-gelique, who put her on speaker with Genny and asked all kinds of questions that Emma really did not want to answer. But her friends did, eventually, give her Louise's address and directions.

It turned out Louise had a modest flat on the second floor of a fieldstone building not that far from Penhallows. Emma found it easily.

If I was smart, I'd turn around right now and call DCI Brent. Emma stood in front of the closed door.

Except what would Emma tell her? That she'd broken into Penhallows to try to determine whether it was Louise who had killed Parker and Victoria, and she'd done it on the strength of what her corgi had told her when he got into the crime scene?

"Emma?"

She needed to give Louise a chance. She hadn't had it easy. If the worst was true, well, at least she deserved a chance to walk in of her own accord.

Or maybe I just don't want to believe it could be Louise, of all people . . .

"Emma!" Oliver barked.

"Give me a minute, Oliver."

"But, Emma . . ."

"What!"

"The door's open."

Emma stared at him. Oliver huffed exasperatedly and bumped the door with his hard muzzle. Slowly, it swung back on silent hinges.

Her heart in her mouth, Emma stepped through the door. "Hullo? Louise? It's Emma!"

Louise's flat was surprisingly up-to-date. Emma had expected someplace fussy, probably with doilies. But the rooms were all light and clean, with bright accent walls and modern furnishings. There were pots and pots of plants too, far more varieties than Emma could name. It was as if Louise was compensating for not having a garden outdoors by bringing nature inside.

Over the pristine white sofa was a whole wall of photographs, some black and white, others in color. There were holiday scenes, home scenes, wedding photos. The man in them was short, round, and plump. He'd obviously gone bald early and exuded an air of active contentment. When Louise stood next to him in those photos, she looked happy.

There were old, faded photos too. Emma had to lean close to make out anything more than a sepia blur, but there she saw Louise, a shadow in all black, and Ruth with her thick glasses. They stood next to a Valkyrie in chunky heels and a wide-lapel jacket, her ginger hair blowing in the breeze. Victoria Roberts.

"Emma?" Oliver grumbled.

"Yes, Oliver."

"Emma, where are the cats?"

Reluctantly, Emma turned away from the photo wall. "What?"

"The cats. Nervous Louise has cats. They're not here."

"Oh. Erm. Maybe . . . she's taken them to the vet."

"But there's no food bowl. Or water." He sniffed.

Emma glanced around the tidy flat. Everything was in its place, and all very clean. That was when she noticed the envelope waiting on the side table, leaning up against a particularly luxuriant philodendron.

Guilt threatened, but Emma didn't let it stop her. The envelope was unsealed, and inside she found a list. It was a list of names, and plants.

Her heart had been hammering. Now it stopped. She dropped the list and strode into the clean kitchen. She pulled open the fridge door. It was empty inside—no milk, no cheese, no half-finished yogurt. Nothing that could spoil. Nothing that needed looking after.

No sign anywhere that the owner intended to come back.

A deep chill dropped down over Emma.

"Oliver? We need to find Louise, right now." She bit her lip. "And I think I know where to look."

The power of motion returned in a rush and Emma bolted out the door and down the stairs, with Oliver barking at her heels.

Just, please, please, please let us be in time.

51

PLEASE. PLEASE. PLEASE.

The word turned into a chant as Emma dashed up the street. Oliver gained on her and bounded ahead and around the corner. She followed him, skidded and stumbled, but did not fall or slow down. They crossed out of the village and onto the barren cliffs. Oliver and his nose found the footpath and galloped down it, with Emma trailing behind.

Please let us be in time.

Emma tried to keep her eyes on Oliver, but she kept straining to see ahead. The streetlights had ruined her night vision, and all she saw was layers of shadow. But Oliver was a pale patch against the dark, bounding forward, nose alternately pointed to the ground or high in the air.

Emma followed, running as fast as she dared. The wind shoved hard against her, and the rush of the waves below drowned out her frantic heartbeat and ragged breathing.

Finally, one shadow separated itself out from all the others, and Emma gasped in relief.

Louise.

Relief faded. Because Louise stood, all alone, right at the cliff's edge. She stared at the ocean and didn't even turn when Oliver bounded up to her.

Emma forced herself to slow down to a walk.

"Louise?" she called cheerfully and waved. "Hullo!"

"Oh, Emma! Hello. Hello, Oliver."

Emma's eyes had adjusted to the dark, and she could see how Louise kept staring out at the sea. She could also see how the older woman stood, hands in her cardigan pockets, feet just a few centimeters from the cliff's edge.

"What brings you out this way?" asked Louise.

"Just walking." Emma hoped the wind and the sea were loud enough to cover the tremor in her voice. "You?"

"The same. I've always loved the cliffs. I'd spend hours out here as a girl, just staring at the sea." She smiled ruefully, but she still didn't look toward them. "There may have been some very bad poetry writing as well."

Emma made herself laugh. "Hazard of being young. That and too much black eyeliner."

"Oh, yes, and silver jewelry. I was quite the Goth girl back in the day. It was an awkward time. The beatniks were long gone and the emos hadn't quite started up yet. Well. I suppose I shouldn't keep you. Goodbye. Goodbye, Oliver."

"Are you headed back to the village?" Emma asked quickly. "We can walk with you."

"No. No. Not at all," she said. "I just . . . I'm very sorry you had to see this, you know. But really, you have the worst timing."

She lifted one foot.

"Louise!" cried Emma. "Louise, stop!"

"Stop!" barked Oliver.

But Louise only shook her head. She lifted her foot higher.

Oliver charged.

"No!" shrieked Emma.

Louise flinched and turned her head. Oliver dove right at her, nose down, teeth bared. Louise screamed and jumped.

Backward. Away from the cliff.

Oliver skirted the tiny distance between Louise and the edge, barking and nipping. Louise screamed again and danced backward. Oliver kept moving forward, nipping at her toes, forcing her backward, circling and angling.

Herding her straight toward Emma.

Emma dove forward and wrapped her arms around Louise.

Oliver sat down and opened his mouth, panting.

"Good boy, Oliver," Emma breathed. "Oh, good, good boy."

"Let me go," whispered Louise. "Please let me go."

"It's all right." Emma held her tightly. "It's all right. I promise it is."

"No." Louise shuddered. Emma felt tears soak through her summer blouse. "It isn't. I did it. I did. I can't . . . I won't be humiliated and dragged through the mess. Please."

"Listen to me." Emma turned her around so they were face-to-face, but she kept both hands on Louise's shoulders. "You don't know what will happen. Not yet. Maybe—"

"Maybe what? Maybe nothing! I killed him! I killed Parker Taite!"

"Did you kill Victoria?"

"What!" Louise cried, indignant. "No! He did!"

"And you figured that out, didn't you?" said Emma. "And you went to confront him?"

"Yes. Yes, I did."

"So what happened? Tell me right from the beginning."

Louise laughed, an entirely unfunny sound. "That's the problem. This isn't the beginning. This is the end. The beginning was forty years ago."

Emma nodded. "I thought it might be. Listen, will you come with me? Just to Nancarrow, I swear. Just for a cup of tea."

Louise sniffed and pulled a crumpled tissue out of her pocket. "Do you know what's truly ridiculous? The whole while I was standing there, trying to work up the nerve to take that last step, all I could think was how much I'd really like a good cuppa!"

"Come on, Louise." Emma put her arm around the older woman's shoulders. "Let's go home."

52

....

A HALF HOUR LATER, EMMA HAD LOUISE SITTING AT HER front room dining table, wrapped in one of the old quilts from the linen cupboard. Oliver, still very much on the alert, was lying across the threshold, blocking the front door.

"Need to be careful, Emma," he said.

Emma was not going to argue. While she was in the kitchen, she made a quick call to Angelique, just long enough to let her know that everything was fine and she'd explain later.

Then she carried the tea things back into the front room and poured out a cup of very hot, very strong tea for Louise, and added sugar without even asking.

She put it into Louise's ice-cold hands and wrapped her fingers around the mug.

"Now." Emma sat down beside her. "Tell me about forty years ago."

Louise sighed. She also took a long, slurping sip of tea. "We were just girls. Me and Victoria and Ruth. Still teenagers, really. We were a little wild, maybe, but we weren't bad. It was a crazy time, wasn't it? The music and the clothes and everything burning down. The whole world was going mad, and we were all dying to get to London so we could go mad with it. Victoria was going to apply to university and everything." She stopped. "People forget how different it was. We were all supposed to finish grammar school, pick some neighbor boy to marry and start having babies. Maybe we could take a bookkeeping course or something if we weren't getting married right off, or if we thought it'd be a help in our husband's shop. We weren't supposed to want lives of our own."

Emma nodded. She'd heard her mother and grandmothers talk in much the same way.

"I wasn't any good in school, so I never bothered with exams. I went to work at Mr. Penhallow's instead."

"The bakery?"

"Yes," said Louise. "Ruth and her mother were trying to talk him into opening a tea room then, but he wouldn't hear of it. Mostly because it was someone else's idea. He was . . . he was what my mother called a hard man. He didn't like anyone, and no one liked him. Not even his wife and daughter." She took another long swallow of tea.

"That's awful," said Emma.

"It was. Sometimes Ruth had bruises, but mostly her mother did. No one said anything, of course. That was something else that was different back then. Everybody just accepted that a man had a right to *discipline* his family. And if there was a quarrel, the first thing anybody did was ask the wife what she'd done to make him so angry." Louise's voice shook.

"I'm sorry."

Oliver got up from his post beside the door and came and put his chin on her toes.

"Yes, well. Thank you."

"Did he ever hit you?"

"No. He just . . ." Louise made a face. "He bumped into me. A lot. And he told dirty jokes when he knew I'd hear, and then he started . . . pinching me, and grabbing me, especially when I was behind the counter and there wasn't any room to get away."

"Oh, Louise!"

"I didn't know what to do. I tried to tell him no, but he wouldn't stop, and then . . . well, he asked me to close up one night and I thought he'd gone home, but he hadn't and . . ." Her mouth clamped shut. "I did get away. But only just.

"I didn't know what to do. After. I felt like I couldn't go home. If I did, I'd just have to pretend nothing had happened. So I went to Victoria's instead. I was pretty sure she'd be alone. Her mother was a nurse who worked the night shift sometimes, and her father was out helping his brother on his boat. Anyway, I told her everything."

Emma pictured her, a slim girl in sleek black, like a Cornish Audrey Hepburn, sobbing on the bed beside a hard-eyed and vengeful Victoria.

"What did Victoria do?" Emma asked, but she had the feeling she might already know.

"She phoned my mum and told her that I'd twisted my ankle and I was fine but I was going to stay at her place so I wouldn't have to try to walk home from the bus. Then she called Ruth and told her to sneak over.

"And . . . when Ruth got there, Victoria told us all what we were going to do. It turned out she'd been planning it for weeks. She knew, you see, how Mr. Penhallow treated Ruth and her mother and . . . everybody. She said there was only one way to stop him.

"She told me I was to go home and pretend I was sick for a few days so I wouldn't have to go into work. She told Ruth she was to go take up the new tiles in the bakery kitchen and that she'd take care of the rest."

Planting the red herrings already, thought Emma. *If Ruth lost her nerve and talked, she'd say the body got buried under the tiles, which of course it hadn't. After that, no one would bother with asking her anything else, because she clearly didn't know what she was talking about.*

In her own very particular way, Victoria Roberts was something of a genius.

"Victoria had always loved gardening, you see, even back then, and . . . well, she knew all about which perfectly normal plants could be dangerous. She made up a mix. There was foxglove in it, I think, and yew berries . . ."

"And lily of the valley?"

Louise nodded. "A belt-and-suspenders brew, she called it. If one thing wouldn't get him, another would."

"Then she called Mr. Penhallow and she . . . well, I don't know exactly what she said, but it was something along the lines of how he must be getting pretty itchy what with his little side bit staying home for so long, and if he was done playing with dolly girls and wanted a real woman for a change, she'd give him everything he could handle.

"He called her names, but of course he said yes. She told him to make sure he was working late and alone, and she'd be there.

"Well, he did. And she showed up at the back door with a bottle of whiskey, and the poison. She got him to drink it and . . .

"She didn't let me and Ruth anywhere near the place. She wanted us to be able to say we'd been together the whole evening. And we were, but what we were doing was packing up a suitcase full of Mr. Penhallow's stuff so it would look like he'd run away. We weighted that with rocks and tossed it off the cliffs.

"And the next morning, it looked to the rest of the world like Mr. Penhallow was just . . . gone.

"Mrs. Penhallow acted like everything was normal for as long as she could. She was . . . more relieved than anything else. Then, when he didn't come back, she didn't encourage anybody to ask too many questions.

"After a while, there were some bits in the local paper and questions from the police and of course the rumors, but . . . really, as strange as it sounds, life just sort of . . . went on.

"Ruth and her mother turned the bakery into a tea room. Victoria went to uni and got her business degree and came back to look after her parents and make a small fortune in local real estate, and eventually look after Jimmy, and none of us ever talked about . . . that night again."

"And you?"

"Me? Well, here I am, aren't I?" She waved toward the hills. "Married. No children, but a good life, and a good home." Then her hand shook. "Until that man came."

Parker had come to Trevena to hear about crimes in the distant past and got handed a much more recent, and juicier, local rumor instead. Emma could picture his eyes lighting up. What if he could solve the crime? Think of the publicity! Think of the telly! Think of his old paper groveling to take him back!

"Did Victoria know what he was really up to?"

"Oh, she knew right away. He'd been talking to Ruth as well as Maggie, you see, and Ruth said some things she shouldn't and called Victoria in a panic. Victoria, of course, told Ruth she'd take care of it.

"She let Parker think she was a harmless old bird like Ruth, and he sat in her front room and chatted away endlessly. When she knew enough, she told him he'd better keep his mouth shut about what he thought he'd found or she'd bring a big enough libel suit down on him that not one word of his ever saw print again."

Which might work, as it would be the second suit he'd been involved in. What publisher or paper would want to take a chance on him after that?

"So Parker decided he couldn't let her jeopardize his chances at a comeback," said Emma.

Louise nodded. "When I confronted him, he laughed about it. Told me how easy it was. He just emptied the poisoned water into the teakettle. And after that, he didn't even have to wait around. He knew she'd be in for her cuppa before too very long." She stared into her mug. "He only came back to make sure it had worked, and you'd already found the body and, well, you know the rest, don't you?"

"When did you realize he was the one who killed her?"

"As soon as Jimmy told me how much he'd been hanging around the house, I saw how it might have gone. Not because I knew Mr. Taite, but because I knew Victoria so very well."

"And you decided to confront him?"

Louise nodded again. "I was going to offer him money to go away. Once I sold Victoria's land, I'd have plenty, you see. I didn't want what we'd done to come back and hurt Jimmy. But I got to Parker's room, and he wasn't there. I think he must have been chasing after Percy and he'd left the door open. Anyway . . ." She paused. "I saw his book full of lies."

Louise's eyes went hard and her whole body shook. "He was writing that Victoria made advances toward Mr. Penhallow and that she killed him when he turned her down! He was going to say she killed herself rather than have her crime exposed!

"He came in while I was still reading. I said I'd tell the police what he'd done. I said I didn't care. I wasn't going to let him twist Victoria's last days when all she'd ever done was try to protect me, and Ruth.

"He was furious. He told me I was not going to ruin his chances. He called me names. And he got his hands round my throat and . . . it was just like . . . just like Nick Penhallow did when I told him I'd scream and . . . I don't . . . I don't actually remember what happened after that. I blacked out, or something, and when I came to again, he was on the floor and there was blood and . . ." She put her mug down and instead pressed her hands against the table's edge.

"I was so calm." Louise lifted her gaze to meet Emma's. There was a look of remembered amazement shining in them. "I couldn't believe how calm. I just washed my hands, and I took the towel with me so no one would see the blood. I cleaned up my foot marks, loaded the manuscript into his briefcase and just . . . walked out. There was a girl hoovering the floors in the great room, and she never even saw me.

"It was when I got home that what I'd done really started to sink in. I decided that whatever happened next, I had to destroy that foul set of lies. So I went to Penhallows and used the old ovens and burnt it."

"And nobody saw you going in?"

"Oh, I'm sure a dozen people saw me parading up and down the street, but who am I?" She spread her hands. "I'm that old damp dishrag Louise Craddock, Victoria Roberts's only friend. Nobody pays any attention to what I do." She smiled. "Besides, Penhallows was going to be leased out soon, for a new shop. Of course I'd have to look it over."

Emma's throat went tight. She took another swallow of tea.

"Anyway, after I'd burnt the manuscript, I took a good long walk, to try to get my head together, you understand. By the time I reached the rift, it seemed to me the best thing I could do for Jimmy and, well, everybody was just throw myself over the cliffs."

"But you didn't."

"No. Because Oliver interrupted me that time too. With Percy. All I could think was I couldn't leave them out there alone. I had to get them home. So I did." She paused. "That's not the entire truth. The truth is . . . there was a moment, when I knew what I'd done, and I knew I had gotten away with it, that I knew I was supposed to feel guilty. I knew I was supposed to want to confess, or die. But I didn't. I just didn't. I just . . . I felt like I'd finally *done* something. Like I'd paid the debt I owed Victoria from all those years ago." She bowed her head. "The guilt didn't come until Jimmy got arrested."

Emma sucked in a deep breath. It was too much. She felt like she couldn't hold even one more revelation, and yet there was still a question that needed asking.

"Louise? Can you tell me one more thing?"

She raised her eyes. "I'll try."

"What happened to Mr. Penhallow's body?"

Louise blinked, and to Emma's surprise, she smiled. "Good heavens, Emma. I thought you knew. Your dog certainly knew."

"Oliver?"

"Yes. You see, Mr. Penhallow's in the rose garden. Right under the Gertrude Jekyll."

53

. . . .

IN THE END, LOUISE LET EMMA CALL A TAXI FOR THEM.
Emma rode with her to the police station. She called Constance on the way, and the detective was there when they arrived. She received Louise gently and asked Emma to make sure her lawyer was called.

She even confirmed that someone was already looking after Louise's cats for her.

There was a lot of paperwork after that, but the charges against Jimmy were dropped, and he was released the next day. Genny insisted he should not be alone, and Emma and Angelique agreed. So did Jimmy, eventually. He packed his bags and moved in with Genny's family.

Louise was charged with Parker's murder, but Mrs. Patel confided that Raj told her there was a very strong self-defense case. This bit of news, it seemed, came under the table from DCI Brent.

Two days later, Kyle Taite arrived by train to collect his brother's things and to take Percy home. He, Emma, Percy and Oliver took a long walk across the hills and talked about family and dogs and choices, both the good and the bad.

Maggie offered to help pay Louise's legal expenses. She

also spent a frantic week on the phone with her skittish developer and every single member of the village counsel. Between them, they managed to put together a new development plan. This time, the papers were signed in a blaze of flashbulbs.

It rained for three days solid afterward. Of course, no one *really* believed that might be Victoria expressing her displeasure from the Great Beyond.

TWO WEEKS LATER A NEW ANNOUNCEMENT APPEARED ON the King's Rest website:

NOW SERVING: CREAM TEAS, WEDNESDAY, FRIDAY AND SUNDAY

Featuring a fresh selection of house-made finger sandwiches, scones, cakes and biscuits by Reed's Cakes & Teas Reservations Required First seating 3 o'clock

THE GREAT ROOM AT THE KING'S REST WAS PACKED.

Normally in the afternoons, the space was deserted, but not today. Today was the first Friday of the new tea service, and most of the residents of Trevena, not to mention a healthy sprinkling of summer tourists, were sitting down to a service of sandwiches, cakes and scones.

Emma couldn't believe it was actually happening. She moved among the tables, checking on the customers, noting who needed a fresh pot of tea and who wanted more sandwiches. Genny's shop assistant, Becca, was helping with the service, along with a friend of hers home from school who had waited tables on other holidays and was looking to pick up a little extra pocket money.

Oliver nosed between the tables, accepting pats and ear scratches and helpfully cleaning up any dropped crumbs.

"Not as good as sausages," he informed Emma. "But there are many, many excellent humans here. But I think that cat is in the garden . . ." And of course, he went to check.

Now, pride bubbled through Emma to see so many people smiling and laughing over her bakes. There wasn't a scone left standing on any of the gleaming new sandwich platters.

Nana Phyllis would be so proud. Although she might not *entirely* approve of the cinnamon and white chocolate drizzle. But Emma thought it went perfectly with the fresh raspberry jam, spiked with a little more cinnamon and some fresh lemon zest.

Just as Emma was setting a fresh pot of first-flush Darjeeling on a tray, the door from the car park opened and Brian Prowse, the taxi driver, walked in.

"Wow," he said as Emma came up to greet him. "I was coming to wish you luck, but I guess you don't need any."

"Always need extra luck," Emma told him. "Did you want a table? I'm sure—"

"No, no," he said, cutting her off. "I'm on the clock. I was hoping you might have something I could take with me . . . ?"

Emma considered. "Follow me," she said.

She ducked back behind the bar. Aware that Genny and Pearl were exchanging amused glances over her head, she swiftly sliced a piece of her new recipe, an apple cake with ginger streusel, and wrapped it in greaseproof paper.

"There you are. On the house. This once."

He quirked a brow at her and opened a corner of her improvised packet. Really, he had no business having eyes that twinkled indoors. Probably he had many other unpleasant traits as well. Probably he didn't even like apples.

He bit a corner off the slice. Chewed, swallowed and stared, first at the cake, and then at her.

Emma's mouth went dry.

"What's the matter?"

"Nothing," he whispered. "I'm just trying to work out if it's too soon to ask you to marry me."

Emma laughed. She also blushed.

"Get along with you, Brian," said Genny loftily. "Some of us are working here."

Brian grimaced, and also made a great show of carefully wrapping up his cake. "Be seeing you," he said as he turned to go. "Very soon."

Emma's blush did not seem to be fading. Genny opened her mouth to make some remark to Angelique, who had not stopped measuring tea into pots, but who also was smiling in a frustratingly maternal fashion.

Fortunately, Emma was saved by Pearl sailing up to the bar.

"We've got another request for that scone recipe!" she announced.

"That's the third!" crowed Emma.

"We'll need to get you your own website," Angelique said. "I'm sure Pearl's designer can set you up."

"Absolutely," said Pearl. She gazed proprietarily over the full, humming dining room.

"Well, Emma, what do you think? Are we in business?"

Emma thought. She thought that in some ways it would be hard to be accountable to somebody else again. The King's Rest belonged to Angelique. She and Pearl would have a say in everything. There'd be negotiations, disagreements, growing pains.

But the morning in the beautiful kitchen had been everything she could have dreamed of. She had mixed and rolled and baked and tasted and smelled and made her notes, her head and her heart full of what she loved. Oliver could not come into the kitchen, but he'd spent the time galloping happily around the garden, making friends with the guests, annoying the local birds and keeping a sharp eye out for cats and foxes.

And now here they were, with a full dining room and happy customers. Oliver zoomed in from the garden.

"We're staying, right Emma? We are? You said you'd think about it. Only, there's that cat, and it should not be allowed free run of that garden. It's not too bad for a cat, but still . . ." He wagged his entire back half.

Emma looked out over the busy scene and realized she could already picture it with a couple of glass cases set up in the corner. Maybe right next to the doors leading to the back gardens. There could be a wall of tea tins where old magazine prints were now, and they could have some pack-aged teas to sell to the tourists, and a whole case of biscuits and buns, and slices of cakes that could be taken out to eat in the garden.

Pearl and Angelique were already talking about adding her bakes and teas to the B&B's catering offerings. Wed-ding parties in the season. New Year's Eve, and Mothering Sunday gatherings.

In the end, it might not work. It certainly wasn't what she'd imagined for herself when she came to Trevena.

But it might just be something better.

Emma looked back to her new friends and partners, and she knew her eyes were shining.

"I'd say that's a yes," said Pearl.

"It's a yes," agreed Emma.

"We're staying?" Oliver jumped to his feet. "Emma? Emma?"

"Yes, Oliver," she laughed. "We are staying!"

"Hurray! Sausages!"

ACKNOWLEDGMENTS

Nobody writes a book alone. I'd like to thank my editor, Jessica, and my agent, Lucienne, for all their hard work; all the very patient members of the Untitled Writers group for their critiques; the members of the Welsh Pembroke Corgi Facebook group for their practical advice: and of course, my husband and son for their unending support.

Ready to find
your next great read?

Let us help.

Visit prh.com/nextread

Penguin
Random
House